$\mathcal{D}$

Home Port

OLIVE
HIGGINS
PROUTY

'From fearful trip the victor ship
comes in with object won.'
WALT WHITMAN

HOUGHTON MIFFLIN COMPANY BOSTON
The Riverside Press Cambridge
1947

Again
to L. P.

1
CHAPTER

WHEN HE OPENED his eyes he didn't know where he was
nor what had happened. He was lying face down, stretched
out at full length, one hand extended straight above his head
as if he were reaching for something. His field of vision was
filled by a granular mixture which looked like brown sugar —
the damp kind with lumps in it and occasional dark hard
nuggets. He turned his head slightly, searching for clues.
There was a long, smooth shaft the silvery gray of wood
ashes, just beyond his outstretched hand. At the end of the
shaft an octopus-shaped object sprawled against the sky.
The octopus-shaped object resembled the upturned roots of
a dead tree and the shaft the stripped trunk of the tree. The
granular mixture was more like wet sand than brown sugar —
coarse, fresh-water sand such as covers what few beaches
there are up here on these lakes in Maine.

Well, at least he was lucid enough to know he was in the
State of Maine, spending his usual two months at camp.
The name of the camp was Tamarack. The name of his
dormitory was Opechee. Obviously he wasn't a victim of
amnesia. He stretched his arm out till his fingers touched
the silvery shaft. Yes! The texture of suede and the punky
consistency of a cork stopper when he pressed the firm blade
of his thumbnail into it. But what was he doing lying on his
stomach in a dazed state of mind on a sandy beach beside
a rotting old tree?

1

Where were all the boys? There were few hours in the day when a bevy of lively youngsters was not his responsibility. Had he fallen asleep? He had no business to fall asleep unless he had put someone else in charge of the boys. He tried to sit up. His muscles wouldn't function! Perhaps he was having one of those nightmares in which you can't move; or coming out of ether; or more likely he was in one of those semiconscious states that occasionally follow a long, deep sleep. He was probably lying in his own camp bed, and the dead tree and the sand were just optical illusions. The best thing to do is to fix your attention on realities and the illusions will disappear.

He closed his eyes and proceeded to visualize his camp-bed — low, narrow, covered with an olive-drab army blanket. It was located at the end of a row of a dozen identical camp-beds all covered with olive-drab blankets. He visualized the whole row. It looked like a range of bare, low-lying hills at night when all the boys were asleep, and he glanced down the line to make sure each bed had its hummock.

Now if he were lying on his right side the first thing he would see when he opened his eyes would be Buddy Plunkett in the middle of the next cot. If on his left side, the log wall of the cabin a few inches beyond his nose. The logs were peeled, velvety to one's fingertips, and in places punky. Again he stroked the surface beneath his extended hand and pressed his nail into it. Of course! His hand was resting against a soft spot on one of the logs at the head of his bed! If he listened he'd hear the ticking of the big schoolroom clock which hung in each dormitory over the counselor's bed.

With eyes still closed he concentrated his attention upon his sense of sound. He could hear no ticking clock. But instead a soft measured swishing like waves lapping the shore. A familiar sound but inaudible from his bed in Opechee. He had better get up. He drew up one of his outstretched legs and then the other. Why, they were wet!

The lapping waves were breaking over his calves! The shock was so great he gave a jerk and sat up.

All illusions disappeared. All doubts as to whether he was awake or asleep vanished completely. He knew instantly what had happened. He had been crossing the lake in a canoe with Briggs — a fellow counselor. A storm had caught them. The canoe had capsized. They had clung to the bottom of the canoe for a while, then had decided to swim for shore. He had succeeded. Briggs had not!

He started to stand up, got as far as his knees and stopped. Gosh! He was going to lose his lunch! A good thing, he thought afterwards. It disposed of a lot of superfluous lake water. When at last he was able to draw a deep breath he bent down to the lapping waves, soused his face and washed out his mouth. Then he crawled over to the bare tree-trunk, pulled himself up onto his feet and leaned against it gazing out over the lake with smarting eyes.

The water was dark gray, dotted with whitecaps, but the storm had passed. The sun was placidly shining now. How long had he lain unconscious on the beach? How had he managed to reach the beach? He remembered the decision to abandon the canoe and swim for shore, but after that it was all just a jumbled mass in his mind of churning water, spray, spume, thunder, lightning, and blinding torrents of rain. Then suddenly the long, white column of the tree trunk now supporting him became disassociated from the mass. Why, this old dead tree had saved his life!

He had never been in such a sea before. The wind and waves and rain were all mixed up. He couldn't see through them. He hadn't known whether he was headed for the shore or not. But he had kept on swimming just the same. It was when he was at the end of his strength, or thought he was, and had decided to give up, that he saw the shaft of a beached tree-trunk piercing the murk before him, like the white tape the last time round the track. It had had the same effect, too. It had forced open his tank of reserve strength, and he had drained it of every atom of will and stamina it contained.

But he shouldn't have collapsed. Ike Dennis, his coach at prep school, used to say, 'Flopping after breasting the tape shows lack of guts.' If Ike were here now he'd tell him to stand up on his own two feet and perambulate under his own power. He took a step or two, then stopped, warned by that peculiar dimming of outlines across his field of vision which often preceded complete darkness. But he mustn't pass out! Not again! 'Usually it's just willingness. Usually you can do what you want to if you want to do it enough.' More of Ike's philosophy.

He pushed himself away from the tree and walked over to a five-foot bank a half-dozen steps away. He grabbed hold of a root and pulled himself up its steep slope. There was a thick tangle of bushes at the top. He pushed his way through them on his stomach. A little way beyond the bushes he saw what looked like a bed of moss. He crawled over to it on all fours and felt of it with his hands. Yes, moss — soft, flat, and springy. He sank down upon it and closed his eyes. But he didn't lose consciousness.

As soon as he felt a little more fit he must start back to camp and report what had happened. But nothing could be gained by hurrying. It would be impossible to reach camp tonight. He was familiar with the geography of the lake, the surrounding trails and paths, and knew his approximate location. He was on the east side of the lake opposite Henderson's Point. Henderson's Point, also on the east side, was a long, narrow, forefinger-shaped peninsula pointing southwest, with a decapitated old tree at the tip of it — a well-known landmark.

Tamarack lay about three miles, south, as the crow flies, also on the same side of the lake. But between him and

Tamarack, Heron Swamp intervened, an impassible morass of decaying stumps and muck. At this end, the swamp merged into the lake, and at its upper end into Long Pond. He must go up around the end of Long Pond and pick up an old Appalachian trail in order to return to Tamarack by foot. A good ten-mile tramp, he should think. There were no trails that he knew of on this side of Heron Swamp. He might run across an old lumber road, however. He'd better be on his way. He had two hours of daylight left, judging from the shadows of the trees. The sky was blue beyond the leafy roof above him. Hard to believe it had been covered with yellow clouds thick as phlegm an hour ago. Or was it several hours ago? What time was it?

He raised his left wrist over his head and focused his eyes on the face of his watch. The watch had been a birthday present from his mother when he was eighteen. It was guranteed to be water-tight and had stood many a test. He had glanced at it just before the canoe capsized. It had been a little before three o'clock then. Its hands were now pointing to twenty minutes past three. What had stopped it? He started to turn its stem. Broken! Instantly he remembered. He had had to hold Briggs's limp body onto the upturned canoe. Every time he hoisted him up higher he'd felt his wrist-watch scraping the canvas beneath and had feared for the fate of the watch. Funny how some trifling detail like that will pierce your consciousness in the midst of some terribly serious situation, and come back afterwards sharply defined, before the important facts and factors get straightened out in your mind.

What were the important facts and factors? He had better find out before he got back to camp. How was he going to explain what had become of Briggs? What was he going to say when Mr. Ben looked at him with those deep-set eyes of his that could be so penetrating and said, 'Tell me all about it, my boy,' his kind voice grave, the expression on his face grave.

At the thought of Mr. Ben's expression another wave of
nausea rose in him, but he controlled it. He must get the
day's events clear in his own mind as soon as possible. Not
only Mr. Ben but his fellow counselors, too, would want to
know all the facts. Also all the campers, even the smallest
boys in Opechee, for whom he stood as an example of all
things desirable, would ask questions among themselves,
and stare at him silent and wide-eyed.

Later Windy must know the facts and pass judgment.
Windy was his older brother. Windy had blazed the trail
for him at Tamarack. He had established a shining record,
first as a camper and then up through all the stages until he
finally became chief counselor and Mr. Ben's right-hand
man. Windy was familiar with all Tamarack's principles and
standards. It had been Windy who had first ingrained in
him what it meant to be a good Tamaracker and explained
the meaning of the camp's motto, printed in Latin on the
camp stationery and carved in wood over the fireplace in
the assembly hall — 'Protege Infirmos' — 'Protect the Weak.'
Not until this moment had the camp motto occurred to him!
He had known Briggs had a weak heart, too! He had been
desperately aware of it, from the first moment he'd noticed
his lips had turned blue, and throughout the whole terrible
ordeal. But not once had the words of the camp motto
entered his head!

If Briggs had been one of the campers, and therefore
one his charges, he would have died in his attempt to save
him. That is one of the laws for all counselors in whose care
parents entrust their children. But Briggs wasn't officially
in his care.

Briggs was the new counselor in charge of Woodcrafts.
He'd never been to Tamarack before. He was a stranger to
everybody. The day before camp opened Mr. Ben had
called all the old counselors together at a special meeting
in his cabin and told them about the new member of their

staff. He said he was the son of a college friend of his, who, shortly before he died last winter, had asked him if he could make room for his son as a counselor at Tamarack, just in case he wasn't around next summer to take their customary six weeks' camping-trip together.

Mr. Ben said Briggs was a splendid fellow, just the right type for Tamarack as to character, standards, sense of responsibility, background and all that, but when he was a child he had had an illness which had left him with a weak heart. He could take part in the regular camp activities — swim, paddle, take short hikes, but it must be positively understood that he must not be placed in a position of responsibility requiring physical endurance over any of the campers. Also he should be protected from all arduous tasks. Mr. Ben had made no reference to the motto, but that was no excuse for forgetting it.

The details of the day's events were still a confused mass in his mind, but at this moment he had a strong conviction that even though he had forgotten the motto, he had not acted unheroically. But would they believe him? There had been no witnesses. He could show them the broken watch-stem as silent proof that he had held Briggs onto the canoe for a while. But countless questions would be asked. How long did you hold him onto the canoe? Why didn't you hold him longer? Why did you leave the canoe? What made the canoe capsize? Why was Briggs paddling stern? Why were you caught out on the lake in a storm that had given fair warning? These were a few of the questions of the inquisition awaiting him.

He sat up and clasped his arms around his knees, his brows drawn into a troubled frown. How was he going to answer the questions when he didn't know the answers himself? At a certain point he had passed out and his memory was a blank. Even before he passed out everything was still a jumble in his mind. He had better go back to the be-

ginning and rehearse the day's events, slowly and consecutively. Then he would find the answers to their questions,
and to his own questions, too. His arms tightened around
his knees, and his expression tightened also as he proceeded
to search for the facts.

2

CHAPTER

WE GOT STARTED about eight o'clock. There wasn't a cloud in the sky. We crossed the lake a little above camp. A light breeze was behind us. It was a hot day and once on the other side we loafed along — hugging the bank, keeping in the narrow border of shade. Briggs paddled forward going up the lake. He performed the conventional convolutions as if familiar with them, his long, white arms inscribing perfectly formed arcs one after another, slowly, rhythmically. Occasionally he'd stop, lay his paddle across his knees, and contemplate the scenery. But the fact is, I didn't pay much attention to his paddling, nor much attention to *him* either. I'd planned to take Tug Tyson with me. Tug and I are old friends. We could have had a swell time. I was feeling mighty sorry for myself that it was Briggs and not Tug seated in the other end of the canoe. It was all Mr. Ben's doings.

This was how it happened. I am the counselor of Natural History at Tamarack and every summer I take groups of campers on research trips lasting several days. I had heard there was a beaver dam under construction on a creek three miles north on the other side of the lake, a short walk inland. Mr. Ben knew I was planning to take a reconnoitering trip to make sure the dam was there and to pick out an overnight camp-site near by, so my boys could watch the beavers at work.

Last Sunday Mr. Ben asked me to drop into his cabin after vespers. There was something on his mind he would like to talk over with me. The 'something' on Mr. Ben's mind was Briggs. None of the old counselors had made an effort to be friendly with him. Mr. Ben had noticed it and wondered why. I told Mr. Ben there was nothing objectionable about Briggs, but that he had been to a prep school in New Mexico and to college in California and there wasn't much in common between him and the other counselors. The fact was, he was a distinct outsider. He'd never seen Tamarack before the day he arrived with his suitcase full of a brand-new counselor's uniform. Most of the counselors at Tamarack have been campers first, then aides, then junior counselors, then full-fledged counselors. Articles of clothing are worn till outgrown and often replaced by hand-me-downs. It was obvious that Briggs had known no one at Tamarack to offer him any hand-me-downs. If he'd been the hail-fellow-well-met type, it wouldn't have made any difference what he wore. But he wasn't! You couldn't be sure but that he preferred to be left alone. Ill at ease with the other counselors, over-anxious to please, and lacking in self-confidence with the campers.

Mr. Ben asked me (in that way he has of consulting, rather than issuing an order) what I would suggest to make Briggs feel more like 'one of us.' And not waiting for an answer he went on to say that he thought that I especially would find a lot in common with Briggs. He had seen me go out of my way to talk to him on several occasions. Before I could explain that it was simply because I felt sorry for Briggs, Mr. Ben remarked that it seemed to him it would be an excellent idea for me to ask Briggs to accompany me on that trip up the lake that I was planning to take in a day or two.

'Briggs is a stranger within our gates,' Mr. Ben remarked. 'You were a stranger once, you know.'

That was true. A mighty unhappy stranger, too! I assured Mr. Ben that I'd do my best to make things happier for Briggs, but I'd already spoken to Tug Tyson about going up the lake with me.

'Tug would understand if you explained it to him. But of course make your own decision. Do as you think best, Bug.'

Whenever Mr. Ben calls me 'Bug' it does something to my feelings. Once Mr. Ben sanctions a nickname by using it, it becomes an epithet to be proud of. Usually he addresses his counselors by their last names only. The campers are required to prefix a mister. When Mr. Ben calls a counselor by a nickname it expresses something bordering on affection. Gosh, I hated not to come up on Mr. Ben's suggestion!

Strolling back to Opechee later that night after an informal get-together of a few congenial souls in the Counselors' club-room I saw a light in the woodcraft shop and dropped in. Briggs was in there reading one of the canvas-covered books from the camp library — *David Copperfield,* I noticed, before he succeeded in covering it up. It struck me as mighty pathetic that Briggs had to resort to that childhood stand-by. Impulsively, against my better judgment, I asked him if he'd care to go with me on a reconnoitering trip up the lake some day soon. He flushed to the roots of his hair when he accepted.

It was my plan after locating the beaver dam to recross the lake, skirt the opposite shore, and pick out another camp-site for my boys somewhere in the vicinity of Heron Swamp. There is a lot of interesting wild life around that swamp. I wanted to poke around in the muck among the stumps and cattails at sundown and see what was going on.

Briggs and I located the beaver dam without any trouble, found a perfect camp-site within a stone's throw of it, took a swim, ate our lunch and were ready to start across the lake by two o'clock.

While I was cleaning up after lunch, Briggs jumped into

the canoe and was already seated in the stern when I appeared. Briggs took it for granted he was paddling stern. It was his turn. I didn't forget about his heart, but I hated to oust him from that seat and hurt his feelings. Anybody with a physical disability is apt to be pretty sensitive. I'd seen Briggs flush when Tug had sung out to him one day to drop a canoe he was hauling up on the beach and then had sent a spindling, twelve-year-old boy to do it.

There was no sign of a storm when we pushed off. The treetops were thick and high and concealed the horizon. We were several hundred yards from the shore when I first noticed the faint outline of a bank of pearly gray clouds crawling up out of the west. The clouds were so far away I figured they couldn't possibly kick up any trouble on the lake till long after we were on the other side. In fact, it occurred to me how wise it was to cross immediately. The wind was fresher than in the morning, but of no importance to a two-manned canoe.

When I realized how slow our progress was, I kept looking around to see if Briggs was resting on his paddle. But he never was. He was always functioning — inscribing those smooth, beautifully formed circles one after another. But they didn't seem to have any core. Like those puffballs one finds in the woods with nothing inside but a cloud of dust. When the wind freshened up still more our course was as zigzag as a drunken man's. Briggs simply couldn't hold to a straight line. I dug in as hard as I could, first one side, then the other, but I was marooned way out in the bow, and my frantic efforts remind me of the futile waving of one of those fox-tails tied to the radiator cap of an automobile. Still, we did make progress.

The lake is about two miles wide where we crossed. Every little while I kept looking at my watch and at both shore lines and making mental notes. The clouds were getting darker and climbing higher and I knew we were in for a storm; but I felt sure we were going to beat it. We would have, too, if something hadn't happened to Briggs. We were within a hundred and fifty feet of the shore when the canoe capsized.

I don't know what made the canoe capsize. Briggs lost his balance somehow. Perhaps he collapsed. Perhaps he was putting more effort into those circles of his than I realized. Perhaps I shouldn't have talked the way I did to him finally. For when we lost the sun and the waves got churlish I began giving Briggs some of Ike's fight-talk. I hollered back things like 'Put more beef into it,' 'Step on the gas!' and 'Give 'er the gun,' prefixing the phrases with occasional 'Damn its' and 'For God's sakes,' to impress on him how important it was. But it didn't seem to have any effect.

I always tell a kid who is scared that falling out of a canoe into warm water is no worse than falling off a bicycle onto soft ground. The bicycle doesn't run off. It stays right there beside you till you get up, mount it again, or push it along home. When I came to the surface the canoe was waiting for me not three feet away. I flung my arm over the bow and looked down the sides for Briggs. For a moment I thought he might be caught underneath. Then I saw him several yards off the stern. I yelled and began pushing the canoe toward him but he didn't seem to hear me. He was making queer, useless motions with his arms. So I swam over to him, caught hold of him, and together we got back to the canoe.

He wasn't unconscious. Dazed, I thought, or just scared, perhaps. His face was grayish white and his lips the blue of crushed blueberries and milk. But he didn't grab hold of me. Briggs may have had a weak heart but there was nothing weak about Briggs above his chin. He didn't lose his head. I certainly must make that fact clear when I tell my story.

With Briggs in a state of collapse I didn't try to turn the canoe right side up. I boosted him up on one side of it, then got around on the other side opposite him and we clasped each other's wrist across the bottom.

When finally the storm broke it gave us a terrible beating. The rain came down in bucketsful and the waves broke over us continually. Suddenly I felt Briggs's grip on my wrists loosen, and then he let go. I got around on his side of the canoe and somehow got him up onto it again. He had passed out! I shoved my left hand under him, got a good grip, and held onto him and the canoe for dear life. His limp body kept sliding down and I kept hauling it up and it was then that my wrist watch got such a grinding.

For a while I was afraid he'd passed out for good and all. I certainly thanked God when he began murmuring, 'Sorry. Thanks. Better,' and his muscles began to function somewhat. With his help I managed to fasten my left wrist to his right. He had his handkerchief handy and I tied two of the diagonal corners together, then twisted the loop into a sort of a figure eight and handcuffed ourselves together. Then I let him down into the water again opposite me, and we continued to hang on, hoping the storm would be a short one. But it wasn't. It seemed to quiet down for a while, then burst forth again worse than ever.

It was I who decided to leave the canoe. We were drifting away from the shore in an oblique line up the lake. It was a big shock to me when during a flash of lightning I caught sight of Henderson's Point with that old dead tree looming up on top of its bare cliff at the tip end. I didn't know we were anywhere near Henderson's Point. We were being carried straight toward Henderson's Falls!

I explained to Briggs as best I could in the uproar that that old tree was like a lighthouse to warn all small craft of the falls that lay at the end of a channel at its right. I told him we must swim for the shore or else we'd be drawn into the channel that would sweep us over the falls.

He said he wasn't up to swimming. I told him all he'd

have to do would be to put his hand on my shoulder, relax, and use his legs if possible. But he shook his head; 'You go alone,' he said.

I refused. He kept on urging me from time to time and I kept on refusing. Finally I told him, with no uncertain emphasis, that we were both wasting our strength for nothing but a plunge over the falls and that it was up to him to make an effort. At last he said, 'All right. Go ahead. I'm ready.' I wonder if Briggs meant he was ready to die. I wonder if he did it to save me when he found my code wouldn't allow me to leave a companion clinging to a doomed canoe to die alone. I wonder.

I untwisted the handkerchief and tossed it aside. We got launched all right. Briggs looked pretty grim but he co-operated marvelously. He didn't cling or clutch or press down. At first I thought we weren't going to make a bad team. The storm was still raging and it was too difficult to get a lungful of air to waste any of it asking Briggs how he was feeling. But from time to time I glanced back at him and could see he was keeping his nose out of water.

I don't know how long it was before his hand slipped off my shoulder — five, ten, fifteen minutes perhaps. At first I thought he was contributing more effort himself. I squirmed my shoulders but couldn't feel any pressure. I glanced back, expecting to see him following under his own power. There was no sign of him! I turned around. I could catch glimpses of the canoe now and then, riding the waves. I swam back toward it. But I caught no glimpse of Briggs. I don't know how far back I swam toward the canoe — perhaps twenty, perhaps forty strokes. Briggs had disappeared completely. Finally I dived, circling around in the murky-green under-water. But with no success. I dived twice. I hunted for Briggs. Before God, I hunted for him! Probably I ought to have hunted longer. Probably I ought to have gone all the way back to that canoe. Perhaps Briggs had tried to return

to it. Perhaps he had succeeded. I don't know what became
of Briggs.

When I came up to the surface after my second dive a
wave hit me in the face and I got a big douse of water into
my windpipe. Then another wave slapped me and my entire
piping system was flooded. I got a little panicky, I guess.
Anyway, I was convinced I couldn't last long floundering
around in a sea like that. I decided I'd done all I could for
Briggs and that it was all right for me to swim for the shore
alone.

After that I don't remember much. It's all a whirling
blank in my mind till I saw the trunk of that dead tree
lying on terra firma. And again a blank till I woke up beside
it.

Wait a minute! I've made a false statement. I didn't
decide I'd done all I could for Briggs. I acted from instinct
— the instinct of self-preservation. I forgot all about Briggs
at the last and put every scrap of energy I possessed into
saving my own skin. So I guess that inner conviction of
mine that I didn't act unheroically hasn't much foundation.
Mr. Ben says it's what a man does in a crisis that is the test
of his courage. The crisis today was when I couldn't find
Briggs. It's going to be tough to go back and say to
Mr. Ben, 'Here I am, alive and well. But the stranger within
our gates you asked me to be kind to I left out in the lake
to drown alone.' It's going to be mighty tough. It's going
to be hell!

3

CHAPTER

HE LAY BACK on the moss again and clasped his hands beneath his head, gazing up into interlacing boughs above perforated by slanting rays of sunshine casting long shadows now. It was nearly suppertime at Tamarack. Pretty soon the clear, clean-cut notes of Freckles' bugle would pierce the still air, and, immediately after, groups of boys, over a hundred in all, would be hurrying through the dappled shadows toward the long, low eating-cabin, their khaki shorts tawny as a deer in the late afternoon sunshine, their abbreviated tops white as the under side of the deer's tail. A pretty sight, he always thought — the happiest hour of the day at Tamarack. Everybody tired, hungry, and clean; the boys' faces shining not only with soap but with the glow of talking over the day's events. There was always more chatter and fun at supper than at any other meal. If they knew about Briggs it would silence the chatter, extinguish the fun. Well, Tamarack was safe tonight. Lucky he had told Mr. Ben that Briggs and he might not return till the next day. He would be back at camp before there was any anxiety. The thought of bearing the news of tragedy to Tamarack made him wince. He loved Tamarack, as did many another who had started in as a boy, passed through all the stages and finally received from Mr. Ben's own hands a roll of parchment which made you 'belong to Tamarack forever, and Tamarack belong to you,' so Mr. Ben never failed to assure each graduating group of boys.

17

Tamarack was one of the oldest boys' summer camps in existence. It had traditions, a reputation to be proud of, and an inspiring leader. You got to feel the same sort of love and loyalty for Tamarack as for your prep school. Sometimes even a greater love and loyalty. Every summer, year after year, various graduates came back in groups, or singly, to see Mr. Ben, talk over their plans with him and problems, and spend a night or two beneath the unforgettable larches. It was because of the larches that Mr. Ben had selected the site and given his camp the Indian name for the trees. Most of the counselors at Tamarack were college boys — freshmen, juniors, and a sprinkling of seniors. But a few like himself kept on returning even after they had graduated from college. He had tried Europe one year, a Western ranch another, but nothing seemed to suit his taste and temperament like Tamarack.

Tamarack had long been a secret refuge for his thoughts when disturbed. Whenever his self-control was threatened he would summon to his mind's eye the vision of the log-cabins huddled among the larches; and to his mind's ear the silky lapping of the waves on the shore — a healing sound, like a dog's tongue lapping a sore place over and over again — *his* sore place. When he was a small boy he used to have inexplicable waves of despair sweep over him. At such times he had tried repeating the Twenty-Third Psalm. But 'green pastures' and 'still waters' and the 'house of the Lord' were just ideas. Tamarack was real. It actually existed. If things ever got too bad for him — if certain situations became unendurable he could always go back to Tamarack, even in the winter, for Ezra the caretaker was there all the year around. Now from sheer force of habit his thoughts sought their old sanctuary. But for the first time the thought of Tamarack brought *qualm* instead of calm.

Presently he heard the hum of a mosquito circling above him, and a moment later the stab of the mosquito's drinking-

tube in his arm made him sit up instantly. He observed her
braced legs and ecstatic gorging for a moment, then swatted
her squarely, smearing his arm with her bellyful of his blood.
She wasn't a solitary mosquito. Her companions weren't far
away. He was soon surrounded by them. He shoved his hand
down into the pocket of his shorts and took out a tube of
pungent grease. It was almost empty. He squeezed it dry,
smeared his face and hands, and tossed the tube aside.

He then proceeded to investigate all his pockets. In one
pocket there was what had once been a bar of chocolate,
which had broken its tinsel wrapping and stained his shorts.
Imbedded in the mushy mass of chocolate was a half a package of Lifesavers and his knife attached to a chain clipped
into a loop. In another pocket there was a swollen pouch
of wet tobacco, a soggy lump of toilet paper, and a wet handkerchief which he spread out on the moss to dry. Unfor-
tunately both his matches and compass were missing. Also
his glasses and pipe.

From one of his rear pockets he drew out his billfold. He
didn't usually take his billfold into the woods, but when he
was dressing this morning he had discovered he was low in
tobacco and had run down to the general store on the main
road and laid in a supply. There hadn't been time to return
the billfold to his suitcase under his cot, so here was all the
cash he had brought to camp.

The billfold was made of pigskin and was old and shabby.
It was now as limp and clammy as a piece of raw bacon. But
the bills inside were unharmed. He began separating them
and laying them out in front of him. Two tens, three fives,
six ones. Forty-one dollars in all. The billfold had a protected celluloid section containing his automobile license.
His signature, and everything written in ink, was blurred
but legible.

The license was dated May 14, 1939. It announced that
he had been born on the 3rd day of the 10th month of the

year 1915. It stated that his eyes were blue, his hair light, his height 5 feet 8 inches. That was wrong! His height was 5 feet 8 inches and *one half!* Every half-inch of his height was precious to him. He laid both the license and the check on the moss beside the bills to dry.

In still another section of the billfold was a heterogeneous accumulation which he emptied in the center of his hand-kerchief, dissecting the pulpy mass with care. A pink laundry check, a dentist's appointment card, an oculist's prescription, an old fishing license, a coat check, several of his calling cards, and two theater-ticket stubs. The theater-ticket stubs were for seats 2 and 4, row E, center aisle left. They were dated November third. They bore the letters S-H-U. That was for Shubert.

He recalled the occasion. His mother had been his companion that night. He'd come in from Cambridge in his car and they'd dined at the Ritz before the theater. Just the two of them. His mother had planned it, in an attempt to recapture the old intimate spirit of the days before his father died, when they had had a common load to carry. Since his mother's second marriage, it was seldom she was free to be his companion alone, and when she did manage it, it wasn't the same. Her need of him had ceased, and his of her had become inarticulate. How hard she had tried that night last November to be gay and comradely and to appear as interested as ever in all the details of his life. And how hard he had tried to respond. But it had been play-acting on both sides. The evening hadn't been successful.

Still gazing at the stubs he visualized his mother. Tall, slender, youthful in spite of the gray hair she boasted. She wasn't the athletic type, but she was full of life, even her voice. Whenever he came home for a weekend she would rush to meet him from wherever she happened to be with an exclamation of delight, anxious to impress upon him how glad she was to see him — overanxious since her second

marriage, it often seemed to him. What would his mother
say when she knew what had happened today! It certainly
wouldn't be very conducive to the pride she was always pro-
testing she felt in him, and always so stoutly defending if
he ever did anything to challenge it. His mother was terribly anxious that all his performances be praiseworthy. His
eyes blurred. Good Lord, he mustn't blubber. He tossed
the stubs aside, concentrating his attention upon the delicate
business of peeling apart the fragile layers of the folded
fishing license.

Beneath one of the layers he was surprised to come upon
a small Kodak picture. It had withstood the water far better
than the fishing license. It was the picture of a girl with
fluffy shoulder-length hair. Daphne DeForest! There she
stood dressed in an abbreviated bathing suit, leaning non-
chalantly against the mast of a sailing boat, smiling at him
in that suggestive way of hers. What a humiliating experience the whole affair with Daphne had been! He
thought he had destroyed everything in his possession that
might remind him of her. He thought he had escaped from
her completely, and here she had been hidden in his pocket,
going around with him everywhere he went. He crumpled
up both the picture and fishing license, gathered together
various other scraps and bits, rolled them into a compact
ball and flung it far away into a tangle of underbrush.

There still remained his calling cards — three in all. They
were as limp as blotting paper. He separated them and laid
them in the palm of his hand in a row. For a long half-
minute he gazed down at the small white oblongs with his
name engraved in black letters on each one — MURRAY
VALE, MURRAY VALE, MURRAY VALE. As he gazed,
that peculiar sense of detachment from his own personality
stole over him, as when he gazed long at his own reflection
in a mirror.

He had never liked his name. It had always embarrassed

him to tell it. It was so short, and with all those soft 'r's' and liquid 'l's,' it lacked stamina. But perhaps he would have felt embarrassed to tell his name whatever it had been, simply because it was his. Well, the poor despised name was certainly a sorry sight now. It looked as if someone had been throwing defiling things at it. The cards were smeared and splotched with dark, tannish stains from the leather. He fitted them together, tore them into small pieces, made a hole in the damp moss, and stuffed them out of sight.

He'd better get started. There was over an hour of daylight left. He replaced the bills and his automobile license in his billfold and returned the other articles to his pockets, even the sweet chocolate, spreading out its crushed tinsel and rewrapping it.

When he stood up he was seized by another paroxysm of coughing. Leaning against a tree-trunk he groped for the Lifesavers, tore of the tinsel, tossed it aside, and placed one of the green disks on his tongue. The sharp, pungent flavor of lime was welcome. The coughing subsided. He turned his back on the setting sun and followed the long shadows of the trees pointing west toward Long Pond.

It was rough going. The trees grew thick — maple, beech, oak, yellow birch, occasional spruce and balsam — some lying prone, some half prone and leaning tipsily against other trees. There was such a mass of dead branches and underbrush that he had to make frequent wide detours.

He wished he had on his dungarees. The counselor's uniform at Tamarack, except on dress occasions, consisted merely of a sleeveless white cotton shirt with a dark-green T on the chest and gray flannel shorts with a dark-green stripe down the sides. Not much protection for climbing over blow-downs, scaling rocks, pushing through entanglements of thorny vines, and sinking ankle-deep, sometimes knee-deep, in leaf-mold and rotting tree-trunks. He still wore his

sneakers. They were so light-soled that they had been no
impediment in the water. They were a merciful protection
to his feet now.

He decided to spend the night in the exact spot where he
had landed after an unexpected eight-foot plunge through
the branches of a stand of sumacs at the foot of a ledge.
He had mistaken the full-leafed tops of the sumacs for the
fronds of a bed of ferns. Dusk had began to fall. His eyesight could no longer be trusted, his common sense either,
evidently. It was ingrained early into every camper at
Tamarack that it was an unpardonable sin to walk in un-
blazed woods in the dark and break a bone. Fortunately,
his fall had simply made him see stars for a moment and
caused another fit of coughing.

It wasn't a bad place for an overnight camp. The face of
the cliff pitched forward so that at its base between the
rock and the slender trunks of the sumacs there was a cave-
like space several feet wide which had been protected from
the afternoon rain. He cut some balsam boughs and piled
them close to the back wall of the rock, then stretched out
upon them.

The storm had been followed by one of those stifling calms
which sometimes follows a summer tempest. But as darkness fell a breeze sprang up. The first intimation he had of it
was in the leaves above him. They began stirring and making silky sounds. The leaves of the sumacs were compound.
So, too, were the leaves of the *Sophora Japonica* at home.
He concentrated his thoughts on the Sophora. Perhaps it
would help put him to sleep.

When he was a small boy he had built his first tree-house
in the Sophora, high up, where the leaves were the thickest,
and had often lain flat on his back like this gazing up. His
great-grandfather had planted the *Sophora Japonica* and
many other rare trees on what had been his farm then,
twelve miles out in the country — a half-day's drive by horse

and buggy from his office in Boston. Now the farm was just
a place in the suburbs — hardly over a half an hour by automobile from State Street. It consisted of a dozen acres of rolling
ground with outbreaks of pudding-stone, surrounded now
by hard-surfaced highways and a constant flow of traffic.

He had built tree-houses in several of his great-grandfather's rare trees. The tree-houses consisted of platforms in
the crotches of the trees at different heights connected by
ladders and cleats. Often he'd taken his filled plate from the
dining-room table and eaten alone in one of his tree-houses,
feeding bits of food from his hand to the squirrels, occasionally a chipmunk, and the bolder birds — chickadees, cat-
birds, and crows. The tree-house in the Sophora had in time
acquired walls and a roof, a door and a lock. In the spring
and summer he used to keep his aquaria there — larvae,
caddis worms, pollywogs and such, in preserve jars and
goldfish bowls.

Windy and his sisters were always urging him to join in
games of various sorts, and there was a raft of cousins who
were forever coming out from town and suggesting tennis, or
touch football. In his heart he hated all ball games, all
games in fact, though he had never admitted it. It was
something to be ashamed of. Once inside his tree-house in
the Sophora, seated at the bench in front of the horizontal
window, he was safer from interruption than anywhere else.
It was at that bench that he did much of his preserving in
formalin, mounting and labeling. In the winter his mother
assigned a heated room in the old carriage-house for his
exclusive use. She had a tier of shallow drawers built for his
mounted specimens, and gave him the folding lens and tin
collecting-box, and finally the microscope, that had belonged
to her father. In those days he had been under the illusion
he might be a genius. It had served as a refuge in much the
same way as the tree-houses. Neither had endured. The
tree-houses had rotted and had been torn down and the

illusion-delusion that he was a second Thoreau or Fabre had
long since dissipated into thin air.

Suddenly there was a commotion in the branches above
him. But it didn't startle him. Chipmunk probably. Later
when darkness fell there would be other noises. He wasn't
afraid of the woods, nor of the creatures that inhabitated the
woods, nor of night, nor of space, nor of solitude. None of
these things ever questioned you or showed up your weak
points. Never censored nor judged, rated or berated.

He had always been rated by his ability to live up to certain standards pronounced desirable, and if he fell too far
short of them he had felt horribly inferior. But here in the
woods Nature imposed no standards upon its creatures, set
no records. No mottoes existed. No Ten Commandments,
no manuals on good sportsmanship. Here each animal, tree,
or plant, lived according to its own nature, simply, serenely
governed by laws of which it was oblivious, and never felt
apologetic for differences in characteristics and behavior,
size, shape or appearance. The low-growing juniper was
without envy of the lofty hemlock. The low-flying partridge
felt no urge to emulate the eagle. Here each living thing
followed its own inclination and suffered from no sense of
shame. It had been from a sense of shame that he had given
up his tree-houses and abandoned the fantastic notion of
becoming a naturalist. He was starting in on his last year at
Law School next fall. The plan now was for him to enter
his uncle's law firm when he graduated.

4

CHAPTER

Iт нар веен Windy who had made him feel ashamed of
his tree-houses. One night at dinner Windy remarked that
even girls gave up playing with doll-houses when they were
his age (he was about twelve then), and that it was high time
for him to be playing football instead of house. His mother
had told Windy that he wasn't playing house, but following
in the footsteps of his Great-Grandfather Vale who was an
authority on trees and his Grandfather Fabyan who had
been a college professor of botany all his life. His mother
was always quick on the trigger to stand up for him. Defending his tree-houses like that was typical.

Windy had had his best interests at heart. After dinner
he had told him in private, following him up into the top
of the Sophora, that he wanted his kid brother to be a
regular fellow, and that sitting around in trees and watching
scum turn into mosquitoes and grubs into cocoons didn't contribute to it. It happened that all Windy's tastes and characteristics did contribute to it. He was a natural athlete, far from
a natural student; gay, affable, kind, and a born leader. Windy
had always been an example to Murray of what he would like
to be but never could. In appearance — tall, blond, and
virile, resembling somewhat that gilded young god in Guido
Reni's 'Aurora,' borne along in a chariot drawn by spirited
horses and surrounded by admirers. Windy had preceded him
everywhere — at kindergarten, day school, prep school, col-

lege, and camp, leaving a trail of glory in his wake that cast its
rosy glow on him plodding along on foot several years behind.
He had only to say that he was Windy Vale's brother to
bring forth a burst of cordial greeting from any host or
hostess who didn't know who he was, and it had a magic
effect on a girl's attitude. 'The brother of my brother. That's
all I am,' he once remarked to his mother.

His mother had recognized the unfortunate difference between her two sons, and for several years had sent him to a
preparatory school which Windy had never attended. But
Windy's reputation was so widespread that it didn't help
much. He was still Windy Vale's brother. He hadn't attempted to vie with the records Windy set up, nor with the
brilliant impressions he made. That would have been futile,
but he had tried to make the contrast between them as
inconspicuous as possible.

A catastrophe had happened to Windy the year before he
went to college. He had been struck down by infantile
paralysis. For days he had hovered between life and death.
For months the doctors had thought the muscles in his legs
would never hold his weight again. It had been a terrific
blow to his parents, to both of them, of course, but it had
been harder for his father. Windy was his eldest son. He
bore his name — Rupert Vale. He bore also the qualities and
attributes to carry on the name. His father was a proud man
to whom appearances meant much, never unconscious of his
stature in the community — the eldest Vale of his generation,
president of an important banking firm, a member of various
distinguished boards of trustees, and a frequent figurehead
at important assemblies.

One day when Windy was still very sick his father had
summoned his unprepossessing younger son into his study
and asked him if he realized what Windy's catastrophe
would mean to his future. Murray had shaken his head,
tongue-tied. He had always been afraid of his tall imposing

father. He was only fourteen at the time, still undersized, still spectacled and still pale and tow-headed. His father had said it would mean that he must assume the responsibilities of his eldest son. 'You must now carry on the tradition and prestige of our family,' he said. 'Even if Windy lives he will always be a helpless cripple. Your position and Windy's have been reversed. You will now be the physically stronger and more fit. Therefore you must immediately prepare yourself for the mantle that will fall upon you.'

For the first time in many months he had wept when he went to bed that night. He remembered it vividly for he was supposed to have outgrown crying. His mother had caught him at it. He told her that it ought to have been *he* who had been stricken down by polio, not Windy. He wished it had been he. He didn't want the responsibilities of an eldest son. He didn't want to carry on traditions or prestige. He didn't want to bear the mantle his father said was to fall upon him.

He needn't have shed those tears at all. His father's predictions proved a false alarm. Windy's handicaps did not reverse their positions nor their fitness for the positions. The disease did indeed destroy certain important muscles below Windy's waist. But it didn't affect his natural agility. The co-ordination between his brain and body escaped unscathed, also the fighting spirit behind it. He entered college only a year later than he planned. Once his greatest ambition had been to pile up scores on football gridirons and baseball diamonds for the college of his choice, but when this was nipped in the bud he didn't sit around and mope. Instead he applied himself to winning competitions in swimming-pools and sculling on water-courses in a specially constructed shell. Windy's gift for leadership also escaped unscathed. Instead of playing on the football team he was Manager of it. He was also President of the Athletic Association, President of his club and Chief Marshal of his class when he graduated. Easily the best-known man in college, the most popular, the most admired and the most cheered.

Windy had attended all the important football games throughout his college course, and afterwards, too. He was a familiar sight in the bowl of the Stadium. Seated in his wheelchair, pushed by devoted comrades, accompanied by Thirp, his dog, he could usually be spotted down in front somewhere on the sidelines on the same level with the players, referees, linesmen, and cheer-leaders. If Harvard won and the victory was important enough for a snake dance to follow, Windy would not be left behind stranded in his chair, but lifted to the shoulders of his comrades as if he were their mascot. It became a sort of symbol of victory to bear Windy Vale aloft from goalpost to goalpost in a twisting course. It was an impressive spectacle.

Murray had gazed down upon it on several occasions. During the fall when he came home from boarding-school for the weekend there would be likely to be tickets for the game in the Stadium. His mother often attended the games. Sometimes his father and several others would be in the party.

Once a friend of his mother's, standing beside him looking down at the exhibition, exclaimed, 'Aren't you proud to be the brother of such a hero?' There were tears in her eyes, she was so moved by the combination of Windy's misfortune and his ovation.

'Yes, terribly proud,' he replied with the proper emphasis.

That night he told his mother that he had decided he did not want to go to Harvard. His mother had expressed no surprise, but she seldom expressed surprise. She asked him where he would like to go. He was ready with his answer. He had been thinking about it for some time.

'I'd like to go to some state college out West.'

'Harvard is a tradition with the Vales,' she said. 'I'm afraid Uncle Lloyd won't approve of sending you to any other college but Harvard.'

This was shortly after his father's death. Uncle Lloyd and Uncle Hilary had taken on the expense of the education of both Windy and him when their father's finances went onto the rocks in 1930.

'Then I won't go to college at all.'

'Windy will be at Harvard only your first year, Murray.'

'It hasn't anything to do with Windy,' he denied stoutly and to convince her still further, he added, 'I'm proud to be the brother of such a hero.'

A pained look shot across his mother's face. He wished she wasn't always feeling sorry for him. Who wants only pity from his mother?

'I heard that woman this afternoon, Murray,' his mother said. 'She's a silly, sentimental person, always slopping over some way. Of course, we're all proud of Windy, but it's more fun to *be* a hero, than to be proud of one.'

'To be a hero, Mother, you have got to have something to be a hero about,' he said.

'Yes, I guess that's true,' she replied, and fell into one of her brown studies. Then her face lit up as if she had an inspiration. 'I'll tell you what I'll do, I'll have a talk with Uncle Lloyd tomorrow.' How his spirits had lifted. 'I'll tell him your wishes, but if he won't consider sending you to another college, perhaps going to Harvard — not turning tail, but seeing it through — will be something for you to be a hero about.'

His mother was very ingenious. In those days she could always swing him around to do something she thought wise. She scarcely ever insisted on her way but sort of ensnared you into agreement. He went to Harvard. He didn't turn tail. He saw it through. But it certainly hadn't made a hero out of him. His career at Harvard had been drab and uneventful.

The only offices he had held had been that of Treasurer of the Biological Society, President of a bird club he'd started

himself, and Recording Secretary one year of his final club.
He had made a final club — Windy's club. Naturally being
Windy's brother. He'd gone out for football and crew both,
but he'd never competed in anything but interclass games
and races. His athletic career had petered out completely
by the end of his second year. A degree had been conferred
upon him when he graduated and a cum laude. But not a
magna cum laude. There had been nothing magna, nor
super, nor extraordinary, about any of his performances at
college. And how he had struggled even to acquire mediocrity. Mediocrity! That was his pigeonhole. Of course he'd
made some good friends at Harvard. Yet come to think of it,
all his best friends he'd known before he entered Harvard,
at prep school and here at Tamarack.

At Tamarack they'd be sitting in a big circle, now, on
Campfire Rock. Darkness had fallen. He could see a few
faint stars shining through the holes of his lacy roof. There
would be a huge bonfire burning in the center of the circle,
the flames roaring and the sparks leaping up out of them
into the sky. They would all be singing. The older boys,
whose voices had already changed or were changing, would
be making a deep roar like the roar of the flames, the high
clear trebles of his little chaps in Opechee mounting up out
of it like the soaring sparks.

It would be time pretty soon for the Opechees to go to
their cabin. At nine o'clock, if he were there, he would stand
up and blow his whistle, and from all directions the
Opechees would come flocking, like young partridges in the
woods when their mother calls to them. He would lead the
way and they would follow after as instinctively as a brood,
some crowding close about him, others straggling, but not a
single one deserting. The thought of the effect of today's
events upon his brood was mighty disturbing. He'd better
rehearse his story again.

He crossed his hands on his chest and closed his eyes as once more he set out on the long journey of his narrative. But he got no further than, 'I'd paddled stern going up the lake, and didn't want to hurt Briggs's feelings,' when his thoughts became blurred, his hands fell limp at his sides and he fell asleep.

It was a profound sleep. When he woke up several hours later he lay perfectly still for a moment, remembering nothing. Then reality began reasserting itself. First, a vague premonition penetrated the fog of his semiconsciousness like the blurred headlight of a steam-engine bearing down upon you on a misty night. Then came the sharp pain that shoots down through your insides just before an impact, and immediately after the impact itself as the truth strikes, followed by a succession of well-remembered facts hurtling over you, like the wheels of a long train of cars, while you lie trapped beneath, conscious and aware. It was better not to go to sleep at all than to repeat the torture of waking up.

He struggled to a half-sitting posture, leaning groggily against the rock. A shiver ran through his body. He drew in his breath. It caught somewhere. He was seized with an attack of coughing. He sank back exhausted. As he lay there breathing cautiously so his breath wouldn't catch again, he heard the high hum of a mosquito. Then of another. They had discovered him again! He drew out his handkerchief and spread it over his upturned face and folded his hands on his chest. Another shiver ran down his spine. Was he having a chill? Didn't you get pneumonia if you carried water around in your lungs?

Pneumonia wouldn't strike you as soon as this, of course, but perhaps by tomorrow or the next day, if he lay right here and waited, he would be too sick to move, and he wouldn't have to tell his story to Mr. Ben or make any explanation to Windy or to anybody. His body would never be found. No-

body would think of hunting for a drowned man several
miles inland! This was an untraveled region. His bones
would lie here undiscovered in their leaf-roofed vault forever, gradually become dust, mix with the leaf-mold and
help feed the sumacs. The contemplation of this thought
gave him a sense of peace. He was all ready, even to the
folded hands and the handkerchief spread over his face. The
shivering stopped, his breathing became measured, and
again he fell asleep.

5

CHAPTER

As soon as it was light enough to travel he was on his feet again, pushing his way toward his dreaded destination. He didn't even remember the mental image of his timely death till he had been traveling for over an hour. When it did recur he relegated it to the realm of daydreaming — an utterly futile device to escape reality, drugging to action, he well knew, and to be avoided. There had been no more chills or fits of coughing. Instead he was aware of hunger when he first woke up. So he guessed he wasn't on the verge of pneumonia!

For breakfast he ate half the sweet chocolate, washed down by brook water, and a handful of edible mushrooms. At least he knew the mushrooms were not poisonous. He munched checkerberry leaves, sassafras bark and Indian cucumber roots as he pursued his way. He hoped to run across some blueberries or raspberries, but the woods were too dense. He doubted if they'd ever been lumbered or swept by fire. However, there were other varieties of berries less juicy and sweet that would fill up space in his stomach — bunchberries, partridge berries, huge, red, winter-seasoned checkerberries. Also there was an abundance of ferns. It was too late for fiddleheads — those tender coiled fronds as tasty as asparagus tips. But there were 'hearts of Osmund' (so called in his fern book) — an ivory-white nugget as crisp as a celery-heart, which lay wrapped up in the center of the hairy roots of the common cinnamon fern.

Clouds had gathered during the night — low, thick, and cottony. He needed his compass badly. The brooks and streams would all be flowing toward the lake, so they were no help in guiding him to Long Pond. The ledge, at the foot of which he had spent the night, faced east. He had started off in the right direction. Deprived of both sun and shadows he had proceeded methodically, selecting some outstanding landmark straight in front of him — a boulder, stump, or conspicuous tree — then plodding his way through or around whatever obstacle intervened. At each destination he paused and carefully selected the next goal. He didn't forget the moss on the trees, and its tendency to grow on the damp side (usually the north side in this part of the world if the tree isn't leaning), but much of the time there was no moss, only lichens.

It was a shock when he came twice upon the same swamp with the skeleton of a tall tree in its center, and a ragged bird's nest in its top. He had been traveling in a circle! Not one of those frenzied circles a man runs around in when he has lost his nerve as well as his bearings, but a wide, slowly inscribed circle.

As the day wore on there was fog as well as clouds. It became so thick he couldn't keep his goals in sight even long enough to go around the insurmountable blow-downs. He climbed several trees but there was even less to be seen from their tops.

Finally he decided to abandon his plan to pick up the Appalachian trail. By nightfall anxiety would be felt because Briggs and he had not returned. As the anxiety became alarm there would be searchers abroad. He concluded to return to the lake shore, where he would soon be picked up by one of the searchers. He had only to follow a stream — one of Nature's ready-made tunnels through the wilderness, to reach the lake. It would be easier traveling than blazing his own trail.

He was surprised when his stream emptied into a good-
sized pond. He circled the pond, but could find no outlet.
Buried, probably. So he plunged into the tangled confusion
of the woods again in search of another stream. It proved
to be the same one! It led him to the same pond! Another
circle!

Well, he mustn't get jittery. He wasn't lost. He had only
to wait till the weather cleared to get out of this maze. Even
though he couldn't locate the Lake nor Long Pond either,
this wasn't a limitless wilderness. It had a boundary around
its entire edge, any point of which was within reasonable
walking distance if he kept going in a straight line. As soon
as the sun came out that would be simple. No reason to be
alarmed. He would neither starve nor freeze at this time
of the year. There were no wild animals to attack him. The
largest animal he'd seen all day was a skunk. Moreover, even
if he were in danger of perishing, why did he object so?
Only last night, passing out of the picture had appealed to
him as a fortunate escape.

Yes, but death from pneumonia is quick and painless,
isn't it? You just lie there, listless and willing, lose consciousness, and it happens. Wandering alone in the woods
for days till you're too weak to crawl is a different proposi-
tion. The combination of fatigue and an empty stomach
sometimes causes hallucinations. You're apt to get panicky.
Some men go crazy. No, thanks! Not for him! He stood up.
He simply mustn't lose his nerve! He must act as if he had
one of his kid campers along who was scared and dependent
on him for courage and wisdom.

It was getting dark. Obviously another night must be
spent in the open. Well, what of it? That's what he'd say
to his camper. What of it? Come on, let's get busy, look for
something to eat and find a comfortable bed while there's
still daylight left. His eyes fell upon a stand of cattails not
ten feet away. Every year he introduced to his new campers

the various edible qualities of cattails. He gathered a supply
of the pithy cores at the junction of the sprouting stems
and managed with difficulty to secure several sections of the
roots packed full of starch. He stuffed his stock in his
pockets and then went in search of a bed.

He had noticed a cover of ferns growing on some flat
ground near the edge of the stream. He made his way back
to them. They were strong, upright brakes standing three
feet high, spreading broad, rugged fronds. He lay down on
his stomach at their edge and burrowed his head and
shoulders beneath their umbrellalike protection. Night-fly-
ing insects would have some difficulty finding him, he hoped.

Sleep was slow in coming. His muscles ached. His skin
was covered with bruises and bites. It itched and smarted,
and no doubt exuded some sort of aroma that attracted the
mosquitoes and other bloodthirsty insects. They soon found
holes in his roof. Time and again he crawled under fresh
fern-fronds in an attempt to escape them. In the morning
the bed of ferns looked as if some terrific struggle had occurred there.

There was a variety of calls and sounds which had not disturbed his sleep the night before — the cry of a loon, the
hoot of an owl, the whirr of wings, the rapid barking of a fox.
Once the crashing of dead branches came to a stop close beside him. This time he lay very still wondering if two glowing eyes were staring at him. If so, the creature thought it
better policy not to interfere, for after a while he heard its
stealthy withdrawal. When finally he did begin dropping
off into lapses of unconsciousness the jar of the transition
seemed to wake him up. However, he concluded that he
slept for longer periods than he thought, long enough anyhow to dream.

One of his dreams was about Briggs. It was brief. Nothing happened. There was no conversation. It was more like

a vision. He couldn't have been completely unconscious, for
he had been aware of the smell of the crushed ferns when
Briggs appeared before him. Briggs was lying on the ground
beneath the overhanging shelf of a hollowed-out bank on the
edge of the lake. On the beach near-by the canoe lay
bottom-side up. Briggs was stretched out on his back with
his face turned up toward a lot of bare, scraggly roots that
were hanging down from his roof. Briggs was alive! He
could see his lashes winking at measured intervals. Briggs
didn't know he was being watched, and very softly, so as not
to startle him, he called, 'Briggs! Briggs!' The sound of his
own voice instantly recalled him to full consciousness.

At first he attached no more importance to this brief
glimpse of Briggs than to a common ordinary dream. But
those winking eyelashes kept returning and claiming his
attention. He had never put much stock in mental telepathy,
but there are people of intelligence who claim that there is
a scientific basis for thought-waves communicating across
miles of space. However, there can be no communicating
thought-waves between the alive and dead. If there was one
theory he considered bunk, it was spiritualism. And Briggs
was dead. Or so he had been assuming. He had no proof
of it.

Suddenly his meandering thoughts were pulled up to a
sharp stop. Briggs might have gotten back to the overturned
canoe! He might have managed to hang on to it somehow!
The canoe might have cleared the falls! It might be lying
there on the beach as he had seen it in his dream, and Briggs
might be stretched out not far away from it, pretty nearly
all in, but alive and winking, thinking of him at the same
moment he was thinking of Briggs, and their thought-waves
crossed. The contemplation of Briggs alive became a hope,
faint, flickering, but not an impossibility; one of these one
chance in a thousand hopes you cling to, just to keep yourself going and your upper lip stiff.

He had decided during the night that if it hadn't cleared
by morning he would stay where he was until the fog lifted.
But after an hour of sitting idle enveloped in a white, motionless shroud which dimmed all sounds as well as objects,
so that the dropping of a cone at his feet had made him
jump as if a gun had gone off, he concluded it was better to
be moving if only for the reassurance of the sound made by
his own footsteps. He decided to follow the same stream
that had led him here, even to its source if necessary.
It would at least prevent him from inscribing circles, and
somewhere along its route something might turn up in the
way of deliverance.

After several hours, while resting on a bank, he was rewarded by the sound of rippling water in the distance. He
investigated and discovered a narrow ribbon of water dash-
ing boldly down a bare incline and disappearing in a direction almost at right angles to his stream. He decided to
follow it. It was something flowing downhill which wouldn't
empty into that damned pond! It was scarcely more than a
brook at first. It widened gradually. Another brook joined
it. Several bubbling spring-holes made their contribution.
In time it became a respectable, full-sized mountain stream,
with pools, rapids and quiet sandy stretches.

Mile after mile, hour after hour, he followed its convolutions. He lost all track of time. He thought dusk was falling
on several occasions but it proved merely that the pall of
clouds or canopy of leaves overhead was temporarily
thicker. He ate very little this second day (or was it the
third day) and began seeing startling shapes and forms in
the rotting stumps, lichened rocks, and leaf-mold. A bear
cub, a man in khaki, a lean-to, a liver-and-white hound, and
once a crouching wildcat. Am I beginning to have hallucinations? That's what happens if your stomach gets too
empty.

I've got to keep my nerve. That little fourteen-year-old

kid who was lost on Katahdin for nine days kept *his* nerve.
I may be lost for nine days myself! There won't be any
planes out looking for me for some time yet. I wish I had
that kid's youth, his ignorance, and a little of his faith. I wish
I could sit down and bawl and relieve my feelings and then
pray to God and feel better for it.'

He was very tired. His body ached. His feet hurt. He
was covered with bites and bruises. He would stop at the
first place where he could spread out flat and stay there
until morning.

He had just arrived at this conclusion when he saw something that brought him to a halt. It looked like a bridge.
He was walking in the center of the river-bed at this time.
Straight in front, spanning the stream and several feet above it
there was a row of black disks which resembled the weathered
ends of the logs of a corduroy road. He approached skep-
tically. Unlike the other illusions, it did not disintegrate as
he drew nearer. When he was within a few feet of the disks
he reached up and touched one. Solid! Real! Grabbing and
scrambling, he hauled his body up onto the top of the
bridge, and then got up onto his feet.

A lumber road. A man-made lumber road. An over-
whelming sense of relief surged up to his throat. It was
like waking up from a nightmare.

He looked first to the right and then to the left. In both
directions he saw inscribed in the fog a gentle curve, open
to the sky above, cleared of all entanglements below. Each
end of the curve disappeared into the atmosphere like the
ends of a rainbow. Yes, the lumber road was like a rainbow.
It was promise of deliverance.

He didn't know which way to turn. One way would
probably lead to an abandoned lumber-camp, the other to
habitation finally. He turned to the right.

How smooth to the feet! How sweet to the eyes! How

neat and well-ordered, as if laid out by a landscape archi-
tect. There was a three-foot strip of tall grass in the center
of the road with a path on each side worn smooth by wheels.
On the outer edge of each path there was a mixed border
of hardy perennials — yarrow, butter-and-eggs, milkweed,
mosquito plant, everlasting, sweet fern, and spikes of dock.
In the foreground, on both sides, the foliage of trees appeared, hanging down mysteriously from out of the fog like
the foliage framing a sylvan scene at the theater. As he
walked, the same scene kept unrolling before his eyes. Occasionally a small bird flew from one tree to another. Once a
brown rabbit darted silently across his path.

He had not thought he could keep going much longer, just
before he had broken out upon the road, but now he felt as
if he were rolling along on wheels, or more as if the road
itself were on wheels, like a moving sidewalk. He didn't
have to use any brain-power even. The effect upon his
spirits as well as upon his body was exhilarating. The little
flame of hope about Briggs, which he'd been nursing all day,
burned stronger.

6

CHAPTER

HE HAD COVERED several miles of the road when he saw a small house ahead of him in a clearing. It had a shaggy shingled roof and an ell covered with tar-paper. There was smoke coming out of the chimney over the ell. That meant a human being! There were white curtains with ruffles at the two front windows. That meant a woman! There was a flat-bottomed rowboat filled with magenta petunias and varicolored portulaca beside the path to the back door. Further indication of a woman.

It might frighten a woman if he were to appear upon her doorstep. He was not a pretty sight — covered with bites and bruises, unshaven for the third day, his shirt bloody, his shorts in tatters. As he hesitated, the door in the ell opened and a woman with gray hair came out. She walked down the path to where he stood beside the rowboat. She didn't appear in the least startled by him.

'I seen you comin'! Had any luck?'

He thought it best to reply in the negative.

'Why you back so early then? And where's the other feller? You said you wouldn't be back till after dark unless you found somethin'!'

'Did I say that?'

She looked at him sharply and came a step nearer. 'Lands! I declare! You all look alike to me in them cloes.' There was a pair of steel-bowed glasses in the pocket on the left of her large, broad, soft front. She put them on and looked at him still closer. 'Yes, you're a new one. Sure enough! Where did you come from?'

He nodded toward the lumber road. 'From the woods.'

'You don't usually look for a drowned man in the woods!'

'I lost my way and was trying to get back to camp by going around Long Pond.'

'Long Pond! For the land's sake! Why, you ain't anywheres near Long Pond.'

'Where am I?'

'You're right on the edge of your own lake. It's about twenty-five yards in front of your nose, behind them birches.'

'Am I anywhere near Heron Swamp?'

'Sure you be! 'Bout quarter of a mile south of it.'

South of it! Then he must have circled Long Pond — missed it completely, and the trail too. 'I guess I've got a rotten bump of direction.'

'This fog would get an Indian mixed up. Ever heard of Jim Billings?'

'He's the game warden, isn't he? Used to be a guide.'

'That's right. Well, this is where he lives in the summer. I'm Missis Billings. The first thing Mr. Ben did when that paddle was found was to get word to Jim to get out his outboard and join the search. Jim ain't had his cloes off for two nights.'

For two nights! Then the paddle must have been found the same night of the storm!

'Jim's out huntin' now with everybody else on the lake that's got a boat or a pair of legs. What portion of the shore was you to cover?'

He hesitated a moment, then risked, 'The portion south of Heron Swamp.' It appeared satisfactory to Mrs. Billings.

'Jim was combin' the east shore of Henderson's Point this mornin'. But he said he'd most likely go on foot down below the falls this afternoon.'

Mrs. Billings hadn't the slightest suspicion of his identity. He couldn't bring himself to blurt it out to her immediately. He would wait anyway till he'd had something to eat. 'I wonder if you'd be so good as to give me a glass of milk?'

'Of course! Glad to! Come right in!'

He followed her into the low-studded kitchen.

'You look as if you'd like to wash up first,' she said and poured him a pail of hot water from the kettle. He accepted it gratefully and followed her into the woodshed off the kitchen. She placed a tin basin on a bench, a piece of Ivory soap in a cracked saucer, and a towel beside it. 'Now make yourself to home,' she said and bustled back into the kitchen.

When he rejoined her he sat down in the chair she indicated at an oilcloth-covered table opposite the kitchen stove. There was a shelf over the stove, in the middle of which was an old steeple clock with the remains of a colored picture in the lower half of its glass door. At first he thought it must have stopped, for its hands were pointing to only half past five, but he could hear it ticking and see its pendulum racing madly back and forth through the bare spots where the picture was worn off.

'Here, you get your nose into that glass of milk,' said Mrs. Billings, and shoved a thick tumbler toward him filled to the brim with a beverage as sweet and smooth to his throat as the wood road to his feet. He tried to drink it slowly but the sensation of the milk going down his throat was too blissful to resist, and he didn't stop once between swallows. Mrs. Billings was staring at him when he put down the empty glass.

'Could you manage with some more?'

'I might.'

She was still watching him closely when he finished the second glass of milk. 'Where is your mate? There was two fellers from Tamarack here this noon and they said you was all working in pairs.'

'We decided to hunt separately for a while. He probably thinks I've joined up with some other pair.' He raised the empty glass to his lips and drained it of the few remaining drops.

'How would some ham and eggs taste to you?'

'Wonderful!'

She disappeared for a moment returning with a slab of pink fatty meat, and yellow bowl full of écru-colored eggs.

'Ham and eggs is what I give the other two fellers who was here this noon. Say, are you one of the counselors or one of the campers? I never can tell the age of boys once they've shot up, and I get those undercloes you wear for uniforms mixed up.'

'I'm one of the counselors.'

'How long you been lost?'

'Since last night.'

'You don't say! I thought you looked pretty well beat up, and bit up, too. Why, then you don't know the latest news!' She turned around and faced him.

'No.'

'They've found one of the fellers!'

'Which one?'

'The sickly one. I got it over the radio 'bout noontime.'

'Where did they find him?'

'On the beach near the end of Henderson's Point.'

'Was he — alive?'

'Mercy, no! The waves tossed his body up there. I never seen a worse storm. The lake just seemed to turn itself inside out. They're figurin' they'll find the other feller's body not far off. You want your eggs sunny side up or turned?'

'It doesn't matter.'

So it was a fact. Definite and final. Briggs was dead. He had known it the first moment he came to consciousness beside that old tree. He turned and gazed out of the window. What a fool he'd been to be inveigled by hope. Neither hope nor sleep were worth the price you paid for their brief intervals of relief. Each interval must be followed by a fresh thrust of reality, like the fresh thrust of a knife into your flesh. To avoid the thrusts he must keep the knife pushed down deep. Never hope. Never sleep. Never forget.

'Help yourself to the doughnuts.' Mrs. Billings placed a plate of them on the table, turning back afterwards to the stove. 'I hear this is the first drownin' accident Tamarack's ever had,' she went on conversationally. She paused but he made no reply. 'Leastwise, so them two fellers who et here this noon told me. I gathered your Mr. Ben set great store by his no-drownin' record. They said he was always talking about not lettin' it get broke.' Again she paused. Again no response. 'Well, it's broke now all right. Seems an awful pity.' Still he was silent. Only a question would rouse him, apparently. 'Was you well acquainted with the poor boys?'

'I knew one fairly well.'

'Which one?'

'The one they haven't found.'

'Oh, the strong one — the Harvard boy.'

He nodded.

'One of them two fellers here this noon was called Tug. You know him?'

'Yes. I know Tug.'

'He kep' callin' the Harvard boy "Bug." Lands sakes! Never heard such outlandish nicknames fer nice educated young men. Tug and Bug! Tug ain't so bad, but Bug — sounds like somethin' crawlin' and pesterin'. What'd they ever call him Bug fer?'

'It's short for bughouse on bugs.'

'Bughouse on bugs!'

'Yes. He used to collect bugs for the fun of it and look at them through a microscope.'

'Oh, one of them natural-hist'ry fellers! Jim guided one once. 'Stead of a rod and tackle he carried a net and a bucket with a glass bottom in it so's he could look down into the water and see what there was to see, and instead of bringin' a string of fish back to camp he was content with a pail of mud. You mean that kind of a crank?'

'Yes. That kind of a crank.'

'Them two fellers here this noon never mentioned it.'

'That was mighty nice of them. But he has gotten pretty well over it by now.'

'Yet come to think of it, I do recollect that feller Tug sayin' Bug was more the quiet studious type than one of these mixers. The two poor boys was alike in some ways, 'cordin' to your friend Tug.'

Murray winced inwardly. Alike? According to Tug? Mr. Ben had intimated it, too, when he said he thought Briggs and he would find a lot in common. Why, he had pitied Briggs! He had felt an element of scorn for his attempts not to offend, and his inability to mix. Well, that was logical. You often dislike in others qualities you despise in yourself.

'What was Bug's real name?' pursued Mrs. Billings. 'The whole of it. They call him just Vale over the radio.'

"Murray Vale.'

'What?' He usually had to repeat it.

'Murray — Vale,' he said more slowly feeling the old embarrassment.

'Oh, I thought you said "Mary." "Murray Vale,"' she repeated. 'That's real nice. I had three boys. I named one of 'em Earl, one of 'em LeRoy, and one of 'em Errol. Murray's pretty-soundin', too.'

'He always hated it!'

'You seem to of been real intimate. Was he a close friend of yours?'

'Well, yes, close in one way. We lived close to each other, but he isn't my idea of a friend exactly.' His tone was edged with ridicule.

'You talk mighty different about him than them two here this noon. Why, they was just full of praise of him. They said your Mr. Ben set great store by him, and that all the little shavers in his dormitory just worshiped the ground he walked on.'

'Stray dogs and cats take to him, too,' added Murray.

'Tug said the little shavers were broke up bad about his drownin' but feelin' mighty proud, too, because it's *their* counselor that everybody is sayin' deserves one of them bronze medals for heroism.'

'Are they saying that?'

'They sure be! Don't you think a feller deserves a medal if he dies tryin' to save another feller?'

'Of course,' quickly he assured her. 'But who knows but that it was the other way 'round?'

'What you drivin' at?'

'Perhaps it was Briggs who died trying to save Vale.'

'There ain't a chance of it! Say, what ails you? Why, Tug said everybody at Tamarack knows young Vale was a strong swimmer and could of saved himself easy if he'd been alone, but he knew about Briggs's weak heart, like all you counselors did, and felt it was his duty to look out for him, 'specially in view of that motto you got at Tamarack, 'bout protectin' the weak. Did you know the Vale boy's folks too?' she broke off.

'We have a speaking acquaintance.'

'I spose he's got a mother?'

'Yes. He's got a mother.'

'Poor woman! I can't help thinkin' about her. I know what it's like. That's a picture of my Errol up over the mantel. He got killed in the last war, and him only nineteen. 'Course his mother will feel proud of him,' she soliloquized, 'but his place at the table will be empty and his room, too, and he won't be comin' in at the door any more and hollerin' "Ma" first thing he opens his mouth, or writin' her letters or anything.' She heaved a deep sigh and turned back to the stove, attacked the eggs with a fork, the spattering increasing, then lifted the frying-pan from the stove and brought it back to the table. 'Come, come, what you starin' at out that window? Here's your eggs all nice and hot. You get onto the outside of this dishful and you'll feel a whole sight better. You act kinder petered out to me.'

He bent over the eggs and began to eat. Mrs. Billings sat down opposite him, folding her hands companionably on the table.

'I've been livin' on this lake over thirty years. There's been a lot of drownin' accidents, countin' 'em all up, but I don't get used to 'em. They always send for Jim first thing to get out his outboard and join the searchers, and bring along his pulmotor, and I have to stay here waitin'. I get awful uneasy. Even when I know there ain't any more hope, like now, and no need of his pulmotor, I can't ever settle down to anything 'till the body is found.'

'Are the bodies always found?'

'Yes, most always. They come floatin' up after a while. Sometimes it's as long as a week. Sometimes two or three. If the lake gets froze over it may not be 'till the ice goes out. I never heard of but one body that wasn't found, and that one went over the falls. There's a pond down below the falls beyond the rapids that used to be a swamp. It's full of a lot of old tree-stumps with roots. Some of the roots are like grapples. If a body once gets caught in one of 'em, it's likely to stay 'till it rots. Old man Keezar had a cow that sunk in some mud on the edge of that pond and her carcass never come up. 'Hello!' She broke off. 'There's Jim drawin' up to the float. He's gettin' home earlier 'n he said. Wonder what's bringin' him. Perhaps they've found the other feller's body.' She stood up. 'I better be gettin' his supper. He'll be hungry. He ain't been back since mornin'.'

Murray shoved back his chair and also stood up. 'I must be going along.'

'No, you mustn't. You set right down again and finish with Jim. I got a lemon sheefon pie I made this morning for dessert.'

7
CHAPTER

J IM WAS tall and rangy, with a lean, seamed face and small, sharp, very blue eyes. He wore leather-topped rubber boots laced up over canvas trousers, and a gray flannel shirt. His hat was a shabby brown felt with several catgut leaders and a fly or two wound around its band.

'Well, what's the news? Have they found the other feller yet?' demanded Mrs. Billings before Jim had a chance to speak.

'Not yet.'

He walked over toward the kitchen sink, pausing when he saw there was a stranger seated at the table.

'This is another of the counselors from Tamarack,' said Mrs. Billings. 'He lost his bearin's and has been out all night.' She turned toward Murray. 'I forgot to ask your name. What is it?'

He hesitated. The psychological moment for revealing his identity had passed. Too late now. But why should he reveal it at *all* to these chance acquaintances? It would cause an avalanche of questions which he would have to answer all over again when he reached camp. These thoughts passed through his mind during the half-dozen seconds between Mrs. Billings' question and his answer.

'My name is Brown,' he said.

'I suppose you got a first name, too.'

'Of course! Thomas,' he chose from out of the blue.

'Tom for short, I suppose. Tom Brown.' (What a fool he'd

been! Might as well have said William Shakespeare!) 'That's
certainly a good plain name!' (Thank heaven for the limita-
tions of Mrs. Billings' education!) 'This is Tom Brown, Jim.'

'Glad to meet yer, Mr. Brown,' said Jim and continued on
his way to the sink. 'I've got to eat quick and get right back,
Myrie. Just heat me up anything you've got handy.' He
placed a basin in the sink beneath the single faucet and
turned it on. Mrs. Billings followed after him with the
kettle from the stove and poured some steaming water into
the basin. Jim proceeded to wash his hands.

'What brought you back so early?'

'I wanted to get my flashlight. Likely to be out late.'

'Ain't anything else been found yet?'

'Yes, the canoe and a pocket handkerchief with the Briggs
feller's name on it.'

'Well, my goodness, why didn't you say so? Where did
they find 'em? When did they find 'em? Who found 'em?'
Her questions tumbled over each other.

'Hold yer horses, Myrie. I'll tell yer 'bout it soon's I wash
up.'

Jim splashed about in the basin like a canary in a saucer,
afterwards wiping his face and hands on a roller-towel
fastened on a door near by, then sat down opposite Murray.
Murray lowered his eyes. There was a coating of drying egg
yolk on his plate which he fell to scraping up with the edge
of his fork.

' 'Twas me found the canoe, and the handkerchief, too,'
Jim announced. 'The canoe was lying bottom-side up under
some alders, stuck fast on a sapling stump underneath her.
What with the fog being so thick and the alders, too, nobody'd seen her.'

Murray reached for a doughnut. In as offhand a tone as
he could summon he inquired, 'Were the alders below the
falls or on this side?' If below the falls, his decision to
abandon the canoe might be justified — but if on *this* side

he would be found guilty on still another count — that of
bad judgment.

'Oh, on this side!' Jim replied. 'Gawdamighty! There
wouldn't be much left of a canoe if it went over them falls.
You know Henderson's Point and that long bar of sand that
runs out? Well, that's where she was, not twenty feet from
the spot where Briggs's body was washed up. First thing
I did after I found her was to send word to Mr. Ben, then
haul her up on the beach and look her over sharp for what
evidence she had to offer.'

Mrs. Billings turned to Murray, caught his eye and
winked. 'You ever hear of Sherlock Holmes?'

Murray nodded.

'Jim thinks he's another one like him. Well, Mr. Holmes,
what did you find?'

'Oh, nothing much, except a lot of marks on her under
side. She'd just been painted. First time she'd been in the
water since. So whatever marks was on her was made that
day. The campers painted her. Amateur job. Her paint was
as soft as the skin of a new-born baby. The scratches were
made by something metal with ribs. In one place there was
an imprint of the ribs as clear as a seal pressed down hard
in soft sealing wax.'

Murray glanced down at the ribbed stem of his watch,
then quickly dropped his hand to his knee hiding it under the
table top.

'You got any notion what made them marks, Mr. Holmes?'
inquired Mrs. Billings.

'Yes, I've got a notion. Mr. Ben says Briggs used to carry
one of them screw-top pencils made of metal clipped into the
front pocket of his shorts. Looks to me as if Briggs made
those marks somehow or other, with that pencil. Perhaps
he was lying on the bottom of the canoe with his arms
round her hanging on like bloody murder. Don't know. Puz-
zling.'

'Where did you find the handkerchief?' asked Mrs. Billings.

'Washed up on the shore not far from the canoe. It's two opposite corners were tied together in a knot.'

'For the land's sake! What do you figure that was for?'

'Might have been he tied it round his head 'stead of a hat. It was a pretty hot day.'

'Too bad there weren't any witnesses,' said Murray.

'It sure is! The only way we know they were crossing the lake was old man Keezar saw 'em when he passed by in his outboard quite a spell before the storm. They were about halfway across then. Me and everybody else have been theorizing about what happened with almost no clues till I found that canoe today near the falls with those scratches on her. *Now* I've got something to base an opinion on.'

'What is your opinion?'

'Well, it looks to me like those boys got scared of the falls. Those scratches show they hung on to the canoe for a while, or anyway Briggs did, but not long enough. Even with their weight I'll wager she'd of landed them safe and sound this side of the falls if they'd stayed with her. Lost their heads is my guess. Mr. Ben says Vale wouldn't of lost *his* head. He says he'd never have left that canoe too soon unless Briggs slipped off and he had to go to his rescue. Maybe that's what happened. They're saying down at Tamarack he was the kind who would consider it his duty not to come back without Briggs. His brother told me today even as a kid he was always driving himself to do what he thought he ought to.'

'His brother! Is his brother here?' exclaimed Murray.

'Yep.'

'When did he come?'

'First minute he got word. By plane yesterday morning.'

'Did his mother come too?' asked Mrs. Billings. 'And are the Briggs feller's folks here yet?'

'Briggs hasn't got any folks except his mother and she's on
her third honeymoon in Europe. The Vale feller's mother
is spending the summer at a ranch out of reach somewheres
in Canada with her husband and kid child. The older
brother is hoping not to tell her about the drowning 'till
we've found the body. Say,' he broke off, 'who do you think
the older brother is, Myrie?'

'Who?'

'That lame feller who used to be a counselor at Tamarack!'

'You don't mean Windy Vale?'

'Yep.'

'Well, for mercy's sakes!' She turned to Murray. 'You
never told me your friend was the brother of Windy Vale!
Everybody up around here was just crazy about him. Lame
'n' everythin'. Yet so handsome and lively and smilin' and
nice to everybody. Is he just the same, Jim?'

'Just the same, even to that dog of his. Full of energy as
a dynamo. Going up and down the lake in the launch with
Mr. Ben. Jumping in and out on his crutches. Tonight he's
joining the searchers again in the launch. It's beginning to
look as if Vale's body must of gone over the falls. Mr. Ben
wants everybody to bring their flashlights and search below
the falls tonight. Hurry up with my coffee, Myrie. I told
Mr. Ben I wouldn't be gone long. Him and Windy Vale are
already there.' He turned toward Murray. 'I'll take you along
with me, if you'd like.'

Appear before them alive, hale and hearty when they were
hunting for his body!

'I think I'd better go back to camp first,' he said.

'Everybody's needed,' urged Jim.

'I want a fresh outfit.' (Even when they returned to camp
and found him it would be ghastly. He could see Windy's
shocked expression!)

'I can lend you some things,' Jim persisted.

'I think I'd better report first.'

'You can report to Mr. Ben when you see him up at the falls.'

'I don't feel too well. I want to get some medicine. I can join you later.'

'He's been out in the woods all night, Jim.'

'Well, suit yourself. You can paddle down in my canoe if you want to. It's shorter than by trail.'

'Thanks.'

'Myrie will give you the key to the boathouse. See you later.'

As soon as Jim had taken his departure Murray inquired of Mrs. Billings how far it was from her house to the main highway.

' 'Bout a mile and a half.'

'I think I'll walk out and take the bus down.' The bus passed within a quarter of a mile of the entrance to Tamarack. 'I happen to have some cash with me. I can even pay for my supper.'

'I'd like to see yer!'

'I'm a pretty tough-looking specimen for a bus. Your husband said he could lend me some clothes. Could you get me something of his that will cover these rags?'

'Of course! I can fix you up fine!'

An hour later, his camp uniform concealed by blue overalls shoved down in rubber-soled laced boots and Jim's canvas hunting-coat, he stood in the dense shadow of a tree at a bus stop on the main highway. Tamarack lay to the south. A south-bound bus approached, stopped, let off two passengers and then disappeared in the dark. It was a north-bound bus which he signaled, stepping out of the shadow of the tree and averting his face as the headlights fell upon him.

He paused at the driver's seat and paid his fare to the end of the route. The bus was half-filled. He made his way down the aisle, head lowered, and sat down in a high-backed, leather-covered armchair next to the window.

He thought he had never felt anything so comforting to his body as that chair. It seemed to nestle him like the arms of a woman her tired child. He slid down deeper into its embrace. The big soft tires of the fast revolving wheels on the smooth macadam road made as soothing a sound as a lullaby. The driver turned out the lights. He closed his eyes, leaned his forehead against the cool cheek of the windowpane and almost instantly fell asleep.

He slept the deep dreamless sleep of physical exhaustion without waking or stirring for several hours. When he finally opened his eyes the bus was shrouded in darkness, humming along the smooth polished highway with the swift unvarying speed of an ocean liner mounting and descending the silky-surfaced hills of the ocean when there is a ground swell.

At present the bus was passing through farming country. The fog had disappeared. From somewhere in the sky the moon was shedding a misty light. Open spaces bordered the highway. Sometimes farm buildings appeared — geometrical-shaped chunks of solid shadow. Occasionally there appeared a solitary light in one of the chunks — blood-orange-colored compared to the few faint silvery stars floating in the dusky blue of the upper half of the window-frame beside him. In the lower half the two horizontal rails of the state-road fence rose and fell, disappeared and reappeared, like endless streamers of ticker-tape constantly unreeling.

When the highway approached a populated area it was lit by frosted globes of light on high poles placed at measured intervals. The globes cast round islands of brightness on the roadbed below. As the bus skimmed from island to island its darkened interior would flare and fade like the pulsing effulgence from the revolving light of a lighthouse. There was something soothing about the rhythmic repetition, and reassuring, too. As long as the lights glowed and dimmed at measured intervals he was safe. He could turn over and go to sleep again.

But before he let himself drift back into unconsciousness he'd better consider what he was doing while there was still time to change his mind. He'd acted on the spur of the moment. When he stopped at Mrs. Billings' he had fully intended to return to Tamarack as soon as possible. Even when her information, and later Jim's, revealed how utterly he had failed to live up to the expectations of those whose opinions he valued most, no other alternative had occurred to him but to return immediately and face the condemning facts piled up against him. It wasn't until Jim announced that Windy was there that the thought of bolting occurred to him. He would rather go back into the woods and lose himself again than to have Windy listen to his stumbling explanations and witness his humiliation.

Even if he could prove he had held Briggs away from the jaws of death for a while, what a paltry claim! According to Tamarack's standards, and Mr. Ben's, and his fellow counselors', and Windy's, too, he ought to be dead. Alan Seeger's lines flashed into his mind. He had had a 'rendezvous with death' and had failed to keep it. Running off would not increase anxiety. All hope of finding him alive had been abandoned. They were hunting only for his remains. Fortunately his mother wasn't worrying even about his remains yet. Perhaps tomorrow he'd wire her. Perhaps he'd telephone Mr. Ben. That was an idea! It would be better for all concerned to telephone first. He would wait until tomorrow night and put in a call for Mr. Ben person to person. No hurry, thank Heaven. He slipped down into the fleshy softness of the chair and went to sleep again.

He ate breakfast in a night-lunch cart with colored-glass windows and shining nickel tanks. Seated on high stools at the same counter were the bus-driver, two truck-drivers, a traffic officer, and a lumberjack returning to his job after a spree in the city. He had taken a fancy to Murray in the early morning, insisting on changing from his chair across the aisle to the chair beside him. He told Murray he looked just like an old buddy of his, and then had informed him he was on his way to a logging-camp north of Millinocket somewhere. It was a good camp, good crew, good boss, good cook, good pay. If he was looking for a job he'd better come along with him.

For a fleeting five minutes Murray dallied with the suggestion. He even went so far as to ask how much the pay was and what experience was necessary. Idle questions, of course. His disguise was but a single layer deep of canvas. If anyone should unzip the front of Jim's hunting coat, a large capital T would appear branded upon his chest.

As he sat at the counter stirring his coffee it flashed over him that he was the only unidentified man in the group. And a hunted man besides. Of course the traffic policeman knew about the drowning and the search now going on. Everybody in the vicinity who listened to the radio knew about it. He began to feel extremely uncomfortable. He wasn't sure, but it seemed to him as if the officer was eyeing him with suspicion. The sleeves of Jim's coat were too short. His hands were too smooth and his nails too well-kept to go with his clothes. He kept his hands hidden under the counter as much as possible. It was an immense relief when the traffic officer finally left the lunch cart, mounted his motorcycle and zoomed away. He decided the next thing for him to do was to dispose of his camp uniform.

The night-lunch cart was located ten miles outside a city through which he had passed by automobile frequently when he was a boy. Every summer the family used to migrate to a certain island off the coast of Maine, and sometimes stopped for a meal at the hotel, famed for its down-East cooking. He left the bus a block or two before it passed the familiar hotel and pursued his way on foot along back streets toward the center of the city.

On one of the back streets he came upon a placard offering rooms for seventy-five cents a night. He was longing for a hot bath and to stretch out flat on a bed. The landlady told him bathtub privileges went with the room free of charge. The room had slanting walls, was small, musty-smelling, and at the top of the building two floors above the bathroom. But he said he would take it, and shortly afterwards was sitting in a bathtub of such abbreviated proportions that his drawn-up knees nearly touched his chin. The water was lukewarm and barely covered his thighs, but the worn-down cake of Ivory soap lathered well.

When he returned to his attic room his nakedness was concealed by Jim's jeans only. His camp uniform he carried in a roll under his arm. There was no bureau in the room where he might hide it in a drawer. But there was a commode. He pulled open the door of the lower part of the commode, letting out a very bad odor, and placed it back of a cracked, white-crockery chamber-pot.

He then stripped and flung himself crosswise on the narrow, white iron bed, shoved the flabby pillow beneath his cheek and slept again.

It was dark when he emerged from the room. That was good! He would be less conspicuous. He stole out to a drugstore, bought a tooth-brush, tooth-paste, soap, and a razor, returned to the room, made use of them all, then went in search of something to eat.

8

CHAPTER

HE DECIDED the railroad station, where strangers attract little attention, was the best place to satisfy his hunger. As he was leaving the lunch-room, walking along the platform beside the railroad tracks, an express train roared up behind him. It didn't stop, but it slowed down and a bundle of newspapers was thrown off. It contained the evening editions of several Boston newspapers. He waited until they were opened and then bought one at the news-stand.

He sat down on an empty bench in a far corner of the waiting room and opened the paper. Almost instantly his eyes fell upon his own name. At the top of the first page appeared a headline in big block letters: 'MURRAY VALE'S PIPE FOUND.' The details followed in fine print, difficult to decipher without his glasses, but not impossible. This is what he read:

> Late last night one of the volunteers searching for the missing body of Murray Vale found his pipe. The pipe bore the initials M. V. McTague Tyson, a close friend and a fellow counselor of Vale's, identified the pipe as the one he saw Vale smoking the morning of the drowning accident.
>
> The pipe was found in a pool beside the rapids at the foot of Henderson's Falls. It was Vale's custom to carry his pipe in an open pocket of his shorts. It is believed that the pipe fell out when Vale's body was hurled over the falls. The pipe was made of briarwood and was so buoyant it did not sink, like the other articles in Vale's pockets.
>
> It is the opinion of Game Warden James Billings and

others familiar with the region, that Vale's body may never
be found. There is a pond below the falls filled with dead
tree stumps. There have been previous instances when
bodies submerged in this entanglement have never come to
the surface.

If such is Vale's fate, there is sufficient evidence to estab-
lish the fact that he died trying to rescue his disabled companion. Vale was a strong swimmer and an excellent oars-
man. The autopsy performed on Briggs's body revealed
that his lungs contained little water, proving that his death
was not due to drowning. Vale was aware that Briggs had
a weak heart. Mr. George Bennington, the head of Camp
Tamarack, had informed all the counselors of this fact. It is
Mr. Bennington's belief that in accordance with the camp's
standards, and Vale's own high regard for duty, he chose to
exert himself. to the limit rather than to abandon Briggs.

Murray Vale was a member of the class of 1937 at
Harvard. He has just completed his second year at the
Harvard Law School. He is the son of Mrs. Barry Firth and
the late Rupert Vale—former president of the firm of Vale
and Firth, investment bankers. He is survived by two
older sisters, Miss Fabia Vale, now residing in New York
City; Mrs. Tuckerman Haverford of this city, who was the
former Miss June Vale; and an older brother, Rupert Vale,
better known as Windy Vale, a familiar figure at all Harvard's recent important athletic events. He is the nephew
of Lloyd Vale and Hilary Vale of the law firm of Vale and
Vale. He is the grandson of—(continued on page 4).

Murray groped for the designated page. He never found
it, for on the editorial page his name again met his eyes in
capital letters, this time at the head of a brief eulogy signed
by initials. But he didn't see the initials. He didn't read as
far as that. 'Murray Vale was a member of one of Boston's
most distinguished families,' the article began. 'His heroic
act revives one's belief in the qualities of the younger generation of the so-called "privileged class." The courage and
high regard for duty revealed by young Vale when —'

Murray read no farther. He had had all he could take for the moment. He rolled up the paper and pushed it into one of the pockets of Jim's hunting coat and walked out on the platform. There was an empty baggage truck at the far end standing in a black shadow. He sat down on it.

What a mess he was in! It was shocking enough to read your own obituary in the newspaper, but to be acclaimed in print as a hero because of an act you never performed was hideous. How could he ever show up in Boston after that article? The very thought of the sensational headlines that would flash across the front pages of all the Boston newspapers announcing the return of a hero whose only claim to heroism was his death made suicide seem preferable.

He had always shied away from suicide. In years past he had often contemplated it as a possible means of escape, and had dwelt in imagination upon its various methods but never with any intention of putting them to use. It had been ingrained in him early that suicide was a cowardly act. But was that always true? Certainly some suicides are justified. Why, if he had gone back for Briggs out there on the lake, he would have been committing suicide — voluntarily putting an end to himself.

It seemed to him that the most self-respecting thing he could do now was to make good those claims in the paper. It was the most altruistic thing to do — the 'greatest good to the greatest number.' He'd been worrying about the effect of his ignominious return on the little chaps in Opechee. Why rob them of their hero? Why prove Mr. Ben's confidence in a trusted counselor false? Why cast discredit on Tamarack's high standards by exposing his errors in judgment and acknowledging his failure to remember the camp motto? Why deprive the family of the only distinguished act he was ever likely to contribute to its record?

His first impulse was to throw himself in front of one of the monster engines that came snorting into the station. But that wouldn't do, even if he had the guts. It would defeat his purpose if it was discovered he had died three days too late. All such available methods as drowning, poisoning, blowing out one's brains, jumping out of a window, must be discarded. He must destroy himself so completely that no mark of identification remained. On his left eyebrow was a telltale scare which he had gotten in prep school playing football. There were also his teeth! The two upper ones in the center front were made of porcelain. Dentists could identify unknown bodies years after death. A dead body is a damned difficult object to hide, especially if it is your own. It would be far easier to conceal his identity if he were able to use his intelligence. He'd better wait till more time had elapsed before doing anything to attract attention. Also it would be well to get farther away from the scene of the drowning.

What about following the suggestion of his acquaintance of the early morning? A lumber-camp buried in the wilds of northern Maine might prove to be the best place in the world for his clandestine rendezvous with death. Lumberjacks were notorious for their rolling-stone tendencies. If a lumberjack disappeared from a camp where he was a stranger, it would make very little stir. There would be no searching at all, he imagined. Certainly no newspaper notoriety.

Why not board the next train going north? The few toilet articles he had purchased would more than pay what he owed the landlady. She would find them all laid out on the commode. The commode! His heart skipped a beat. Good Lord, he had forgotten about his uniform inside the commode!

He jumped down from the truck and hurried back to his room. What if the landlady had been doing a little tidying up during his absence? What if she had unrolled the wad of rags behind the chamber-pot and discovered the big capital T on the shirt? His heart was in his mouth when he yanked open the door of the commode. Thank God the uniform was still there and apparently had not been touched. Gosh, that was a close shave!

He wrapped it up in the Boston newspaper. A half-hour later it lay at the bottom of a lilypad-covered pond a short distance out of the city, anchored to its last resting-place by some stones.

An eerie proceeding. Like disposing of a dead body. He knew now how a murderer felt. He was filled with misgivings as he retraced his steps to the city. Perhaps after all he had better make a clean breast of everything and get out from under this awful burden of guilt which was getting heavier and heavier. He could at least enjoy a clear conscience. It would require less nerve. Also it would release him from that dreaded rendezvous.

When he arrived at his room he lay down on the bed, flat on his back, staring up at the low ceiling dimly illuminated by a light in the hall showing through a wide crack at the top of the sagging door. For hours he could not go to sleep, his thoughts ranging far and wide, weighing pros and cons. He wondered if his mother knew about the tragedy yet. If not, she would soon. Mrs. Billings had said his mother would feel proud that he died a hero. That was true. Of course she'd feel badly at first about his death, but once the shock was over the healing process would begin. There was no need for Mrs. Billings to worry about his empty place at the table. He was at home only for occasional weekends and brief portions of his holidays. Barry Firth was always amiable, and his mother always cordial, but his presence cast a shadow of constraint. As for his empty room — a big rambling sunny apartment on the third floor — it would not be empty long. Christopher, his little step-brother, had long wanted it for his.

Christopher was another argument in favor of his clearing out. It would be tough on Christopher when he went away to boarding-school or to camp and new acquaintants talked him over. 'Oh, yes,' they'd say, 'brother of Murray Vale, that fellow the newspapers reported died doing his duty and then turned up alive!' Nice sort of inheritance to pass on to Christopher! Not even the prestige of being the brother of Windy Vale would make up for the stigma of being the brother of Murray Vale.

Luckily there was no girl in the picture to consider. His relationship with Daphne was definitely finished. Daphne and he had been engaged for six months — one of those experimental engagements that had never been announced and never should have been put to test. The memory of it brought only chagrin to them both. To Daphne because her charms had failed to accomplish their object. To him because he had fallen so far short of her expectations. Daphne expected to be made love to, in one way or another, practically all the time when they were alone and unobserved. It used to fill him with a horrible sense of inadequacy when the unmistakable invitations she made with her eyes, voice, and posture left him cold. It got so that unless he had several cocktails, or their equivalent, he felt no desire to treat her as an engaged girl has a right to be treated. He had had to tell her so finally. It was a terrific blow to her pride; to his pride, too.

Daphne was a débutante of the preceding season when he had met her at Nantucket. June and Tuck had rented a cottage for the summer down there, and June had asked him to spend a fortnight with them during August. One night soon after his arrival when Tuck was up in town he had become confidential with June. They had had one of their periodical heart-to-heart talks. The subject had swerved to girls. He told her he could never seem to get beyond the acquaintance stage with them and deplored the fact. He didn't know why it was.

'It's because you never make love to them,' June had replied.

'That's exactly what I'm telling you! I never get to know a girl well enough to make love to her.'

'Oh, my goodness gracious! It's far easier to make love to a stranger than a girl you know well. In these days a girl expects a little harmless hand-holding the first night you take her out and a good-night kiss when you leave her.'

'In cold blood?'

'Certainly not in cold blood! Don't you ever get a thrill from a stranger? What's the matter with you, Murray?'

He sometimes wondered himself. Ever since his first year at boarding-school when one day in the shower bath the boys made fun of the size of certain parts of his body, he had been afraid that something might be the matter. He had again been haunted by this fear his freshman year in college. Nichols, his worldly-wise cousin, had told him that acquaintance with 'the facts of life' from experience, not merely hearsay, would give him self-confidence and the reassurance that he was a perfectly normal red-blooded human being. He had followed Nichols's advice, or tried to. It had been a miserable failure.

The humiliating event had occurred in New York where he had gone with a bunch of classmates to celebrate after one of the big football games in New Haven. One of the fellows knew a good safe place to go where there were some girls. They'd all had a good deal to drink except himself. He hated the stuff. He had stayed for a while. It was a place where you danced with a girl and then went upstairs to a small room. The name of the girl who fell to his lot was Lilly. She had very light platinum-blond hair and huge pale-blue eyes, globular shaped, like glass marbles.

The first minute they were alone in the room she unzipped her dress (the zipper ran from the hem to the top of the low-cut neck) and stepped out of it completely naked. She didn't have on even one of those things her sister Ruth called 'a bra.' It was the suddenness that shocked him. He felt as embarrassed as if her clothes had dropped off by mistake in the street. She still wore high-heeled dancing slippers,. dangling earrings, and a long rope of imitation pearl beads. All these trappings made her nakedness stand out as still more glaring. She certainly didn't look anything like his dream of a girl ready to go to bed.

When he told her he wasn't staying her eyes seemed to protrude still farther out of their sockets and flash with scorn as she turned and hurled names at him that seared like a hot branding iron. She was still loudly berating him when he turned the knob and fled.

He had never owned up to the other boys what a quitter he had been. They were not in the dancing-room, thank God, as he threaded his way across it and finally escaped.

That attempt at sophistication had made him more ill at ease than ever with girls. But it wasn't an experience he could discuss with June, nor with anyone else for that matter.

'The trouble with you is,' June went on with older-sister frankness, 'you never unbend, loosen up and forget yourself. You never get worked up into a mood that makes you do and dare things. I never saw you take but one cocktail in my life.'

'I hate the taste of them.'

'Too bad, little boy! You hate the taste of coffee, too. You always take milk — two glasses every morning, and never a demi-tasse at night. When are you going to grow up?'

'For the Lord's sake, June, I see no reason why I should drink or eat anything that doesn't suit my palate.'

'All right, old thing. Don't then. But it's darned uncompanionable. If anything I hate it's to be with someone who hasn't touched a drop when I'm a little high. I assure you it would be lots easier to break the ice with a girl if you could ever bring yourself to get down a third cocktail. Most men don't need any such stimulation. But you're one of those on whom I bet it would work like magic!'

'You're wrong! Alcohol simply makes me sleepy as a rule, or sick.'

'Like a great big fat cigar! Oh, Murray, Murray, don't you see that remark shows you're naïve and inexperienced? And so sort of righteous, too!'

'Not at all. I'm perfectly glad to give it another tryout.' Perhaps she was right. Perhaps if he'd had a drink or two that night in New York it would have been different.

'You mean it?' June followed it up.

'Sure thing. I'm game.'

The nexth day June invited Daphne DeForest to come over from the Vineyard for the weekend. Daphne was very pretty, very feminine, the clinging-vine type and full of sex appeal. The first night Daphne arrived June planned a picnic supper on the dunes preceded by old-fashioneds and accompanied by dividends. There were no other guests, so it was easy for June and Tuck to leave Daphne and Murray alone to watch the moon come up.

Daphne's weekend was prolonged for as long as Murray remained. June's scheme worked to perfection — too well, in fact. Murray was still in college. She hadn't planned on an engagement. Still Daphne was a perfectly good match, as far as family and background were concerned. She did lack gray-matter, true, but perhaps a girl with limited mental capacity would give self-confidence to a man, and clinging-vine tendencies make him feel like an oak. These arguments in favor of Daphne had seeped through to Murray.

When six months later he told his mother the affair with Daphne was over and had been a ghastly mistake she had said calmly, 'Oh, no, not ghastly. Just natural. You and Daphne had only one interest in common and it has run its course now.'

But it hadn't run its course with Daphne! 'It was my fault. Not Daphne's. It was I who ducked out, Mother.'

'Next time you'll be wiser and start with a mutual interest; then you won't want to duck out.'

'There'll be no next time,' he had replied. 'Two failures are enough, thank you.'

'Two?'

'Yes, two,' he assured her curtly. He knew he could trust her not to pursue a confidence he preferred to let pass as a mere reference. 'Evidently I'm not a lady's man, Mother,' he added lightly.

Did she suspect the facts — surmise his fear? 'Don't jump to conclusions, Murray,' she had said quietly.

That affair with Daphne had been finished for over two years now. He had felt horribly restless and vaguely despondent for a while after the engagement was broken, though God knew he didn't want anything more of Daphne. He had become wakeful at night and began cutting classes in order to sleep in the daytime and because they bored him to extinction. His appetite fell off. His mother had noticed it.

One Sunday when he went home for the weekend Doctor Jaquith, an old friend of his mother's and a psychiatrist of high standing, came to dinner, by chance — or so his mother would have him believe. She had often suggested that he talk things over with Doctor Jaquith, who had an office in Boston now to which he came for a day every other week. Murray had always opposed his mother's suggestion. He didn't intend to rubber-stamp himself by asking any psychiatrist how to meet his problems and swallow his peculiarities. What if someone he knew should see him in the waiting-room? His mother hadn't pressed it. On that Sunday she had managed to leave him alone with Doctor Jaquith for a short time after dinner, also as if by chance. But her scheme hadn't worked out as she planned.

The conversation had opened with a perfunctory comment from Doctor Jaquith about Murray's graduation in June, followed by a casual inquiry about his plans for next year.

'Your mother says you haven't decided yet what you're going to do.'

'Oh, yes, I have! I'm going to the Harvard Law School.'
Until that moment he had been painfully on the fence. 'My
uncle wants me to go into his firm later. It's a wonderful
opportunity and I'm keen to do it.' He spoke with such confidence and enthusiasm he hoped he convinced Doctor
Jaquith he was in no need of a psychiatrist's advice or guid-
ance on that or any subject. At that moment Windy
dropped in. As often before, he welcomed the opportunity
which it gave him to become inconspicuous. He withdrew
instantly into the merciful shadow which Windy's magnetic
personality always cast. Five minutes later when Doctor
Jaquith and Windy were eagerly discussing the baseball
game which they'd both attended yesterday he sneaked out
of the room and departed for Cambridge in his car, by a
rear driveway. That explained why he had chosen a lawyer's
career — if you could call it a choice.

He would start for Millinocket tomorrow. But first he
must get some clothes. He had promised Mrs. Billings to
return Jim's outfit. If he failed to do so she might ask Jim
to drop in at Tamarack and inquire for them.

In the morning he visited a second-hand shop called
'Abe's' and outfitted himself in traveling clothes as nearly
like those worn by his bus acquaintance as he could remember — long, baggy trousers, shabby coat that didn't
match, faded blue shirt, stringy red necktie, limp-brimmed
felt hat, thick-soled, heavy-toed boots, and a red-and-black
plaid mackinaw.

He wrapped Jim's clothes in stout brown paper, printing
the address in small letters, stamped it and took it down to
the railway station. It must bear a postmark that could be
explained. There was a junction near Tamarack where a
certain express train stopped several hours after the regular
Boston mail train had left. It was the custom practiced not
only by the counselors at Tamarack, but by many of the

residents in the vicinity, to ask the friendly conductor on the express to mail letters and packages upon his arrival in Boston. Therefore, if there was a Boston postmark on the bundle, and Mrs. Billings observed it, it would arouse no suspicion. So now he waited till a Boston-bound train rumbled into the station, and asked the conductor if he'd be so good as to drop his stamped package in a Boston mailbox.

When he paid for his room before leaving, the landlady looked at him sharply. 'I took note you didn't have any bag when you come. Been doing a little shoppin', I see.'

'Yes,' he acknowledged, uncomfortably aware that she was staring at his far from new clothes. 'I picked up most of this stuff in a second-hand shop. I'm a little short of cash at the moment.'

'Seen better days! That's as plain as the nose on your face. The stylish way you talk gives that away. Sayin' "short of cash" 'stead of "broke," and "at the moment" and such like. What's your name, young man, and where you from?'

'My name is Tom Jones.' He was prepared this time.

'Where you come from?'

'A place out West.'

'What place?'

'A little place in Wyoming.'

'What's the name of the little place?'

'Jackson Hole.' He knew such a place existed in Wyoming. He had attended a rodeo there once.

'Humph!' snorted the landlady. 'You'd better think up a more stylish-sounding name than Tom Jones to go with your talk, if you want anybody to believe you, and a likelier-sounding place to come from than some hole out West. I don't know what you're up to, but it don't look like anything good to me. Well, it ain't any of my business. I've got my chores to do.'

That was lucky. Once on the sidewalk outside her closed door it was all he could do not to break into a run.

9

CHAPTER

ONE DAY in October Jim Billings started off early in the morning with his gun and Black-Eye his dog to hunt for partridge. He was familiar with their haunts. North of Heron Swamp there was a stretch of flat ground with clumps of alder, dwarf birch and blueberry — excellent cover for birds. He decided he'd have a look there first.

He tied his boat to the trunk of a dead tree sticking out into the lake. That dead tree had been serving him as a float for years. He and Black-Eye made their way along the trunk of the tree and jumped lightly down on the sandy beach. Black-Eye leaped up the high bank from which the tree had torn away and stood alert at the top, while his master followed more slowly, pulling himself up by roots and branches. Jim was on his hands and knees when he reached the top of the bank. He was about to stand up when he saw something shining in front of his eyes.

He picked it up. He rubbed off the dirt and grime. It was a glasses case made of aluminum. Inside the case there was a pair of rimless spectacles with silved-colored bows. The case was lined with velvet. Printed in gold on the inside of the cover was the name and address of a Boston optician.

He closed the case and slipped it into his pocket, then stood up. There was a comfortable bed of moss beneath a tall tree not far away. He went over to it with the intention of sitting down and examining the glasses more closely. And there, lying right on top of the moss, if there wasn't something else shining! A piece of tinsel. Inside the tinsel was a scrap of green paper with the word 'LIME' printed on it. At the foot of the tree trunk of the tree there was another foreign article — an emptied metal tube squeezed dry.

He might never have found the torn cards if it hadn't been for Black-eye nosing around. It was Black-Eye's investigating nose that poked down into the moss and unburied the clotted scraps of cardboard. They were damp and punky. About the consistency of a toadstool when he tried peeling the layers apart. There was printing on the cards. With the help of the small blade of his knife he separated the layers. The cards had been torn into small pieces. He laid his gun in front of him so its butt would be level and proceeded to fit the torn edges together on its smooth surface. It was like a jigsaw puzzle. Like three jigsaw puzzles, all identical. When he had finally finished, the name MURRAY VALE appeared three times repeated before his amazed eyes.

'What you back so early fur?' demanded Mrs. Billings, when Jim and Black-Eye appeared in the early afternoon.

'I ain't been pa'tridge hunting.'

'What have you been doin'?'

'Body-hunting.'

'Well, I 'spose you'll tell me what you been up to when you get good and ready. In the meanwhile I ain't goin' to waste my breath askin' yer.'

'I been hunting for the body of that young feller, Murray Vale.'

'Humph!' was Mrs. Billings' only comment, and she crossed to the stove where a large kettle was emitting the spicy perfume of boiling grape-juice and sugar. She began stirring it with a long wooden spoon.

'You think I'm joshing you.'

'I know you be, or else you're touched. You find it mighty amusin' to get my curiosity het up over nothin', but my curiosity is het up sufficient at present about whether or no this is goin' to jell, so I'm in no mood to be obligin' yer by askin' foolish questions.'

'Come over here, Myrie, I got something to show you.'

There was a quality in his voice that made Mrs. Billings look at him sharply. She shoved the kettle to the back of the stove and walked over to him.

He placed the glasses case on the red and white plaid tablecloth, the empty tube and the bit of tinsel, and then, with great care, the pieces of one of the cards beside it and fitted them together.

Mrs. Billings was struck dumb. First she stared at Jim and then at the articles on the table. Finally she murmured, 'What's it mean?'

'I haven't decided.' And he told her in detail where he found the articles. 'My first thought was he'd crawled up there pretty near all in and must have passed out for good near-by, so me and Black-Eye looked around for quite a spell. Then it struck me that if he had the strength to pull himself up that high bank, eat Lifesavers, and tear up them cards, he had strength to walk and perhaps he'd set out to walk back to camp. The only way to get there on foot is up around Long Pond. Looked to me as if he might of lost his bearings. That being the case it was foolish for me and Black-Eye to hunt around that bank. So I came home.'

'Long Pond! Why, that's where that feller said *he* was aimin' for when he lost his bearin's last summer.'

'What feller?'

'Why, don't you remember? That counselor who stopped here for something to eat, a day or two after the drownin'?'

'What was his name?'

'Brown. Tom Brown. I remember it because it was so plain. Don't you remember he borrowed some of your cloes?'

'Oh, that feller! Yes, I remember *him*. Wouldn't take my canoe to paddle back to Tamarack. Look here, what if—' He stopped abruptly. 'My cloes came back all right, didn't they?'

'You know they did. By parcel post. You got 'em yerself up at the post office.'

'You usually save wrapping paper and string, Myrie. You got the paper the cloes come in?'

'What you thinkin', Jim?'

'Nothing. Just you go and get me that wrapping paper.'

She found it finally in the bottom of a cupboard in the pantry, spread out underneath some kettles and pans. She had cut the paper to fit the space but the address and postmark were there, faintly legible through some soot and a grease ring. The address was printed in small block letters. MRS. JAMES BILLINGS, CROFTON, MAINE. The postmark was blurred. Only the date, July 31, 1939, was legible.

Jim studied the paper in silence, his brows drawn into a frown. 'No return address if not delivered,' he remarked finally, then folded the paper carefully and laid it on the table beside the other articles. 'Well, if that's the case, we'll be spared searching the woods for his body.'

'If what's the case?'

'I ain't saying yet.'

He crossed the room to the wall-telephone. 'I'm going to talk with Ezra,' he announced, took down the receiver and began turning the small handle on the side of the black-walnut box.

Ezra Verity lived at Camp Tamarack all the year round in a small cabin of his own. His modest title was Caretaker, but Guardian Angel better described him. Ever since Tamarack had started, Ezra had kept constant watch over its cabins summer and winter, day and night, and felt a similar sense of protection for all those inside the cabins during the season. Ezra knew all the counselors by name.

'Hello, Ezra,' said Jim when finally he had him on the line. 'How things going? Many birds down your way? Thought I might come down some day soon. Sure. Maybe.' There were long pauses between each sentence. 'Oh, say, I want to get the address of one of your counselors so as I can send him some birds I promised. Brown was his name. Yes, Brown. Tom Brown. Never heard of him? Now that's funny. Shucks! Guess I got it mixed up with somebody else — one of the summer sports, maybe. Did you get that bear yet that was bothering your supplies? I saw tracks of a big feller up this way and set my trap last night. Oh, Myrie is feeling real good, thank ye. Drop in on us some day. Good-bye.'

Myra had been standing motionless over her kettle on the stove and had heard every word Jim said.

'Well. Guess that settles it,' Jim remarked after he'd hung up the receiver.

'Settles what?'

'That it was him.' He shoved his hands into his coat pockets and looked off into space, his eyes squinted speculatively. 'And all the time he was setting here, I ain't got a doubt but he knew what made them scratches on the canoe.'

Several days after the canoe had been found Mr. Ben had procured the silver pencil, which sure enough had been found clipped in Briggs's shorts, and Jim had compared it with the scratches and imprints. To Jim's chagrin the ribs of the pencil-end were too big. Whenever one of Jim's hunches proved wrong it whetted his curiosity to find the right explanation of a clue he had misinterpreted. 'Yep, I bet a dollar he knew what made 'em, yet he never made a peep to set me right.'

'Oh, for goodness' sakes, stop goin' on 'bout them everlastin' old scratches when I'm all excited about this stuff you've found. What you thinkin' about it? What's it mean?'

'Nothing good,' said Jim and proceeded to gather up the

articles on the table. 'Looks bad.' He heaved a sigh, shook his head. 'Tearing up his calling cards and burying 'em. Getting rid of all identification marks. Premeditating escape — that's pretty clear. Must be a motive. Must of done something pretty bad.'

'What you think he did?'

'Haven't made up my mind. They found mighty little water in Briggs's lungs. Said he died of heart failure. No telling what gave him the heart failure.'

'You hintin' the Vale boy did somethin' he shouldn't to Briggs? Is that what you're accusin' him of, James Billings?'

'Keep your shirt on, Myrie. Who's doing any accusing? I'm just trying to figure out why he was so anxious to escape. Staying out in the woods like that for two days and nights while we were all hunting for him!'

'He couldn't help that. He was lost.'

'So he *said*. What a feller *says* who gives a false name don't amount to a hill of beans.'

'You goin' to let on 'bout what you found today?'

'Of course.'

'What's the use of makin' trouble?'

'You want me to be an accomplice to something what looks crooked, Myrie? Guess you're forgetting my position as defender of the law in these parts.'

'Don't put on airs. What I'm *not* forgettin' is that Vale boy's mother, and how proud she was 'bout all the things everyone was sayin' 'bout her son that day she dropped in here. You couldn't help findin' the things, but you can help blabbin' about 'em.'

'My conscience wouldn't feel easy. Not for long, that is.'

'I suppose keepin' your conscience feelin' easy is more important than smashin' a boy's reputation.'

'It wouldn't be right keeping facts like that hid.'

'And how you proposin' goin' about tellin' the facts?'

'I haven't been down to Boston for quite a spell. Thought

maybe I'd take these things down to his mother and let her do what she wants about 'em. I can't go till the end of next week but there's no call to hurry about exposing facts that have been lying in the woods for over two months, far as I see.'

'Ain't no call to expose 'em at all far as *I* see.'

That night, after the supper things had been cleared away and Jim and Myra were seated close to the glass-shaded lamp on the table, Myra remarked, 'I've been thinkin'.'

'You ain't sick, are you?'

'Stop yer teasin'! I got an idea.'

'Well, now, that's real interesting. Let's hear it.'

' 'Stead of you goin' to Boston and settin' off a bomb in that poor boy's own home, why don't you write Mr. Ben about your facts? That will clear your precious conscience, won't it? If Mr. Ben don't want to tell 'em, it ain't any of your business.'

'That's worth considering,' said Jim after a pause, and a minute later, 'Yes, Myrie, that's worth considering. Get me the pen and ink.'

10

CHAPTER

Lisa Firth sat in the library waiting for her tea guests
to arrive. She sat by the window that commanded a view
of the winding drive to the house, so she could watch for
approaching cars and reach the front door before the bell
rang and one of the maids got ahead of her. Murray's portrait had arrived yesterday. She had hung it in the big
square entrance hall and wanted to be present when her
guests first saw it.

There were to be very few guests — the family chiefly,
Lloyd and Hilary, her first husband's two brothers; their respective wives, Rosa and Justine; his sister, Charlotte; and
Charlotte's house guest, Doctor Jaquith. She had used
Doctor Jaquith as the excuse for her tea invitation. She
hadn't mentioned the portrait, but it was the real reason for
this gathering. None of the family had seen the portrait.

Lisa had hung it over the mantel above the fireplace in
the hall, between a pair of family heirloom candelabra. That
place of honor had been occupied ever since Lisa had come
to this house as a bride, by a Sargent portrait of Grandmother Vale when in her prime. Lloyd and Hilary might
disapprove of the new location of their mother's portrait on
the side wall over a sofa, but she doubted if they would
dare say so.

Lisa rose from her chair by the window and walked over
to the door into the hall, pausing on the threshold to gaze at
the two portraits and experience again that wave of satisfac-

tion which the sight of them aroused every time she passed
through the hall. Oh, if only Murray could see where he
was enthroned!

The family's estimate of Murray had never been high.
Murray had been a shy, self-conscious little boy who would
hang his head and scowl at all advances of friendliness. He
was the youngest of Rupert's and her children and different
from the others. He had none of Fabia's charm, Windy's
athletic ability, or June's gay self-confidence. He was different from his Vale cousins, too, lacking utterly that manner
of superiority with which they all had been born, along with
silver spoons in their mouths. He had lacked also the physical characteristics of the Vales. When Murray was a little
boy he was pale-skinned, with tow-colored hair that sprouted
in a rugged line from his forehead and stood up stiff and
straight. When the light shone through it it had an oyster-
white cast and resembled somewhat a seeded dandelion.
June used to call him 'Dandelion Top.'

Murray had been the victim of many nicknames, 'Sawed-
off,' 'Shorty,' 'Fish-eyes,' 'Professor,' 'Bughouse,' 'Bug.' His
cousins took particular delight in using them. When they
came out from town on Saturdays Murray would disappear,
explaining afterwards he was hunting for specimens or busy
in his laboratory. He never joined in their rough-and-tumble
games if he could help it. 'Lacks spunk,' was Grandmother's
dictum.

Sometimes Grandmother Vale came out on Saturdays,
too. She enjoyed watching her grandchildren at play, noting
with satisfaction various traits and characteristics that revealed their Vale or Nichols inheritance. Grandmother had
been born a Nichols. But she could see no trace of either
Vale or Nichols in Murray. He didn't look like a Vale, nor
act like a Vale, either. There had been occasions, too, Lisa
was aware, when he hadn't been treated like a Vale.

Once at a sub-deb dancing-party when Murray was six-

teen, Lisa had seen Cynthia, one of Hilary's and Justine's
three daughters, aged also sixteen, nod curtly to Murray as
he approached and then move quickly away so that she
wouldn't have to acknowledge any kinship before her
friends. But now Cynthia was boasting of her kinship to
Murray! Lisa had heard her only a day or two ago. Now all
the family were recognizing him as one of them. Murray
had added honor to the name, unprecedented honor. Murray
was the first Vale on record to die performing an heroic act.
In the First World War no Vale had gotten any nearer the
fighting-line than Washington, D.C. In the Civil War no
Vale had seen duty outside of New England. The Vales
were not warriors by nature. Their gifts lay in other fields.

Murray's portrait was life-size. It showed his figure to a
little below the knees — a slight, erect, well-proportioned
figure now. He was bareheaded. His hair was no longer
tow-colored nor did it stand up straight. When Murray's
legs had mercifully begun to grow, his hair had turned to
a light, earthy brown and had become amenable to a hair
brush. He was seated on something low, his chin lifted,
looking off into space. The background of the picture was in
shadow. You didn't notice its details at first, but if you
looked closely you saw the bark of a tree trunk behind
Murray, and in the recesses farther back a blurred gray-
green mosaic of geometric figures made by the shooting
branches of needle-covered larch trees. He didn't wear his
glasses, but there was a glimpse of their familiar platinum
bows in the breast-pocket of the blazer of his camp uniform.
The artist whom Lisa finally selected had never seen
Murray. He had painted the portrait from photographs and
Lisa's suggestions. Lisa had spent much time with the
artist while the portrait was in process of creation. It was a
form of sublimation. When all hope was abandoned of re-
covering Murray's body she found consolation in trying to

recreate on canvas not only his body but something of his spirit, too.

He was looking off into space in the portrait, his chin lifted, his lids squinted slightly, an expression on his face as if he were listening to something that gave him pleasure. It was literally a 'speaking likeness.' She could hear the very words he was about to speak — 'Listen, Mother.' Murray and she used to go bird-hunting every spring.

They used to go cocoon- and pollywog-hunting, butterfly-netting, egg-collecting, too, when he was a little boy (though Murray never took but one egg from a nest). Their pilgrimages had not been confined to fields and streams. As he grew older they often went to the theater together, or to a concert, a movie, or a ball game. Lisa had tried to cover up Murray's frequent lack of a companion by being ready to act as a makeshift whenever necessary. Certain habits and customs had been formed which her marriage to Barry Firth had interrupted. She had tried to protect the old intimacy with Murray, but he himself had made it difficult. She should have tried harder. Not once since her second marriage had she risen at five A.M. to go bird-hunting with Murray. Suddenly her eyes filled with tears. Come! Come! That wouldn't do. She gave her head an impatient shake, and turned from Murray to Grandmother Vale, glaring fiercely out of her rococo frame. Murray's portrait was framed in smooth, plain, pickled pine.

Grandmother Vale had had her portrait painted many times. She must have been well along in her fifties in this portrait. There she sat stiffly upright, her thin lips tightly compressed, her features as rigid as if cast in iron. Lisa's eyes turned back to Murray.

What a contrast were Murray's pliable contours, flexible flesh, full lips slightly parted. What a pity Murray had died before character-lines had become permanent in his flesh, and before character qualities had made their final impression on his personality. Everything had been in the process of formation — his powers untested, his problems unsolved, many of his fears and anxieties proved groundless. Well — better to die too young than too old. Better to die like Murray, exerting himself to the utmost performing a fine act, than like Grandmother Vale, exerting herself to the utmost to prolong a merciless tyranny.

She turned away. At the same moment the telephone bell rang. She walked across the hall and answered it herself. An operator's voice asked for Mrs. Barry Firth. Mr. George Bennington wished to speak to her. Mr. Ben! Calling from out of town about some detail in regard to the chapel probably. Windy and she were giving a log chapel to Tamarack in memory of Murray. But Mr. Ben was not calling from out of town. He was passing through Boston on his way back to New York. At the moment he was at a near-by country club with the father of one of his campers. If she were to be at home this afternoon he'd drop in and see her. No, they hadn't started building the chapel yet. He was having a little difficulty about getting the logs.

Lisa told Mr. Ben to come as soon as possible. She had something she wanted to show him. A portrait of Murray! She had hung it only yesterday. Wasn't it a coincidence that he should appear today! Wouldn't he stay for dinner? Well, possibly. He'd see.

Ten minutes later Lisa was still awaiting her guests, not seated by the window now, but at the oblong table in the center of the room, with the plans of the memorial chapel spread out before her. Mr. Ben hadn't seen the finished sketches yet.

Also he hadn't seen the contents of a portfolio which she had placed on the table within easy access of anyone passing. The portfolio contained her collection of written tributes to Murray — clippings from various newspapers, an

article that had appeared in the last Harvard *Bulletin*, also
a careful selection of letters she had received from individuals.

She was studying the front elevation of the memorial
chapel when she heard a familiar sound, like a breaker rolling
in on a long sandy beach. It was an automobile approaching
the house on the gravel-surfaced driveway. A fawn-colored
roadster flashed from behind the bare branches of the purple
beeches, advanced rapidly and came to a stop with the crash
of a breaking wave as its wheels dug into the gravel. The
crash was accompanied by a shrill screech. Would Windy
never get that brake fixed?

It didn't require the brakes' screech to recognize Windy,
and from a long way off, too, in that conspicuous roadster of
his with its bright-red trimmings and low-hung body, designed for his particular requirements. Windy could get in
and out of his car without lifting a foot. He could drive his
car without lifting a foot. The driving gear had also been
designed for his particular requirements. In the back of his
car he sometimes carried a wheelchair especially designed
to fold up and fit in the rumble. Certain important muscles
below Windy's waist had been out of commission for eight
years now, yet the word 'cripple' did not seem applicable
to him. He was just as quick of motion and as happy of
nature as he had always been.

As Lisa passed through the hall she could hear Windy
honking his horn. That meant he did not intend to come in.
But he must, if only for five minutes, to see Murray's portrait.

Windy wasn't alone. The minute Lisa opened the door
she recognized all four of the occupants, or rather five,
counting Thirp. The collapsible top of the car was down.
Windy was seated behind the wheel as usual. Barbara was
beside him. Barbara was his wife. Barbara was the first
girl he'd wanted to marry. She had accepted him the first

time he'd asked her, and because he wanted her to marry
him soon she had given up her last year at college without
demur. It was a happy marriage. They had two children,
a boy first, then a girl. As ordered. Ever since Windy's illness everything happened as ordered, as if Fortune were
trying to compensate for the knockout blow it had dealt him
the spring before he went to college.

In the back seat of the car sat Thirp, a German police dog
of large proportions. Beside Thirp, June, and on the outside
Tuck Haverford. Tuck Haverford had fallen in love first
with Fabia Vale. But Dan Regan had appeared on Fabia's
horizon at the same time, and Fabia was blind to everyone
else. So Tuck had begun pursuing June instead. Many men
had pursued June. Lisa had about concluded June might
never settle down to any one man when she announced that
she had decided to marry Tuck a month hence. June's
marriage was also a happy one, apparently, though Lisa confessed to Barry she was keeping her fingers crossed.

Fabia had never married. Her love affair with Dan Regan,
a young Irish doctor, had occurred the year she came out.
It had been of a violent nature, and when it went onto the
rocks she had fled to New York and plunged into the time-
and-thought-consuming activities of becoming a trained
nurse. She had lived in New York ever since.

Fabia had always been shy with the opposite sex. She had
never made friends quickly with even her own sex. In both
these respects she was like Murray. They had other simi-
larities, too. Both were individualists, different from their
contemporaries who had been born and brought up in the
same environment. This difference had branded Murray
with the term 'misfit,' but it had given Fabia distinction.
When Fabia came out, her difference from the other débu-
tantes attracted many admirers. She was lovely to look at,
possessed charm and extraordinary poise, but she was timid

beneath the poise, and so unlike the herd with which she must mix and run that Lisa had likened her to a white fawn — one of those rare, exquisite creatures one sees occasionally in the woods.

One day, to console Murray who was suffering keenly because he could not mingle with his group at school, Lisa told him of her simile.

Murray had flushed darkly. 'I don't want to be a white fawn or any other freak of nature,' he had replied. 'They're called "sports" in botany. *That's* not the kind of sport I want to be!'

11

CHAPTER

LISA did not stop to put on a coat, although it was late October and the sun had already begun to set. She ran across the terrace as light-footed as a girl to the purring car drawn up at its edge. There was a chorus of staccato greetings, and Thirp gave two brief sharp barks as she approached.

'We're not coming in, Mona,' June announced.

For years June's name for Lisa had been 'Mona.' June had a flair for nicknames. Their etymology was usually interesting. 'Mother Lisa' had become 'Mona Lisa' when June was a child and first heard of the famous painting. Both Tuck and Barbara had adopted 'Mona' as the perfect appellation for their mother-in-law.

'We stopped to drop these.' June held up a shapeless bundle wrapped in tissue paper. 'Your silver slippers, darling. I borrowed them one day last week when you were out,' she announced blandly. 'Thought you might be looking for them. We are on our way to the Cape for the weekend.'

Lisa took the slippers without comment and tucked them under her arm. 'You must all come in.'

'Sorry,' said Windy. 'It's getting late and we've got to go round by our place.'

'Our place' referred to a quarter of a mile of meadow, pasture and woodland ten miles farther out on one of the bends of the Charles River, and a house and other buildings

clustered close to the river's edge, all of which had been a
wedding present from Barbara's parents. Another of Windy's
strokes of good luck! When Windy asked Barbara to marry
him he knew nothing of the Freemans' financial status.

'You needn't stay long,' urged Lisa. 'Tea is all ready.'

'Can't be done this time, Mater,' said Windy. 'I haven't
packed my stuff yet and neither has Frietchie.'

All Barbara's intimates called her 'Frietchie.' It was another of June's nicknames. When the name of the lady with
the 'old gray head' first struck June's sensitive eardrums,
'Barbara Freeman' became 'Barbara Frietchie.' That was
years ago when June and Frietchie became members at the
age of ten of the carefully chosen entering class at a certain
exclusive day-school in which their names had been entered
for years.

'You simply must come in for a minute. I have something
to show you. Something very special.'

'What is it?'

'Murray's portrait!'

Oh! A change passed over their faces. Windy stopped
the engine. 'Of course we'll come in!' He swung open the
low door beside him. 'All right, Thirp.'

Thirp leaped out of the rear seat and stood at attention
close beside Windy's opened door. Thirp was a tall dog,
lean in his hindquarters, thick and muscular in his shoulders
and neck. His proportions suggested his master's. He wore
a harness supporting a stiff brace, similar to those worn by
Seeing-Eye dogs.

Windy pivoted in his seat, swung his legs outward, planted
his cane on the ground, placing his free hand on Thirp's brace
and got out of the car. The muscles of his legs were now
strong enough to support him if he stood still. To propel
himself required some sort of support on both sides. He preferred crutches, but he sometimes used two canes, and sometimes, as now, only one cane and Thirp. Slowly Windy and

Thirp mounted the several low steps to the terrace, Thirp filled with importance, Windy nonchalant, casual, pausing on the top step to light a cigarette. Thirp stood motionless as his master hooked his cane onto the brace, so that both his hands were free.

When they reached Lisa the other occupants of the car were gathered close around her. Again Thirp took over the cane while Windy leaned and kissed his mother on the cheek, putting his arm around her shoulders and giving her a comradely squeeze.

The group was moving toward the front door when another car emerged from behind the beeches. It was Mr. Ben. There were vociferous greetings. Tuck as well as Windy had been an old Tamaracker.

'They're coming in to see Murray's portrait,' Lisa announced. 'I'll go ahead and turn on the lights.'

A gray pall shrouded the hall now. Lisa pushed only the buttons that controlled the concealed bulbs installed long ago to illumine Grandmother Vale's dark shadowy portrait. Murray's portrait was the opposite from dark and shadowy. There was a shaft of sunshine just above his head piercing the needled larches. When Lisa pushed the buttons and Murray appeared over the mantel the effect was spectacular. Never had the lighting radiated such brilliance. Some of the glow seemed to be emanating from Murray himself, as he sat there looking up, alert, eager, glowing.

The group inside the vestibule were literally struck dumb for a moment. The comments that followed were all exclamatory and brief — muted expressions of surprise and wonder. 'Marvelous! Wonderful! Amazing!'

It was June who finally relieved the tension. Her voice was shaky at first but when she finished it was strong and almost savage. 'Poor kid, I've seen him look exactly like that — all excited and sort of inspired just listening to some darned squirrel.'

'He isn't listening to any squirrel!' retorted young Christopher who had appeared in the group. 'Mummy says that Murray's listening to some very rare bird up in that tree.'

'How did the artist ever catch that expression of his?' It was Windy speaking. 'I've caught it when he wasn't looking, but not often. None of his photographs have it.'

'Mona posed for that portrait,' June announced.

'Indeed I did not! I provided the artist with numerous photographs of Murray and occasionally told him how Murray used to look sometimes.'

'Well, I never realized before how much he looks like *you*, Mona,' said Frietchie.

'Why shouldn't he? He's my very own son!' Her tone rang with pride.

'I remember when he got that scar on his left eyebrow!' said Tuck, who hadn't spoken until now. 'I was coaching at Whitley that year.' Tuck had been a famous football star in college. After he graduated he had coached football for several seasons for diversion. 'I pulled the poor kid out. He was conscious, but in bad shape. Face mashed in. Bone crushed, looked to me. Lots of blood. Lots of sand. I helped the doctor pick the sand out. Long job. Painful. No ether till we got a surgeon to fix him up. Had to wait hours. But not a whimper from the kid. Mighty plucky.'

June said, her tone still savage, 'Murray would never whimper. I used to pinch him or bite him or something of the sort till it hurt, the way sisters do sometimes to make their brothers cry for mercy. I did it to Windy too. Windy would holler right off and I'd stop. But Murray would just set his jaw and take it and I wouldn't stop until I got good and ready. Made me mad. Oh, I used to be perfectly horrid to him sometimes.'

'I was there, too, when he got that scar,' Windy remarked. 'I went up to Whitley especially to see him play in that game. It was his first big one.'

'That's right,' said Tuck. 'You were mighty anxious to make a football player out of him. You were at me all the time to give him all the practice I could. I did my best for him because he was your kid brother. But Murray never liked football. Nor physical combat of any kind. Yet he kept at it season after season as if something was goading him. Why, three weeks after his face was mashed in he was back on the field again, hating it like poison, but standing up to it. He certainly was no quitter.'

'*That* fact has been proved beyond all doubt!' said June. 'But what good is it doing Murray? If I'd been in Murray's place I'd have thought twice before I gave up my lovely life for a stranger who couldn't live long anyway — not one of the campers, no one who was my responsibility — just to prove to you people I wasn't a quitter! Or to live up to some darned Latin motto either! Oh, I'm sorry, Mr. Ben, but Murray might be alive today if it hadn't been for that Tamarack motto of yours about protecting the weak.'

Mr. Ben was standing in the rear of the group. He hadn't spoken since they'd entered the hall. Murray's glasses and the torn calling cards were in his left breast pocket, wrapped in a pasteboard box. He could feel the box pressing against his chest. 'I have something I'd like to say to you all,' he began, and paused. Everybody was silent. 'That boy up there lived up to the camp motto every day of his life. He was always protecting the weak — whether it was an animal, a bird, or a bug, or one of his little chaps in Opechee. That's why I put him in charge of our youngest campers. That's why I asked him to be kind to Briggs. He'd already been kinder to him than any of the counselors at camp.'

Lisa was glad it was so dark in the hall. She was afraid she was going to cry.

'I've already told your mother, but I'd like to make it clear to you all,' Mr. Ben continued, 'that I was responsible for Murray's taking Briggs with him that day. He'd planned to

take Tug Tyson. Briggs was new at Tamarack and wasn't
fitting in well. He was looked upon as a weakling — treated
like one, too, I'm afraid. Murray was in the very act of protecting the weak when he started out that morning. Whatever a man may do at the finish, it can't rub out the day in,
day out record of his life.'

As the children were leaving, the invited guests arrived in
two cars, almost simultaneously. They, too, stood in an awe-
stricken group just inside the vestibule door, silent for the
first minute or two. Their first remarks also were brief and
exclamatory, followed by encomiums spoken in low tones
by one and another. Lisa had heard most of the speeches
before. The portrait drew them out again. Her tea-party
was turning into a second memorial service to Murray. She
snapped on the other lights and suggested moving on into
the library for tea.

There was no reference made to the location of the portrait till Lisa boldly asked Lloyd if he approved of the place
where she had hung it.

'I think it very understandable that you, as his mother,
would wish to place Murray's portrait in the most important
place in the house,' he said stiffly. 'Only — '

'Yes, Lloyd? Only what?'

'It would seem to me more appropriate if Mother's portrait remained in its old position. I would suggest over the
mantel in the dining room as a dignified location for Murray.'

'I'll consider it, Lloyd,' said Lisa.

'I don't think Mother would mind being on the sidelines
so as to give her place to a grandson who had died a hero,'
said Charlotte.

12

CHAPTER

IT WAS not till after nine o'clock that evening that Mr. Ben had an opportunity to be alone with Lisa. She invited Charlotte and Doctor Jaquith to stay for dinner. Barry was in Chicago on a business trip. They were a congenial quartette and old friends.

Charlotte and Lisa had first met at a boarding-school on the Hudson River. Doctor Jaquith and Mr. Ben were also schoolmates. There were other bonds, too. Lisa had first known Doctor Jaquith when she had sought his advice professionally about her unhappy first marriage. Charlotte also had first known Doctor Jaquith professionally.

Charlotte had been the victim of her mother's domination, and for years had suffered from a slowly progressive neurosis which had finally resulted in a serious nervous collapse. She had spent six months at Cascade, Doctor Jaquith's sanatorium in Vermont. Her cure had seemed miraculous. It had released her from all sorts of repressions and inhibitions. At the age of forty Charlotte Vale had become an independent, self-confident, unafraid human being. And a useful one, too. When her mother died Charlotte Vale had become an enormously wealthy woman, and had given a building to Cascade especially designed for children. The building was called Fairways. Doctor Jaquith and she had met often during the construction of Fairways, and had become warm friends. Charlotte was now one of the trustees

of Cascade and a very active one. When Doctor Jaquith
came to Boston he usually stayed with Charlotte in the big
Vale mansion on Marlborough Street where she lived alone
now.

After dinner Lisa steered Mr. Ben and Doctor Jaquith
into Barry's oak-paneled room-of-his-own to smoke their
cigars alone. Charlotte and she withdrew to an open fire
in the library. Mr. Ben frequently consulted 'Jake' about the
various problem-boys at Tamarack. Mr. Ben and Doctor
Jaquith belonged to different schools of thought, due to a
fundamental difference in their natures. Mr. Ben was an
idealist, Doctor Jaquith a realist. But their object in dealing
with one of Mr. Ben's problem-boys was the same — to correct his maladjustment, and they worked well together on a
case. However, they did a lot of amicable disagreeing.
 Mr. Ben believed in appealing to a boy's 'higher instincts.'
Doctor Jaquith reminded him that instincts were all on one
level, preconceived before birth, all integral parts of human-
nature and none to be despised. Mr. Ben held up patterns
and ideals for his boys to copy, and rules to follow. Doctor
Jaquith contended that no one who confined himself to copy-
ing, or was restricted by rules, developed his own potentialities. Mr. Ben was constantly repeating slogans to his
boys as guides to conduct. The Bible was his chief source.
The Golden Rules was his favorite verse. Doctor Jaquith employed slogans occasionally, too. His favorite was 'Know
yourself.'
 'Know yourself' was Doctor Jaquith's advice to anyone
who was in a psychological snarl as the first step to take to
get out of it. Study the mechanics of your emotions, as you
would the mechanics of an automobile you've got to run
and keep in order. 'Trust yourself,' was the second step.
Get into the driving seat and take over. 'Direct yourself,'
was the third step! Decide upon your goal and route, and
get started. Self-knowledge, self-confidence, and finally

self-direction: these were Doctor Jaquith's prescription for intelligent living.

'Nothing but self, self, self,' Mr. Ben had objected one day long ago in the early history of their debates. 'No mention of service to others, which is the secret of happiness, in my humble opinion. And no reference to prayer, or to God.'

Mr. Ben was a religious man. Every Sunday during the summer he stood behind a birch-bark pulpit, read the Bible, prayed and preached a sermon to his boys. He maintained there was in every one of his boys — in every human being — 'a wish to be good' which he claimed that Jake, the rank materialist, couldn't tabulate as instinct, emotion, or thought — 'fish, fowl, or good red herring.' Mr. Ben called it a 'spark of the divine,' and meant it literally. In other words, it was God Himself demonstrating His presence in man. Doctor Jaquith called it the spiritual element in a human being, which was the result of the higher development of his intelligence.

Doctor Jaquith tried to avoid religious disputations with Mr. Ben, or with anyone whose faith in a personal God was a conviction and a source of comfort and strength. But Mr. Ben was continually citing examples to prove his theory.

For instance, how did Jake explain the phenomenal power of endurance that so often comes to the rescue of a man or woman during some sorrow or terrific ordeal? What else was that hidden source of strength but God revealing His divine presence? Doctor Jaquith explained the familiar phenomenon in banking terms. Every normal human being has a reserve fund of spiritual force similar to a reserve bank account which comes to his rescue in a financial crisis. The amount of one's reserve fund of spiritual force depends upon one's experiences and one's intelligence as a depositor. A man or woman who has had much sorrow to bear — sickness, defeat and difficulties — and has done so courageously, is far richer than he or she upon whom fortune has only smiled. It was

life's compensation for misfortune. That was a fundamental
part of Doctor Jaquith's philosophy.

Lisa placed a box of Barry's cigars within easy reach of her
two guests before she left them seated in armchairs on each
side of the burning logs, stirring their black coffee.

'How well did you know Murray Vale, Jake?' Mr. Ben
inquired a brief half-minute after Lisa's departure.

'Chiefly through Lisa, as one of her problems. I've observed him carefully, however, when I've been here off
and on.'

'He was never a patient?'

'Never to his knowledge. Murray felt it was an indication
of weakness to ask a psychiatrist's advice. I've always supported Lisa a hundred per cent in not pressing him to see
me, or doing anything that robbed him of any of his self-
esteem or independence. However, she managed to leave
us alone once for a brief period in this very room.'

'What happened?'

'We were interrupted by Windy after about five minutes,
but I got a good deal of first-hand material to support my
opinion of him.'

'What is your opinion of him?'

'Let's hears yours first, Ben. You know him as an individual, and from the viewpoint of a trusted friend. I know
him as a type, and from the viewpoint of a diagnostician,
and an unwelcome one at that.'

'That's true. I've known Murray ever since he first came to
Tamarack when he was ten or twelve, or thereabouts. He
became one of my most reliable and responsible counselors.
I trusted him utterly. I never knew him even to shade the
truth. He had an extremely high sense of duty and an exceptionally sensitive nature. How does that tally with your
opinion?'

'We aren't so far apart fundamentally. It's chiefly our
terms that differ. I'd define an "exceptionally sensitive nature,"

as a neurotic personality in his case, and "his high sense of duty" as an extremely uncomfortable New England conscience dominated by fear and precedent. You say he never even shaded the truth with you, but he wasn't above putting up a bluff with me last spring. When Lisa left us alone, he pretended to be keen about going into the law. An excellent sign, I pointed out to Lisa. Any human being who is incapable of putting up a bluff when he wants to is in a pretty bad way. You see, Lisa was afraid Murray might be on the edge of a nervous breakdown as a result of the failure of that engagement of his, and another similar failure to which he had only referred to Lisa.'

'Another girl?'

'So I assume.'

'You mean — not of his own class?'

'I wouldn't be surprised. Lisa said he didn't go into the particulars. It's consistent with his conclusions about himself, which he mentioned to Lisa. A highly sensitive boy can be so shocked by his first experience with sex that it may result in a complex, and the false conclusion that he is doomed to impotence for life.'

'In such a case I suppose you'd advocate a psychoanalyst?'

'Not necessarily. Not even a psychiatrist. Another girl of the right sort would probably do the trick. Of course, if he had been married and another girl was out of the picture, then a doctor should be consulted. I advised Lisa to leave it to time and Nature.'

'Lisa has always been a tremendous influence in Murray's life,' remarked Mr. Ben reflectively. 'During his first years at Tamarack I used to wonder if he didn't have something of a mother complex.'

'Possibly. Many boys at that age do, but in the majority of cases it does no harm. It passes if the boy has an intelligent mother, which Lisa is. Her marriage to Firth acted as an excellent cure of Murray's tendency toward the Oedipus complex, and I strongly advised it. Murray's greatest handicap in like was his brother complex.'

'Brother complex?'

'Certainly. Any young boy who had Windy for an older brother would have to be pretty hard-shelled not to have such brilliant success and outstanding popularity result in misgivings about his own potentialities. It's no wonder to me that Murray recoiled from competition and sought inconspicuousness and nonentity at times. He gave me an excellent example of this when Windy interrupted our interview last May. Shut up like a clam and disappeared. One suffers for a boy caught by fate in such an unfortunate brother-relationship.'

'Unfortunate! Why, Windy has been the greatest influence in Murray's life in making him a normal, all-round good fellow. When Murray first started in at Tamarack, Windy, who was a junior counselor then, wasn't there for the first several weeks, and Murray had a pretty mean time of it. Couldn't swim. Couldn't play ball. Hated all games. Stayed by himself. An introvert, *you'd* call him. When Windy arrived on the scene he took him in hand. Devoted hours to him. And gradually Murray learned to be a good sportsman and a good sport, too, and did a mighty fine job in shaping himself into the type we hold up as our ideal at Tamarack.'

Doctor Jaquith laid down his cigar. 'A bit of verse occurs to me,' he said:

'I shape the vessel of my life,
Hammer it cold, hammer it hot;
I try my best to make of it
    What it is not.

Blow, bellows, blow!
Burn, fire, burn!
I try to shape a silver vase
    Out of a copper urn.' *

* 'Misdirection,' by Eleanor Slater, reprinted from *Quest* by permission of the Yale University Press.

'I get the point. But your poem doesn't fit this case.'

'Not accurately, you're right. It was the other way round with Murray. Everybody was trying to shape a copper urn out of a silver vase.'

'Good Lord, Jake, if there hadn't been some shaping done and hammering, too — Murray would have been utterly un-equipped for life. When he first came to camp he was such a meek, weak, undersized little specimen, the boys nick-named him "Johnny-Jump-Up." When Windy learned they meant "Little Pansy" he said he'd knock the daylights out of anyone he ever heard call Murray that name again. Which he did, too, once! But once was sufficient.'

'What kid wouldn't hate a brother who fought his battles for him?'

'But Murray never hated Windy! He adored him and looked up to him as a model and ideal.'

'Lisa told me Murray used to have frequent dreams that Windy was dead. You know your Freud well enough to know what that signifies, Ben.'

'Oh, Freud!' Mr. Ben spat the word out. 'Let's leave Freud out of this! They were two of the most devoted brothers I've ever seen in my life.'

'All right, Ben, old man. Have it your own way. But I still contend that Windy would have done his brother a greater service if he had made him feel pride in his own talents, even though they were different from Windy's and those of the average popular young men of his acquaintance.'

'Whatever a boy's talents are, he's got to be taught to be a good sport, Jake.'

'A "good sport." Quite a frequent term of yours. Exactly what do you mean by it?'

'Well, I tell my boys, being a good sport is taking what's coming to you with your chin up.'

'The athletic field isn't the only place to learn that! Pluck doesn't require muscle or brawn or physical skill, or popularity, or being a leader, or a good mixer, or any of those admirable assets you specialize in developing in a boy at Tamarack.'

'Glad to hear you acknowledge they *are* assets,' laughed Mr. Ben.

'Sure, they're assets. But there are plenty of examples of able men of great value to this world who've got pluck and power of endurance, who never played football or baseball or any other kind of damned ball, and were never what you call good mixers.'

'Oh, come, come, Jake, you know as well as I do objective activities are desirable. One of the first pieces of advice you give a repressed patient is to get out of his shell.'

'Yes, but in some way that will put his own talents to use. One of the most valuable by-products of developed talent is the self-esteem it gives one, and the confidence to act on one's own judgment. I wouldn't be a bit surprised but that the reason Murray isn't alive today is because he was afraid of falling short of Windy's standards, and yours too, and didn't act on his own judgment.'

'Jake, listen!' said Mr. Ben in a lowered tone. 'He *is* alive!'

He related in detail Jim's story, stealthily exhibiting the articles in his pocket and returning them to their hiding place again.

'What do you think I had better do, Jake? My plan was to tell Lisa tonight, but when I arrived and saw the portrait and what the general attitude was, I thought perhaps I wouldn't tell her at all.'

'Lisa is the kind of woman who prefers to know the truth.'

'Well, wouldn't it be better to wait till her husband returns to help her take it?'

'No, Ben, tell her tonight. Lisa doesn't need her husband or anybody to help her take facts.'

13

CHAPTER

Lᴇᴛ's ɢo into the library, Mr. Ben,' said Lisa after bidding Charlotte and Doctor Jaquith good night. 'The light is better there. At last I can show you the plans for the chapel.'

Mr. Ben followed her across the hall, pausing a moment to glance up at Murray's portrait, dreading the task before him.

The plans had been put away. Lisa produced the long tube containing them and laid it on the center table, then sat down. Mr. Ben sat down opposite her. Instead of opening the plans Lisa reached for the red portfolio.

'I've been making a collection of some of the things that have been written about Murray,' she said. 'Before we start on the plans I'd like to read you a few paragraphs I've marked here and there. That is, if you don't mind.'

'I'd like to hear anything you have to read me. But first I have some news to tell you.'

'News? About Murray?'

'Yes, something has been found.' His voice was grave. His eyes, too. Instantly Lisa jumped to the conclusion that the tentacles that had so long been holding Murray's body a prisoner beneath the surface of the water beyond the falls, had finally released it. Mentally she braced herself.

'I am ready. What has been found?'

'His glasses.' Mr. Ben reached into his breast pocket and took out the pasteboard box.

'Oh! Only his glasses.'

'And also we have some of his calling cards torn up into small pieces.'

'His calling cards torn up into small pieces!' Lisa repeated.

Mr. Ben unwrapped the glasses from their tissue paper and passed them across the table to Lisa. He then emptied the bits of cardboard from their envelope into the palm of his left hand. First fitting a few of the fragments together he stretched out his palm at arm's length across the table for her to see.

Lisa gazed first at the glasses in her hand, then at the mutilated name, lying crooked, ragged-edged, and stained on Mr. Ben's outstretched palm. Her brows were drawn into a perplexed frown.

'Where were these things found?'

'On the top of a bank opposite Henderson's Point where Briggs's body was lying.'

'When were they found?'

'About two weeks ago.'

'Who found them?'

'Jim Billings, the game warden. He wrote me immediately, but I was in Canada and didn't get his letter till I returned three days ago. I went up to Tamarack immediately to investigate. Jim found the glasses lying under some bushes on top of a five-foot bank. They couldn't have been washed up there. The torn cards were buried in some moss near-by.'

'Buried! Who could have done such a thing?'

'Possibly Murray.'

'Murray!' Clouds of puzzled dismay spread over her face.

'It looks as if we had been mistaken about what happened to Murray,' said Mr. Ben.

'You mean there's a possibility Murray wasn't swept over the falls?' He nodded. 'And didn't drown?' Again he nodded. 'You mean Murray may be alive?' For the third time Mr. Ben nodded.

'Why didn't you call me up instantly? Why did you wait to come to tell me such wonderful, wonderful news?'

'I didn't know how you'd take it.'

'How I'd take it! How would any mother take the news that the report "dead" about her son was changed to "missing"? For that is what you're telling me, isn't it?'

'Yes.'

'Where is he now?'

'We don't know.'

'You mean you're afraid Murray lost his way and died in the woods? Why, that's a worse death than drowning.' She sat up very straight and clasped her hands on the table-top. 'Is that what you think happened to Murray?'

'No! It is not! Positively! I have proof that it is not!' He took out a piece of brown wrapping paper from another pocket and passed it to Lisa. 'Even I recognized this as Murray's printing.' All his specimens were labeled with the same flawless lettering. 'Notice the postmark. Part of it is blurred, but Jim has had it examined and there's no longer any doubt about the place where it was mailed. The date is clear — July 31. Four days after the tragedy. Murray was alive when he addressed that package. It was mailed right here in Boston.'

Lisa stared at the brown paper long and silently. 'Please tell me everything, Mr. Ben.'

Mr. Ben did so slowly, quietly, and on Jake's advice, as matter-of-factly as possible, offering no sympathy except that conveyed by the tone of his voice. He related in detail the Billings' account of the counselor's call at their camp on the third day after the tragedy, repeated Mrs. Billings' description of his physical appearance and the fragments of conversation which she could recall. When he had finished Lisa inquired calmly:

'Do you think Murray did something cowardly?'

'I wouldn't put it as harshly as that.'

'Why do you think he ran away?'

'Well, it looks to me as if he probably became panicky. It was a very severe storm. He knew his companion had a weak heart and couldn't help himself. The combination was enough to strike fear to anybody's heart. In a crisis like that, if fear gets the upper hand, ideals are apt to be forgotten. Murray had the highest of ideals, but —'

'Don't try to spare me. I can take the truth.'

'I only wish I knew the truth. If only Murray had trusted me more! If only he'd come straight to me and told me what he had done, then I could have explained — made allowances. But in the face of all this unfavorable testimony I'm helpless to defend him against the conclusions that may be drawn.'

'What may they be?'

'Jim Billings has developed quite a talent as a private detective. He's pieced together all this fresh evidence with what we already had, and has worked out a series of events that he thinks pretty close to the facts. His conclusions seemed pretty far-fetched to me. You must bear in mind it's only *one* man's opinion.'

'Go ahead, Mr. Ben. Tell me.'

'Well, those buried cards indicate to Jim that Murray was destroying all marks of identification. If he had any other articles on his person bearing his name, they, too, according to James's opinion, are buried somewhere in the vicinity. Jim thinks he dropped his glasses by mistake when he was hiding under the bushes at the top of the bank.'

'Hiding?'

'Yes, that's Jim's theory. He points to a number of facts that lead to his conclusion that Murray was guilty of something that made him extremely anxious not to be found. As you know, there was practically no water in Briggs's lungs. Often it is necessary for a rescuer of a drowning person to break his grip by a blow, and so be less hampered. It occurs to Jim that Murray's blow might have proved fatal. In any case, he deserted Briggs. The bank he climbed was on the other side of the cove from the beach where Briggs was found. Then, after destroying all marks of identification, he disappeared. Do you follow Jim's reasoning?'

'Yes, I follow it,' said Lisa. 'Please tell me how Jim explains, if Murray was so anxious not to be found, that he turned up two days after the drowning at his camp?'

'He points out that Murray couldn't hope to escape in his camp uniform. Murray was familiar with camp customs. He knew that as soon as anxiety was felt all our campers would be out on the lake and combing the shores, so he had to keep himself hidden until he could pass himself off as one of the searchers and borrow some clothes, which was exactly what he did.'

'Does Jim Billings think Murray thought that all out and hid in the woods for two days and nights, under bushes and behind trees like a criminal, when he knew we were hunting for him and terribly anxious?'

'That's Jim's idea.'

'Well, I don't believe it! It isn't like Murray.'

'I agree. But Murray *did* give a false name. And he *has* disappeared. Those who don't know Murray as well as you and I will be likely to accept Jim's theory when this fresh evidence comes to light, I'm afraid.'

'How many know about what Jim has found?'

'So far only Jim and his wife, Jake, whom I have just told, and now you.'

'Must anyone else know? I shall tell Barry, but why should we tell facts that may give a false impression of Murray's behavior? Can't Jim Billings be persuaded to say nothing of these few poor paltry bits of paper that would be lying up there in the woods now, and until they rotted, if his dog hadn't dug them up?'

'Yes, I think Jim would keep still if I asked him to. But

what's your idea? Don't you intend to try to find Murray?'

'I think not. I'm speaking from impulse. A poor one, perhaps. But my first reaction to your news is a strong intuitive wish to help Murray in the decision he has made. Of course it may be just maternal instinct. Any mother would want to hide her fugitive son, I guess. I may be wrong, but —'

'I'm not so sure you're wrong. Jake said to note your first reaction to my news. Women's intuitions are usually pretty sound. But in this case there are complications. Murray is being regarded as a hero on false grounds.'

'But we have no proof that Murray wasn't heroic.'

'Running away isn't heroic.'

'I know! I know! But absolute heroism or absolute courage or absolute any fine quality is never wholly attained. All virtues are just approached. I feel sure that Murray was courageous up to a certain point. The fact that he is being regarded as a hero by a small circle of people isn't hurting anybody, is it? It isn't depriving anyone else of credit due him. And it's so transient. It will all soon be forgotten.'

'But you know the saying, "In the end the truth always conquers." It's Nature's law.'

"Well, if it's Nature's law why not leave it to Nature?'

'Nature can be very cruel at times left to itself. For example, a painful illness without medical assistance. If Murray should return it will be a very painful experience for him. People resent being deceived about their heroes. Remember Cook and the North Pole? They are more scornful of frauds than of a man who fails to rise to heroism in a crisis. Won't you be sparing him some of the pain of his return if you take his friends into your confidence and let the truth be known?'

'It's Murray's life, Mr. Ben. He's no longer a child. Isn't it better for him to meet the consequences of his own decision in his own way, and at his own time? Who am I to interfere?'

'His mother.'

'That's true. But the time comes when the wisest thing a mother can do is nothing. No, Mr. Ben, I'm not going to interfere, and I hope you and the Billingses and Jake will all stand with me and keep the knowledge of these articles a secret.'

'What would you have done about the chapel?'

'Oh, I forgot about the chapel! Of course you can't accept it now.'

Mr. Ben shook his head. 'I've already instructed the lumberman not to cut the logs.'

'I'm sorry about the chapel, Mr. Ben.' She reached across the table and picked up the plans — symbol of the monument that was to have perpetuated Murray's heroism. Useless now! Never to exist except on paper. Beautiful in design and purpose but dead before it ever lived. She shrugged and tossed the tube aside. 'How am I ever going to explain about the chapel? What excuse can I give to Windy?'

'Aren't you going to tell even Windy the facts?'

'No. I think Murray would rather I wouldn't.'

'Very well. Leave it to me. I'll say the logs I wanted couldn't be found so we've postponed the work till spring. Perhaps by that time Murray will provide an explanation.'

The next day, with the help of the chauffeur, Lisa returned the Sargent portrait of Grandmother Vale to its old location between the silver candelabra in the entrance hall. She hung Murray's portrait over the mantel in her private sitting room upstairs.

14

CHAPTER

Murray never reached Millinocket. The driver of the truck in the back of which he lay asleep on a pile of burlap bags made a wrong turn. When Murray started out upon his journey he decided he couldn't afford to travel by either bus or train. It might be some time before he would be receiving a pay-envelope in a lumber camp. Hitch-hiking was a new experience to him. But he soon learned the technique. He made no overtures to touring cars, selecting only trucks and utility vehicles of various sorts, and only when they were stopping at a gas station, or slowing down for a traffic light.

He was surprised at the cordial response of the drivers. To receive such greetings from strangers was a new experience. It was because of his clothes, he supposed. His apparel proclaimed him to be a member of the unprivileged class with no pretensions to superiority. He had never realized to what extent the mere veneer of raiment could invite or forbid good-fellowship.

The first driver he approached sang out lustily when he appeared from behind a tree and Murray shyly made the familiar gesture, 'Come on up, Bud.' And when Murray was seated on the straight-backed driver's seat, with a super-structure of logs towering behind, the driver inquired, 'Where yer bound, Pal?'

Murray had never been addressed as Bud and Pal before. It was warming to the heart. It was reassuring, too. His apparel roused no suspicion, nor his method of travel. Self-confidence increased with every hour.

His progress was slow at first. By noon he had covered only fifty miles of the approximate two hundred and fifty to his destination. The first several vehicles he boarded were going his way for only a short distance, each engaged in local business of some sort. One was delivering a load of live chicks in crates to the nearest railway express office. Another was conveying a cow to a neighboring farm.

It was after he had eaten his midday meal consisting of a frankfurt buried in a damp, mustard-smeared roll, produced from one of the pockets of his mackinaw, that a covered moving-van hove in sight as he stood at a crossroads scanning the highway for likely prospects.

It slowed down to a crawl when Murray stepped out from the side of the road. The driver was seated inside a glassed-in cubbyhole, in a separate unit painted bright red, attached to the front of the van. He stuck his head out of the open window. Several faces appeared framed behind the glass windshield. 'Plenty of room in back,' he hollered and brought his vehicle to a stop. 'Where you tryin' to get to?' Murray told him. 'Fine and dandy! We're bound for the border. Our route goes right by the road into Millinocket. Hop in behind. There's a drunk in there somewheres but he's harmless. We'll let yer know when you get to your gettin'-out place, but it won't be for some time yet.'

Murray hoisted himself up into the interior through a small opening at the rear. It was so dark he could see nothing at first, but the place sounded empty. As soon as his eyes became readjusted, he discovered a pile of furniture-mover's pads in one of the forward corners. On top of the pads lay a man, face down, arms and legs sprawled out in grotesque angles, as if it were a dead body tossed there just as it had chanced to fall. In the forward corner there was a pile of burlap bags. These were unoccupied.

Murray made his way over to them, rolled up one into a bolster and lay down. Not a single ray of light penetrated the walls and roof of the van. The roadside was completely obliterated. All he could see of out-of-doors was an unchanging rectangle of blue-white sky through an open section at the rear. It was like traveling in a tunnel but making no progress. The entrance to the tunnel neither receded nor approached. It was monotonous.

He fell to reviewing the day's events. The very thought of the landlady's suspicion gave him gooseflesh. He must think of a better name for himself — one that was more consistent with the 'stylish way he talked' — unless he could change the way he talked, like the girl in that play, *Pygmalion,* who acquired a new vocabulary, inflection, and quality of voice by sheer determination and effort. He was familiar with down-East vernacular because of those summers spent off the coast of northern Maine when he was a kid. He wasn't half bad at imitating it. He had often regaled his campers with his down-East stories. There was a man at home — a member of his club at college, one of the older graduates — who was famous for his Vermont dialect and in constant demand as an after-dinner speaker. His name was Sumner Bryant. He was a lawyer and a brilliant one, an aristocrat born and bred, but he could discard his natural accent at a moment's notice. His ability to reproduce the soft nasal tones and cryptic humor of the Vermont farmer whom he personified when he told his stories (always the same farmer — Jess Judkins by name) kept his listeners in a state of constant chuckling. Often he would drift into the rôle of Jess Judkins in an ordinary conversation and without warning. Murray had heard it said his friends couldn't be sure when he opened his mouth which it would be who would speak — flat-toned, ungrammatical Jess Judkins, or his antithesis. If Sumner Bryant could shed his 'stylish way of speaking' at will, why couldn't he?

Of course it would take time. Until he had acquired the knack, a name more consistent with his natural accent would be wise. No need to discard Jones. All that was necessary was to combine it with a more distinguished first name. What about Eliot Jones, or Lowell Jones, or Kirkland or Leverett or Dunster Jones? He ran through the entire list of the freshman dormitory houses at Harvard. Any one of them did the trick — had the desired effect upon Jones.

Also he'd better change the place he came from. He had mentioned Jackson Hole simply because it was the only town or city in the State of Wyoming he could think of when the landlady had pinned him down to be specific. To anyone who was familiar with Jackson Hole this claim could easily be proved false. He didn't know the name of a single street, shop, or inhabitant there. A big city would be a wiser choice. How about Chicago? No! That landlady would have insisted on his street and number if he'd mentioned Chicago. A far distant country would serve his purpose better. Why not claim India or Burma or China as his birthplace? A native village too remote to have been heard of here. He was reminded of a little chap in his class the first year he went to boarding-school, who had been born on some island off the coast of China. The island had an outlandish name which only the little chap himself knew how to pronounce. His parents had been missionaries there and died of some tropical fever. Such circumstances were feasible. Why not say his parents had been missionaries and likewise had died when he was a child? How ridiculous! How utterly haywire to be choosing his name, birthplace, parents, and fate up to date. He turned his thoughts elsewhere.

Presently he sat up to relieve an odd sensation in his chest — a sort of burbling, like something boiling down deep in the bottom of the cavity. Hadn't he gotten rid of that lake water yet? Afterwards he lay down again, curved an arm

beneath his head, and joined his traveling companion in
sleep.

He was awakened by someone tugging at his leg. 'Hi, kid,
wake up! We got to part company. 'Less you want to come
along to Rivière de Loup. We made a wrong turn back at
Bangor, so we ain't on the route that goes by your road.
Forgot all about yer till just now. Durned sorry, son.'

Murray said it didn't matter. He'd pick up another car
going back to Bangor, spend the night there and start out
fresh in the morning. He'd had a fine sleep. Thanks a lot
and good-bye.

The van dropped him opposite a roadside tourist camp —
a long row of miniature houses as identical in shape, size, and
color as a row of birds all of one species seated on a telegraph
wire. They were tall and narrow with peaked tops, painted
light blue, trimmed with flaming red. Their narrow front
doors were bright yellow. They suggested a row of parakeets
of some exotic variety, but the name of the camp, announced
on a large electrically lighted sign, was 'The Blue Bird.' The
sign also announced that the cabins rented for a dollar a
night per person, were equipped with hot and cold water
and beauty-rest mattresses.

The Blue Bird appeared to be doing a good business today.
Automobiles were already parked between more than half
of the cabins. There was just enough space between them
for one car. Murray longed for the touch of cool sheets and
the feel of resilient springs beneath his body. But no telling
whom he might run into. Lots of fellows he knew put up at
tourist camps when on an automobile tour. Besides, his
shabby clothes would arouse the suspicions of the proprietor.
He slept on a stack of second-crop hay in a field behind the
camp that night.

Before retiring to his haystack he mapped out a far shorter
route to Millinocket from his present location than via

Bangor. The van had dropped him a few miles west of
Moosehead Lake — a quarter of an inch north of Greenville
on the road-map. A service man at a gas station near the
tourist camp pointed out the exact spot on the road map.

The spot was some fifty or sixty miles west of Millinocket
in a straight line. But there was a lot of impassable stuff on
the map intervening — the sprawling body of Moosehead,
unattached blue blobs beyond, mountains, streams, swamps.
There was no road indicated, but the serviceman said that a
road existed. It was not so much traveled as a state road
of course, but he'd have no difficulty in getting lifts. There
was a C.C.C. camp located up that way somewhere, working on one of F. D. R.'s crazy projects. All kinds of trucks,
vans, tractors, and whatnot were wearing out the road from
morning till night.

Murray traced the route in pencil on the road map. From
Greenville the pencil line slanted northeast to Kokadjo, then
climbed more steeply north to Ripogenus, crossed the Ripogenus dam, then turned slightly south, following the faint
hairline of the Ripogenus River, weaving its way along
Mount Katadin's foothills — widespread sunbursts on the
map.

It began to rain in the night. He could keep drier walking
than lying down. He was upon the road before daylight.

It was still raining twelve hours later when he was grimly
plodding along the road on foot, with Millinocket lying
thirty miles or more ahead, he figured. He had spent more
hours hiking than hitching. The serviceman had been right
about opportunities for a lift provided by the C.C.C. boys.
There'd been plenty of traffic as far as their camp, but that
was located way back on the Greenville side of Kokadjo.
Since leaving its vicinity he had contacted no vehicles except
two dump-carts full of gravel and a road-scraper.

He had arrived at the Ripogenus dam seated on the road-

scraper. Since he'd left the dam ten miles back he had seen
nothing on wheels going in either direction. Nothing moving
at all, except on four legs — a deer, a fox, several rabbits. Or
on wings — occasional crows, a fish-hawk, two aeroplanes.
The last human being he had seen was the man stationed at
the gate across the road beyond the dam. An official-looking,
officious-acting individual, who demanded where he was
going and what his business was there, eyeing him sharply
from head to foot as if he suspected him of designs on the
dam, and of having some dynamite concealed somewhere.
If it weren't for the attitude of that gate-man he'd go back
and ask for a night's shelter in one of the little houses he'd
noticed near the dam. Daylight would be folding up on him
before long, and he was feeling lousy — hot, cold, shivery,
sweaty, all at the same time — and to add insult to injury, his
stomach had gone back on him. He had provided himself
with some good nourishing food at Greenville, to eat en
route — thick ham sandwiches, filling doughnuts, and a slab
of cheese. But it wouldn't stay down. Soft! That's what he
was, he guessed. Couldn't stand up to roughing it on the
road for three days! Had to go and get a stomach-ache
like some of his camp kids brought up in cotton wool.

He walked with his hands shoved deep in the side pockets
of his mackinaw, raising his feet as little as possible, and
with head bent. He noticed that in the middle of the road
there was a growth of short grass. That road-scraper fellow
couldn't have been along here with his blade for weeks.
This couldn't be the main road to Millinocket. Had he made
a wrong turn? Whenever he had come to a fork and had
been in doubt which way to go, the telegraph poles had
been his guides. He glanced up in search of one of the tall reassuring sentinels, bearing cross bars and numerous cables.
Instead his eyes met a slender slanting rod, no bigger than
his arm, tapering at the top and bearing a single wire. Gosh!
How far back had he made his mistake?

He turned around. Doggedly he began to retrace his
steps. He hadn't gone far when he came to another road
turning off sharply at his right. It was a narrow woods road
— with tall grasses in the center. There was a sign nailed to
the trunk of a dead tree on one corner. The sign was badly
in need of fresh paint. It read: 'Fiddle Pond Camp, 7 miles.'

If he could keep going seven miles more why not spend
the night at Fiddle Pond Camp? It might prove to be an
abandoned camp, but the road led to some destination inhabited by humans because the long grasses in the middle
were streaked with grease from the under-side of an
automobile. Perhaps it was a private camp. Private or public, there was the risk of running into somebody who would
recognize him. He was staring up at the sign, cogitating,
when his ears caught the chug-chuggety-chug of an automobile engine running on fewer than its allotted number of
cylinders.

It proved to be a touring car of a vintage before he had
become automobile-conscious. It had a chunky body,
perched above the wide high running-board, wheels with
spokes, and a collapsible top. The top was raised, the canvas
hanging limp on its frame. It chugged up to Murray and
stopped.

A man with a ragged mustache and a wizened face, leaned
out from behind the wheel.

'So you're here!' he remarked in a soft flat tone.

'Yes,' Murray agreed.

'I've been way down to Millinocket to meet yer. What
did you do? Come in by Greenville?'

'Yes.'

'How did yer get here from Greenville?'

'Hitch-hiked.'

'You should of called up and let me know.'

'I'm sorry.'

'Well, come on, get in.' Murray started to do so. 'Where's
your kit?'

'All the kit I've got is on me.'

'But you said you was bringing your own camping-kit.'

'Did I?'

'You know durned well you did!'

'I guess you think I'm somebody else.'

'Ain't you the new guide?'

'No,' Murray replied, and after a pause, slowly, meticulously, 'I ain't.'

'Ain't yer name Silus Hicks?'

'No, it ain't.'

'Well, yer medium tall and light-haired, like he said he was, and got a red and black mackinaw. That was how we were to tell him at the depot or if we met him walkin' in. If yer ain't him what yer doin' in here?'

'Tryin' to get to Millinocket. Guess I got off the main road.'

'Well, you keep on goin' and you'll get back on it again, after a mile or two.'

The man withdrew into the shadows of his collapsible top, pulled out one button then another, pushed down on a pedal and began pumping it up and down. The engine gave a few hoarse coughs, then stopped. Murray walked up closer to the car.

'Is the camp where the guide was expected Fiddle Pond Camp?'

The man nodded, and repeated his operations, with the same results.

'Is it a private camp, or open to the public?'

'It's a club.' For the third time the man pulled, pushed, and pumped. Presently there was a deafening paroxysm of explosions. The man's body stiffened as he leaped into action with both legs and arms. The engine collapsed into silence. The man dropped his hands to his knees and sat back.

'Mixture's wrong. Gotta let her set awhile.'

'If it's a club, then I don't suppose a stranger can get in.'

'If *I* say so he can.'

'I'd be glad if I could get a bed for the night. I can pay for it.'

'It would suit me better, if you could *work* fer it.'

'I can do that too. I'm looking for a job.'

'Ever do any guidin'?'

'Yes, I've been guidin' for years.' Hadn't he guided a bunch of irresponsible kids on camping-trips every summer ever since he was a senior counselor? What was more, he had not only guided but had *been* guided, and by some of the best guides in the fishing world. For the last few years he'd always tried to get in a week's fishing somewhere in the wilds — on the Allagash with Tug last June before camp opened. Three years ago in Nova Scotia with his mother, after camp closed. He had no license, but he'd cross that bridge when he got to it.

'The job I got to offer ain't just guidin'. It's hired-man sort of work, too. Ed, my regular feller, has broke his leg. I got a full camp and want someone to lug wood, haul ice and help any way I have a mind to want him to, when he ain't guidin'.'

'That suits me.'

'Can yer drive a car?'

'Yes.'

'Can yer milk a cow?'

'Yes.' He had tried it once. He would have said he could walk a tightrope, so urgent had become his desire to get into a bed under a pile of blankets.

'Come around the other side and get in. We'll talk it over as we go along.'

15
CHAPTER

THERE WAS a bundle of mail tied with fine loosely twisted hemp string on the seat beside the man. The man tossed it into the back of the car and began pumping, pushing, and pulling again. Finally the balky car burst into vociferous response and consented to move, turning its nose sharply to the right and proceeding jerkily along the narrow woods road. Nothing was said for the first ten minutes.

Murray realized he was running a risk showing his face at a Maine fishing-camp about which he knew nothing. He had never heard of Fiddle Pond Camp. The fact that it was a club suggested an exclusive clientele, and added to the chance of running into somebody who would recognize him. Why, he might be headed straight for Doctor Warburton — for years the family adviser on all things medical. Doctor Warburton belonged to several fishing-clubs and one of them was in northern Maine. Murray had heard him talk about it. He'd better ask a few questions before it was too late.

'I remember one man I guided once talked a lot to me about a club he belonged to in this region. Is one of the members a doctor?'

'Ye-up. One.'

'Is he a surgeon from Boston?'

'Nope. A vet from Rumford Falls.'

'Where do most of the members come from?'

'State o' Maine folks mostly.'

'Any from Massachusetts?'

'One.'

'Where does he live?'

'Suburb of Boston, so he sez.'

'What's the name of the suburb?'

'Dorchester.'

'What does he do?'

'Manager of an A. & P. store down there. Say, young feller, how 'bout *me* askin' *you* a few questions fer a change?'

'Fine! Go ahead.'

'What's your name?'

'Jones. Eliot Jones.'

The man repeated the name, 'Eliot Jones. Eliot Jones,' softly, twice, as if feeling of it with his voice. 'I don't think much of "Eliot" fer a name fer a guide, or fer a hired man either. How 'bout callin' you "Joe"?'

'Suits me all right.'

'My name is Watts,' the man informed Murray. 'Seth Watts. "Seth" to the members. "Mr. Watts" to the help.'

'Yes, Mr. Watts,' said Murray respectfully.

'Where you come from?' asked Mr. Watts.

'I came from Bangor today.'

'H'm-m-m! In other words you don't care 'specially about tellin'?'

'Well, the fact is, I'm sort of a rollin' stone,' Murray began and stopped. He was aware of an approaching wave of nausea. He must be ready for it — ride it like a rising comber and not let it sweep him off his feet.

'Rollin' stones have to start rollin' from *some* place,' Mr. Watts remarked.

'Oh, you mean where I was born?' And then, somewhat to his own surprise, he heard himself saying, swallowing desperately, 'I was born in China.'

'China! You mean China, Maine, or China where the tea comes from? And the Chinks in the laundries?'

'China where the tea and the Chinks come from.'

'You don't say! Well now! Well now! China! That's real inter*es*ting.' His tone was mocking. It discredited Murray's claim completely. His next remark held it up to derision. 'I suppose your old man was a sea-captain on one of them clipper-ships with sails.'

'My father was a missionary! What's so funny about that?' Murray retorted. Thank God, the wave was receding.

'Nothin'. Nothin'. Suits me fine. Fact is, I don't care where you come from, nor what yer old man was. All I care about is how you do your chores. I'm in a kinda pickle. As I said, my regular helper broke his leg week or two ago and Rufus, another feller helpin' me out, went back on me two days back, and now Silas Hicks don't show up. Mr. Brock — he's one of our members — him and his daughter are goin' to feel mighty disappointed when I don't turn up with Silas tonight. You say you're a guide, where you been guidin'?'

'Nowhere around here. Up in Canada mostly. On the Restigouche, and the Moisie, and the Grand Cascapedia.'

He hoped *that* list would impress Mr. Watts, and that the region was far enough away to evade investigation.

'I suppose you've got references?'

'Well, no, not with me.'

"Mighty funny.'

'I wasn't plannin' to do any more guidin' this season.'

'Well, goldurn it, I can't palm off a guide I don't know nothin' 'bout on any of the members. You may be a jailbird that's got loose fer all I know.'

'Well, I'm not.'

'Likely you'd tell me if you was! What was takin' you to Millinocket?'

'I thought I'd try to get a job in a lumber camp. I've got to kill time somewhere till spring comes and the salmon season sets in again.'

'Hev, hev you?' There was a long pause. 'Ever do any trappin'?'

'Yes, some.' He'd trapped insects and butterflies.

'I stay up here at Fiddle Pond winters and do a little trappin' on the side. If you measure up doin' the chores I might hev a winter job for yer. No tellin'.'

Murray was silent. Another wave of nausea was approaching. The waves were increasing in frequency, in power, too. Water began flowing into his mouth from some hidden source. Experience had taught him that when that stage arrived it was time to take quick action.

'I've got to get out a minute, Mr. Watts,' he said abruptly. Once out of the car he plunged into the bushes at the side of the road. 'Don't stop the engine — I won't be but a minute,' he managed to call, and pushed his way farther into the tangled undergrowth, hoping not to be heard above the chugging engine. Then he crouched on all fours like a dog and gave himself up to his pressing necessity. The retching, once started, was as automatic as the gesticulations of a mechanical toy. It was followed by an attack of violent coughing, also automatic once started. When he returned to the car he felt better.

'Say, you ain't got T.B., hev yer?' Mr. Watts inquired when they were under way again.

'No, I ain't!'

'I don't want to bring anythin' catchin' into camp.'

'I haven't — I ain't got anything catchin'!' That cough is just a hang-over from a cold. And I ate somethin' last night that upset my stomich. I'll be all right now.'

It had stopped raining. The oyster-white pall that had hung low all day was lifting, and forming into cauliflower-like clouds with folds and contours, taking on a bright, translucent quality over to the left. The road was running in a northwesterly direction, and according to Murray's calculation, Mount Katahdin was close beside them on the right, towering up five thousand feet behind the clouds. When the road turned away from the brightness and bore

north it seemed to Murray to be pursuing a course around
the mountain, climbing up and down its outflung buttresses
one after another. There were many sharp rises and
descents. He ventured to inquire if Mount Katahdin could
be seen from the camp.

'Nope,' was Mr. Watts' brief reply, his attention fixed at
the moment upon a rippling sheet of water that appeared
straight ahead, down into which the road dipped and disappeared. Shifting into low gear he nosed the car straight
through the middle, and for a hundred feet or more it
splashed and sprayed like a shying horse fording a stream.
Two minutes later he again shifted the gears into low, guiding the car over a bridge badly in need of repair. It required
a steady hand to keep the four wheels on the narrow planks
laid end to end, like a pair of tracks, spanning the soft spots
where the logs were rotting, and the gapping holes where
they were missing.

The seven-mile drive provided samples of all the existing
varieties of a Maine woods road-bed — grass, gravel, rock,
clay, water, mud, corduroy, and planks laid on corduroy.
There were samples, too, of all the varieties of landscape and
physical geography that border such a road — woods dense
with underbrush; woods open as a park; stretches of spruce
and fir; stretches of deciduous trees — birch, maple, beech,
and ash; lumbered tracts spotted with stumps; burned tracts
covered with sweet-fern, blueberry, and low scrub; an
abandoned farm with nothing left but a few gnarled apple
trees on a cleared tract of land, some scraggly sumacs growing in the cellar-hole and a clump of lilac bushes at one
corner.

There was a continuous string of ponds, streams, and
swamps. There was also one of those desolate slate-gray
sheets of water, surrounded by dead tree trunks, stripped
of their leaves, bark, and most of their branches —
a nursery of 'dri-ki' — those mummified specimens of stumps

and broken fragments of trees, often found miles away from their source. Spring freshets and floods sweep through a pond such as this and carry away the floating pieces of wreckage of the trees, depositing them high up on beaches or on sand bars or on top of banks, or sometimes on inland hillocks and knolls. There they remain year after year exposed to sun, rain, frost, snow and ice, slowly turning to the ash gray of bleached bones and to a similar state of ossified preservation. Their surfaces become as smooth as if rubbed down with sandpaper. They seem to lose all relationship to a tree, assuming strange shapes and contours, many resembling animals — grotesque monsters, a rearing dragon, a serpent with wings, curious birds and fish, sometimes human beings, or parts of human beings — a head, a torso, a giant's arm.

The road passed within a stone's throw of the murky water in which the dead trees were standing, tipsily leaning or lying prone one on top of the other, their roots exposed. Like a pile of jackstraws after the first throw, it occurred to Murray as he gazed upon them. His body was supposed to be imprisoned under a pile of dead trees similar to these. What a safe hiding-place for a dead body! Even your own! Last night the problem of disposing of his own remains had been his object for postponing immediate action. (Or his excuse. Which?) But here was a solution. It would be easy to crawl out on a low arm of one of the fallen trees, fasten some rocks about his body and topple off into the water below. Tomorrow or the next day he could easily wander down here after sundown and never be heard of again, never be searched for even. He could leave a note for Mr. Watts saying he was leaving and going out on foot. He made a mental note of the location of the pond.

Not two minutes later another signboard appeared nailed to a dead tree. It read 'Fiddle Pond Camp, one mile,' and presently the road began climbing up a long, straight, steep

ascent with no curves or undulations. A thick growth of firs,
pyramid-shaped, with church-steeple tops, shut out the
scenery on each side. Twice Mr. Watts changed gears. The
car was crawling at a snail's pace when it finally broke out
onto a bare shoulder of rock at the top. Mr. Watts brought
the car to a standstill, 'to let her cool off.'

A broad valley lay before them. In the west the horizon
line was visible. Just above it the setting sun was shining
through a slit in a mauve-colored bank. Other rays had
found a hidden route behind and were tinging pink the
white clouds higher up so that a warm glow was cast over
the panorama of treetops below — stretching away as far as
one could see, so dense they looked like a down puff in
various shades of green. Sunk down deep in one of the puffs
appeared what resembled an oval-shaped nugget of silver.

'That's it. That's Fiddle Pond,' said Mr. Watts.

'Pretty,' said Murray.

'It's from here you can see best why it's called Fiddle
Pond,' Mr. Watts went on. ' "Muskrat" used to be its name.
Looks kinder like a muskrat, too. But a lady visitor changed
it some thirty years back.'

Murray could see the resemblance. The oval-shaped nugget was narrower in the middle and from one end extended
a long, narrow strip of water. 'A river?' Murray inquired.

No. Just a creek. See that little round shinin' patch at
the end of the creek? That's Frog Pond. The same lady
changed it to Scroll Pond, but I always call it Frog. Goes
by both names. See that smoke risin'? That's where the
camp lies. We'll be there in another ten minutes now.'

They started to move again. They hadn't gone more than
a few jerks when a long-drawn-out, 'Yah-hoo!' reached their
ears. A human voice — strong and strident. Mr. Watts
stopped the car, turned off the engine and waited. Crackling sounds of approaching steps could be heard in the
thick scrub growth on the right. 'Coming,' the voice called.

16
CHAPTER

A MOMENT LATER from behind a huge boulder emerged a khaki-clad figure, male or female it was impossible to tell. Even as it approached Murray wasn't sure. A young boy, he thought, hot and disheveled, his shock of red-brown hair so awry that it hung down in clotted bangs on his forehead like a girl's. There was a diagonal scratch across his nose, and blood-stained daubs on his chin. When he was near enough the car to be heard he said nothing at first, standing with feet well apart and his hands on his hips, breathing hard. A lumpy canvas pack was strapped on his back. Two fishing rods in cloth cases were sticking out of it.

'Gosh, I was afraid I wasn't going to make it!' were his first words. 'Dad's coming. We want a lift back to camp.' He raised one arm, bare to the elbow, crooked it up over his forehead and swabbed off his face with the back of his wrist. Then tossed his head, the bangs falling backward.

It was that toss of the head that made Murray look sharper. It was not a boy's gesture. The figure approached with long confident strides leaping lithely over the prone tree trunks edging the road.

'I heard you start up the long hill. I bet Dad I could head you off, and, by Jiminy, I did!'

The face glowed with that look of elation which immediately follows the accomplishment of a difficult feat. The voice was elated, too. It was a low-pitched voice with a husky quality, as if hoarse from a cold. It might well be a boy's voice in the process of changing. But no boy Murray had ever known had a throat and neck like that. No bulging Adam's apple, no cordy muscles, no sign of a collar-bone except a shallow depression between the almost invisible knobs. All such anatomical details were buried deep beneath a layer of that smooth, resilient quality of flesh confined to the female of the species. Even thin girls had that kind of bone-concealing flesh.

She shoved her hands into her trouser pockets and placed one foot on the running-board.

'Well, I see you got him, Seth.'

'Ye-up.'

She addressed Murray. 'Your name is Silas Hicks, so Seth told us.'

'This ain't Silas. This feller's name is Jones — Joe for short.'

'Drop in at our cabin right after supper, please, Joe. The name of our cabin is "Old Crow." Our name is Brock. Are you familiar with this neck-of-the-woods?'

'No, he ain't,' said Mr. Watts. 'First time he's been in here. I advise you to wait for Silas. I expect he'll be showing up in a day or two.'

'We want somebody tomorrow. These long hikes are too much for Dad now, Seth.' Then to Murray, 'What I want to do is put my father in the bottom of a canoe and go off for a trip of a week or two. We don't need another guide. I'm as good as another guide myself.'

She stated the fact for information only. No suggestion of bragging. But naturally she wouldn't brag to a person in his position. Her manner was self-confident and assured, as if she was accustomed to making plans and carrying them out.

'Are you acquainted with the Allagash River, Joe?'

'Yes. Fairly.' He and Tug had paddled down the Allagash as far as Fort Kent last fall. But he couldn't possibly undertake a guiding job in that wilderness. Another bridge to cross later!

'Oh, good! Dad and I have our car so we can get up to the head of Moosehead all right. Where do you think it's best to start in?'

For the next few minutes Joe answered a fast volley of questions forgetting completely his dialect in his attempt to appear intelligent about the region. Suddenly she turned around, cupped her hands around her mouth, raised her chin, and let forth an ear-splitting 'Ya-hoo.' Then listened, chin still lifted. From somewhere in the valley came two shrill whistles.

'That's Dad!'

Seth said to Murray, 'You get in back. You'll have to climb over. Can't open the door, I got it so full.'

Murray pulled himself, head first, over the high back of the front seat, distributing his body — legs, arms, and torso — as best he could on top of the pile of bundles, bulging paper bags, and various unwrapped articles; managed to turn himself right side up, and let himself down on a burlap bag full of what felt like potatoes, his half-drawn-up legs sprawled out in front of him, straddling a smoked ham, a bag of flour, a carton of toilet paper, two broom handles, and the upthrust shin bone of what he discovered was a side of beef. His head almost touched the sagging top. His first sight of Mr. Brock was from under one of the overhanging side-flaps.

Mr. Brock was some thirty feet ahead of the car in process of climbing over one of the roadside logs. The log was broad and high. Mr. Brock's legs were fat and short. He was sitting up straight as if mounted on a broadbacked horse. It appeared as if he were stranded for the moment.

'Wait a jiff, Dad,' called his daughter and ran over to him. 'Here, give me your hand.'

He shooed her away, rolled over on his stomach, and

slowly let himself down backwards onto the ground. He
was a bulky, hydrant-shaped man — thick-necked, slope-
shouldered, with the gait of a bear walking on his hind legs
as he lumbered toward the car. His face was the red of
stewed tomatoes, and wet with sweat. He leaned heavily
against the nearest mud-guard, and began mopping his face
with a dark blue-and-white-print handkerchief.

'Je-hoshaphat!' he gasped at last. 'Some climb!'

He too was dressed in khaki — long, baggy pants, open-
necked shirt unbuttoned halfway down the front, exposing
a vigorous crop of rust-covered hair growing in wiry curls on
his rose-pink chest. On his head was a once-white canvas hat
with a limp, green-lined brim hanging down like a ruffle.
His breathing was labored. He placed the palms of his hands
on each side of his chest, just under the armpits, and pressed
hard.

'Sit down on the running-board, Dad,' said his daughter.
'Take it easy for a little.'

He ignored her. After a moment, 'Where's the guide?' he
demanded of Seth, pulling off his hat and wiping his shining
head. He was bald down to his ears — his ears were insig-
nificant little coils of gristle with soft pink lobes clinging
close to the surface of firm fat which merged cheek, jaw,
and neck into one thick column.

'He's in back,' said Nora.

Mr. Brock gave Murray a quick glance from out of two
shiny bright spots, buried in pink puffs of flesh. A conversation followed similar to that with his daughter a few minutes
before. His manner, like hers, was self-confident and
peremptory, but there was no arrogance. The use of the
imperative mood was simply his way of getting done what
he wanted done as quickly as possible — a grammatical habit
of his.

'Open the door, Seth,' he commanded and pulled himself
into the car. 'Move over farther. Take that pack off your

back, Nora. Give it to Joe. Take care of it, Joe. There's a
damn nice trout in it. Clean it and give it to the cook. Get
in, Nora. Start your old tin lizzie warming up, Seth. Get
going.' This rapid-fire series of orders was spoken with
brusque good-humor. When the car, after its usual pre-
liminary of noisy objections, finally began to move, Mr.
Brock said, 'This car is fit only for the dump. Disgrace to the
club. Disgrace to you too, Seth, you damned old tightwad,
you.' And he patted Seth on the knee.

He treated Seth Watts like an intimate friend, which was
his attitude, Murray was to discover, toward everybody of
whatever class and in whatever position. According to Sam
Brock's category, all human beings are human beings, just the
same as all dogs are dogs. If you like dogs, then you like *all*
dogs, whatever their breed, training, or condition.

Mr. Brock planted his spreading bulk next to Mr. Watts.
His daughter jammed herself sidewise into what space remained, thrusting her arm behind her father and holding
to a rusty lap-robe attached to the back of the seat a
few inches in front of Murray's eyes. The bones of her wrist,
bent at a sharp angle, were rigid. The muscles of her arm,
bare to the elbow, were taut. But the skin was of the same
soft, silky, feminine texture as her neck and throat. Something a little touching about it somehow, Murray thought.

No more remarks were addressed to Murray. The conversation was monopolized by an account of the fish inside
the creel he held in his hands, and was addressed to Seth
Watts. At first Murray didn't listen closely but he caught
familiar words and phrases. 'Too rainy — too windy — too
late — too early. Not a rise. That pool where the big fellows
lie.' Dusty Miller — Parmachenee Belle — Silver Doctor. Not
interested. 'We'd decided to reel in when all of a sudden
Nora gave a squeal. There was something tickling her inside
her blouse. She fished down and brought up a live cricket,
about the size of a small Black Gnat. She stuck the little

black sonofabitch, still squirming and kicking, onto her hook. Walked back and made a long, pretty cast, into the wind, too! There was a rise ten inches this side of the big boulder. She cast again, and by golly, there was a strike! She hooked him. He leaped, mad as the devil. Lively fellow. Put up a damn good fight. Beauty! Two and a half pounds. Perhaps more. I tell Nora she's got to carry live crickets inside her shirt, whenever we go after those old geezers. Takes something with a lot of sex-appeal to rouse the old boys.'

Seth chuckled. Sam chuckled, too, then lowering his voice and leaning closer to Seth's ear, 'Listen to this one.' There were more chuckles. Nora sat with her head turned away from her father and Seth, deaf to their conversation, serenely surveying the landscape.

The road approached the camp along a high bank edging the pond, so Murray's first view of it was from a balcony seat, extreme right of center. It looked like a typical Maine fishing-camp. There were a dozen or fifteen small cabins, and one long cabin of barracklike proportions, set back from the water about a hundred feet on a slight rise. The cabins were made of peeled logs weathered to a smoked pearl gray. Their slanting roofs were shingled and had the ruffled feathered appearance of split cedar chips. Most of the cabins stood in a row closely huddled, but there were occasional stragglers. Ribbons of smoke were curling out of several of the stubby chimney tops. The trees in front of the cabins had been cut down, but the stumps remained and none of the rocks had been removed. All landscaping had been left to Nature. All planting, too. No patches of cut grass. No paths except those worn by feet.

The cabins varied slightly in size and detail but were all built on the same general design except two steep-roofed cabins the logs of which were vertical. They stood side by side and were connected by a covered porch. They were

named 'The Siamese Twins.' All the cabins had names. The
names appeared in capital letters made of silver birch twigs
nailed onto a board over the entrances. It was still light
enough for Murray to read the names. The names were not
what you would call literary. There were 'Whaddayaknow,'
'Stay-a-while,' 'Reelax,' 'Beano,' 'Sidecar,' 'Old-Fashioned,'
and 'Old Crow.'

Seth stopped his car in front of 'Old Crow.' Mr. Brock and
his daughter got out. Murray hoped they wouldn't speak to
him. He was having a chill, he guessed. If he unclenched
his teeth to reply they might notice it.

'Don't clean that fish until after supper, Joe,' said Mr.
Brock. 'I want to show it to the crowd. Just wash it off
and put it on a platter.'

'Very well, sir,' said Murray, through tightly clamped teeth.

'Come over to the cabin about eight o'clock, and we'll fix
up.'

'Very well, sir.'

'And drop the "Sir." '

Murray was silent.

'You heard me, didn't you?'

'Yes, I'll remember,' he managed to bring out finally, but
he couldn't keep his voice from shaking. 'Sorry.'

'Don't mind Dad, Joe,' said Nora Brock kindly.

Seth drove on in silence, not speaking until he drew up at
the kitchen door. Murray crawled out. Seth piled his arms
full of articles and told him to give them to the cook. 'Tell
her I'll be in in a minute.'

Murray got inside the kitchen door all right, but decided
it was better policy to wait for Mr. Watts to do the talking.
His legs warned him to lay down the heavy articles on a
table beside him and lean against it as he waited.

No one seemed to notice him. Night had already fallen
upon the kitchen. There were several kerosene lamps in
iron brackets attached to the log walls. The lamps were lit,

but their small yellow flames were swallowed up in so much murkiness.

It was a long, narrow room. Its ceiling was high and slanting. It was supported by heavy log rafters, unpeeled, and crossbeams. Clouds of smoke and steam were rising from various kettles on the stove and disappearing in the dense space above. A tall, raw-boned woman was standing over the kettles. A meal was in progress in the adjoining room. There was a swinging door between the two rooms. The door was suddenly pushed open by a rounded hip, and a girl appeared bearing a large oval tray piled high with dishes. She deposited it with a great clatter on a long trestle table running down one side of the room.

Murray was leaning against one end of the table. But she didn't see him. At the other end the hunched figure of a shock-headed, ragged-bearded man was seated, his hands hanging down at his side and his head hanging forward, staring up at Murray from under shaggy brows. Across the room, in front of a black iron sink, a man was standing on crutches.

Presently Seth Watts appeared. He went over to the stove. 'Here are the pork chops,' he said to the raw-boned woman.

'Too late now,' she replied, not looking up. 'I see you're alone.'

'No, I ain't. I got him! He's here!' He turned toward Murray. 'What's the matter with you, Joe? Scairt? I told you to give the stuff to the cook. This is her. Her name is Mrs. Scully. You're to do anything she asks you to. Him over there by the sink, that's Ed. And this is Elta.' The waitress gave him one of those long, from-under-the-eyebrow looks that always made him feel uneasy with a girl. She was short and dark, very full-bosomed, very red-lipped. 'Elta is the cabin girl and you help her with the heavy work. This is Joe, everybody. Joe Jones.' No reference was made to the hunched figure at the end of the table. 'Mrs. Scully

will give you some supper later. Ed will show you where
you are to sleep. You'll be in the cabin next to Ed's.'

'No, he can't be in there, Mr. Watts,' said Ed. 'MacGregor
showed up 'bout noon-time.'

'Did, eh? Well, then, guess we'll have to put Joe in with
Danny.' The hunched figure looked up suddenly like a dog
who hears his name spoken. 'Or else in with you, Ed. Or up
in the pickers' cabin.'

'I've already had Elta take some blankets up there,' announced Mrs. Scully.

'That's good.' He turned to Joe. 'It's a cabin we let the
blueberry pickers stay in sometimes. Kind of rundown now.
But it's got a bed. MacGregor is the fire warden. He don't
usually stay but a night or two. Now come on out to the car
and help me unload.'

'The first thing I must do,' said Murray, once safely outside
the kitchen, 'is to wash that fish for Mr. Brock.'

'Oh, no, it ain't, Joe,' replied Seth in that soft tone of his,
especially soft when insinuating a reprimand. 'The first
thing you must do is what *I* want done. That's always the
rule here at Fiddle Pond. We'll start with the cases of drinks
first. They're in the back under the seat.'

Murray tackled the unloading with all the strength he
could muster. Some good stiff physical exercise might tighten
up his muscles so they'd stop shaking. Like tightening a wire
that gets to vibrating. He thought he was going to see the
job through without flopping. Flopping is usually just
willingness. 'You can do what you want to if you want to do
it enough.'

It was when he was carrying one end of the side of beef to
the ice-house that he collapsed. He tripped on a root and
fell sprawling with the carcass on top of him. He tried to get
up but couldn't. The muscles of his legs simply wouldn't
function. Finally, Mr. Watts propped him up against the

carcass and went for help. Events were vague after that.

When he regained full consciousness he was lying on a
wide bed with log footposts and a pile of blankets on top of
him. His shoes and socks had been removed. Also his tie,
and his shirt collar was unbuttoned. He turned his head
slightly. His mackinaw, hat, and tie were hanging on some
wooden pegs sticking out from one of the horizontal logs of
the walls. The logs were lit by the dim light of a kerosene
lamp with its wick turned low — so low he could smell it.
The lamp was placed on the wooden seat of a chair with its
back broken off. There was a big kitchen stove with a bulging stomach on one side of the room. Opposite was a rusty
kitchen sink minus faucets or pipes. On a shelf beside the
sink there was a tin pail and a battered white enamel wash-
basin.

He had stopped shivering. He threw off the blankets and
sat up. He was dripping with sweat! What time was it?
Gosh, that fish! He hadn't done a thing about it yet. He got
out of bed and crossed the room.

17
CHAPTER

THE DOOR of the cabin was open. He walked out onto a porch as black as ink, and stepped down onto a rough rock. Damn! He'd forgotten his shoes! He took a cautious step or two. It hurt like the devil.

'Come back here!' It was Seth Watts' voice. There was nothing soft or gentle about it now. 'Where do you think you're going?'

'To clean that fish. Isn't it all right for me to do it now?'

'No, it ain't! Come back here!'

Murray obeyed.

'I've been settin' here fer a dog's age waiting for you to come to enough so's to have a talk, and the first minute I drop off to sleep you try to sneak out on me barefoot!'

'I wasn't trying to sneak out. I forgot my shoes. I've got to clean that fish, and then go and see Mr. Brock. He's expecting me.'

Seth took hold of Murray's arm and gave it a sharp shake. 'Snap out of it! You ain't right in your mind, young feller.'

'I'm not?' He glanced down at his naked feet and raised his hand to his open shirt. 'Where am I? What time is it?'

'Past midnight! And I've been here since ten o'clock and before that Ed set here for a spell.'

'I'm afraid I've made you a lot of trouble.'

'Get on back into that bed.'

Murray offered no more objections. Seth sat down beside the bed on an empty soap box turned up on end.

'You're sick and you know it! This ain't no place for a sick man. The best thing for you to do is to go on down to Millinocket, like you planned, where there's doctors. If you don't feel up to walkin', I'll take you down to the main road in my auto and see you get a lift in. We'll start early before the crowd gets up. I'll go now and we'll both get a few hours sleep. Mrs. Scully has left a glass of milk and a dish of food on that shelf by the sink. And there's water in the pail.'

'Water?'

'Lie down.' Seth filled a thick tumbler and gave it to Murray. Propped up on an elbow he drank every drop. Seth refilled the glass and again Murray drained it.

'Thanks,' he murmured and dropped back. 'Mr. Watts, listen. I don't want any doctor, nor any care, nor any food. All I want is just that pail of water near enough to reach. I won't make you any trouble. I don't know a soul in Millinocket. If you'll just let me lie here till I get over this, I'll be darned grateful. What I've got doesn't last long.'

'What you got?'

'Pneumonia, I think. I got drenched in a thunderstorm a few days ago and chilled through. Pneumonia acts quickly.'

'Pneumonia! That's bad! You might pop off.'

'If I should, it needn't bother you. All you'll have to do is dig a deep hole in the woods and dump me and my clothes into it. There's nobody to notify.'

'Look here, young feller, you're talkin' crazy again. Strikes me you're mighty sick. You say you ain't got no parents livin' but there must be somebody had ought to know where you are.'

'There isn't.'

'This ain't no time to be lyin'.'

'I'm not lying. There isn't anybody, anywhere, who ought to know where I am, or who is even wondering where I am, or how I am, and that's God's truth. I swear to you on the Bible that's God's truth, Mr. Watts.'

'Well, calm down. No need of getting het up over it.'

'Listen,' Murray went on fumbling in his pocket and bringing out his billfold. 'I'm not asking you to let me stay here for nothing. This is all the money I've got. It isn't much. A little over twenty dollars. But it's all yours. Here, take it. Take it now.' He held the bills out to Seth. 'And will you please give me another drink of water?'

Seth gave him the water. 'I don't want your money. Put it back in your pocketbook. Go on! Do as I say! I'm the boss here. I'll be up in the mornin'. You'll probably feel better after a good sleep. I'm leavin' the pail of water close to your bed.'

Seth blew out the lamp and went out of the cabin. He closed the door, making it fast with a wooden peg on the outside, just in case Joe got another notion to clean that fish.

Murray, left alone, sat up in bed. While he still had the strength, he'd better destroy his license and that American Express check. Also get rid of his wrist-watch. It might be used as a tracer to his identity. The license and the check he'd burn in the stove, the watch bury outside. He got out of bed, groped for matches, but could find none. He'd have to bury all the stuff. He felt his way to the door. It was locked on the outside! He stood leaning against it, trying to think of some place inside the cabin where these articles could be concealed forever. His knees were wobbling. The shivering had started in again. He must act quickly. He began feeling of the log walls. They were packed with dried moss. He found a soft cavity, pulled out the moss, stuffed the license, check, and watch into the cavity, replaced the moss, then crawled back into bed.

Seth was plied by questions the next morning. The club members were buzzing with curiosity about the new guide who had passed out cold soon after his arrival. Bill Mac-Gregor had helped carry him up to the berry-pickers' cabin.

A half-hour later Seth had come into the dining room in search of Sam Brock who was finishing supper late. Several other members were lolling about the oilcloth-covered table. Seth told Sam not to expect the new guide to drop in tonight because he was in no condition to talk. That expression 'in no condition' caused an exchange of glances. Plastered, eh?

Seth didn't say anything to correct the supposition. Seth could shut up like a clam when he wanted to. 'Maybe,' 'Don't know,' 'Search me,' 'No telling,' or just a shrug, were his typical answers to all inquiries. When asked if the new guide would be showing up later in the day he had replied, 'Shouldn't wonder.' But he didn't show up later in the day, or in the evening either. Many opinions were expressed. If it was just a hang-over why was Mrs. Scully going up to that cabin with sheets and a pillow and things covered up on a tray? One of the members' wives had caught her in the act.

About noontime Seth had a telephone call from Silas Hicks. He had reached Millinocket too late last night to meet Seth, but had gotten a lift as far as the road into Fiddle Pond. He was telephoning from a farm house. Seth told him to start walking in and he'd run down and meet him.

This would be good news for Sam Brock. Sam Brock had received a letter in the mail last night that made it necessary for him to be back in Detroit on a certain fixed date. He had just time enough to work in a few days on the Allagash if he could get started tomorrow. Therefore he was mighty anxious for Seth to get a guide somehow.

When Seth dropped Silas Hicks at Old Crow shortly before noon, Sam Brock shouted, 'Good boy, Seth! Trust *you* to deliver the goods! Come here, Nora. Here's our guide. Here's Silas Hicks! You look all right to me, Silas.'

Silas was a big, blond, Swedish-looking Nova Scotian, slow-moving, slow-talking — *right*-talking for his job. No 'sirs' from Silas. Inside of five minutes he was engaged.

Both Sam and Nora were busy all the afternoon packing

their duffle bags for the Allagash; and their suitcases for the trip home. They were not returning to Fiddle Pond. After supper a group of members gathered on the porch of Old Crow for a good-bye drink with Sam. It wasn't long before the conversation swerved to the occupant in the berry-pickers' cabin.

'Seth acted the same tight-mouthed way when he lugged Danny in here,' said Alf Mullins.

Alf Mullins was one of the charter members of the club. Next to Sam Brock he was the most prosperous. He'd been a plumber once, but now he owned a store on the main street of his home city and sold plumbing fixtures. The store had two plate-glass show-windows where he exhibited bathtubs, wash-bowls, toilet seats and other bathroom equipment. Several of the cabins at Fiddle Pond were now equipped with wash-bowls and flush toilets — gifts from Alf Mullins.

'Don't you chaps remember,' Alf went on, 'how Seth hid Danny up there in that same shack for nearly a week, with us all thinking it was a dog or some kind of animal Mrs. Scully was taking food up to all the time?'

'That's right, Alf,' said another voice from behind the glow of a cigar in a dark corner. 'And when he did get around to talking, he told us that fishy story.'

The fishy story Seth had told was that he had run across Danny just by chance wandering along the road, whimpering and frightened, unable to tell his name. So what else could he do but pick him up, the poor creature? Seth had acted very much surprised when it turned out the poor creature was Mrs. Scully's own son! The story was she'd left him to be taken care of by a family down at the dam and he'd run away.

'It's always been my opinion Seth forced Danny on us,' Alf said. 'No telling but what he's lugged another like him in here for us to have to stomach. My wife is more afraid of meeting Danny on the trails than a bear.'

'Oh, tommyrot! Danny's harmless.' It was Nora Brock's voice from the far end of the porch where she sat on the railing, her legs twisted into the bars underneath.

'My wife says there's no telling what an idiot will do. They may go stark, raving crazy at any moment.'

'Boloney!' said Nora. 'Danny is no idiot! He is just feeble-minded.'

'Well, in any case, Danny is no addition to this club, and I think all you fellows will agree.' He excluded Nora. She was the only woman present. 'I get mighty sick of Seth's being so Godalmighty independent.'

'Well, if we don't like it we know what we can do,' remarked Sam Brock. 'Seth made it clear to us from the start this is *his* camp.'

'Which it isn't. Seth doesn't own an inch of the land.'

It was quite true. They all knew it. The land was owned by a large and prosperous paper company to which Seth paid a small yearly rent.

The conversation on the porch of Old Crow had turned to another subject when Seth appeared on the path in front of it, passing by on his way elsewhere.

'Hello, Seth. Hyuh?'

'G'evenin',' said Seth not pausing.

'Hold on! Wait a minute,' called out Sam Brock. 'How's Joe?'

'Gettin' on pretty good,' said Seth and disappeared into the darkness.

Nora withdrew her feet from the railings, swung her legs outward and jumped noiselessly down to the ground. She followed Seth, overtaking him just as he was turning onto the trail that led up to the berry-pickers' cabin.

'Wait a minute.' Seth stopped. 'I want to know what's the matter with that kid you brought in yesterday afternoon, Seth.'

'I don't know.'

'Well then, I'll come along with you and find out.'
'I don't think you'd better.'
'Go on. Get started.'
'I'm afraid he's pretty sick. You might catch somethin'.'
'What are you doing for him?'
'Mrs. Scully's lookin' out for him.'
'Has he got a fever?'
'Uhuh. So she sez.'
'What's his temperature?'
'I don't know. She ain't got one of them thermometers, and don't know how to use it if she had. Anyway, Mrs. Scully says they don't do any good.'

'Well, I know how to use a thermometer. I'll go and get mine and be up at his cabin in a minute.'

18

CHAPTER

Nora read the thermometer by the light of the kerosene lamp on the barrel table. It registered 104 degrees. His pulse was 120, his breathing short and rapid. Nora Brock was neither a doctor nor a trained nurse, but she had a flair for anything medical. Sickness and suffering never repelled her, but aroused her interest and acted as a challenge.

When Seth had told Joe that someone was there with a thermometer Joe had made no reply. He hadn't even opened his eyes, just parted his lips and closed them gently on the familiar crystal shaft, trying not to cough during that interminable three minutes of waiting. He was lying on his left side facing the lamp. The sharp spot of yellow flame hurt if he raised his lids.

'Please, somebody snap off that light,' he murmured when the thermometer was withdrawn.

Nora placed the lamp on the floor so close to the head of the bed Joe couldn't see the flame. She then sat down on the soap-box beside the bed and proceeded to take Joe's pulse. His arm was outstretched, his hand conveniently upturned. She placed her three fingers firmly on his wrist.

He opened his eyes instantly at her touch. The lamp on the floor illumined her face. Were his eyes playing him false? It looked like that Brock girl! His gaze traveled downward and paused on her bare forearm — yes, that same silky texture — then leaped to the open V of her blouse. She was leaning forward a little. He could see the gentle rise of the mounds of her breasts.

'What are you doing here?'

'Taking your pulse, at the moment.'

'But why?'

'Keep still. You've made me lose count.'

When at last she withdrew her fingers he said, 'I'm sorry about that fish.'

'Forget it.'

'I tried to clean it, but Mr. Watts wouldn't let me.'

'Don't talk.' She sat back on the soap-box and folded her arms, listening to his short, labored breathing with a glowering expression.

'What time is it?' Joe asked.

'Nine o'clock.'

'That's what he's always askin',' Mrs. Scully remarked from the foot of the bed. Mrs. Scully and Seth were both looking on. 'What time is it, over and over again. Not knowin' seems to bother him no end.'

'That's easily fixed,' said Nora and unstrapped her wrist watch, which she used only in the woods. Her mother had given it to her one Christmas when she was in her early teens. Her mother had had her first name, 'Leonora,' engraved on the back of it. The strap was adjustable. She let it out, then leaned down, lifted Joe's upturned hand, and attempted to strap it on his wrist. 'No use! It won't go round,' she said. 'Never mind. I'll leave it here. See? Right beside your water.' She propped it up against an empty cup, then reached down into the pocket of her trousers, drew out the flashlight and pushed it underneath his pillow. 'There you are! Next time you want to know what time it is, all you've got to do is to reach under your pillow and look for yourself. Mrs. Scully will wind the watch for you. It's all wound for tonight. It's got an alarm, in case you've medicine to take at a certain time.'

He made no reply, just kept staring at her, but she
doubted if he was seeing anything, much less taking anything in.

'Do you understand what I've been saying, Joe?' she asked
ever so kindly, and put her hand on his burning forehead.

'That feels good,' he murmured and closed his eyes.

Outside on the porch Nora said, 'You're right, Seth, he's a
pretty sick kid. He's got a bad bug of some sort in the region
of his lungs. One of the pneumonias, I think.'

'That's what he said it was — pneumonia. You had ought
to of been a doctor.'

'Well, I'm not! And he needs one. It's my guess he ought
to have some sulfa, and have it quick.'

'Sulphur? That's a new one! I got some in a bag down at
the barn.'

'It's not that kind, Seth. And a doctor has to give it. Look
here, who is this kid, anyway? It's high time you stopped
being so cagey and came out with the facts.'

'The only fact I've got to come out with is, I've got stung.'
And suddenly Seth became confidential, pouring out all the
details of his chance meeting with Joe on the road, and Joe's
claim to having been a guide for years and handy at any
job, and his story about his parents who had been missionaries in China and were now dead.

'And you let him pull that on you? Gosh, I didn't think
you were that gullible. That kid is hiding something, Seth.
We'd better search his clothes.'   •

'I done that already. This mornin' Mrs. Scully got him undressed and into one of Danny's nightshirts. And I took all
his stuff out here on the porch — pocketbook 'n' everythin',
and looked 'em through thorough. There warn't a thing to
point to a thing. I don't like it no more'n you do, but I
don't see the point in tellin' the whole club I got into this
pickle, pickin' up any old bum I ran across on the road.'

'I won't leak, Seth. But he doesn't strike me as a bum.'

'Nor me neither. But I'm stuck with him just the same. Looks like I got to let him lie here and let Nature take its course. But there's no call for you to be hangin' around here any longer. Mrs. Scully is goin' to fix him up for the night pretty soon.'

'All right, I'll go along then. By the way, meet me down at the main camp in twenty minutes. I've got to put in a long-distance call.'

The porch of Old Crow was empty when Nora returned. Her father was inside seated at the table with a siphon and whiskey bottle beside him and a half-filled glass. There were several other empty glasses on the table. Sometimes whiskey made her father mellow, but sometimes cantankerous. There was no time to test his mood before announcing her intention. She told him she had seen Joe and was going to telephone for a doctor. She would tell Seth to charge the doctor's bill to Sam's account. The doctor would probably make several trips. The after-effects of sulfa had to be watched.

Sam's face flushed deep red. He had never heard of such damned foolish nonsense. Did she think he was made of money? Doctors didn't make trips into the wilds for nothing! Years ago she'd bamboozled him into paying that Boston specialist a hundred dollars to examine Danny and it hadn't done Danny a mite of good. And here she was up to the same trick. What kind of a damned fool did she think he was anyway?

Nora had discovered long ago that to repeat her father's strong language, often had a mollifying effect. She replied calmly, 'I think you're one of the kindest, most generous damned fools in the world, Dad.'

'That's no language for a young girl to use.'

'Don't blame a parrot for the language it uses, Sam.' She often called him Sam. That, too, had a mollifying effect.

'Listen, Nora. Be sensible. That guide up there is a total stranger to us.'

'So is a stray dog lying beside the road bleeding to death. But if you came along and saw him there wouldn't you pick him up and stop the bleeding if you could?'

'But Seth has already picked up the dog.'

'Seth doesn't know what to do for him, and *I* do.'

'Well, if you want to spend your life butting into other people's business, because you think you know how to run it better than they do, go ahead. For God's sake, go ahead! But don't ask me to put up the money for it.'

'All right, Dad. I *will* go ahead.' She walked toward the door.

'Where are you going?'

'Over to the main camp. Seth's there waiting for me to put in that call.'

'You're going to do just as you damned please, eh?'

'I'm going to do just as I damned think best. But,' she added, 'I'd be a whole lot happier if you approved, Sam.' Her tone was wheedling.

'No soft-soaping! No soft-soaping! I don't approve! And I won't pay a red cent of the doctor's charges. That's final.'

'All right. I'll tell Seth to send the bill to *me*. Thank Heaven for my nest egg.'

The nest egg was a trust fund Sam had deposited for Nora when she was eighteen years old, yielding an income of about a thousand a year, so she wouldn't be dependent on the allowance her mother gave her, out of the alimony he had been paying her ever since her divorce.

Nora had been four years old when Myrtle decided to make the separation final. Sam was spending most of his time in Detroit then. Myrtle and Nora were living in the little house he'd built for Myrtle the first year they were married. But Myrtle and Nora didn't live in it long after the divorce was granted. The house was in Augusta, Maine, not

far from the farmhouse on a back road where Sam had been
born, and where his old man was still living, all alone with
his hens, a cow, a pig, a horse, two dogs and countless cats
and kittens. Myrtle told Sam she didn't want her daughter
to grow up anywhere near such a disreputable old relative.
He let the hens into the kitchen and looked like a bundle of
dirty rags when he drove to the nearest general store in his
tumble-down buggy. Nora had taken a great fancy to the
old man and was always begging to go out to his shambles
of a farm. Myrtle said she considered it her duty to save her
child from such a back-country background.

She moved first to an apartment in Brookline, Massachusetts, next to a hotel apartment in Bronxville, New York, then
Chicago, then Pasadena, then Washington, then Providence,
then back again to Massachusetts — Cambridge this time —
then New York City. Sam had lost track of the number of
places where his wife and daughter had lived since Nora was
four. Instead of a 'back-country background,' she had no
background at all! God knew he couldn't give her any background. He lived in a hotel in Detroit. It was no place for
a kid, even for the few weeks she spent with him each year.
And the crowd he played around with, especially the women
— he couldn't expose Nora to *them* even once! So he'd
brought her to Fiddle Pond year after year, where the air
was pure and the women, too.'

'I suppose,' said Sam as Nora pulled open the screen door,
'this nonsense of yours means our plans for tomorrow are
off, as far as you're concerned.'

'Not a bit of it. Mrs. Scully is looking out for Joe. My job
is over as soon as I put a doctor in charge. You bet I'm not
going to let our camping-trip be ditched!' She spoke without
a trace of ill-humor. 'You sweet old crosspatch, you!' she
finished and dashed out of the door.

19

CHAPTER

Left alone Sam poured himself another drink and took a swallow or two. No regard for his opinions! No respect! No obedience! Stubborn as a mule! Wouldn't budge an inch. Holler at her, swear at her, it rolled right off. Goldamndest girl! Couldn't even get her mad! Mighty different from her mother! Couldn't say as much as 'darn' to Myrtle but she'd get up on her hind legs. God! Myrtle was a touchy woman. Everything you said or did that wasn't up to her standards got her goat something terrible! He took another swallow or two from his glass. Myrtle had standards for everything — the way you dressed, the way you ate, the way you talked, your work, your fun, even your friends. The Fiddle Pond Camp members were so far below Myrtle's standard of friends that she wanted him to resign from the club and drop them. But heck, those chaps were his friends before he'd ever laid eyes on Myrtle. You can't drop your old friends any more than your old man. Myrtle had wanted him to do that too, believe it or not! His dad wasn't up to Myrtle's standard of dads! The Fiddle Pond Camp members were fine fellows — the salt of the earth — family men most of them, good, honest State-of-Maine stock; and their wives were fine women — damned fine women, even if Myrtle did turn up her nose at them because their grammar wasn't always up to her schoolmarm standards.

Myrtle was a schoolteacher when Sam met her. She was

148

teaching the sixth grade in the public schools in Lowell, Massachusetts. Myrtle's name was Myrtle May Cook. Mr. Cook was the head bookkeeper in a mill where Sam was the building contractor for an addition under construction. Sam was a stranger in Lowell and Mr. Cook asked him to supper one night. The Cooks lived upstairs in a two-family house with an upper porch lined with flower boxes filled with red geraniums and hanging vines. Myrtle was their only child and they treated her as if she were something very rare and special.

Sam was looking around for some nice woman to marry who had more refinement and education than he. He was forty years old and making good money then, and bound to make more. He wanted a wife whom he wouldn't feel ashamed of, however great his success, and someone who would be a good mother with refined tastes for the bunch of children he wanted to have. The first night he had supper at the Cooks, Myrtle May played two showy pieces, which she knew by heart, on a grand piano in the parlor; referred to the Symphony concerts she sometimes attended on Saturday nights in Boston; and later, seated on the porch, told Sam how devoted she was to all her kiddies in the sixth grade, even the naughty ones. After her parents withdrew she let him sit with her in the hammock and hold her hand. It seemed to Sam that Myrtle May was the perfect little woman for him, and he promptly fell in love with her with all the strength and capacity of his strong, wholesome nature.

Myrtle was over thirty then, and was beginning to feel anxious about the future. She didn't intend to be a schoolteacher all her life, and she didn't intend to marry anybody who couldn't provide her with a front door of her own. The two-family house had always been a source of embarrassment to Myrtle. When Sam asked her to marry him she didn't keep him waiting for her answer ten minutes.

Sam was very careful to do nothing to shock Myrtle's parents during the courtship. Mr. Cook was a teetotaler and a deacon in the Congregational Church, and Mrs. Cook taught in the Sunday School. Sam told no smutty stories and refrained from all profanity in their presence, also from all intoxicating beverages when he was in Lowell. It wasn't too great a strain, for his visits to Lowell were short and the courtship brief. He met Myrtle in June and they were married in September.

He was careful also to attempt no love-making that might offend Myrtle's delicate sensibilities. She was a dainty, pink-and-white little thing, and very pretty then.

'Like a piece of Dresden china, *we* think,' her mother said to Sam shortly before the wedding day, 'and should never be roughly handled.'

Sam thought he knew what she meant, and solemnly assured Mrs. Cook she needn't worry.

Sam ought to have known, he supposed, that Fiddle Pond Camp was no setting for a piece of Dresden china. He took her there on their honeymoon. They motored up in Sam's car, spending several nights at different hotels en route.

Sam had talked at length to Myrtle about Fiddle Pond Camp. He was terribly anxious for her to like it and to feel a little the way he did about it. But all she felt was disgust. She had never been to a fishing-camp before, and she hated it all, and complained of it all, too — the damp, dark little cabins, the smelly kerosene lamps, the tin pails for hot water, identical tin pails for slops, the agateware wash-basin, the crockery chamber-pot under the bed (there was no plumbing then) and the big ugly bed itself, with its four fat posts made of stripped logs sawed off at the top like piles.

The bed stood in a corner of Old Crow. It was still there, half hidden by a curtain. Sam turned and regarded the bed dolefully, tears of self-pity in his eyes. Of all the offending objects at Fiddle Pond that innocent old bed was the most maligned. It was the symbol of the climax of Myrtle's out-raged sensibilities. It was in that ugly old monster, she often reminded Sam, that she had lost her girlhood illusions! And when she was a bride of only a week, too!

Sam had not disregarded his promise to Myrtle's mother. He had remembered the Dresden china warning and had treated Myrtle like his little sister until she was settled in Old Crow. How long should he have waited? Why, Myrtle had blushingly told him one night in the hammock that she knew all about the 'marriage act' (that was what she called it). But evidently not as enacted by *him!* It was a terrific surprise to her. Even after they'd left Fiddle Pond and the surprised stage had passed, it was always unwelcome.

Sam was hurt and at a loss to know what the matter was. In the early spring he consulted a Boston doctor whom he had never seen before. The doctor told Sam it was probably just a case of nerves with his wife, sometimes mistaken for per-manent 'frigidity' (Sam had never heard this term before) and advised Sam to be patient till after the baby was born (Nora was then 'on the way') and his wife would probably thaw out all right, but if she didn't, to send her down to him sometime and he'd look her over. Sam followed the doctor's advice, but Myrtle never thawed out. When he suggested that she consult the Boston doctor, let him look her over, she was as indignant as if he had proposed something indecent.

Just Sam's presence became unwelcome to her in time. Sam consoled himself as best he could by working at his job night and day, playing around with his men friends and drinking more than was good for him. His strong breath was revolting to Myrtle, so was the strong language that usually accompanied it, and the course vulgar stories he told. Sam spent very little time beneath the roof he had built for Myrtle. He made bids on contracts that were far removed from Augusta, Maine. Finally he landed a big contract in Detroit. Then another and another. By the time Myrtle

asked for her divorce he was spending most of his time in
Detroit, making money hand-over-fist and not knowing what
to do with it all. Sam gave Myrtle her divorce without any
argument. She certainly had grounds enough for it by that
time. He had never remarried. Once was enough.

For years Myrtle didn't remarry either. Not till Nora had
decided to live her own life and share an apartment in New
York with a couple of girls did Myrtle change her name.
Myrtle was now Mrs. Harry Willow. Sam had heard she had
met Willow on a train crossing the continent. She was traveling all alone, and Willow's only companion was nailed up in
a box in the baggage car. Willow was an undertaker in
Springfield, Ohio. Sam often wondered if Willow had been
able to thaw out Myrtle. Perhaps having had so much to do
with dead bodies had made him lose his taste for live ones,
and he'd married Myrtle just to have someone around to
speak to.

Nora was six years old the first time Sam brought her to
Fiddle Pond. She had taken to it like a duckling to water. She
had found nothing to criticize about the women. She loved
them all and they loved her. Nora had found nothing dis-
gusting about the smelly kerosene lamps, the water pails,
the slop pails, or about himself either, God bless her. God
bless that girl! He raised his glass and drank a silent toast
to Nora.

He'd better be getting into bed, he guessed. He rose un-
steadily and turned toward his curtained corner. Outlines
were dim and shrouded. He sat down in his chair again,
closed his eyes tight, then opened them. His eyes smarted
like hell and he couldn't see anything but shifting darkness
and a streak of red fire. Was he going blind? Damn it, was
there poison in that bottle?

'Nora! Nora!' There was no answer. 'No — ora!' Still
no answer. Where was that girl? Oh, .yes! Over at the

main camp telephoning that damned doctor! Ignoring his advice! Disregarding his wishes! All right, all right! Then he'd disregard *her* wishes, even if it was poisonous liquor. She hated to have him get dead drunk. He poured himself another drink, stronger this time, and drained the glass. 'Tit for tat. Tit for tat, young lady.'

When Nora returned she found Sam slumped down in his chair and breathing heavily. The Aladdin lamp was smoking. The inside of the chimney was coated with soot. A long red tongue of flame was belching forth black clouds. She blew out the flame and placed the lamp with its charred mantle still smoldering on the porch outside, then opened all the windows wide, lit a candle and shook her father gently.

'Wake up, Dad.'

'What's happened? What's happened?' he asked blinking at the candle flame.

'You let the lamp get to smoking. Come on, stand up. It's time to go to bed.'

She guided her father to his bed, pulled back the blankets, then with infinite patience helped him to undress.

'What about that doctor?' he murmured as he sank down onto the pillows.

'I got him. He was delivering a baby but he'll be here early in the morning.'

'Do as you please!' he went on after a moment, his voice thick and blurred. 'If I don't like it I can lump it. Might's well be dead and buried for all I count. Pretend you don't want your poor old dad to drink himself to death, but don't really give a hang. Don't give a tinker's damn, just so you ——'

'Shut up, Dad. I'm not listening.'

By the time Nora had cleaned up the worst of the particles of feathery black soot, Sam had sunk into a deep sleep and was snoring. There were particles of the soot on his

face and bald head. Nora wet the corner of a bath towel and
wiped them off, then got him sufficiently awake to swallow
a little water into which she had mixed a spoonful of bicar-
bonate of soda.

A few minutes later she pulled on her pajamas (once-blue-
now-faded-to-gray affairs) and crawled into her low cot,
placing an alarm clock on a chair close to her pillow. She set
the alarm at five-thirty. The doctor said he thought he
would get there about six. But he arrived an hour earlier.
Seth took him up to the berry-pickers' cabin. The doctor
had already finished his examination and was standing outside the cabin on the porch giving his opinion to Seth when
Nora's alarm clock went off.

'Not a Chinaman's chance, I'm afraid, Seth,' he said, shaking his head. It was good old plain-speaking, plain-dealing
Doctor Folger whom Nora had finally persuaded to undertake this errand of mercy. 'Perfect wild-goose chase, my
traipsing way up here with sulfa at *this* stage of the game!
Or at any stage of the game, it looks to me, as far as that
boy is concerned. He's got pneumonia, all right, as the girl
thought, but I doubt if sulfa will touch it. Sulfa's mighty
choosy. Still, I've given him a big dose of it, and will leave
some tablets just to please that girl he's engaged to. I certainly do hate telling *her* there's mighty little hope for her
young man.'

Seth glanced away from Doctor Folger's honest blue eyes.
It went against his grain to be a party to deceiving a man
like Doctor Folger. But he couldn't let Nora Brock down,
could he? Last night he had been her silent accomplice. The
first doctor she'd called had refused to make the long journey
for an unknown hitch-hiker Seth Watts had picked up on the
road. When Nora got Doctor Folger on the phone, she had
closed one eye and given Seth a long slow wink, as she explained to the doctor her relationship to the patient. Once
Nora Brock made up her mind to do something which she

believed ought to be done she usually did it. If a little harmless deceit was necessary in its accomplishment it didn't
bother her.

When Nora appeared coming up the trail to the cabin
Seth withdrew. Her father and she were spending a night
at a resort hotel en route to the Allagash and she was dressed
in traveling clothes — a yellowish-gray tweed suit — short
snug-fitting jacket, short snug-fitting skirt, long snug-fitting
silk stockings, pumps with Cuban heels, and a perky little
tweed hat that matched her suit. Seth went around to the
back of the cabin and stole down the hill by another route.
He always felt uncomfortable with the women-folks at camp
when they put on their city duds. Moreover he didn't want
to sit in on any more putting-it-over on Doc Folger.

Nora received Doctor Folger's report about Joe as gravely
as he gave it.

'And the worst of it is,' she replied, like Seth, looking
away from the honest blue eyes, 'I can't stand by. My father
is taking me away by automobile right after breakfast. He
disapproves of my engagement to Joe. So I'll have to leave
him in your care, Doctor Folger. Joe is a mystery to everybody here. But not to me. I've known him before. He came
up here hoping to see me. He has no money at present. That
explains why he's in this rundown old cabin, and why I'm taking care of his doctor's bills. Send your bill to me personally,
please. Not to Dad. At this address.' She passed Doctor
Folger a card. 'And please do all you can for him. Oh, if
only I didn't have to go!' She produced her handkerchief
and held it up to her eyes.

Doctor Folger put the card in his pocket. Then in a voice
so kind Nora began to feel pricks in her conscience he said,
'I will do all in my power for the boy, my dear. And remember this, your presence or absence will make no difference in the outcome.'

She asked him several penetrating questions. He replied

simply, gravely, holding out but little hope. But finally forcing a brighter note into his weary voice, 'But miracles sometimes happen,' he reminded her. 'And now, my dear,' he broke off, 'go in and see him.'

Nora hadn't anticipated this. 'Wouldn't it be bad for him?'

'He won't know it. I've given him something to make him sleep.'

'He might wake up.'

'He won't recognize you. He thinks I'm someone he calls Mr. Ben. The fever has clouded his brain. I just thought for your own satisfaction you'd naturally want to say good-bye to your young man.'

'Naturally.' Still she hesitated. Should she tell him the truth?

'Don't you *want* to?' the doctor looked at her sharply, his eyes bright and piercing now, and suspicious too.

'Of course I want to!' And she turned on her heel and went into the cabin. Far better a little more deceit than to let this fine, kind, genuine man (so tired-looking, too, and far older than she had imagined) guess that she had made him come way up here in the middle of the night on a false pretext.

Doctor Folger didn't move away from the spot where he was leaning against the porch railing opposite the open door in full sight of the log bed in the corner. Nora felt he was watching her. She went over to the bed. Joe was lying on his back, both arms above him, in a posture of surrender. His hands, palms upturned, lay on the pillow each side of his head. His eyes were closed. He appeared to be in a deep sleep. Nora leaned down over him, smoothed back a damp lock of hair, placed her lips on his forehead keeping them there long enough, she hoped, to convince Doctor Folger that she was saying an appropriate good-bye. When finally she raised her lips and stood up she was amazed to find Joe's eyes were open and gazing at her.

At the first touch of her lips upon his forehead Joe had opened his eyes. The cabin walls were completely hidden by a yellowish-gray screen a few inches above his face. It wasn't until she raised her head and stood up that he discovered that the screen was the brim of Nora Brock's hat with the sun shining through it. He stared at her with all the concentration he could summon, noting such details as the tiny bunch of feathers (red, yellow, and green) stuck in the side of her hat, and that the hat was made of the same material as her suit — a yellow and gray plaid. Surely if he could see and note such minute details, she was no hallucination.

His open eyes were disturbing to Nora. They had a glazed appearance, however. Probably he wasn't seeing her.

'Good morning,' she said brightly.

'Good morning,' his lips replied.

'Do you know me?'

There was a slight nod.

'Who am I?'

He turned his head toward the watch on the table and a suggestion of a smile stirred his lips. 'Leonora.'

So he'd discovered the engraving on the back of the watch!

'Leonora! Who in the world is *she?* And who's Mr. Ben?'

'Is Mr. Ben here?'

'No, he isn't. But you think the doctor is somebody by the name of Mr. Ben, and now you think I'm somebody by the fancy name of Leonora. You're wuzzy.'

'Aren't you Nora Brock?'

'For the love of Mike! Now I'm somebody else! Nora Brock! What in the name of heaven would *she* be doing here? Honestly! Look here, Joe, listen. You've got a fever and are befuddled. Imagining all sorts of perfectly crazy things. My advice to you is to go back to sleep and wake up clear-headed.'

She was standing close beside the bed, the gray and yellow skirt was easily within his reach. He stretched out one hand and stroked it. Yes, fuzzy tweed and solid underneath.

At his touch she moved quickly beyond the range of his fingers, then leaned forward and gave his shoulder a sharp shake. 'Come, come,' she said brusquely. 'Wake up! You're dreaming!' and turned and went out of the room.

20
CHAPTER

It was an early morning in September two years later. There had been a frost the night before. The patch of cleared ground in front of the cabins was covered with a coat of furry white when Joe came down from his camp to begin his daily round of duties. The pond was covered with white, too. A thick blanket of fog, nicely tucked in around the edges, completely concealed its shining surface. The blanket looked like a dropped cloud, but there were no clouds in the sky. The sun would soon be up and about its business of defrosting and defogging. By the time Joe had filled his pails of hot water from the boiler in the kitchen and started forth with a couple of the pails for the two cabins farthest away, the white blanket was tinged pink on top and beginning to stir and form into billows. By the time he set out with his last couple of pails it had become a diaphanous mass of silvery mist and rose-colored clouds fast rising.

Throughout the process of pail-carrying Joe kept close track of the time. At six o'clock he must ring the rising bell. The bell was a brass schoolbell with a sharp, brilliant tone. The bell was hung in the top of a high hemlock behind the row of cabins. It had a long wire attached to it with a pull handle located near the kitchen door. It was like lighting the fuse of a skyrocket, Joe thought, whenever he pulled the wire and a sunburst of brilliant notes, like stars with peaked points, broke against the silence of the woods.

Joe carried a pail of hot water this morning to all the occupied cabins, even those with plumbing, for the pipes were laid on top of the ground and the water had gotten caught somewhere. He left his pails outside the doors of all the cabins but one. When he came to the cabin called 'Jackpot,' he opened the door, carried the pail inside, knelt down before the Franklin stove and proceeded to build a fire. 'Jackpot' was occupied by the Mullins at present, for whom he was acting as guide this week. Joe had become very popular among the Fiddle Pond members. He was so much in demand as a guide that Seth had had to shift a lot of the general work onto Ed and Silas Hicks.

After Joe had started the fire he placed the pail of water close in front of it, then proceeded to close the sliding sashes of the windows. He was about to leave the cabin when Mr. Mullins called out from behind the curtain which concealed the sleeping quarters.

'Good morning, Joe!'

'G'mornin'.'

'How's the weather?'

'Nice.'

'Where had we better go today?'

'I was thinkin' Little Hawk Pond, maybe.'

'Suits me. We won't start too early — around eleven or so. And say, round up a steak for us. We've asked the Hinckles to come along.' The Hinckles were new members in the club. 'So bring enough grub for four.'

'All right. Anything more?'

'No. Guess not. Yes, there is, too! Wait a minute.' There was a creaking of bed-springs, and a moment later Mr. Mullins, tousle-haired and frowsy, appeared from behind the curtain in wrinkled pajamas. He held a pair of rubber hip-boots in his hand. The feet were caked with dry mud.

'Clean these waders some time today.' Joe took them. 'And remember, if anything happens Mr. Brock doesn't want you tomorrow you're hired by me. I wouldn't be surprised if he'd be too tired to start right out the first day fishing. He isn't so well lately.'

'For goodness' sake, Alf, let Joe go.' A woman's voice called from behind the curtains. 'I want my coffee.'

'All right, Joe. Go along.'

Five minutes later when Joe returned bearing a tray of clinking white crockery, Mr. Mullins was in the process of shaving by the front window. The curtains that hid the sleeping-quarters had been drawn back exposing the double log bed to full view. Beneath a faded cotton quilt appeared the hump of Mrs. Mullins' generous-sized body. She was lying on the inside of the bed. She struggled to a sitting position when Joe appeared. Her short iron gray hair stuck out from her head straight and stiff. She stretched out her arms to take the tray. They were bare to the shoulder. The skin was dough-colored and crepy.

'Thanks, Joe. Pass me that sweater, I'm nearly frozen to death.'

It no more occurred to Mrs. Mullins to feel apologetic to Joe for her appearance than as if he had been a steward on a ship, or an orderly in a hospital. Joe had soon discovered that his job as guide was supposed to divest him of all feelings of embarrassment, surprise, interest, curiosity, repugnance or its opposite, whatever intimate sight or scene he witnessed. He kept his eyes turned away from Mrs. Mullins as he passed her the tray, and afterwards the sweater, sparing her all but that first fleeting glance.

As he walked away from the cabin his thoughts turned to his mother and the vision of her drinking coffee in bed — her hair lovely, her shoulders covered with a shell-pink negligee, the bedclothes concealed beneath a silk and lace blanket-cover. His mother always looked attractive in bed. Even when they went camping that fall to Nova Scotia she observed all the niceties. Funny, but there was some-

thing about Mrs. Mullins' disregard of her appearance before
him that he liked — that made him feel comfortable and at
ease. It made no demands on him. Perhaps the reason why
his existence here at Fiddle Pond was so congenial was because it made no demands beyond his ability to meet. Ambitions no longer nagged him. Much unhappiness is caused
by one's ambition being greater than one's ability. Here at
Fiddle Pond the pain of competition was practically elimi-
nated. He was an outstanding success as a guide. The members all preferred him to either Ed or Silas. Seth said he was
the best worker he'd run across in years, not a lazy bone in
his body, and mighty smart about catching on to jobs new
to him.

There had been plenty of jobs which were new to him! It
had taken some time to persuade Nellie the cow to let down
her milk when she felt his untrained hands yanking at her.
He was awkward with a saw at first. Nothing to boast about
with an axe and he'd never set a beaver, mink, or otter trap
before in his life. Joe had hated the trapping at first. Killing
wild life was not to his taste. But he had to get over being
thin-skinned in that respect if he wanted to remain with
Seth Watts the year round.

When finally he had emerged from the dark cabin two
years ago, weak-kneed, weak-lunged, and weak-blooded, he
was in no condition to take to the road again. Doctor Folger's
sulfa drug had squashed the pneumonia-bug in short order
but it would have nothing to do with the boggy mess in his
lungs. For a long series of days and nights, merging un-
counted one into another, he had lain in the big log bed in
the dark cabin, hopefully awaiting an end that didn't come.
Seth had kept his water-pail filled and his slop-pail emptied.
Mrs. Scully had brought him food and a clean nightshirt occasionally. The cabin was musty and often damp. He ought
not to have survived, according to all the books.

The first day he crawled out of the cabin he lay stretched out on a bed of moss too weak to stand. He was like a moth that has just crawled out of its cocoon — sluggish, inert, unable to use its legs or to spread its sticky wings. He couldn't open his eyes at first, the light was so blinding. But, oh, the warmth of the sun! The freshness of the air! The good clean smell of the earth! He could hear wind blowing through trees, waves lapping, the chirp of a bird.

After a while he had crawled into the shade, propped himself up against a soft, rotting stump, and turning his head slowly first this way and then that, gazed about him with wonder and excitement. It was the first time he had seen the cabin from the outside. Its roof had a long overhang and a gentle pitch extending out over the porch across the front like a wide-brimmed sunbonnet. It was located on a shelf twenty feet above the lake. It backed up against a stone wall with rock ferns growing in its cracks. It looked out over the lake through the top branches of trees — maple, birch, and beach — with a few rugged firs piercing their black spearheads through the soft leaves. It seemed to him he had never gazed on such beauty before.

Several hours later when Seth came to fill his water pail he was still lying against the stump.

'Guess I'm going to get well,' he remarked.

'Looks so.'

'I've been lying here thinking. I want to work for you for nothing till I've paid back every cent I owe you, Mr. Watts, and that doctor too. If that winter job is still open and you can see your way to letting me stay on here in this cabin, I'll be everlastingly grateful.'

Seth had said he'd think it over.

Joe usually ate his breakfast at the long trestle table in the kitchen, between the first breakfast-bell at quarter of seven, and the last at seven. But this morning he had eaten earlier because he had so much to do before starting off with the Mullinses.

It was Joe's responsibility to keep the woodpile in the corner of each cabin well-stocked. Whenever there was a cold snap the woodpiles shrank like snow-banks in warm weather. He must pile them high today. Joe was in the open doorway of the woodshed near the main camp filling his wheelbarrow with short chunky logs of shaggy birch and split hardwood when the club-members began passing by on their way to breakfast.

They all gave him a cheery greeting. 'Good morning, Joe.' 'Hi-yah, Joe?' 'Cold night, Joe.' 'We'll be needing those logs today, Joe.' 'Sun feels pretty good, Joe.'

The note of friendliness was unmistakable. Never before — at home, at school, at college, nor at Tamarack either, had he drawn forth such genuine and general good-fellowship. It was as if he had died, when he was so sick, and had been born again with a more likable personality, more likable to himself as well as to others. Far pleasanter to live with. If only his former existence as Murray Vale could be erased as completely as in the transmigration of a soul at death then he would be happy to remain as Joe the guide indefinitely, he believed, living here in the woods close to Nature, free, detached, a member of no family, no community, unshackled by pride, ambition and rivalry, performing homely tasks for plain, unpretentious people. Liked and liking. Unenvied and unenvying.

Joe's response to the members' greetings were brief, sometimes only a smile and nod. He applied as much conscious effort to the use of few words, as to the colloquialisms and inflection he tried so hard to imitate. The less he conversed the less opportunity for his natural habits of speech to break out when he was off guard. Moreover, brevity is characteristic of the typical Maine guide. To speak briefly and in a vernacular consistent with Joe's job helped to make Joe more of a reality to himself. It was said of Sumner Bryant, the famous impersonator of a native Vermont farmer, that the minute he began to speak like old Jason Judkins, he got right inside his skin, and thought Jud's thoughts and felt Jud's feelings.

When speech was necessary Joe was particular not to exaggerate the vernacular. He had taken Seth Watts as his model. Seth didn't drop all his g's, nor always substitute 'ain't' for 'isn't.' What rubber-stamped Seth was his tone and inflection, and slow rate of speed. Joe had also copied Seth's clothes and the way he wore them. He tied his tie, when he wore one, loosely like Seth's, adopted suspenders and raised his pants' line. His haircut resembled Seth's, too, ragged at the back, long at the temples, and he had abandoned daily shaving. He had even managed to acquire Seth's slouch, and could reproduce his table manners without a slip.

By the time Joe had replenished the woodpiles, breakfast was over and Elta appeared on the path in front of the cabins with her slop-pail, broom and mop and can of kerosene, to begin her daily chores. Seth had told Joe that he was to help Elta first thing after breakfast today to get Old Crow ready for the Brocks. The furniture must be arranged the way they liked it and their trunks hauled out of storage. Many of the members left their camp clothes and fishing gear at Fiddle Pond the year round. Seth said Nora Brock had called up late last night from Greenville. No telling what time they'd reach camp.

This was the first visit the Brocks had made at Fiddle Pond since Joe's illness. Last year they had gone West to try their luck fishing in the Canadian Rockies. Tomorrow would be the first time Joe had seen Nora Brock since those few brief glimpses he had had of her two years ago when his brain was so befuddled by fever, and his eyes so untrust-

worthy that he wasn't yet sure what had been dream and
what reality, what delusion and what fact.

It was no delusion that she had taken his temperature and
pulse. Mrs. Scully had been witness to that. And she had
given him her watch and flashlight. He had them still as
proof. He had asked Seth for the Brock's address so he
might return them but Nora had left word, Seth said, that
they were both articles she always left at camp with her
fishing clothes.

It was no hallucination either that she had telephoned
Doctor Folger. Doctor Folger had told him that she was
responsible for saving his life. Also that she had instructed
him to send her a bill for whatever medical expenses were
incurred. Thank Heaven that had not been necessary. The
one redeeming feature about his recovery was that he would
be able to pay his own doctor's bills, and somehow make it
up to Seth Watts for all the trouble he had caused him.
Doctor Folger had made no reference to Nora Brock's pretended engagement which Seth had finally confessed was
all bunk. Joe was in complete ignorance of this particular
detail.

Joe's recovery had been rapid once he was on his feet
again. He grew strong by leaps and bounds. Tone returned
to his muscles, edge to his appetite, and rest to his sleep.
The fog that had lain so long on his sea-of-consciousness
lifted. Memories returned clearcut and vivid.

But there was one memory that baffled him — Nora Brock
standing in a shaft of sunlight beside his bed and kissing him
long and tenderly on his forehead. That last visit — or vision
(whichever it was), was vividly impressed upon his consciousness, but by that time his fever had mounted high. He
had mistaken Doctor Folger for Mr. Ben. His final conclusion was that Nora standing in the shaft of sunlight had also
been an hallucination. Her costume with all its well-remembered details was probably something dug up out of his

subconscious — perhaps a colored picture in a nursery book, or fashion magazine, imprinted upon his retina when he was a child.

After Joe had finished helping Elta he hauled a load of ice, fed the hens, collected the eggs, and changed an inner tube on the tin lizzie. It was after ten o'clock when he climbed the sharp ascent to his camp to make his bed and tidy up.

The outside of the cabin looked much the same, but inside it had undergone an amazing transformation. It was no longer dark and musty. There was a long, oblong-shaped window in place of the two small openings over the iron sink. The sink had disappeared, also the kitchen stove and log bed. In one corner there was a built-in bunk which Joe had found in an abandoned lumber-camp near-by. In another corner a cupboard, also from the lumber-camp. There was a Franklin stove opposite the big window. There were shelves hewn into the face of the logs beside the stove. There were books on the shelves. On the floor were pelts of a deer and moose. Another pelt served as the seat and back of a long, low-slung chair of the folding beach-chair variety. The chair was drawn up close to a shiny white-shaded Aladdin lamp on a table covered with red oilcloth.

In front of the big window and running its entire length was a bench with a tier of shallow drawers underneath it at one end. On top of the bench, close to the window, there was a row of preserve jars, and screened boxes filled with animal and vegetable life, at various stages of development. Once inside his cabin Joe had the same blissful feeling of detachment that stole over him when he used to escape to his first tree-house in the Sophora at home. Which explained the name that finally appeared in birchbark letters over the door of his cabin.

Everybody, including Mrs. Scully, said he must name his

cabin. Mrs. Scully's cabin was named 'Cozy Nook,' Seth's 'Single Bliss,' Ed's 'Bella,' after his dead wife. Silas, who had now become a fixture at Fiddle Pond during the busy season, had chosen the name of his girl in Nova Scotia for his cabin, 'Nettie.' Joe considered 'Ivory Tower' for a while, but the name that finally appeared in birch bark letters over his door was 'Sophora.'

The first time Silas saw it he said to Joe as they both stood gazing up at it, 'Never heard that name before. How do you say it?'

Joe repeated each syllable slowly, softly, 'So-fo-ra.'

'A girl, I suppose?' Silas queried with a sly smile at Joe.

'Yes, a girl, Silas,' Joe replied, his eyes still on the name. 'A girl with birds' nests in her hair.'

'Oh, yeah!' drawled Silas, and looked at Joe sharply. He must be off his nut.

'A girl,' Joe went on, ' "Upon whose bosom snow has lain." ' He paused a moment, then added, ' "Who intimately lives with rain." '

Oh, she was dead, suddenly it dawned on Silas. Being snowed on and rained on in some cemetery. That's what he meant, of course. 'Gee, that's too bad, Joe,' Silas murmured and quickly changed the subject.

21

CHAPTER

At eleven o'clock Joe appeared in front of the Mullins's porch with a bulging pack strapped on his shoulders. The pack contained provisions for one of his famous meals in the woods, and the utensils — frying pan, tin cups and plates, coffee-pot, spoons, knives and forks; also a number of articles of the Mullins's — a couple of sweaters, a camera, a tin fly-box, a box of candy, Mrs. Mullins's knitting bag, and two thermos bottles. When Joe arrived at the cabin Mr. Mullins gave him two rods in canvas cases, and at the last minute, decided to take along an extra sweater. Joe tied it around his waist.

The route to Little Hawk Pond followed the main road for a while, then picked up a trail through the woods to a cove where there were a couple of canoes tied up. The party walked single file — Mr. Mullins leading, Joe bringing up the rear. It was a steady climb at first. They stopped to rest and admire the view when they reached the bare rock from which Joe had first seen Fiddle Pond. As they stood there, the sound of an approaching automobile climbing the long hill reached their ears.

'I'll bet that's Sam Brock!' exclaimed Mr. Mullins. 'Let's wait and see.' Two minutes later a big gray touring car emerged from the dark fir-lined tunnel. 'It is! Jiminy Crickets! It's Sam!'

Mr. Mullins ran toward the car waving his arms, Mrs.

Mullins following. The car came to a standstill. Nora Brock
was at the wheel, and beside her sat her father, red-faced
and grinning. There was a vociferous exchange of greetings
between the two men. Nora sprang out from behind the
wheel as Mrs. Mullins approached panting and stumbling.
Nora threw both arms about Mrs. Mullins, kissed her and
exclaimed, 'Gosh, it's marvelous to be here!'

The Hinckles remained with Joe, withdrawn to one side
of the road. Mr. Mullins turned finally and called out to
them. 'Come here, you Hinckles, and meet the high muck-
a-muck of this club — Mr. Samuel Brock of Detroit, Michi-
gan, and his daughter, Miss Nora Brock, of New York City.
James W. Hinckle, Junior, our new member, and his better
half. From Manchester, New Hampshire.'

Nora came forward to shake hands with Mrs. Hinckle.
Until now she had been hidden from Joe by the car. He could
hardly believe his eyes as she approached. She was wearing
a suit of gray and yellow plaid! Her hat was made of the
same material. When finally she turned, there appeared on
the left side of her hat a little bunch of feathers — green,
yellow, and red! He stepped still farther back into the
bushes, but she spied him.

'Hello, there! Come here. Why, it's Joe!'

He tried to square his shoulders as he approached her,
feeling like a humpback under his pack. She shot out her
arm to him. He dropped the rods and they shook hands.

'Come and see Dad. Dad, here's Joe. All ready to start
with us tomorrow, Joe?'

He nodded.

'You're looking swell. Some difference from the last time
I saw you.'

All day long the last time she saw him and the last time
he saw her he reviewed over and over. It hadn't been a
dream! It was Nora Brock herself who had imprinted that

costume on his retina and that long kiss on his forehead. It had been the brim of the same gray and yellow tweed hat she was wearing today that had screened the cabin from view as she leaned down over him; her lips that had aroused him from a state of coma to lucid awareness; her firm, solid flesh that he had felt beneath his investigating fingertips when he reached out and touched her skirt. No delusion! No fancy!

Throughout the process of preparing lunch — making the fire, boiling the coffee, turning the flapjacks, cleaning up, packing up, and afterwards tramping back to camp, his thoughts were in a state of turmoil. He reviewed each time she had touched him. He remembered them all. The first time was when she took his pulse; the second when she placed her hand on his forehead; the third when she kissed his forehead; the fourth when she shook his shoulder. Today was the first time they'd shaken hands. What a strong grip she had! Something electric about it. Something electric about *her*, so that every time she touched him a current passed through him which instantly woke him out of sleep, or snapped him out of torpor. Good heavens, he wasn't in love with her, was he? Of course not! Ridiculous! Girl he hadn't seen for two years, and then for only three brief glimpses. But there was something about her — he'd better be careful. Nothing could be more unfortunate than to get tangled up with a girl at this stage of the game. One of the first clues a detective follows in searching for a man in hiding is a woman. That was proverbial. *'Cherchez la femme.'* He must watch his step.

By four o'clock Mrs. Mullins and Mrs. Hinckle announced they had had enough and asked Joe to take them back to camp, leaving the men to follow later. Once when they stopped to rest their conversation drifted to Nora Brock. Joe overheard it.

'How does she know you so well — kissing you like that?' asked Mrs. Hinckle.

'Oh, I used to sort of mother her when Sam brought her
here. I've known Nora ever since she was a little tot. This
place used to be full of children in the summer. Like a big
family. Now the young people are grown up and scattered.
Nora is just my Gertrude's age. Trudie and Nora used to
be great chums and they still keep up.'

'What is she doing in New York? I thought you said her
mother lived in Ohio some place.'

'Oh, Nora and her mother parted company long ago.
Nora got a job in New York in some law office. A stenog-
rapher. Smart as a whip, they say. She doesn't *have* to
work. Sam can support her all right, but she wants to pull
her own weight, she says. She lives in one of those dingy
old apartments down where Fifth Avenue starts in. I've
been there. She asked Trudie and me down to supper with
her one night when we went to New York once on a spree.
Nora's awfully loyal to Trudie.'

'Does she live all alone in the apartment?'

'Oh, mercy, no! There are three of them. All working.
One's an actress when she has a job, and one does something
or other in a department store. Trudie and I didn't like them
very much. We thought they were kind of fast. The things
they said right out! And slathers of lipstick and layers of
stuff on their nails, and smoking cigarettes all the time.
Funny, Nora doesn't seem to get that way. She just seems
to stay herself, no matter what. I never knew a girl who
has had a worse bringing-up, yet it doesn't seem to have hurt
her a mite. Of course she's slangy and kind of rough, in a
way — just the opposite from my Gertrude. But she's *had*
to be sort of hard shellac, I guess. Divorced parents and all
that, and no real home ever to feel safe in. Dragged all over
the country. Her mother was always putting her into one
school and then another. Nora was crazy to go to college
with Trudie. We sent Trudie to Bates, but oh, no — her
mother wouldn't think of such a thing. A common ordinary

college in the State of Maine was not select enough for *her*
daughter. She had her eye on one of those fashionable board-
ing-schools where they teach horseback riding and have to
wear uniforms and speak French at meals. She got her into
one of them finally. Nora stayed just two weeks.'

'Did she break the rules?'

'No. Just ran away, and told her mother she'd run away
again if she sent her back, so her mother had to put her in
the nearest public high school. Nora hasn't had any sort of
education.'

'Just another victim of divorce,' sighed Mrs. Hinckle.

'Well, I don't know. Nora has never seemed to me to be
a *victim*. There's a kind of fighting spirit in her that doesn't
get beaten. Perhaps not having things easy has developed it.
Having to get out and fend for herself has sort of toughened
her. Now, Trudie — well, sometimes — I wish Trudie would
be a little more independent.'

Joe left Mrs. Mullins and Mrs. Hinckle at their cabin
doors, then went over to the kitchen to clean up his kit.
When he climbed up to his cabin shortly after sundown,
Danny came running out to meet him. Whenever Joe was
off on a day's trip, it was a habit of Danny's to go up to his
cabin in the afternoon and wait for him. Danny's devotion
to Joe was like a dog's — a one-man dog whose master is
also his god. All other human beings, his mother included,
were as nothing to Danny when Joe was in the vicinity.
Joe was the first human being who had ever attempted to
teach him anything, or to think him capable of understand-
ing a command. Joe had taught him to fetch, to carry, to
come, to go, to follow and stay. He had also taught him to
perform simple tasks — shell peas, scour pots, turn the handle
of the ice-cream freezer, wipe dishes, knead bread, scale fish.

Danny's favorite occupation was knitting worsted reins
on a spool which Joe had fixed for him with staples. Danny

loved the bright-colored worsteds, and pulling the rope bit by bit out of the bottom of the spool, but the chief source of his delight, Joe maintained, was the thrill he got in making something himself. Later there was the added thrill of making something for Joe! After Danny had filled a bushel-basket full of reins, Mrs. Scully conceived the idea of braiding them, and one day Danny presented Joe with an oval-shaped afghan for his bed. Pure wool, thick, warm, and lightweight. Danny was now working on his third afghan for Joe.

Danny was no longer shaggy-faced and unkempt. Joe kept his hair cut. Mrs. Scully kept his face shaved. He had objected to having his face as much as washed till Joe intervened. But now he would bring his mother the soap and safety razor and make grunting noises that meant 'please.' He was as proud of his appearance after a haircut and shave as an Airedale after a plucking.

When Danny saw Joe coming he loped toward him. He was an ungainly figure, long-armed, short-legged, and slightly humpbacked. Guttural sounds gurgled out of his mouth as he approached. He was trying to tell Joe something. He waved his arms in the direction of the cabin. He seemed excited.

'Good boy! Good Danny!' said Joe in a soothing tone. 'Calm down, old fellow. Nice Danny.' He walked across the moss lawn in front of the cabin, Danny at his heels. As he drew nearer he saw a figure dressed in khaki approaching. It was Nora Brock.

'Hi, Joe! Dad wants you to set up his rod sometime tonight and look at his reel. He thinks it isn't working right. Here they are.' Joe took them. 'What a nifty place you've got here! I was going to take a peek inside, but Danny objected. He's the best watchdog I ever saw.'

At the sound of his name Danny began making more inarticulate sounds.

'Be still, Danny,' Joe said. 'She can come in. Down!' He pointed to the low step of the porch. Danny sat down on it. Joe took off his canvas coat and laid it across Danny's knees. 'Stay there!' Then, turning to Nora, 'Come in,' he said and pushed open the screen door.

She stepped over the high threshold.

'Why, how perfectly lovely!' She exclaimed in her low, husky voice as she gazed about her, taking in the details — the Franklin stove (before which Joe leaned lighting a fire), the built-in bunk covered with a red and black horse blanket tucked in as neatly as a soldier's cot on inspection day, the pelts on the floor, the curious chairs, the big oblong window through which was shining the afterglow of the setting sun casting a deep amber tinge on everything in the cabin. The peeled log walls, that had been weathering for years in a continuous gloaming until Joe cut the big window, were the color of an old pigskin wallet — a warm, golden brown in the combined light of the setting sun, flaming logs, and the lamp which Joe lit.

'What perfectly enormous logs!' Nora exclaimed.

'Virgin timber, Mr. Watts says.' Joe's cabin had been built by an old cruiser years before Fiddle Pond Camp was thought of.

'I never noticed them before, it was so dark in here. What's become of the kitchen stove and the iron sink?'

'They're in the back room.'

'And where's the big log bed where I left you so sick?' (Where you kissed me, too, Joe thought.)

'Mr. Watts has got the bed stowed away some place. Miss Brock —' He broke off. 'Miss Brock —' he began again. 'I want to thank you for all you did that time I was laid up.'

'All I did was to put in a long-distance call.'

'If you hadn't put it in I wouldn't of pulled through, the doctor said. I don't know why you took so much trouble for me — a stranger, but I —'

'Oh, for goodness sake! I'd have done the same thing if
you'd been a sick dog or cat. Forget it. Wherever did you
get such a gorgeous big window?'

'Oh, it's just four old winder-frames off an old farmhouse
made into one.'

'How awfully clever! It's terribly attractive. The whole
place is attractive, Joe!' Her eyes darted from one side of
the cabin to the other, and up and down too, like an investigating searchlight pausing here and there while she made
comments. 'I love your bed tucked away there in the corner.
So low and cozy-looking, like a built-in bunk on a boat. And
your rugs — simply perfect! Deer or moose, which are they?
All the furniture looks as if it was native — grew here. What
kind of a chair do you call this?' She crossed over to a wooden
armchair. Its straight back was made of round split rails.
Its arms were smooth and polished, tapering to delicate
spool ends.

'That's made out of peaveys.'

'Peaveys?'

'Those poles with hooks lumberjacks use to handle logs.'

'Oh, I know! Who made it?'

'Well — I did.' Joe had to acknowledge. 'It's just a copy.
I saw one in a lumber-camp.'

'Let me try it.' She crossed over to the chair and sat
down, stretching out her hands along the arms and stroking
them. 'So soft! And polished by the palms of men's hands!
Just think!' She hitched forward, raised her heels to the
bottom rung, leaned back and gazed up. One of the burning logs broke. Flames leaped high, lighting the space
above. The mellowed cedar ceiling slanted to a peak. Huge
rafters supported it. Dim shapes played upon it like cloud
shadows on a hillside.

'Nice!' she murmured. Then abruptly, 'How do you keep
warm here all winter with all that space up there, and only
a Franklin stove?'

'That old kitchen stove's good's a furnace. The heat comes just pourin' in over that low partition.'

She closed her eyes and let both arms hang down limp. 'It must be heavenly here in the winter!'

Joe looked at her in silence as she sat there in her dungarees, her heels on the rung, her knees spread man-fashion — her bare throat, parted lips, tapering nostrils fully exposed to his gaze. He might have been some harmless species of dumb animal, gazing at her, as far as she was concerned. She appeared to be unaware of his presence. How different from Daphne! Daphne's constant tricks and devices to lure used to make him feel like some sort of sissy when he failed to respond. This girl with no tricks and no devices aroused feelings that were anything but sissy. He was filled with a crazy desire to go over to her sitting there in his peavey chair, completely unaware of him as a man, and *make* her aware.

Presently she stood up and walked over to the bench in front of the big window. 'What's all this mean?' she asked, looking at the row of preserve jars and other containers.

'Nothin' — just some old stuff I must throw out.'

'For the love of Mike!' she ejaculated suddenly. 'Look at this!' Her eyes had fallen upon an open drawer at one end of the bench, pulled out almost to its full capacity. 'How perfectly marvelous!' The drawer was lined with long neat rows of shallow boxes, each containing a winged insect mounted on cardboard, an inscription in tiny letters beneath. 'It's like a tray in a jeweler's showcase! Wherever did you get them?'

'I collected 'em. It's a hobby I had when I was a kid. Like collectin' stamps.'

'You mean you send for them? They come by mail?'

'Not these. These are all native. I caught some of 'em and raised others.'

'They're marvelous! You're some kind of genius is my guess.'

'No, I'm not — I ain't,' he corrected. 'I have to have somethin' to do up here. The evenin's are kinda long in the winter. That's when I do a lot of my mountin' and labellin'.'

Luckily, thought Joe, the open drawer hid the other drawers underneath. Nora turned away and wandered over to the rows of books on the opposite wall. Most of them were small and in similar bindings — Modern Library volumes chiefly.

'Where did these all come from?'

'From a bookshop in Bangor.'

'Let's see what your literary taste is.'

'They're not my taste. I have to take what's on the list.'

'Gosh! Listen!' and she began reading off the authors in the order they chanced to stand. 'Henry James, Henry Adams, Marcel Proust, Virginia Woolf, Wilde, Tolstoy, Schopenhauer — Holy Moses! Most of these are just names to *me*.'

'To me, too, two years ago.' Joe assured her, 'I was just tryin' to get a little learnin'. Some of 'em I don't fancy much.'

'Well, I'll know where to come if I get hard up for something to read. Here's one I'll take right now. I've never read a word of this chap Thoreau, except in collections, and once I had a Thoreau calendar somebody gave me. Mind if I borrow this?' She held up Joe's copy of *Walden*.

'No, but it's kinda shabby, I'm afraid. It got rained on once, and it's all pencil-marked.'

'Oh, I don't mind.' She tucked it under her arm. 'Now, about our plans,' she broke off. 'Dad had a heart attack last spring. We've got to see to it that he doesn't overdo. We'll take only short day trips, usually. But I'm dying to spend a night in the old cabin at Spot Pond. Tomorrow I thought we'd try Big Hawk. By the way, Mrs. Scully says you have been taking breakfast over to Mrs. Mullins. I'll have breakfast with Dad in the dining room, but I would adore a cup of hot coffee before I get up. 'Round half-past six. Black and two lumps.'

'I'll bring it over.'

She pulled open the door. 'Oh, gosh, I forgot all about
Danny. There he is sitting out there with your coat across
his knees. I've heard about the effect of that coat. I've been
talking with Mrs. Scully this afternoon and gotten all the
dope. She says when she and Danny went out from camp
last fall he felt so badly that for days he wouldn't eat and
was terribly hard to manage. Then you sent him your coat
to wear and he was all right. She says he simply worships
you. I can see why. I think you've done a simply swell job
for Danny, Joe. It isn't often anybody bothers to show kindness to anybody like that.'

'It really wasn't kindness so much as interest in his reac-
tions.' He stopped abruptly. This was not the language of
Joe the guide. 'I mean it was real inter*est*in' to me, Miss
Brock.'

'No need of talking that farmerish way to *me*, Joe. I guess
you've forgotten that we had a conversation before you tried
to go native.'

'When?'

'That first day you told me about the Allagash River trip.
I told Dad that night I didn't know whether your accent was
Harvard or English or Boston or what.'

'I must've been putting on airs.'

'Nonsense, Joe, I'm no fool. By the way, I saw the name
of your cabin when I came up here. I hear you told Silas it
was named after a girl — a girl with robins' nests in her hair.'

'Yes, I did say some such fool thing to Silas — just for a
joke.'

'Of course I know that poem of Joyce Kilmer's, even
though I haven't been to college nor read all those highbrow
books of yours over there. I've heard of a Sophora, too, but
I never saw one that I know of. Tropical, I have an idea.
Why name a cabin way up here in northern Maine for a tree
like that?'

'I thought it had such a pretty-sounding name for one thing. *Sophora Japonica* is the whole of it.'

'Japonica!' she ejaculated. 'Japanese, is it? I begin to see the light. You picked a name that would go with that crazy yarn you told Seth about being born over there in Japan or China — whichever it was. Method in your madness! I see! I see!'

'No, you don't! I named it Sophora simply because when I was a kid —— ' He paused. No harm telling her about his tree-house, was there? But he must proceed cautiously. 'There was a Sophora tree near where I lived when I was a kid, and — you're right, it was a fool name to pick for my cabin, but when I was a kid —— '

'Oh, never mind, Joe. Don't try to explain. It's none of my business. I must hustle. Dad will be wondering where I've disappeared to. Thanks for the book.' She turned again toward the door.

'Just a minute, please. The watch you lent me and the flashlight. I'll get them for you.'

'Oh, there's no fire. They can wait till tomorrow.'

Nora had spied the watch. Mrs. Scully had told her where to look for it. It was hanging on a peg at the head of Joe's bunk. Mrs. Scully had said that he laid great store by the watch. Never let it get run down. Once it had broken and he had had her send it to some jeweller he knew about in Boston, and had given her the money to pay for the repairs when it was returned collect. The repairs had cost the whole of fifteen dollars!

'I was going to mail you the watch and flashlight,' said Joe, 'but Mr. Watts said no, you'd rather they were left here.'

'That was right. Well, see you in the morning.' She pulled open the screen door.

Danny was still seated on the low step — a black blotch now on the night-shrouded porch. Joe called out to him to come into the cabin. He instantly obeyed. Then to Nora he said, 'I'll see you down the hill. It's dark.'

'I'm not afraid of the dark.' She stepped down off the porch. 'Besides, it isn't so very dark. Is there a moon?' She walked out onto the open space in front of the cabin, searching the sky for the source of the peculiar blue-green glow in the air which grew brighter even as she crossed the clearing.

Joe followed behind her at a respectful distance, waiting for her in the shadow of a tree trunk when she stopped on a bared promontory behind the screening branches on the edge of the cliff over the lake.

'Joe, come here,' she called out sharply. 'Look! Look!' she exclaimed when he stood beside her. 'Northern Lights!'

For a full minute they stood side by side facing the north, gazing silently at the streaks of white light rising and falling, swelling and shrinking, flushing pink and fading again. Suddenly the long, lonely call of a loon broke the silence.

'God, I love this place!' Nora murmured.

22

CHAPTER

Joe was usually in bed with the lights out by half-past nine, the alarm hand of the watch beside his bunk set for five o'clock. The peg on which the watch hung was close to his head, because its bell was so faint. Its birdlike trill was muted by two tightly closed lids, giving it a furry quality, like the voice of the girl whose name was engraved on its back, as if she herself were calling to him.

She never failed to wake him up. Once last fall he had taken the watch with him on an overnight hunting-trip. When he crawled into his sleeping-bag at night without undressing he had slipped it into an inside pocket. The bell was buried under several layers of canvas and wool and he couldn't possibly hear it. But at the hour set he had felt its gently whirring vibrations against his ribs like something alive and had waked up instantly. After that, whenever in doubt about hearing the bell, he slipped the watch into a pocket close to his body.

He had come to have a sentimental feeling for the watch. Often after winding it, he would gaze down at it in his palm, its upturned face seeming to smile at him, then turning it over, he would contemplate the name on the back, sometimes saying it aloud, 'Leonora, Leonora.' A beautiful name, he thought. So definitely feminine! The only feminine thing in his cabin, or in his life now!

He had procured another watch for daily use. Tonight he went through his nightly performance of winding both

watches as usual, first turning the protruding stem of his
two-dollar wrist-watch, then the small corresponding one
of the silver watch, locating the delicate disk deep-set in its
rim with his exploring fingertips. It couldn't be handled
roughly, nor forced. Once when he was in haste he had used
his blunt thumb-nail to raise the disk and had broken it.

Tonight he wound the alarm bell to its limit. He didn't
want to lose a fraction of the blurred voice on the last
morning that it would call him to consciousness. He must
return the watch in the morning. The blatant blare of an
alarm clock would jerk him awake hereafter. This would be
the last time he would wind the stem, the last night he would
gaze down at the lovely name. He was about to hang the
watch on its peg beside his bed when he changed his mind
and slipped it in the pocket of his pajamas.

When Joe opened the door of Old Crow the next morning
bearing a cup of hot coffee both Nora Brock and her father
were asleep. Mr. Brock was snoring. The burlap curtains in
front of Nora's portion of the cabin were drawn only three-
quarters of the way across the pole. Joe caught a glimpse of
her bare arm extending out into space from her cot, fingers
upcurling.

He placed the coffee on the table with the saucer on top
of the cup, tiptoed to the wood-box, lifted some kindling and
logs, and laid them down gently, one by one, on the floor
close to the Franklin stove. Then he squatted and began
feathering a piece of kindling with his sheath-knife.

A few minutes later Nora opened her eyes. The most
beautiful sound in the world to hear first upon awakening,
Nora thought, was the crackling of leaping flames in a fireplace; and the most beautiful sight to *see* first was the
flames' shadows playing on log walls chinked with dry moss.
She lay perfectly still for a moment, watching and listening.
Presently through the open space of the half-drawn curtains
she caught sight of the cup of coffee on the table.

'Oh, Joe,' she called in a drowsy tone hoarse with sleep.
'Yes.'

'Bring my coffee in here, will you?'

He kept his eye steadfastly on the cup as he approached the cot.

'Put it on that chair.'

There was a wooden-seated kitchen chair beside her pillow with a kerosene lamp and a nickel alarm clock on it. Joe pushed aside the lamp and clock, and put down the cup of coffee six inches from her head. She was lying on her back, arms raised, rubbing the sleep out of her eyes with her fists. One of the sleeves of her striped pajamas was shoved up above the elbow. Her mop of hair was tousled. Like Mrs. Mullins, she completely disregarded her appearance before him.

But unlike Mrs. Mullins, Joe thought, as he left the cabin a moment later, the skin of her bare arm was firm and smooth, the strands of her tossed hair thick and coiling, and the traces of recent sleep — the flush of her cheeks, the sleepy hoarseness of her voice were disturbingly attractive. It wasn't going to be so easy to be blind, deaf, and impervious guiding *this* party. Of course, if he were a bona fide guide he'd be as immune as a doctor with a patient, he supposed, whoever the woman was, and however intimate the services he performed. But he was playing a rôle. Underneath his disguise he was at liberty to look upon Nora Brock with the freedom of any man of her own world — whatever that world was. Not *his* world, he imagined, not his old world, that is. Difficult to place her. He felt pretty sure her name wouldn't be found in the Social Register or on the Junior League list of any city, and she herself had informed him it wasn't in the catalogue of any college. She was like some species of wild life that he'd never run across before and couldn't classify.

It was a pleasure to watch her in action in the woods —

swinging ahead of him on the trails, lithe and long-strided; fording a stream, nimble and sure-footed; springing in and out of a canoe with never a pause or slip. She was powerful with a paddle, digging it deep into the water and giving it a powerful, jujitsu-like twist at the end of each stroke — over and over again as she knelt in the bow of the canoe in front of him. She ate greedily. She drank ravenously — refusing the tin cup he offered her when they stopped at a spring, dropping down on all fours at the edge of an amber-colored pool and plunging her face down into the dark, cold water like a thirsty deer. She made beautiful casts. Her form was flawless. The tiny fly at the end of her line seemed to soar through the air toward its goal, dimpling the bull's-eye of the target, skimming lightly over the surface, then rising again as if on its own wings. Her patience was untiring when casting; the eagerness of her expression glorious to behold when her line was taut and the rod bent. If the fish got away her disappointment burst out in an explosion of expletives as spontaneous and as relieving as an unrestrained sneeze. She was simple and natural in everything she did; and in everything she said straight-to-the-point and unhesitating.

There would, however, be some squeamish individuals whose delicate sensibilities would be shocked by her breezy, slapdash manner and free-flowing speech. For instance, certain members of the Vale clan. Thank God, he was no longer one of them! He could just see Aunt Rosa's and Aunt Justine's raised eyebrows and compressed lips as they looked down their noses at Nora Brock if he ever brought her to one of the clan's sacred Thanksgiving dinners as his guest — a privilege open to all friends and members of the family and a test to all prospective members by marriage. Nora Brock would make no effort at adaptation, he felt sure. She would use whatever phrase, term, or expletive best suited to express herself at the moment, irrespective of her audience. Even his mother would cringe at her frequent 'Goshes,' just as she

used to when June was going through the Gosh era. Nora
was seldom profane and she had a far cleaner mind than
June. Surely his mother, who always looked beneath surfaces, could not help seeing Nora Brock's genuineness and
freedom from fraud and smut.

Each day followed the same general pattern as long as the
clear weather held. Every morning after breakfast the trio
set out for some lake or stream not too far distant for a
single day's journey. A different destination was selected
each day until all Sam Brock's favorite fishing-grounds had
been revisited. Most of the trips started by trail through the
woods with Nora leading, Sam Brock following and Joe last
in the line. Frequent stops were necessary for Sam Brock, a
fact he tried to hide from Nora, but he never resented Joe's
suggestion to rest if made out of her hearing.

During the rest-periods Sam did a lot of talking, Joe a lot
of listening. Sam's topics of conversation ranged from fish
yarns and the latest Mae West story to politics and the war
in Europe, now entering its third year. He liked airing his
opinions on Roosevelt, third terms, Churchill, the plucky
British, the flighty French, the lucky U.S.A. with its two
protecting oceans, and especially Isolationism versus Stick-
ing-our-necks out. He often asked Joe what he thought, but
Joe never committed himself. He had learned from Seth
how to evade expressing an opinion.

He had never imparted even to Seth what his ideas were
about the war. But underneath his apparent indifference to
all events outside the radius of his life at Fiddle Pond he was
aware of a buried seething deep underneath his routine acts.
Every time the war was discussed the seething increased,
grew louder as if coming up nearer and nearer to the surface.
He had a feeling that the war was creeping up on him, not
from the outside but from within; not because of laws made
in Washington and enforced by government officials, but

from a source of authority within himself enforced by his own unescapable conscience.

He hated the very thought of war. Physical combat of any kind, even on the football field, was distasteful. He was in a position to sidestep the draft. Murray Vale, according to the records, had been dead for over two years and the name of Eliot Jones was recorded nowhere. But the inner seething had made him walk into the local draft-board at the time appointed and ask for a registration blank. It was now on file somewhere, filled out in full, even his birthplace — a small island he'd never heard of off the coast of China picked out at random in an old atlas. He hoped the island was inhabited.

There was usually two hours' fishing for Nora and her father before their midday meal. After eating, Sam Brock invariably took a full hour's nap. During these long siestas Joe and Nora were alone, and as unheard and unseen by Sam as if he were back at camp asleep in his own bed.

Lunch the first day was eaten on a sandy beach beside Big Hawk. Afterwards Sam Brock stretched himself out close to the sun-warmed flank of a tree trunk. Nora lay down flat on her back on the sandy beach, while Joe cleaned up. She took off her khaki hat and placed it over her face, perched one foot on a drawn-up knee and closed her eyes. The sun's rays at midday were warm and penetrating. It was as dark and musty beneath her hat as a closed attic room. The smell of the leather sweat-band and the hot canvas was pleasing to her nostrils. She grew drowsy. Her foot slipped off her knee. She slept for ten minutes, woke, slept again, and then sat up and looked around.

'Joe!' she called. He was sitting at a respectful distance at the top of a bank behind her. He approached. 'What about a little casting while Dad sleeps?'

'All right. I'll put the canoe in.' But he made no move to

do so. He had slipped her watch into his pocket before
starting out. 'Miss Brock,' he began, fumbling inside his
pocket, 'I've got your watch here.' It was wrapped in tissue
paper. He unwrapped it. 'I hope you'll find it's all right.'

'Mrs. Scully said it went on the blink. No wonder. It
hasn't been cleaned since it was given to me when I was a
kid.'

'It didn't go on the blink. I broke it. But I've had it fixed.'

'So I heard. To the tune of fifteen dollars! You certainly
got stung. I don't believe it cost over twenty-five bucks in
the beginning.'

'Oh, yes, it did! It is a beautiful little watch. It's a Patek
Phillipe.'

'What's that?'

'A make of watch.'

'How do *you* happen to know so much about makes of
watches?'

'A man I guided once had one. He —— ' he hesitated.
Damn it! Always putting my foot in it!

'Never mind, Joe. I prefer *this* good old Big Ben of mine
to any of your Patrick Philleep's.' She thrust out her arm.
There was a man-sized watch encased in leather strapped to
her wrist. 'It's got more guts.'

'But it hasn't got an alarm.'

'Humph, that measly little faint-voiced thing was always
letting me down. Give *me* an alarm clock. In fact, give me
two!'

'It has never let *me* down.'

'Well, it's yours if you want it. If you've put fifteen dollars
in it, half of it belongs to you already by rights.'

'Of course it doesn't!'

'Oh all right, all right. It's okay by me! Pass the watch
over if you don't want it.' She reached out her hand.

'I do want it,' he said stiffly and wrapped it up again.
'Thank you, Miss Brock. Thank you very much.'

'Forget it.'

'Is it your name on the back?'

'It's the name my mother saddled me with at birth.'

'Don't you like it? I think it's a beautiful name.'

'It doesn't go with *my* type. How would you like it if *your* name was Lancelot? Come on, let's get a move on.' She stood up. 'I'll give you a hand with the canoe.'

23
CHAPTER

Sam never knew what they would be up to when he woke
up from his midday nap. Once he discovered them standing
thigh-deep in a small pond, waders pulled up to their hips,
investigating the construction of a beaver dam; once on
their knees poring over the bare mound of a large ant-hill;
another time in the branches of a tree dislodging an abandoned bees' nest the size of a football. It appeared that Joe
knew a lot about the habits of beavers, ants, bees, skunks,
porcupines, loons, owls — all birds, in fact all flying creatures
from eagles to midges.

'Nora has always had a bump of curiosity about animals,'
Sam told Joe one day. 'We never had a guide before who
knew half the answers. When she was a kid she was always
teasing for a puppy or kitten or rabbit or guinea pig or God
knows what.'

It was the lunch hour. They were gathered around one
of Joe's small concentrated fires built in a groove between
two rocks beside a brook. Joe was making flapjacks, squat-
ting down close over the hot bed of ashes. Nora and her
father were leaning back against two comfortably inclined
boulders watching him.

A week had passed since the Brocks' arrival. There was
no longer any doubt in Joe's mind about the state of his
feelings for Nora Brock. He was in love with her! He still
realized the menace of any such involvement, but he did

190

nothing to avoid it. It had occurred to him to ask Silas or
Ed to take over his job with the Brocks, and stay at a deserted camp he knew about until their departure. But he
couldn't bring himself to do it. He had never been in love
before and didn't know the power it had to make everything
else dwindle into insignificance. A smile from Nora Brock,
the sudden changing of her voice from brusque to gentle,
a glance from her eyes, the slightest touch of her fingers, or
grazing arm or knee — the daily possibility of these was more
important to Joe than anything else in the world. He was
very careful not to betray his feelings to her, and felt sure
she did not suspect them. She gave no sign of it. No sign
either of the slightest reciprocation. Whenever Sam Brock
got to talking about Nora, Joe egged him on. He had an
insatiable curiosity about the object of his desire.

'You were saying your daughter was crazy about animals
when she was a youngster,' he reminded Sam, sliding a
velvety golden-brown flapjack onto a hot enamelware plate
and passing it to Sam.

'Yep, she was! Always looking into pet-shop windows, and
at a circus would rather hang around in the animal tent than
see the show. And when she got older she got a notion in
her noodle she wanted to be a vet.'

'An animal doctor?'

'Sure thing. Hell-bent to go to some college with a lot of
men to learn how to take care of sick cows and horses. But
I couldn't see it. That's one thing I agreed with her mother
about one hundred per cent. But Nora harped on it for years.
She's stubborn as a mule when she gets her mind set.'

Nora didn't mind her father's poking fun at her before
others. It was an expression of affection. If she got too much
of it, and he wouldn't stop when she asked him to, she would
get up and move away, like a dog who gets bored with too
much playful poking.

'Why didn't you let her be a vet?'

'I would have if she'd been a boy, but for a girl to be going around to kennels and stables and cowbarns with a bag of instruments — why, I'd as soon have her a plumber lugging around a box full of tools, fixing kitchen sinks, cleaning out catchbasins and God knows what.'

'Oh pooh, pooh, pooh, Dad!'

'Well, anyhow it wasn't fit work for *my* girl. No, siree!' He paused to convey half a flapjack wrapped around his fork to his wide-open mouth, closing his lips upon it and sucking in escaping streams of syrup and melted butter.

'What made you want to be a vet?' asked Joe, glancing up from the creamy surface of an unturned flapjack in his frypan.

'Oh, I don't know. Animals are so pitiful when they're sick.'

'What got her started wanting to be a vet,' said Sam, 'was something that happened when she was a kid.'

'Ring off, Dad. Joe isn't interested.'

'Yes, I am. Please go on.'

'Well, she was always teasing for a puppy or a kitten, as I was saying. So one day when I dropped in to see her (her mother and I weren't making our home together at the time) I stopped at a pet-shop and bought her a kitten.'

'Dad, *please!*'

'Angora. Pure white. Cute little thing.' Sam went right on. 'And she — '

'And she killed it!' Nora cut in. 'She put the cute little thing into a shoe box, and wrapped it in a lot of newspapers so it couldn't get any air and it smothered.'

'Now, now, Nora! You tell it right.'

She got up and walked away, seating herself on a log above a noisy waterfall far enough removed from her father and Joe so she need not hear their conversation, and frowningly regarded the sparkling spray.

'She wrapped the box up in newspaper,' Sam explained in

a lowered tone. 'So the kitten wouldn't freeze — the way she'd seen florists wrap up flowers. You see, her mother didn't like kittens — especially in an apartment, and one day after she'd had the kitten about two weeks and gotten fond of it, Nora heard her mother telephoning someone to come and get the kitten next morning while she was at school. So Nora gets a box, puts the little beggar in it and hides it down in the cellar of the apartment-house. When she gets home from school, in the late afternoon, her mother is looking all over everywhere for the darned cat. Nora never lets on, you bet. She has to wait till her mother's gone to bed before it's safe to go down to the cellar with some milk, and when she gets there — well, you can guess what had happened. She took it mighty hard. Of course in time she got over it okay. But it left a kind of soft, punky spot in her about animals in trouble — even flies on sticky paper, and humans if they are down and out enough.'

After her father had withdrawn for his nap, Nora called to Joe. She was still sitting on the log above the waterfall. She was still in a frowning mood. 'Sit down.' She motioned to the empty space beside her. She was silent for a while. Neither spoke. A bird chirped on a branch above them. A chipmunk passed by.

Finally she remarked, 'It always makes me furious to have dad tell about what I did to Twinkle.'

'Twinkle?'

'That was the kitten's name.'

'That's a pretty name for a kitten.'

'I named her Twinkle because that's what she did — just *twinkled*, especially evenings when the corners of the room got dark. She'd flash in and out from under chairs and tables playing with shadows. Sort of sparkling all over, even her whiskers and eyes. She had the longest whiskers. Like aigrettes. And fur like eiderdown.' She was reminiscing to

herself, and Joe did not interrupt. 'Her fur sort of wilted
when she died. I never saw anything so dead as a dead
kitten. I'll never forget when I opened the box. She'd been
so helpless and trusting when I put her in. It was a terrible
thing for me to do.'

'You didn't know any better.'

'I should have. I was nearly six. I was an idiot — a fool.
My mother was simply horrified when the janitor told her
what I'd done. I tried to get Twinkle alive again and she
found me down in the cellar pouring warm milk down
Twinkle's throat. She punished me for torturing animals
and playing with their dead bodies and said such children
grew up to be fiends.'

'How cruel!'

'Oh, I didn't mind! I didn't mind anything except that
Twinkle was dead. I simply adored her. I shall never have
a baby I adore so much, I shall never let myself adore any
living thing so much.'

'I know,' Joe murmured, struggling with a desire to take
her in his arms.

'Oh, well,' she shrugged. 'Forget it. I'm all over it now.'

'Except for the soft spot.'

'Oh, so dad divulged that crazy theory of his!'

'It's not crazy. It's absolutely sound. And explains why
you did what you did when you said good-bye.'

'What are you driving at?'

'When I was so sick two years ago. You know as well as I
do.'

'When you were out of your mind, having hallucinations?'

'It was not an hallucination. I know just how the sunlight
looks shining through the brim of that tweed hat of yours.'

'Oh, heavens, are you by any chance referring to that long
and tender kiss I implanted on your brow?'

'Yes, I am.'

'Why do you think I did it?'

'I think the soft spot was touched.'

'Nothing of the sort!' Her blunt honesty rode roughshod over the tender soil he'd just turned up. 'I did it to fool the doctor!'

'To fool the doctor!'

'Sure! I'd had to tell him I was engaged to you so as to make him come way up here in the middle of the night and I had to act the part when I said good-bye to you.'

'I see,' said Joe, turning his face away.

'I didn't want to let the doctor down. The poor thing looked terribly tired.'

'Oh, it was the poor doctor that touched the soft spot! Say, that's a good one on me!' He could feel one of those waves of hot blood threatening him. Not a mere flush, but a slowly rising, long-drawn-out flood of crimson that would mount to the very roots of his hair. It had been years since he had given one of those humiliating exhibitions. He picked up a loose stick lying on the ground and placing his elbows on his spread knees began poking in the soft leaf-mold, head bent, shoulders stooped. She couldn't see his face but there was no way to hide the back of his neck. 'What a fool I am!' he muttered.

'No, you're not!' Any man's bowed head filled Nora with a wave of compassion, whether it was a minister seated in his pulpit-chair silently praying just before his sermon, or a drunken man slouched on a park bench, head sunk in the misery of a hang-over. 'Drop that old stick. Sit up, and look at me, Joe.'

But he kept on doggedly digging, his stooped shoulders jerking at each poke. The painful crimson gradually crept up over the edge of his shirt collar, his bare, defenseless ears turned the color of coral. Nora's soft spot was touched *now* without any shadow of doubt! She reached out her hand and laid it on Joe's knee. He dropped the stick instantly, sitting perfectly motionless staring at her hand as if unable to believe his own eyes. She gave the rough cloth a tiny stroke to assure him her hand was no apparition. He grasped it and pressed it down hard against his knee. For a full minute they sat thus, neither speaking or moving. The bird in the tree twittered again. The chipmunk returned from his errand. Joe's hot wave of chagrin receded and disappeared.

Nora was the one who broke the spell. She made no motion of withdrawal, however. 'Isn't it about time you let go of my hand?' she inquired.

Instantly he released it. 'I'm sorry. I shouldn't have done that. I forgot who I am.'

'Who are you, Joe?'

'Your guide. I'll go and finish cleaning up.' And he walked away.

That night after her father had gone to bed Nora sat a long while before the burning logs in Old Crow deep in thought. For years her first impulse had always been to withdraw from a man's touch. If there was the least suggestion of sex, a wave of aversion would sweep over her. She was haunted by the fear that she might have inherited her mother's inability to respond, of which her father had told her. (There was little Sam didn't tell Nora when he had had several drinks.) But today when Joe had grasped her hand and pressed it hard against his knee, no antipathy had risen up in her. Instead she had felt breathless anticipation.

Lying awake in her cot she relived the scene on the log. Down deep within her there was a locked room to which she had lost the key. The door to the room had swung open without any forcing at all as she sat there beside Joe this afternoon, and the spell over the Sleeping Beauty inside had been lifted by Joe's touch. It had been sort of like that. Every girl is born with a sleeping beauty in a locked room inside her, she guessed. Some wake up early, some late, and some have evil spells cast over them.

That night it wasn't of Joe Nora dreamed, but of Oscar Bergen, a boy she'd known at one of the high-schools she had attended. She was supposed to be Oscar's best girl. Oscar used to take her to the movies and out in his father's car sometimes. He was always urging her to be like other girls. He said she was missing a lot of fun, and she could never hope to be popular if she never loosened up. One night they went into the woods. Could it be that that miserable experiment and failure with Oscar had cast an evil spell over the beauty in her locked room? She had fought Oscar like a wildcat, and ever since had been repelled by men who wanted to touch her.

The next day was Sunday. There was never any fishing at Fiddle Pond on Sunday. Many of the members skipped breakfast entirely, making their first appearance at dinner. When Nora woke up in her cot at half-past six the cabin was shrouded in a thick brown dusk. After the burst of the rising-bell notes had faded into silence she was aware of the purring patter of rain on the roof. She loved its monotonous murmur. No need to get up. She could stay here till noon. She turned over, and closed her eyes, but she couldn't doze off again. Joe would be arriving any moment with her coffee. She was wideawake when she heard his step on the porch, and a moment later the creak of the door. Her cot was entirely hidden by the curtains. She had drawn them close together last night.

'Good morning, Joe. Just leave my coffee on the table, please. I'll get it later.'

Why didn't she want Joe to see her all tousled and mussy in bed? Hiding behind curtains from her guide till she made herself pretty! She was disgusted with herself!

It rained hard all day. The members luxuriated in the enforced idleness, took frequent naps, read old newspapers, wrote letters, smoked, ate, drank, played cards. In the late

morning Sam strolled over to the main camp and got into a
poker game that continued all day. Nora, left to her own
devices, washed out some of Sam's socks and B.V.D.'s and
several pieces of pink underwear of her own, hanging them
up to dry on a string she stretched between two chairs; then
she washed her hair and stretched out in front of the fire
to dry it, flat on her stomach, her elbows planted far apart,
her chin cupped in her hands, and on the floor an open book
lit by the logs' flames. The book was Joe's copy of *Walden*
which she had borrowed a week ago and not opened until
now.

She had always thought of Thoreau as one of those strict,
straight-laced old codgers who had a lot of ideas about living
but had never lived much himself. Pretty dry reading if
taken in large doses. But she became immediately engrossed.
She didn't turn the pages consecutively but skipped from
chapter to chapter, and back and forth, pausing where Joe's
pencil lines appeared in the margin, and reading what came
before and after.

The first marked passage was in the introduction. This
was it: 'What he chiefly sought for himself was freedom.
To him freedom meant escape from the bondage of petty
gods, the chance to live life fully, the leisure to think and
ripen, and enjoy.' My goodness, that's what I want, too, she
thought, and read it again. Many of the marked passages
dwelt on freedom and independence. Such as: 'I would
have each one pursue his own way, not his father's or his
mother's or his neighbor's instead.' And later, 'Let every one
mind his own business, and endeavor to be what he was
made.' And again, 'If a man does not keep pace with his
companions, perhaps it is because he hears a different drum-
mer. Let him step to the music which he hears, however
measured or faraway.' Several of the passages he had
marked with a double line. This was one: 'Our moulting
season like that of the fowls must be a crisis in our lives.
The loon retires to solitary ponds to spend it.'

She read the book until the dinner-bell rang, and again in the afternoon curled up with it in a corner of the old couch. She had exchanged no words with Joe all day. She had seen him at a distance helping Elta, pushing his wheelbarrow piled with logs, passing Old Crow occasionally without glancing up. She felt sure he was avoiding her. At about four she put on her slicker and sou'wester, pulled on some old overshoes and set forth to find him.

Underneath her slicker she wore a silk shirtwaist and a skirt, and underneath the overshoes, snug suede pumps. She liked to get out of bulky dungarees and stiff canvas on a rainy day at Fiddle Pond. After a week of camp clothes she loved the contrast of silk against her skin and the absence of thick canvas between her legs when she lay stretched out before a fire. Like a cat, Nora delighted in orgies of warmth, softness, and relaxation. It was not for Joe's edification that she was dressed in feminine attire, she assured herself, as she climbed the slippery trail to his cabin.

24

CHAPTER

She had contrived a plausible excuse for her call. She wanted some information about a specimen of wild life which she carried in her creel, held carefully upright under her arm. The top of the creel was strapped down and the hole in the top stuffed with paper.

She had to knock twice before she heard his 'Come in.' His back was toward her. He was seated in the low-slung beach-chair, slumped down so deep she couldn't see his head. All that was visible were his extending arms and legs.

Joe also had exchanged his stiff canvas for comfortable lounging raiment. He had obtained the outfit at a second-hand shop in Bangor during one of the rare visits to the metropolis which he had risked making in the company of Seth. It consisted of loose gray flannel trousers, a shabby soft-collared white shirt, a pair of dirty, rubber-soled saddle shoes, bulky, and white woolen socks, worn garterless.

'That you, Ed?' he called drowsily, and when there was no reply, 'That you, Danny?'

'It's neither of them!'

He drew in his sprawling antennae and stood up. A pipe, an ash-tray, and a book rattled to the floor. He turned around and faced Nora. He was wearing a pair of horn-rimmed glasses also obtained in Bangor. Nora was struck instantly with his resemblance to a certain type of American young man she had seen before. One year she and her mother had occupied an apartment in Cambridge overlooking the Charles River. They had come as strangers to Cambridge and had left as strangers. But Nora had seen countless boys dressed in the same raiment Joe was now wearing.

'Why, Joe, I didn't know you wore glasses!'

'I don't!' and he snatched them off. 'Only for fine print. Is there something you want?'

'Yes, I've got something here I want you to tell me about.' She held up the creel. Yesterday's event had meant nothing to her, Joe concluded. She was ignoring it completely.

'Have you been fishing in this weather?'

'Yes, but only in my wastebasket. Can't I take off my coat? I've come to make a call.'

'Yes, of course. Wait till I pick up some of this mess,' and he fell to gathering up his pipe, book, tobacco-pouch, and the pages of a dismembered newspaper strewn over the floor. Nora took off her oilskins and overshoes and went over to the bench with her creel.

'Come here and see my fish! I want you to tell me whether it's domestic or wild.' Joe walked over to the bench. 'We've got to be darned careful or he'll get away.'

Joe saw the glint of fun in her eyes. 'What have you got in there?'

'A mouse,' she announced.

'Alive?'

'You bet it's alive, and quick as greased lightning.'

'How did you catch it?'

'The way I always catch the little scamps when I hear them rustling around in wastebaskets. Fling a towel over the top of the basket, then reach my hand in and feel around. This little chap ran up my arm trying to get out, and I caught him as easy as anything in my other hand.'

'Gosh! And you a girl!'

'It takes far less courage than chasing them around till you get them in a corner, then torturing them to death with a broom or a poker.' She lifted the cover a little way and they both peered in. Their shoulders grazed.

'Is she aware of it?' Joe wondered.

'Is he aware of it?' Nora wondered.

'Look at him staring at us,' she said in a half-whisper. 'Frozen with fear, the poor little thing!' The captive made a dash for freedom. In a flash Nora hugged the basket close to her body, and thrust her hand inside. 'Cover up the edges, Joe, that's right! Just a minute. I've got him! Let go.' She withdrew her hand. 'Here he is! Take him.'

Joe curved his hand beneath her extended fist and placed his other hand on top. Nora slowly dilated her fingers and the warm little ball of life dropped into Joe's palm. He held it like a bird at first, then by the scruff of the neck like a kitten, turning toward the light so Nora could see.

'It's a field-mouse,' he said. 'It's got a shorter tail than a house-mouse, and a browner coat.'

'Is it a male or female?'

'It's a nursing mother. See?' and he pointed to the tiny teats.

'Oh, the poor little thing! She is worried to death about her babies. I'll take her back.'

'She can find her own way. I'll put her outdoors.'

'No, it's too far. She might get lost. Put her back in the basket. You poor, frightened little darling! I didn't know you had babies! But I'll look out for you. Don't be afraid.' If the mouse had been human she couldn't have expressed tenderer concern.

The soft spot was susceptible to the distress of *any* creature — mouse or man. She had a weakness for weakness — a pity for pathos of whatever variety. Her sympathy was as simple and natural as a child's and as promiscuous. The reason she was ignoring yesterday's scene on the log was because it had made no more impression on her than as if she had patted a hurt dog, and he had licked her hand.

These were Joe's conclusions as he put the mouse back into the basket and again stuffed the opening with paper.

'I want to speak to you about something, Joe,' later Nora remarked matter-of-factly.

'Yes? What is it?'

'Your private affairs are none of my business but your job as our guide *is*. I'm a pretty straightforward person myself and I like dealing with straightforward people. It makes me feel uncomfortable to come up here to speak to my guide and find an undergraduate college boy sitting here instead. That's what you look like to me.'

'Well, I'm not!'

'Well, you certainly know how to dress the part all right! How many other costumes have you got tucked away? See here, Joe, you're not really and truly a guide, are you?'

'I'm really and truly trying to be a guide to the best of my ability. How am I failing?'

'Oh, you're not! You're marvelous! But you're not fooling me nor the other members either. They're all onto you.'

'What do you mean, "onto me"? This is the first I've heard of it and I've been here two years.'

'Oh, don't be an ostrich! I'm the only one who's got the nerve to talk straight out from the shoulder to you, but they all hash you over in private, swapping theories, trying to solve the big mystery.'

'What are the theories?'

'All sorts and varieties. Do you really want to know?'

'Yes please.'

'Well, one theory is you're a victim of amnesia. Got knocked in the head by a hit-and-run driver or something like that. Another is you're an escaped prisoner and scared stiff you'll get caught. A third, an escaped mental patient with delusions, which would account for that crazy story of yours about China and your missionary parents. No man in his right mind would tell such an unlikely whopper. Of course it's been suggested there's a woman at the bottom of it. Perhaps you've got some girl into trouble. After dinner today several of the women got to hashing you over with the new member — Mrs. Hinckle. Her theory is, you're hiding up here to avoid the draft.'

'That's false!' Joe ejaculated. 'On the face of it, it's false! Why, when I came in here two years ago there wasn't any draft to avoid!'

'Why, that's so!'

'What right has the Hinckle woman to say a thing like that? I've already registered at our local board. You tell that woman the facts, please.'

'I will! I will! I'll squash such libel the first chance I get, and tickled to pieces to do it, too.' She paused briefly. 'I wouldn't want *that* to be your reason,' she added, her voice performing one of those sudden changes from brusque to gentle, her eyes from bright to soft, which brought Joe's heart up into his throat. 'Today after dinner they all wanted to know what *my* theory was, after a week in your company.'

'What did you tell them?'

'I didn't tell them. As luck would have it I'd been reading that book of yours. It seems to me marked passages in a borrowed book are sort of confidences. So I had to keep mum.'

'That was mighty fine of you! Will you tell *me* what your theory is?'

'I might. Let's sit down. Any objections?'

'No, let's.' He drew the rawhide chair closer to the fire and she sat down in it. He squatted in front of her on an old milking-stool, knees spread far apart, elbows on knees, hands clasped loosely between. 'Now what is your theory?'

'Well, it's still kind of vague. It dawned on me when I was reading that book of yours, and the things you marked. It strikes me, Joe, you're an awful lot like that old duck,

Thoreau. He loved the woods and animals like you, and went off to live alone in a shack he made himself on the edge of a lonely pond, like you.'

Joe gave a short laugh. 'That's funny! My mother used to say I was like Thoreau, to console me when I was a kid because I wasn't much of an athlete. But that's no theory to explain why I'm here now.'

'Yes, it is! Thoreau wanted to be free and independent and live the way he wanted to live and judging from the things you marked in that book I bet a dollar *that's* the chief reason you're here. In a nutshell, my theory is you are up here just to get away from conventions and life in general and be yourself.'

'I'm sorry. You're wrong, entirely wrong. I didn't have Thoreau's courage or self-confidence, or guts either, I guess, to break away and live independently. I had to wait till something happened that forced me to it.'

'Well, anyway, you love the woods and this kind of life, and whatever happened that made you decide to come here I don't believe was anything very horrible or tragic.'

'But it was! It was! And I didn't *decide* to come to the woods. I just happened to land here. I was running away. Any safe hiding place — a lumber-camp, a coal-mine, or the hold of a ship would have served my purpose. Things happened. I was in a terrible situation. And I still am! God, I wish I could tell you about it!' He got up and took a turn up and down the room and came to a halt in front of her. 'No, I can't. I can't. I mustn't! It's impossible! It involves others — everyone who ever knew me. If my mother should find out that I am alive and living here, it would absolutely ruin her memory of me, and her opinion, too. I can't let her down like that! It would be unfair to her, and to everybody who ever had a good opinion of me, to tell anyone in the world who I really am. I try not to acknowledge it to myself even.' He stopped abruptly. 'I don't know what I'm thinking of, telling you

things I've never mentioned to a living soul! I must be mad!'
His brow drew into a painful frown. His whole face became
crisscrossed with distress.

'It's all right, Joe. I'm safe with confidences. Safe as a
priest. You haven't confided much anyway, only that you've
got a mother, and people somewhere who've got a good
opinion of you. I love knowing that! You don't have to tell
me anything more. Come on, let's forget it. Too bad I
don't smoke or I'd ask for a cigarette. But I love the smell
of a pipe. Light up for me.'

'No, thanks. I don't want to smoke now.'

'What about a cup of tea? Or haven't you the mixings
here?'

Unlike any other guide Nora had had before, Joe frequently served tea in the late afternoon, brewing it over a
can of Sterno in the bottom of a boat or canoe, or anywhere
they chanced to be, pouring it strong and hot into folding
cups, and passing a box of fig newtons with it as a rule.

'Yes, I have the mixings. I'll go and make you a cup.' He
started toward the back room.

'Wait a minute. Make yourself a cup too, then come and
sit down and drink it with me.' Joe was very particular to
observe all the proprieties of his position. In spite of Sam's
urging him to join Nora and him at lunch in the woods he
had always refused, eating alone later. 'Do you understand?' Nora followed it up.

Joe smiled and nodded.

'Cut out the guide act,' Nora went on, 'as long as you're
in that college-boy costume, and treat me as you would any
girl who'd risked her reputation to come and see you in your
room on a Sunday afternoon.'

'Well — all right,' he agreed. 'But — remember, you asked
for it. I'm warning you.'

'I'll run the risk. Go on, hurry up. I can't stay all night.'

When Joe returned five minutes later Nora had piled fresh

logs on the fire, lit the lamp, and was stretched out at full length in the rawhide chair apparently asleep. He had poured the tea into thick white crockery coffee cups. He knew how she liked it — strong and clear. On the saucer of each cup there were two fig newtons. He placed Nora's cup on the table beside her, then sat down again on the stool, placing his cup on the floor. She didn't open her eyes. She didn't stir. She was as relaxed as a child asleep, her lips slightly parted, the corners of her mouth drooping, her hands hanging down limp from the ends of the chair-arms.

Dressed in these soft feminine clothes he was surprised to discover how slender she was, small-hipped, small-waisted, with a firm, compact little torso. The short skirt had crawled up over her sleek bare knees, and the silk shirtwaist was open in front down to where the first rises of her breasts began. There was certainly nothing now to suggest his first impression of her — that she was a boy, or even a tomboy.

He ought to get up, pull down a shade, open a window, do anything to interrupt the tide of emotion rising in him. But instead, cautiously, warily, he moved his foot so that the sole of his shoe rested against hers. Instantly her breathing became measured and deep. She was feigning sleep! He moved nearer till his knee touched hers. Thus they sat for another of those long, vibrating silences. Finally she stirred slightly and raised her lashes, gazing at him from beneath them without speaking for a moment, then smiled slowly.

'Hello, Joe!' she whispered.

'Hello, Leonora!' he whispered back.

A twinge shot through Nora as the name she had discarded as a ridiculous misfit for her fell from his lips. She closed her eyes quickly so they wouldn't betray her feelings and resumed the measured breathing. He locked her foot in the soft vise of both his rubber soles then, and his shin grazed the soft flesh of her calf. Another minute slipped by. A log broke, fell apart and a flash of crackling flames burst forth. Joe stood up then, gazed down at her for half-a-dozen pounding heart-beats, then leaned and kissed her on the lips — gently — as if fearing to wake her up. She made no protest. Her body didn't stiffen, her lips either. She gave a little start — that was all, as if in doubt as to what had happened, then sat up, and looked around with a dazed expression.

'Good heavens! I guess I fell asleep! Where's my tea?'

'On the table beside you.'

'Where's yours?'

'On the floor.'

'Well, come and sit down and be sociable.' She took a sip or two from her cup. 'Delicious! Nothing like a cup of hot tea to go to the spot! Wherever did you get these heavenly little angel cakes, Mr. Jones?' She lifted one of the fig newtons and took a nibble. 'They're simply divine!' She was trying to get back onto firm ground again with Joe. But he didn't respond. He sat on the stool in front of her with his cup of tea, taking occasional swallows and contributing nothing to her artificial prattle.

Finally he placed his cup on the floor and blurted out, 'I don't think I ought to be your guide any more. Silas is free. He can take my place.'

'Why, Joe, what is the matter?'

'I'm in love with you,' he announced quietly.

'Of course you're not in love with me!'

'I'm sorry if I've shocked you, but you told me to forget I was your guide.'

'You haven't shocked me. But it's crazy to think you're in love with a girl you've known only a week, and,' she added, 'kissed only once for a stunt.'

'I didn't kiss you for a stunt. I've known you for two years, and I've been in love with you for two years.'

'That's ridiculous!'

'Ridiculous or not, it's a fact. I'm in love with you.' His

tone was dogged. 'I'm in love with you,' he said for the third time. He seemed to like to repeat the phrase.

'Well, it's no crime. Why so lugubrious?'

'Because it can never lead to anything.'

'Oh! Are you already married?'

'No. Worse.' He gave a short mirthless laugh. 'I'm already dead. There's a gravestone with my name on it in the family lot at home, or ought to be by this time.' He got up from the stool and shoving his hands in his trouser pockets stood gazing down into the fire. 'I've made a big mess of things in my life.'

Nora stood up, too. 'Don't you say that! You haven't made a big mess of things *here*. Everybody *here* thinks you're a wonderful guide, and a wonderful guy, too. From Danny up — they all think you're *simply* wonderful! *I* do, too!' Her voice was more than soft and tender now. It was fierce, and trembled a little. It swept away all Joe's precautions.

'You wouldn't think I was wonderful if you knew the facts. I'm going to tell them to you. I'm going to tell them to you, *now*.'

'No, you aren't! I won't let you!' She felt suddenly too protective of his peace of mind to endanger it simply to satisfy her curiosity. 'If you told me the facts now you might worry afterwards. Wait till you're dead sure you can trust me.'

She crossed the room and put on her coat and hat and overshoes, slung the strap of the creel over her shoulder and came back to Joe.

'I'm going now. Thanks for the dope about my mouse. Where do you think we'd better go tomorrow if it doesn't rain?'

'Do you still want me for a guide?'

'Silly! Why shouldn't I? I told you to play the part of your costume, didn't I? And you did it, darned well too.

Tomorrow you'll be in your guide's costume and play *that* part. Of course I want you to be my guide, Joe.'

She knew the way out of all difficulties. 'You're wonderful! You're simply wonderful!' Joe murmured.

'Copycat! That's what I said about *you*. For Pete's sake, can't you express yourself more originally?'

'Yes, I can! Shall I?'

'Sure! Why not?' she flung back with a mischievous expression of 'I dare you' in her eyes.

'All right, I will!' and he grasped hold of both her shoulders, holding her away from him at arm's length for a minute, looking straight into her pupils, then drew her body close to his, put his arms around her and tried to kiss her again. It wasn't so easy this time. She fought like an infuriated little demon, but there was no fury in the gasps of laughter that burbled forth as she struggled. It was an exciting battle — tense and taut, but as amicable as two boys wrestling. Her creel dropped to the floor, her hat, too. Strands of hair fell down over her eyes in wild disarray, as she pulled and pushed, turned and twisted, braced and strained. Joe was amazed at the fight she put up. He could however have ended it in short order, had he chosen. He prolonged it on purpose, loathe to terminate the mounting exhilaration. She was aware in the first few seconds it was futile to resist, but she persevered until Joe had backed her up against a wall, with her hand pinned down close to her sides.

'All right, let go,' she panted, laughing and weak.

'Say, "uncle." '

'Uncle.'

Even then he didn't release her immediately. He kissed her first. Again on the lips. Not gently this time, but roughly, triumphantly, with the gleam of a conqueror in his eyes, such as never had shone there before.

Nora stepped away from him, hot-faced and disheveled. 'Gosh,' she exclaimed under her breath, and set about repairing her damaged appearance — pulling her disarranged coat into place and smoothing her hair. 'I've never been so man-handled before in my life! I'm simply ruined! And you *hurt* me, too! I'm not used to cavemen.'

This time Joe didn't say he was sorry. The gloating gleam didn't fade from his eyes as she went on grumbling.

'What's become of my hat? And where's my creel? Good gracious, it's a wonder I haven't lost my virtue, too.' He picked up the hat and creel from the floor and handed them to her. The creel was empty. The paper had fallen out of the top. 'And my mouse has gone! You let her run away!' She pulled her hat onto her head with a savage jerk, shoved the creel under her arm, and stomped to the door. 'Open it!' she commanded, glowering at him from beneath contracted brows.

He was afraid she was going to leave him on this note. In fact he began to wonder if her indignation might not be genuine, but one of those lightning changes occurred as she stepped out onto the porch. Just after she crossed the threshold she turned back abruptly and looked up at him. The porch was shrouded in darkness but a spurt of flame from the logs inside lit up her face. Her eyes were luminous and full of tender fun, transforming the harsh epithets she flung at him into terms of endearment.

'Good-night, you brute! You browbeater! You old bully, you!' she said, and ran off into the lavender rain.

25

CHAPTER

SAM was ensconced in an armchair smoking his pipe when Nora pushed open the door. She kissed him twice on the top of his bald head, then took off her oilskins and crowded herself onto the narrow shelf of his knees, removed his pipe and kissed him again, this time on one of his sandpapery jowls, afterward rubbing her cheek against them kittenlike.

'Come, come, come!' he grunted. 'That'll do, that'll do.'

'Dear adorable daddy!' she purred and fell to twisting the hair behind his ears — the only long hair he possessed, into tiny outstanding spirals. When she was a little girl this act had been a demonstration of deep filial affection.

'Get away! Get away! Leave me alone,' he grumbled just as he used to. 'What's up? What's happened?'

'Nothing. Nothing. Just happy.' And she sprang off his knees and disappeared into her curtained cubicle, threw herself down onto her cot and lying there, hands folded beneath her head, stared up at the dim rafters above.

Just happy! Just terribly, deliriously happy! The magic quality of Joe's touch wasn't temporary. She wasn't going to be like her mother! During that terrific wrestling match she had been aware that down in the depths of her being some sort of spontaneous combustion was in process of development which she didn't want interrupted, vague and blurred, but definite enough for her to know she wasn't going to be cursed for life with frigidity. She was perfectly normal! Her reactions were like those of any healthy girl who is in love.

Am I in love? Have I actually fallen in love? All of a sudden like this, out of the blue? Or is it just some freak sex attraction? Perhaps one of those chemical reactions which Tweak (one of the girls she lived with in New York) was always talking about. They occur sometimes, Tweak said, between two strangers on a railroad train, or in a crowded bus, without a word being spoken, the only essential being proximity. Would Tweak's chemical theory account for the compassion Joe aroused in her, the loyalty that had already sprung alive, the maternal feeling that swept over her every now and then?

Presently her reflections were interrupted by the clanging of the supper bell. Joe was pulling the cable. He was hundreds of yards away. No chemical reaction requiring proximity could account for the choking wave that rose up in her as the bright notes fell on her ears.

Sam Brock noticed no difference in Joe's manner or attitude during the days that followed. Nor in Nora's either. He had no suspicion of what was transpiring underneath his very nose — hourly, daily, and often in the evening, too. For Nora suddenly developed an enthusiasm for evening fishing. Sam had had his fill by nightfall and preferred a game of poker or bridge with the men. So Joe and Nora went alone. Sam finally did observe a tendency in Nora when fording streams on slippery rocks, or stepping in and out of a canoe, to accept Joe's help. Once when Joe was carrying practically her whole weight across a brook easily leaped over, Sam asked if she'd turned her ankle, or what did ail her. She said she guessed she'd caught a little cold — her bones felt achy. Sam also observed that during his midday nap hour Nora and Joe spent their time in less strenuous activities than casting, or visiting beaver dams in hip-boots. They were always within calling distance when he woke up, but never in sight.

Nora usually was as straight as a die with her father but she concealed what was going on between Joe and herself by all the tricks and subterfuges at her command. The minute her father knew she was in love with Joe (and what was more, intended to marry him) he would fume and rage, and it would be all over the camp in no time. What was more serious, he would insist on knowing all the facts about Joe's past, and use sledgehammer methods in obtaining them. She could run no such risk.

Nora didn't know the facts of Joe's past for nearly a week after she had told him in her honest, straightforward way that she had fallen in love, too. He couldn't be any more surprised than she was herself, she said. She had never done such a thing before, she was inexperienced with the symptoms, but she knew it was the real thing. Nora made her announcement after she had lived with the turbulent knowledge for nearly forty-eight hours. She made it impulsively, on the spur of the moment, unable to hold it in a moment longer. Her father was only ten yards away casting from a boulder.

There was no opportunity for Joe to see Nora alone until after lunch the next day while Sam was asleep. They wandered off to a shaded grotto, and almost immediately he tried to pour out the facts of the mystery shrouding him. While Nora was still tremulous from their first licensed kiss he started to tell her his real name. But she stopped him.

'No, no! Not yet. Please. I don't care what your name is. You're *you*, whether you answer to Joe, or Tom, Dick, or Harry.'

'But it isn't fair to you to let you get in too deep with me, till you know what I've done and why I'm here.'

'It is, too, fair! I *want* to get in too deep with you, and I want you to get in too deep with me. I want us both to get so tangled up with each other that nothing short of death can untangle us. That's my object. I'm a scheming woman, Joe.'

She smiled at him teasingly, trying to break through the clouds of gloom on his face. He was lying on the ground flat on his back. She was seated close beside him.

'All I can offer you,' he said in a tone of deep dejection, gazing up at a scaly network of needled branches close above his head, 'is shame and disgrace and dishonor, and notoriety of the worst variety as soon as I'm discovered.'

'Sh-sh! Keep still! I won't *let* you treat my happiness like that when it's scarcely two days old! You ought to be more protective of the poor little just-born thing. It's no way to treat your own child, Joe.'

He smiled wanly at that. 'But you've got to know the facts *sometime*, Nora.'

'Of course I have! And I *want* to! I want to know all the facts there are to know about every little inch of you. And I want you to know all the facts there are to know about every little inch of *me*. But I want to *begin* with a few common ordinary facts. What is the date of your birth, Joe?'

'October third 1915.'

'Then I'm older!' she crowed. 'By nearly two weeks. So I shall be the boss, at least I shall be the boss of *you*. Not of our children. I think it's better for children if their father is the authority. What do *you* think?'

The clouds on his face broke up and scattered. 'Kiss me,' he exclaimed and drew her down to him. Afterwards, 'I agree with you,' he said. 'We'll let the facts of my shady past go hang for a while.'

The next day during Sam's nap hour Joe tried again to make his confession, and again Nora staved it off. This time she was lying on the ground with her head on his shoulder. His arm was around her, and her hand was shoved under his canvas coat, lying on his flannel shirt just over his thudding heart.

'Oh, Joe, don't tell me *now*,' she said dreamily. 'I don't

care a fig whether you have forged a check, or cheated at
cards, or murdered somebody and buried the remains in a
cellar under cement. As for that awful newspaper notoriety
you say is in store for me, what of it? I'm a free lance. No
family or setting, nobody it will hurt. Whatever it was
landed you at Fiddle Pond, thank Heaven for it! Or else I
wouldn't be here with you now, like this. That's the only
important fact in the world to me.'

'Why don't you want me to tell you my secret if you're not
afraid of it?'

'Because *you're* afraid of it. To you it's still more important than *us*. Last Sunday you talked about your mother and
all those people whose good opinion you've got to consider.
You have got a background. That's clear, and you're not
nearly as unprincipled as I am. So I've decided it's wise
before hearing any more about your darned old secret, or
your duty to others, to make myself one of your duties —
your most important duty, except your country.' She withdrew her hand, rolled over on her stomach and propped herself up on her elbows. 'Of course,' she added giving him the
sly smile, 'I hope I won't be obliged to get myself into a
family way to make you realize I'm your chief duty, but I
warn you I'll stop at nothing.'

He stretched out his arm on the ground toward her. 'Come
back here!' he ordered.

'No, thanks!' she replied, tilting her chin skywards to
watch the flight of a faraway aeroplane. Planes often went
over on their way to Canada and private camps further
north.

Presently she turned back. He was still gazing at her.
She leaned down over him. 'Don't wink,' she said and proceeded to study his eyes. 'I never noticed those brown
specks before. Your eyes are sort of hazel, aren't they? Your
eyebrows are very distinct. They look made up. They're
several shades darker than your hair.' She made these com-

ments in an impersonal tone. 'Lie still a minute. I'm curious
about something.' She reached out her forefinger and drew
it exploringly over each of his eyebrows. 'Yes, there *is* a
ridge under that scar! I've often wondered. What a lot of
things there are to find out about! How did you get that
scar, Joe?'

'Just playing football.'

'Tell me about it.'

'I was only a kid.'

'I'd like to hear about it.' She resumed her former position. 'Oh, what fun it's going to be! I've heard that the
discovering stage of falling-in-love is thrilling, and that love
sharpens your curiosity about the smallest details. And it's
true! Have you ever been psychoanalyzed, Joe?'

'No. Never. Have you?'

'No. Let's psychoanalyze each other! I want to know all
about when you were a little boy — your dreams and first
memories, where you went to school, what games you
played, and about your brothers and sisters, if you had any,
your mother and father, and where you went to college and
what girls you've known, and how well you knew them, and
how many affairs you've had — oh — just everything, Joe.
And I'll tell you about when I was a kid, and what a little
devil I was in every school my mother sent me. And I'll tell
you about *my* sex life, and we'll compare notes.' She paused,
burrowed her head more securely into the hollow of Joe's
shoulder and closed her eyes. 'Well, go ahead with the story
about the scar. I'm listening.'

Joe hadn't gotten very far when with no intention on his
part, and no expectation on Nora's, his identity emerged. He
had been careful to omit all last names as he recounted his
football accident, and even withheld the name of the school
he was attending. But he did use authentic nicknames — Ike,
the coach, and several times he referred to Windy, another

coach, 'who was particularly anxious to make an athlete out
of me.'

'Windy? That's an unusual nickname. What's it stand
for?'

'For breezy, I guess. That's what he was like — a good,
stiff breeze. A fair breeze. Never nasty. He was a marvelous
football player till he got struck down.'

'Struck down? By what?'

'Infantile.'

Nora sat up. 'Wait a minute! Are you referring to Windy
Vale by any chance?'

'Yes. Do you know him?'

'I know *about* him. My mother and I lived in Cambridge
one year. We got tickets once to a big game in the Stadium
and Windy Vale was wheeled in in his chair and the cheering
section gave him a rousing cheer as he passed by. I was
terribly impressed. I used to see him running around Cambridge in his car often after that, smiling and waving to
everybody he knew, with that great big dog on the seat
beside him. A kind of perpetual hero in a parade, he seemed
to me. So Windy Vale was your coach in football!'

'Yes, and my brother, too!' It slipped out as inevitably as
a ripe seed from an open pod.

'Windy Vale is your brother!'

'That's right.' He smiled wryly, drew up his legs and
stood up. Nora also stood up. 'Is your last name Vale?' she
groped. He nodded. 'What is your *first* name?'

'Murray.'

'Murray?'

'Yes. People seldom get it the first time.'

'Are you suggesting that you are Murray Vale?'

'That's right.'

'But that's impossible! I know about *him* too. It was in
the New York papers. I read every word printed about it
because he was Windy Vale's brother. Why, Joe, Murray

Vale died two years ago — a greater hero than his brother. He was drowned trying to save a friend of his up here on one of these Maine lakes.'

'Was his body ever found?'

'I don't know. I remember they were hunting for it, and thought it might never be found because it had gone over some falls and had gotten caught under a lot of dead trees in a swampy pond at the bottom of the falls.'

'The body didn't go over the falls. Murray Vale isn't dead. I am Murray Vale, Nora.'

Her eyes narrowed. A look of pity flickered across her features. 'How long have you had this idea of yours, Joe?'

'It isn't an idea. It's a fact! I can give you proof of it. I have my license back at the cabin with my signature on it. It's still legible. You've *got* to believe me. Listen, Nora, I didn't die trying to save Briggs. Far from it! As soon as he got knocked out and couldn't hold on, I left him to his fate, swam for dear life and saved my own skin. You've got to face facts.'

Knocked out! Nora heard the words clearly. Did he mean he had knocked Briggs out in order to save his own skin? She straightened her shoulders a little and swallowed, neither speaking nor moving. It was as if a bomb had gone off in her consciousness. Until the debris had settled a little and she could see through the clouds of rising dust it was best to say and do nothing. When she did speak it was calmly, with no tremor.

'Let's go over and sit against that big rock, Joe, and you tell me all about it.'

No sooner had she spoken than Sam's bellow interrupted, 'No - o - ra! Jo - oe! No - o - ra.'

'We'll have to wait till tonight,' said Nora. 'Meet me on the wharf right after supper. Bring the rods and a blanket.' She turned around and let forth a long, raucous 'Com - i - ng!' then turned back to Joe and added, her voice performing one of its miraculous metamorphoses, 'Don't look like that, Joe. It's going to be all right.' She took a step or two toward him and laid her hand on the sleeve of his coat. 'I told you that *whatever* you had done you would still be *you,* and you still *are!*'

26

CHAPTER

THE AFTERNOON seemed endless to Nora. The necessity of masquerading before her father for several hours, and before Joe, too, so as not to reveal the turmoil of her thoughts and growing suspicions, wasn't easy. They were fishing from a canoe that afternoon. She insisted on sitting in the bow perched high, and paddling as they moved from pool to pool and rise to rise. This had the advantage of not facing Joe and her father.

Knocked out! She remembered now that the newspapers had said that no water had been found in Briggs' lungs, so he hadn't died from drowning. The papers said he had suffered for years from a recognized weak heart. Such a possibility as foul play hadn't occurred to Nora as she had read the newspaper articles. They all lauded Murray Vale, a strong swimmer, for the supreme sacrifice he had made for his disabled companion. But what would the papers say if they knew Murray Vale was alive? Quickly her thoughts rushed to his defense. Briggs had probably grabbed hold of Joe with one of those viselike grapples she had heard about. It wasn't foul play to break such a hold by a knock-out blow. But possibly, it occurred to her with the startling shock of another exploding bomb, the knock-out blow had been too hard. Possibly it had been fatal! Would that mean Joe was guilty of murder?

As the afternoon wore on this possibility seemed to Nora

more and more likely. Why, otherwise, had Joe run away
and remained in hiding for over two years? A bitter taste
rose in her mouth as she stiffened herself and reinforced her
defenses to met such a reality. As the canoe headed down
Fiddle Pond for the three-mile home stretch a stiff wind
was against them. Nora sat very straight in her bow seat in
scowling silence, digging her paddle down deep into the
water, and ferociously, the epitome of defiance. One thing
was certain! She wasn't going to let this rob her of Joe. Two
can stay in hiding as well as one.

Joe told Nora his story that night under a canopy of stars
before the smoldering embers of a driftwood fire. They were
seated side by side on a sandy beach leaning against the
canoe drawn up on the shore, with a large horse-blanket
wrapped around their legs. Before Joe began, Nora thrust
her arm through his crooked elbow and interlaced the fingers
of her right hand through his left. 'Now fire away,' she said
feigning unconcern.

'Briggs and I were both counselors at a boys' camp called
Tamarack. Briggs was a new counselor. I'd never known
him before. We started out one morning on a reconnoitering
trip, to be gone possibly two days. We got off about eight
o'clock. There wasn't a cloud in the sky. We crossed the
lake a little above the camp . . .' Almost word for word
Murray repeated the account he had rehearsed two years
ago. The details came back to him clear and well-defined.
He stated the facts accurately and in sequence.

Nora listened silently, asking no questions, making no
interruptions, but with such a mounting sense of relief that
she grasped his fingers tighter and tighter in her attempt to
hold in her swelling joy. When he had reached the place in
his story when he had come to consciousness beside the old
tree-trunk on the beach she could stand it no longer. She
tugged her arm free. Tears were running down her cheeks.

She tried to stop them with the backs of her hands. 'Have you got a handkerchief?'

'What's the matter?'

'I'm so happy.'

'Happy!' he ejaculated increduously.

'The papers weren't wrong. You're just as great a hero as they said you were.'

'Of course they were wrong! What do you mean? I didn't die.'

'Lots of heroes don't die.'

'But they don't sneak off and hide for two years! Wait till you hear the rest of my story.'

'The rest is unimportant. Nothing else matters to me now.' She shoved her hand through his arm and clasped his hand again.

Joe resumed his narrative from where he left off, describing the three days he was lost in the woods; his joy when he came upon the log road; his astonishment when Mrs. Billings, the guide's wife, informed him that Murray Vale was already a hero. 'Even when Mrs. Billings told me how proud my mother would be, and Mr. Ben, and all my kid campers too, still I had no other thought but to go back and own up. But something happened. All of a sudden Mrs. Billings said Windy was there! I think I intended just to postpone going back. I'm not sure. That night is all a kind of blank. But I *am* sure I lost my nerve and beat it. Like a man running away from a battle line he's scared of. That's the kind of hero I am!'

Nora said quietly, 'After the swell job you did with Briggs on that lake, and being so plucky for three days in those woods, you had a right to lose your nerve for a minute, and jump off the deep end.'

'Jump off the deep end! You've said it! That's *just* what I did! I jumped off the deep end.'

'Well, you can swim, can't you?' Nora retorted holding tight to his hand, for he was trying to draw it away. 'It doesn't matter how deep the water is to a strong swimmer. The papers said you were a strong swimmer.' She paused. 'I'm a strong swimmer, too, Joe.'

'Oh, I can't drag *you* into my mess.'

'I'm already in your mess. I've jumped off the deep end too, Silly.'

'I ought to clear out of here tomorrow morning before breakfast and never see you again.'

'And leave me to drown, you fiend! Say, *that* would be heroic! Oh, Joe, Joe, don't be so tragic! Why, we're going to have a wonderful life together!'

Joe couldn't share her elation nor understand it. He had no inkling of the fear from which she had just been released. 'You don't appreciate the situation, Nora, or else you couldn't treat it so lightly.' There was a note of reproof in his voice. 'Don't you realize that when I acknowledge my identity everybody will question my motive for running off, and there'll be suspicions of the worst kind.'

Her own suspicions were proof of his statement. She was instantly sobered. 'Why acknowledge your identity?'

'Do you mean you'd have me go on like this? Hiding? Using a false name?'

'Actresses and authors often use false names. That's no crime.'

'But, Nora! Why, Nora! You're so honest yourself that I'd have sworn you'd have no respect for a man hiding and sneaking, telling continuous lies.'.

'Oh, I'm no George Washington, Joe! I hate hypocrisy and putting on false airs and a lot of senseless little lies, but I can tell a whopper when it serves my purpose without turning a hair. Seems to me a purpose is more important than how it's accomplished. If you've got a darned good purpose I don't believe God minds a few harmless misstatements.'

'It isn't just the misstatements. It's more fundamental. It

is the fact that I'm not genuine — not myself here.' He
paused searching for the right words. 'I'm living a lie, letting
a lie live, Nora.'

'It strikes me you're far more genuine here and far more
yourself too, than when you were trying to be a football star
and a second Windy. As for "letting a lie live" — Goodness!
In my opinion lies are like dogs. If they're sleeping and
doing no harm — for Pete's sake, why stir them up?'

'Good Lord, you can make black look like white!'

'It isn't my plan that we'll live incognito all our lives, Joe,
but I'm dead sure it's the best way to start.'

'You can't be serious, Nora! It simply isn't practical. Unless — ' he stopped abruptly. 'Do you mean to — to start
without getting married?'

'No, I don't mean that! I'd be willing to, though, if I
couldn't get you any other way. But why shouldn't we get
married?'

'There are such things as a marriage license to consider,
Nora. I haven't any name to give you unless I go back and
claim it. No birth certificate. No address. No family. No
background. No money. Nothing!'

'You got by with the draft board somehow. Jones suits
me perfectly for a name, and China for a birthplace. I've
never had any background nor family worth mention, and I
shan't miss it. In fact, I think I might find it a nuisance, especially the family. The Vale family sounds sort of snooty to
me. They might highhat Dad and my poor little mother.
She doesn't make too good an impression sometimes and I'd
hate that! I think I prefer Joe's missionary parents to
Murray's. Dead in-laws are lots easier to get along with.
As to that objection you mentioned about money, forget it.
Dad says I'm going to have oodles sometime, and I've
already got a neat little nest-egg we can start on.'

'Oh, I couldn't touch your money, Nora!'

'Don't be antediluvian! You'll have to touch it if you

touch *me*. I refuse to be carved up and have you select only
the tidbits that suit your Puritan tastes. You'll have to take
all of me — fat and lean, tender and tough, gristle, sinews,
skin, even my bones and my shekels, or you can't have as
much as one little tiny kiss. It's *all* or nothing! Which shall
it be?'

'All!' he replied instantly, a low laugh escaping him like a
waterfall in a brook, breaking through a coating of ice. She
was dissolving all of his resistance. He claimed the kiss.
There was no opposition.

Afterwards — some time afterwards — Nora exclaimed,
'Do you know what I'd simply love?' They were lying down
under the blanket now. Joe had piled more wood on the
fire. Hot red sparks were flying up to the cold white stars.

'What would you love?'

'To be the wife of a game warden!' she announced.

Joe laughed again, from pure astonishment this time. The
way she jumped from one breath-taking idea to another
reminded him of the leaping of a mountain goat from spur
to spur on a mountainside.

'I think you'd make a marvelous game warden, Joe,' she
went on. 'You'd look wonderful in those nifty uniforms they
wear. Game wardens have lovely log cabins to live in. It
would be a wonderful place for you to collect your specimens and study them, and perhaps some day you'd write a
book — something like old Thoreau's. You'd have done something *then* to make your family sit up and take notice!
Something far more worthwhile than drowning with a dead
man. He must have been dead because there was no water
found in his lungs. Doesn't that prove he didn't draw a
breath after his hand slid off your shoulders and he disappeared? So that notion of yours that he quietly slipped away
so as to save *you* is all nonsense.' She paused a moment. 'I
don't think much of that camp motto of yours.' And for the
next several sentences she meandered leisurely down a side

path of philosophical reflection. 'The motto is all right for a
boy's camp, I suppose. Some boys are such little brutes and
get a kick out of torturing the weak, like some dogs who
worry poor defenseless sheep till they die. But a grown-up
human being with responsibilities to the strong as well as
the weak must use his common sense. When I was a kid
I used to want to protect every weak thing I saw — stray cats
and dogs, wounded birds or bugs, or even worms cut in two.
It was just foolish. Lots of weak things are better dead than
alive and should be left to Nature to take care of. Nature
knows a lot better how to do it than some sentimental little
protector of all the world.'

Joe made no comment. His attention was too concentrated on Nora's proximity to listen to what she was saying.
Her rays had penetrated beneath the surface of mood and
state of mind. Her warmth was striking down into the very
depths of his being mingling with his warmth. He was
keenly conscious too, of her softness and the satisfying
solidity of her body.

'Do you see what I mean?' Still he said nothing. 'Answer
me, Joe.'

'Don't talk.'

She understood instantly and was silent.

It was a quiescent silence. She never took the initiative
when he was in a mood to make love to her, and was free
from all coquetry, waiting with something like curiosity for
him to proceed in his own way and own time, and respond-
ing warmly, generously, and with no trace of false demure-
ness. There was a quality of awed wonder in her manner,
verging on worship, because this man possessed the magic
power to re-awaken again and again the sleeping beauty in
her. Daphne had never showed awed wonder. Daphne had always expected more from him than he gave, and used all
the devices she possessed to lure him to bolder caresses.
Nora, on the other hand, limited the extent of his caresses
and made him feel he was being too audacious.

'I don't want things to happen till the right time for them to happen, Joe,' she cautioned. 'Don't go so fast.'

This attitude, combined with her quick response to him, filled him with a sense of power and effectualness. It was just as Doctor Jaquith had prophesied, the right girl would cure him of his false fear as well as any doctor.

He told her in detail about both Lilly and Daphne. Nora's suggestion that they psychoanalyze each other had worked like magic. The mere talking to another about long-concealed facts discounted their importance. There was nothing that seemed to surprise or shock Nora and nothing that bored her. No detail about his childhood or boyhood was too trivial to command her attention. Her keen interest whetted his own, to delve into his past and unfold and reveal.

When it came Nora's turn to delve, unfold, and reveal, she was equally unrepressed. She told him about Oscar Bergen with no hesitation or fear of his disapproval. Also about a certain summer spent at a girl's camp when several of the younger girls had crushes on her. It had pleased her at first and made her feel important.

'I was about sixteen then and it was a new experience to me to have a lot of admirers. But one of the older counselors pricked my shiny little soap-bubble in short order. She said I was popular with the kids simply because I was the strong, athletic type and had a mannish voice and manner. She told me what a misfortune it would be if I should turn out to be one of those queer sexless women. One of the crushes got terribly violent. I was frightened and ever since then, I've steered clear of any friendship with a girl that gets over-sentimental. Of course if I'd been born that way, it would not have been my fault, and I wouldn't have let it ruin my life. There are some perfectly wonderful women who are born that way, but I'm darned glad I don't happen to be one!'

That fear had disappeared in time, but there was another fear which had hung on and on, the fear that she was cursed with frigidity like her mother — her poor little mother with a soul about the size of a peanut and inflated social ambitions the size of a balloon. There was nothing she concealed from Joe about either her mother or father. She told him all about Sam's weakness for liquor, and his various amours. She also described her beloved old grandfather who lived in the ell of his tumbledown old farm house with rags stuffed into broken windowpanes. Neither hid any fact from the other or felt any shame in revealing it.

'We are like Adam and Eve, Joe,' she said one day. 'Not ashamed of the nakedness of each other's truths. Wouldn't it be horrid if some old snake sneaked in and made us hide our confidences from each other? Let's never let it!'

27

CHAPTER

THERE WAS one confession which Joe postponed making to Nora from day to day till nearly two weeks had slipped by. He hated to interrupt any of their limited periods of intimacy with its chilling effect. He came out with it finally following an exposition of hers on the subject of cities — New York in particular.

'I'm sick to death of the place. All that cement! Like one of those plaster casts on a broken arm or leg. I suppose way down underneath the crust there's softness and dampness and good brown earth of some kind, but you can't see it or feel it or even smell it, and the sun can't touch it nor the rain soak into it. They say lots of the parks in New York have been carted in, like those gardens in the flower shows. I'm crazy to get out of New York. What I'm getting at is, why do we dawdle? There is a war on in Europe. And there's a draft on here. Frankly, Joe, I don't want the draft to get you, before *I* do.'

'The draft won't get me.' Each time she had referred to the draft he had veered away from the subject, but he must make a clean breast of it sometime.

'Why won't it get you?'

'Because I've enlisted. I've enlisted in the Navy.'

'Enlisted! Why, Joe, I didn't know you were so anxious to go to war, any sooner than your country needs you.'

'I'm not. I hate the thought of it.'

'But how splendid of you then!'

'Splendid! Nothing of the sort! Nora, listen. I prefer the Navy to the Army. I think I'll enjoy life more on a ship than in a hole in the ground. And I'd rather drown than be horribly crippled for life. My motive was purely self-protective. I was again thinking of my own skin.'

'Joe darling! You've got a perfect complex about your own skin! However did you get by with a false name and phoney address when you enlisted?'

'All right. There's nothing false about the fact that somebody called Joe Jones exists and has existed for two years, or nothing phoney about his address — Fiddle Pond, Maine, nor his occupation either — guiding and trapping. On the blank form you fill out they ask for references. I was able to give two perfectly good ones — Seth Watts and Bill McGregor, the fire warden. They both said they'd be glad to vouch for me when I registered. If my birthplace and dead parents aroused any suspicion I never heard of it. China is a long way off to send for a verification, even if records of such facts existed in the little village where I was born. Funny, my saying "I" like that! It's come to seem like such a reality — as if I actually had been born there. I even have a dim picture in my mind of my parents. Like one of those faded daguerreotypes. I was five when they died, you know. My mother was little and frail and my father tall and lanky with a sad, kind face, something like Abraham Lincoln's. When I filled in those forms I felt no compunction. It's like being two men, each with a different history and set-up. The only trouble I had in getting by was because of my eyes.'

'Of course! I saw you in those glasses! I've heard the Navy is terribly particular about eyes.'

'That's right. I drank can after can of carrot juice. Someone told me it helped poor vision — I've heard since, though, the theory is all bunk. But anyway, they finally passed me.

The doctor who examined me knew how crazy I was to get in. I told him the job I had in mind for myself didn't require much eyesight. I told him I was going to apply for a cook's job. I've had some experience. Last winter the cook at a lumber-camp near here broke his leg and I filled in for six weeks. He lay there in a cast and taught me all the tricks. I'm a darned good cook, if I do say it, and I told that doctor so. Also I reminded him I was going to be just a common ordinary sea-man. He said none of my arguments held any water, but by some stroke of luck I got by.'

'I think it's fine of you, Joe — starting in as just a common sailor!' said Nora.

'Oh, fiddlesticks, Nora, don't you see it's self-protection again? There's less danger of recognition if I'm one of a million. And the sooner I'm off the better. There's going to be a big rush for commissions. By the time any friend of mine who might spot me in the rank and file gets his stripe, I hope to be far away from here on a big battleship — a mere dot in an anonymous horde of white hats and sailor-collars.' He gave one of his short self-deprecatory grunts supposed to be an expression of amusement. 'Sorry to pour cold water on your hero, Nora, every time you try to applaud him.'

'Why do you do it then? It's an obsession — running your-self down all the time. Another complex. Like "your own skin." '

'I do it to be honest. I'm simply stating facts. For two years now I have been a fugitive. I'm a confirmed victim of it. Fear of discovery haunts me constantly. The object of all my acts is to escape discovery.'

'That's not true, or you'd have dodged the draft. It would have been a cinch. Murray Vale is dead, Joe Jones has never been born. You had only to step across the border into Canada and take on another name to evade the draft en-tirely.'

'Maybe you're right. I considered it. It would have been the surer way to escape discovery, I guess, but —'

'But what — ?'

'I couldn't do it. I simply couldn't do it — evade a law like that which is going to hit everybody, some mighty hard — get out of all the fear and dread now and all the horrors later. Go scot-free. No, I couldn't do that! Even if I am a fugitive I've still got some self-respect.'

'Oh Joe, Joe, Joe!' she ejaculated. 'I knew it! Pour all the cold water you want to on my hero. It won't hurt him. He's carved out of marble. Your water simply washes off the dust and grime and makes him stand out clearer and brighter to me. You couldn't dodge the draft because of your self-respect!' she mimicked, 'and in almost the same breath you say the motive of all your acts is escape discovery. You're contradicting yourself, Joe darling! Don't you see your self-respect as you call it (I'd call it your *self*, your own wonderful self) won't let you do anything really shameful? But I'm wasting my breath, it's so obvious. And our precious time, too. Dad will be waking up any moment now, and I've thousands of questions. Where will you be sent to train?'

'I haven't a notion.'

'And *when* will they send you?'

'I've waited a month already. No telling.'

'Goodness gracious, it begins to look as if I was going to be the wife of a sailor before I'm the wife of a game warden!'

'I shan't let you do that! The reason I have not mentioned my enlisting till now is because I didn't want to spoil what was happening between us by telling you we'd got to break it off so soon. My orders may come any day. I may be gone for years. I may *never* come back. You have your life to live. I must leave you free. But we've had these few weeks anyway. That's something — something I've never had in my life before — something I'll never have again — something I'll carry with me wherever I go — something — '

'Oh shut up, Joe,' she interrupted, 'I'm not interested. I'm not even listening. I'm too busy planning. I guess I'd better

tell Dad about us tonight and write my boss in New York
and give notice, and break the news to the girls I live with —
that I'm engaged to be married — engaged to be married to a
man in the Navy! My, Joe, that sends shivers up and down
my spine, I'm so proud! Look!' she broke off abruptly and
gazed skyward. 'Look at that plane. Isn't it flying awfully
low?' They both stood up and walked to the edge of the
high bank on which they had eaten lunch beside Little
Hawk Pond. 'It's making a circle, Joe. They never make
circles here.'

'Looking for a place to come down, possibly. But this
pond's too small. It may be in trouble. Guess not, though.
She's climbing now. She seems all right. There she goes!'

The plane disappeared into the September haze, also all
further thought of it. Neither Joe nor Nora had the slightest
suspicion that a few minutes later the circling plane made
a forced landing and lay on its side with a broken wing
jammed against the float of Fiddle Pond Camp. There was
no messenger to convey the news, nothing to warn them
that that which Joe had said was his greatest fear in life —
discovery — was lying in wait for him like a timed bomb.

They started back to camp at four o'clock. Little Hawk
Pond was only three miles from Fiddle Pond by plane but
by boat, canoe, and automobile, it was over five. This morning they had covered the first two miles in Sam's car. They
had left the car on the side of the road at the crest of the
hill near the bare shoulder where Joe had first gazed upon
Fiddle Pond. Joe figured they would reach Sam's car well
before dark. The last mile was a steady climb by trail. Nora,
as usual, took the lead, traveling at twice her father's speed.
She hurried tonight because the pink-washed sky over the
top of the wall of trees on her left gave promise of a glorious
sunset.

She arrived on the shoulder twenty minutes before her

father and Joe joined her. A brief five minutes after she sat
down on one of the logs that fenced the road she heard the
wheezy chug of Seth's tin lizzie approaching from the direction of camp. Silas Hicks was at the wheel. He brought the
car to a halt and leaned out.

'Heard the news?'

'What news?'

'Great excitement back at camp. Plane came down.
Engine trouble. Nobody hurt, but the plane got a smashed
wing. Rich folks. They're stayin' all night. Seth's sendin' me
for more grub.'

'We saw that plane!' She came up close to the car. 'Is it a
private plane? How many were in it? Who are they?'

'Yup, private plane. Four was in it. You might say five.
One of 'em is a dog. One of them police dogs. He was the
first one out, jumped off onto the float, barkin' before any of
us got down there. The next off was a big tall feller on
crutches and the next, his mother, I heard tell. An older
lady. Name of Firth. Then there was a kid, and last the
pilot, the feller who owns the ship. Seth's put 'em into
"Beano"and "Relax." Lucky it's the end of the season and
we'd got room enough. They're the particular Ritzy type.'

'How long are they going to stay?'

'Search me! I heard the lame feller was heard sayin' to
the pilot not to mind the accident, he'd always been crazy to
fish this district. They've got their tackle and stuff. They
was on their way to some private camp up in Canada some
place. They was askin' about guides — they want two. You
got Joe hitched up for as long as you stay?'

'Yes, we've got Joe hitched up. You better hustle along,
Silas.'

The chugging car disappeared into the dark tunnel of
firs. Nora walked slowly back to the log. Joe must
not show up at Fiddle Pond tonight! It would be a calamity
for all concerned. His identity must not become known,

now, and like this — accidentally, by force of circumstance, like an undesired abortion. Joe wasn't ready for his rebirth into his old world. His self-confidence was still in process of development. He had hardly any self-pride yet, nor defiance either. They were there in the embryo of his new personality, but they needed more time to mature — more days of the nourishing warmth of their love, to make them expand and develop. These were the reasons for the gripping conviction that Joe must not return to Fiddle Pond tonight. How could she prevent it? She must avoid taking her father into her confidence if possible. He'd make a scene, and even if finally won over, he was too impulsive to be trusted with any such secret knowledge. If plied with questions about Joe's failure to return to camp he'd be sure to let the cat out of the bag somehow.

She was still desperately searching for some way out, when she heard Joe's long shrill whistle by which it had become his habit to announce his approach with her father. She whistled back, resisting the impulse to go and meet them.

'Come rest your weary bones, Dad,' she called when they were within speaking distance. 'There's still some sunset left.' She waited till they joined her than turned to Joe. 'I'm sorry, but I've got to ask you to go back,' she said casually — a little too casually.

'Back where?' Sam demanded.

'To Little Hawk Pond where we had lunch.'

'What in hell for?' Sam demanded.

'For my writing-case.' It was an article familiar to both Sam and Joe — a red morocco portfolio which she carried in her pack. Often she sat on a bank afternoons while Sam and Joe fished and occupied herself with her pen, writing letters, or in her diary.

'Joe can get your precious writing-case in the morning,' growled Sam.

'I don't want it to stay out all night. It may rain, and

there are important things in it that will be ruined if they get soaked — my diary — my checkbook and letters.'

'Look here, Nora, you aren't actually suggesting that Joe trek back three miles over that mean trail to Little Hawk and back to camp again, with night coming on, are you?'

'No. He doesn't need to come back till tomorrow. Once he gets my writing-case he can spend the night in that old shack near where we ate.'

'I won't stand for such damn fool nonsense,' sputtered Sam. 'You're not to go, Joe. I'm the boss.'

'You *are* to go, Joe! I'm the boss, too!' Nora's voice was hard and steely, her eyes, too. They conveyed no secret message to Joe. He was puzzled. There was a quality of desperation about her insistence which he couldn't understand.

'I think I'd better go, Mr. Brock, if you'll allow it. I'll turn the car around for you and change the stuff in my pack.'

'I'll help you,' said Nora.

Hidden behind the body of the big gray car, with Sam still grumbling seated inside it on the front seat, Nora said to Joe, 'You're not to go back to Little Hawk. That was just an excuse. See that big rock down there? Hide behind it till I come back later with more facts.' Then in quick, short, low-spoken sentences she told him what Silas had told her. 'Dad and I will know nothing of the accident when we get there. I shan't mention the fact I've seen Silas. Seth will think you've gone back for my portfolio and will show up tomorrow. But you won't! You mustn't!'

'What excuse will you give Seth when I fail to show up?'

'I haven't had time to think of that yet.'

'Nora! Nora!' Sam called. 'Where in God's name are you?'

'Coming, Dad.' Then to Joe, 'Don't expect me till you see me. I'll have to wait until Dad's in bed, and he may get into a late card game. Wait till I come. I won't fail. Now go so Dad can see you starting off.'

28

CHAPTER

THE SUPPER BELL was ringing when Sam and Nora drove into camp. Stars were pricking the mauve sky, darkness was fast falling, but the outline of the spread wings and the long sleek body of the plane tied up at the float was plainly visible. Both Nora's and Sam's surprise was entirely convincing to Seth, also the reason for Joe's absence.

'But I need him pretty bad. I hope he'll make it early in the mornin'. There's lots of chores to be done 'round here. Some of these folks think they'll be staying till the plane's fixed maybe. I've put 'em at the table with you in the dinin'-room.'

The tables in the dining-room were all large octagons, five in all, covered with figured oilcloth, with the usual collection of articles in the center of each table — a bottle of ketchup, a cruet for vinegar, pickles in a jar, a covered dish of butter, a bowl of sugar, a tumbler full of spoons.

Before supper when Sam was washing up, and without Nora's knowledge, he took a double quota of drinks to fortify himself for the visitors. He'd got to represent the hospitality of the club. The visitors were already seated when Nora and her father put in an appearance.

'Good evening,' said Sam before sitting down, 'Welcome to our club!' Then drew out the chair beside Lisa and sat down. 'My name's Brock. Rhymes with dock. "Hickory Dickory Dock." And this is my daughter, Miss Brock. What are your names, strangers?'

'Vale.' The elder of the two men replied curtly.

'Rhymes with trail. "It's a long, long trail," ' Lisa added, smiling at Sam. She had smelled the recent whiskey on his breath, but she showed no offence or even condescension. 'We're terribly apologetic for descending, four strong, on a private club like this. You're awfully good to take us in. We think you have a beautiful location.'

Tact was instinctive with Lisa. Kindness was instinctive with her, too. The combination was the formula for her charm which the years had not robbed of its luster. It had a mellowing effect on everyone at the table. Instantly Sam Brock felt not only at ease with Mrs. 'Trail' (as he thereafter jocosely addressed her), but the inhibitions which usually cramped his style when in the company of a highly cultured woman whom he was in mortal terror of offending, fell away from him. His natural good-fellowship expanded to its full capacity. Before the main course of meatballs and baked potatoes was over he was telling Lisa his latest shady story, leaning toward her confidentially, shaking with suppressed laughter. Lisa laughed, too. By the time the canned-pears course had begun, Sam was telling similar stories to everyone at the table, and everyone was laughing. Everyone except Nora. She sat in glowering silence. These people were not laughing *with* her father but *at* him! The older young man was egging him on.

'Come, Dad, let's go,' she said abruptly and took him away.

Joe had a long wait for Nora behind the big rock. It was nearer one o'clock than midnight when he finally heard Nora breaking through the thick underbrush surrounding his hiding place.

'I came as soon as I could,' she said after they had clung together for a moment. There was a pack strapped on her back. Joe couldn't get his arms around her satisfactorily. Between them they removed the pack and embraced again.

Then they sat down on it close together while Nora poured
out her information to Joe.

'There are four of them, your mother, your brother Windy,
Nichols — that cousin of yours — and your little step-brother,
Christopher.' She knew them all by name. She was familiar
with all the characters who stalked through Joe's memories
of his former existence. 'Seth put them at our table,' she
went on. 'You never told me your mother was so young.'

'Mother's not young — in her fifties by now. How does
she look?'

'Lovely! Slim as a rail, but not scrawny. Sort of smooth
— suave is the word. Even her hair. No fuzz. No fluff. Lies
flat, like a bird's feathers.'

'Has it gotten very gray?'

'No. Reminds me of one of those cinnamon-colored
pigeons you see sometimes in a flock of gray ones, with
streaks of white on his wings. She was lovely to Dad. Windy
was all right, too, and Christopher is a sweet kid, but Nichols
— well, excuse me! I sat opposite him at the table and
wondered if he didn't like the smell of the oilcloth. He
warmed up a little later when Dad got to telling some jokes,
but it was as plain as the nose on your face that he considered the Fiddle Pond Camp members a bunch of rough-
necks. Your mother did her best to make up for it. After
supper she stayed around a while, talked to Seth just as if
he was on her own level, and made a great hit with Mrs.
Mullins, asking her about the pattern of those doilies she's
always crocheting.'

'There was no talk about you. Seth didn't smell a rat.
Nobody was excited about your not turning up except
Danny. He gave me the scare of my life. As soon as I could
get away from the crowd, I went up to your cabin to get
the stuff into this pack — your college-boy costume and some
shirts and shoes and things. I took my flashlight and was
rummaging around in the dark when I heard a step on the

porch. Gosh, I was scared! It was Danny. He'd been hiding
in the bushes waiting for you to come back. He gibbered
and jabbered when he found it wasn't you, and the only way
I could quiet him was to get an old coat of yours and put
him out on the porch with it. He was still there when I left
the cabin, poor soul. I had to wait till Dad went to bed to
get money for you. He changed for supper tonight because
of the visitors, and his billfold was in the coat he put on. He
may not discover the money is missing till we leave. Time
enough to explain when he puts up a holler. I left him two
or three tens and am giving you fifty dollars, and my cash-on-
hand — twenty-five. That will be enough to keep you going
till we know what's best to do next.'

'Keep me going! Where? Good Lord, Nora, how long are
they staying? I know of an old shack where I can hide for
a night or two, but —'

'No telling how long they're staying. The plan is for
Nichols to go down to Boston and bring back the parts
needed for the plane, and a mechanic. Nichols may be coming and going for days yet. I heard your mother say she
thought a week of the real woods here was better for Christopher than the de luxe camp they were bound for.'

'What camp were they bound for?'

'It's in the Laurentians somewhere — a private camp
owned by the father of the girl Windy married — the girl
you call Frietchie. She's up there now with their children.
I got this all from your mother after supper. Nichols and
Windy were flying up for the last two weeks. Two others
were going in the plane but dropped out, so at the last
minute Windy called up your mother and suggested she
come along with Christopher, for the trip. That's the whole
story, and all I know up to date.'

'It's a lot! Gosh, I do get into the worst jams!'

'Have you told Seth that you've enlisted in the Navy, Joe?'

'Yes, I mentioned it to him and to Bill McGregor, too, in
case some Navy official referred to them. Why?'

'It makes it simpler. I've got a plan. Where was the recruiting station where you enlisted?'

'In Bangor. What's your plan?'

'My plan is for you to write to your recruiting station that
you've changed your address to "General Delivery, Bangor"
and for you to go on down there and hang around till your
orders come, then scoot. Perfectly simple.'

'But Nora, how in God's name shall I explain to Seth my
running off without a word?'

'Don't explain. Just send a brief telegram to Seth tomorrow that you're off to war. I'll tell him you told me your
orders had come and you hated good-byes. You can get
away with it because you're still such a mysterious character.'

'I believe it may work! You're simply wonderful! You've
saved me! But for you, I wouldn't be any use in the Navy or
Army or in any branch of the service in the war. I wouldn't
want to hold my head up if I'd run into Windy and Mother
and the others *now*, when I haven't done a damned thing
yet to prove I've got any guts. I've got a chance now — a
second chance — and it's *you* who's giving it to me. I hope to
heaven I don't flub it. Even if I don't come back.'

'Stop saying that, Joe. You've *got* to come back. I refuse
to be left holding the bag.' Abruptly she started off on another track. 'I've put all the clothes I thought you'd need in
this pack. Tomorrow I plan to go up to your cabin and
strip it of everything that might be a clue, except for a few
small things you'd like me to keep.'

'Darned lucky I showed you that place in the wall where
I hid my license and that check and my watch. Better burn
the license and check, but the watch — ' he paused. 'It's no
good as a watch. Perfectly useless — but — but it's all I've
got that's gold and lasting to give you, Nora.'

'I shall simply love it, Joe darling! I'll have it made into
a ring, and some day you can buy a huge diamond for it.'

'Where's your watch?' Joe demanded. 'It was hanging by
my cot.'

'It's in the pack. You'll find it wrapped up in your shaving things. You bet I wouldn't let you leave behind a single scrap of me that you could take along. We've exchanged watches now, Joe. This is a double-ring service.'

'Oh, Nora — Nora, there's no girl in all the world like you!'

Later she said, 'What shall I do with your beautiful specimens, Joe?'

'Burn them. They're of no value. But you might keep my notes, I suppose.'

'Your notes! You never showed me any notes! Where are they?'

'They are in a box under my bunk with some reference books I sent for. They're written on theme paper inside one of those loose-leaf notebooks. But after all, why bother? God knows what you could ever do with them. Better burn *them*, too, with the other stuff. That chapter of my life is finished. Oh, Nora! This is our last night together.'

'Our last night until our *next* one, Silly! I've got your address — General Delivery, Bangor. You'll be hearing from me as soon as I can mail a letter safely, which won't be until we get out of Fiddle Pond Camp where addresses on letters are anybody's business. Dad doesn't know it yet, but he and I are moving on just as soon as I can possibly manage it. Come, you'd better be on your way now, Joe.'

'What's the hurry? No one will be passing now. Silas went by on his way back long ago. There's a kind of cave I found further down the slope where I built a fire to keep warm till you came. Come down there, and let's be together for a while.'

The three big jewels in Orion's belt and Sirius the Dog Star — the dawn star at this time of year, were shining brightly in the northern sky when Nora trudged back along the rough gravel road-bed to Fiddle Pond. When she reached the slope that dipped down to the crescent of cabins, the horizon in the east was faintly lemon-colored. The cabins were wrapped in a gray chiffonlike pall. Not a single lighted window shone through it. Not a single ribbon of smoke rose from it. When she shoved open the door of Old Crow its hinges gave a sharp squeak. Her father's deep snoring stopped for an alarming moment, then reassuringly began again in a different key and on another theme. Nora undressed quickly, crawled into her cot and almost instantly fell into a deep dreamless sleep, which a brief hour later was interrupted by the clanging of the rising-bell. Drowsily she called out to Sam that she was skipping breakfast today.

She was again wrapped in sleep when Lisa made her startling discovery.

29

CHAPTER

L<small>ISA AND</small> C<small>HRISTOPHER</small> set out for a tour of inspection of Fiddle Pond Camp as soon as they had seen Windy and his guide off for the day in a canoe — still one of Windy's favorite means of locomotion. Lisa and Christopher inspected the cabins first and chose their favorites. 'Choosing Favorites' was an old game of theirs. They also inspected various short trails. One led to the ice-house, one to the spring, one to the dump, one to a patch of old corn-stalks and pumpkin vines, and another climbed up a sharp incline to a shelf overhanging the pond. There was a cabin at the back of the shelf, built close against the face of a cliff.

'*This* is my favorite!' Christopher announced.

'Mine, too,' Lisa agreed. 'It must be the absent guide's. Mr. Watts told me last night there was a nice view from here.'

'What a funny name it's got!' said Christopher, looking up at the birch letters, and repeating them slowly one by one. 'S-O-P, sop, H-O-R-A — horror, Sop-horror. What's that mean? Oh! I see! Sophora! Why, that's the name of our tree at home!'

'Ours isn't the only Sophora in the world,' said Lisa, a puzzled look on her face.

Thirp had accompanied them on their tour of inspection. Presently he gave a sharp bark. He repeated the bark . He had run up onto the porch of the cabin. There were two armchairs on the porch and a canvas coat thrown over the arm of one of them. Thirp was barking at the coat. He sniffed it investigatingly, darted out to Lisa, barked at her twice — sharply, peremptorily, then dashed back to the porch again, Christopher and Lisa following.

'What's got into Thirp?'

'Perhaps there are some partridge or woodcock in the pocket of this coat,' Lisa replied, lifting it from the chair.

'Thirp's not a bird dog.'

'Maybe one of his ancestors was.'

Thirp was making short whining sounds now as he gazed up at Lisa.

When Thirp became a member of the Vale family, it had been Murray who had brought him from the kennels. Windy was confined to a wheel-chair then. He couldn't even use his crutches, so Murray had fed Thirp, and sometimes taken him on tramps. Devotion to Murray was imprinted deep in Thirp's dog-consciousness. After Windy married and took Thirp away, the sound of Murray's voice in the distance would make Thirp stop short and prick up his ears, and once he got his scent he would become ecstatic with joy.

'Let's put the coat inside where he can't get it,' said Lisa.

She pulled out the wooden peg which made fast the door on the outside, pushed it open and stepped inside. Thirp's excitement increased as he circled the room, nose close to the floor, darting from spot to spot, sniffing, snuffling, frantically searching. Lisa's heart was beating as excitedly as Thirp's. There was a long bench in front of the big window. Along the back of the bench there was a row of preserve-jars and screened boxes. The bench was almost a replica of the workbench in the old carriage-house. There was even a tier of shallow drawers underneath one end of it!

'Thirp's acting crazy,' said Christopher. 'Look at him! He's gone into that back room. He's hunting for something.'

Lisa made no reply. She was still staring at the drawers.

'What do you suppose he's hunting for, Mummy?'

'A porcupine, possibly.'

'In here?'

'Or a bear.'

'Oh, boy! A bear? I guess I'll go outdoors.'

'That's right, Chris. You scamper out. I'll get Thirp and come in a minute.'

As soon as Christopher had crossed the threshold Lisa went quickly over to the drawers, and drew out the top one. There, spread out before her eyes, were long neat rows of butterflies, moths and other winged insects mounted in shallow boxes such as Murray used to make out of cardboard. Each specimen was labeled with Murray's small meticulous lettering. She stood gazing down at the display, transfixed.

'Mummy! Mummy!' called Christopher from outside. 'Why don't you come?'

Lisa tried to push the drawer back, but one side stuck. She pulled it out a little to straighten it in its tracks, but it stuck again.

'What are you doing?' Christopher inquired from the open doorway.

'Just putting this coat where the guide will surely find it when he comes back.' She laid it so that it concealed the open drawer. Christopher must not catch so much as a glimpse of its contents.

He couldn't fail to see the similarity to the collection Murray had left in the drawers in the old carriage-house. The drawers had been moved into Murray's room and were now a part of Lisa's memorabilia of her absent son. Occasionally, under her supervision, Christopher was allowed to look at the rows of fairylike bodies but never to touch them. Christopher's voice was always filled with awe as he pointed and exclaimed over the flawless handiwork of his dead hero-brother.

Lisa left both Christopher and Thirp in her cabin and went in search of Seth Watts. Seth Watts had said the

absent guide was expected back in the morning. She must
act quickly. She must warn Murray — forestall the violent
shock in store for all three of her sons — or soften it somehow.

Seth was in the main camp seated at an ancient roll-top
desk.

'Oh, Mr. Watts, I wondered if that guide you call Joe had
come back yet?'

'No, he ain't.'

'Well, when he does perhaps he can help me set up my
rod, if Mr. Brock will be good enough to lend him to me for
half an hour.'

'He ain't coming back today,' said Seth. 'I've just been
calling up Sourdnahunk and got hold of a guide up there.
I'll send him over when he comes. Maybe some time yet.'

'When is Joe coming back?'

'No tellin'.'

'Why, I thought he was one of your standbys here! Mr.
Brock was speaking of him last night. It must leave you
rather in the lurch.' She paused. Evidently she would get
no information from this man without direct questions. 'Why
didn't he come back?'

'He's gone to war.'

'Oh, he's been drafted?'

'Amounts to the same thing. The Navy's got him.'

'Has he gone for good?'

'Looks like it.'

Lisa made her second visit to the cabin on the shelf in the
afternoon. It drew her like a magnet. She left Thirp tied
up to a log bedpost in her cabin, and Christopher tied up to
a log pile in a flat-bottomed row boat, with a fishing rod.

She was surprised to see smoke coming out of the chimney
of the cabin as she approached it. She knocked on the door.
There was no answer, so she pushed it open.

'Anyone here?' Still no answer. She glanced down at the smoking ashes in the Franklin stove. There was a lot of charred paper, a smoldering book-binding or two, Gray's *Botany*, she read on one, somebody's *Anatomy* on another. There was a piece of window screening and some broken glass. The preserve jars and all the other containers too had disappeared from the bench. The drawer she had left open was closed. She crossed over to the bench and drew out the drawer. It was empty. All the drawers were empty. Her eyes fell upon two canvas-covered suitcases on top of the bench. She lifted the cover of one. The specimens were inside, packed carefully in layers. Newspapers several pages thick were spread between each layer. They were held firm by thumb tacks so that they were almost as stationary as trays. It must have taken a long time, thought Lisa.

It had indeed taken a long time! From eleven o'clock in the morning when Nora arrived at Joe's cabin, conscience-stricken to be so late, until midafternoon. It had taken a lot of strategy, too, to convey two suitcases from the back of the automobile to Joe's cabin. She had had to make her way through thick underbrush to avoid a possible encounter on the trail.

Nora had now gone to get Danny (who would ask no questions and answer none) to carry one end of the suitcases, which must be kept level, and help her put them into the back of the car.

Danny had disappeared, Mrs. Scully said. She had found him late last night sitting on Joe's porch beside the coat. She had lured him home by calling Joe's name and pointing down to their cabin, and then had locked him up. But he'd gotten away somehow. She wasn't worried. He'd come back when he was hungry enough.

Nora returned to Joe's cabin alone. When she opened the door Lisa turned around and smiled at her as she paused on the threshold.

'It's Miss Brock, isn't it?' she inquired.

Nora nodded and made a sound in her throat.

'What a delightful cabin this is! No one answered when I knocked, so I wandered in.'

It was obvious. Nora made no comment.

'Mr. Watts told me this is where the guide called Joe lives. He's been guiding you and your father the last few weeks I believe.'

Still Nora said nothing.

'Mr. Watts said he'd enlisted in the Navy, and had to leave all of a sudden yesterday. What a shame for you and your father!' It was not often that Lisa was disconcerted. Such a long, silent, hostile stare was a new experience to her. She glanced away. 'I've been admiring this big window. Such a beautiful view from it.'

'Were you in this cabin this morning?' Nora asked point-blank.

'Yes, I'm the guilty one!'

'Were you hunting for Joe?'

'Oh, no! My little son was with me and we were hunting for bears. We were on an exploring expedition,' she went on, persistently amicable. 'Playing a sort of game. Our dog barked at something that seemed to be in here, so we took the liberty of coming in.'

'Was it you who opened that drawer?'

'Guilty again!'

'You weren't hunting for bears in a drawer, were you?'

'No. For hidden treasure *then*.'

'Did you find your hidden treasure?'

'Yes, I found it,' said Lisa quietly.

She knows! I was too late. I failed him. She knows!

'I thought the hidden treasure was so beautiful,' Lisa went on, 'that I came back this afternoon to look at it again. But the drawer is empty. All the drawers are empty.'

'You should have looked in the suitcases.'

'I did. You've packed them beautifully. How kind of you to take such trouble for your guide. Have you known him long?'

'Several years. I told him I'd put his stuff away when he had to go.'

'Oh! you knew he'd enlisted, and was likely to be called?'

'He'd mentioned it.'

'Do you know where he has gone to train?'

'No, I don't, and frankly, Mrs. Firth, if I did, I'm not telling you nor anybody else. I'm not a perfect fool! Nobody goes poking into a stranger's cabin and opening drawers unless there is some good reason for it.'

'There *is* a good reason for it,' said Lisa, shedding all her artificiality. 'But frankly, I'm not telling you or anybody else what the reason is.' Lisa could be as outspoken and brusque as Nora when she chose.

'I know what the reason is.'

'I wonder.'

'Joe has told me everything, Mrs. Firth. You don't have to beat around the bush with me.'

'What has he told you?'

'Enough for me to be surprised that you can be so calm when you discover all of a sudden your son isn't dead.'

'I've known it all along. All I've discovered is his hiding place. But I don't want the others to discover it. My son, Christopher, may come in search of me at any moment. What are you going to do with those specimens?'

'Put them in the back of our car, and store them some place later. But it takes two to carry those suitcases and keep them level.'

'I'll take one end.'

'Christopher would ask questions if he saw you, and everybody else, too.'

'You're right. But they mustn't be left here. Where can we hide them?' The 'we' slipped out unexpectedly. With-

out intention, plan or warning they had become fellow conspirators.

'They'll be safe for a while in the back room,' said Nora.
'I'll cover them up with a blanket. We'd better move them
in there now.'

30

CHAPTER

Neither Lisa nor Nora was aware, at the moment, of the significance of this ordinary little act of conveying the suitcases, each bearing an end, to a place of safety. Neither knew that a bond had been conceived.

'Is this his kitchen?' asked Lisa, gazing about her after she had helped Nora tuck the blanket around the suitcases. 'His shelves? His dishes? His pots and pans? How clean! How neat! But how lonely for him — how terribly lonely!'

'I don't think he was lonely.'

'Did he stay here all winter? Has he been here all the time? What did he read? What did he do? But how could *you* know?'

'I *do* know. Come into the other room and I'll show you something that he did. Something he never showed even me.' Lisa followed after Nora to the tier of drawers. 'You saw all the specimens, but what do you think I found in the box under his bed? A lot of heavy old scientific books, and this. His notes, he called it. It's like a book. It's got a title and chapters, too. And here's a whole lot of sketches that go with it.' She had drawn out the shallow, trundlebed-shaped box under the cot and taken out two loose-leaf note-books with stiff black covers.

Lisa opened one of them. In Murray's characteristic lettering, she read on the title page 'Winged Animals I Have Known,' by Eliot Jones. 'Eliot?' she queried when she dared trust herself to speak. 'Your father said his name was Joe Jones.'

'It's Eliot when he signs it.'

Lisa turned back to the title page. In the lower left-hand corner, in parenthesis, appeared the information 'For Youngsters Chiefly, by an Amateur.'

'This ought to be good,' she remarked. 'Murray knows a youngster's point-of-view perfectly. For years he was a counselor for little boys at a summer camp.'

'I know that. But notice that word "chiefly"? His book is a lot more than just a story-book for little boys, and if he's such an amateur why bother with all those scientific volumes I burned up? In my opinion the reason Joe said for "youngsters" and "by an amateur" is because he's apologetic about everything he does, except his cooking. He's got a terrific inferiority complex.'

'You seem to know Murray well, Nora,' said Lisa. 'May I call you that? Those are very perceiving comments of yours. By the way,' she broke off, 'if you haven't any special use for this manuscript, I should like to keep it very much. Naturally,' she added, 'being his mother.'

'But I *have* got a special use for it.' Did this woman imply that the fact that she had borne Murray gave her certain rights and prerogatives?

'What do you mean to do with it?'

'Keep it till Joe gets back, and if he doesn't get back, give it to his child.'

'His child! Oh!' She paused, and added, 'I thought there must be some special reason why you were taking such beautiful care of Murray's things. So that's it!'

The very gentleness of Lisa's tone conveyed the conclusion she had jumped to. It was like gasoline on the still smoldering resentment which Lisa's presence here had kindled in Nora.

'No! It's not it!' she flared. She was seized with a paradoxical impulse to shock the woman whom she wanted so terribly to please. 'But it's *going* to be it, just as soon as I can work it. I wasn't going to tell you, but you might as well know the truth first as last. Joe and I are going to get married at the first minute it's possible. But if he's run over or killed some way before we can get to a minister's, don't think for a minute you're going to be embarrassed by having a little grandson left on your doorstep. I'm not that kind of person, even though my name isn't in the Social Register. If I was in such a jam you may be dead sure you'd never hear from me. Never! Never! Never!' she stopped abruptly, more shocked herself at her outburst than Lisa.

Lisa replied, 'I don't blame you a bit for hitting back at me. I had no business to draw such a conclusion. I didn't know anything about you. I made a mistake and I'm sorry.'

It was an apology — simple and straightforward. This experienced, self-possessed woman was not too proud to admit a mistake and say she was sorry. In spite of herself, Nora felt her rage giving way to admiration. But she made a few more thrusts.

'You haven't got to have me as a daughter-in-law, Mrs. Firth,' she went on, 'I'm marrying Joe Jones — Eliot Jones on the marriage license, not Murray Vale. Joe and I are going to start a line of our own. None of the Vales need be afraid they've got to have Dad around. I saw how you all felt about Dad last night. The way that nephew of yours treated him wasn't lost on me.'

'Nor on me, either. Nicholas is impossibly rude at times. I liked your father. I think he's sort of a dear. And I like *you*, too. What's more, I admire you, Nora. You're so fearless and self-confident.'

'I'm not really self-confident, and half the time that don't-give-a-hang manner of mine is just a bluff — so I won't get hurt. I've had a lot of snubs in my life.'

'And you're beautifully honest!' Lisa exclaimed. 'We're going to get on!'

'Joe said you were like this.'

'Like what?'

'Could make anybody like you, if you wanted to.'

'Well, I want very, very much to make *you* like me, Nora. Will you come over to my cabin tonight after Christopher is in bed, and tell me more about Murray?'

Lisa's cabin was divided into two rooms. There was no danger that Christopher would hear the conversation on the other side of the partition, should he wake up. The partition was made of logs and ran to the ceiling.

Lisa and Nora sat one on each side of the Franklin stove, conversing in guarded tones. Nora asked the first question.

'How did you find out that your son was alive, Mrs. Firth?'

Lisa described Jim Billings' discovery of Murray's glasses and other clues, and Mr. Ben's call on her just after the hanging of Murray's portrait in the place of honor in the hall.

'I had the portrait hung upstairs in my own sitting room the day after Mr. Ben brought me his news.'

'Oh, you thought that your son, instead of being a hero, had done something cowardly or worse, didn't you?'

'I didn't know,' Lisa replied candidly. 'Jim Billings thought it looked that way. But if Murray did do anything that seemed cowardly or unethical, I feel sure it was simply because he got panicky. It was a terrific storm.'

'He didn't get panicky,' said Nora. 'Not during the storm. Not till several days later, when you'd all put him up on a pedestal. He couldn't bear to knock himself down before Windy and the others.'

'Has Murray told you what happened on the lake?'

'Yes, everything!'

'Will you tell me?'

'Yes, I'll start at the beginning the way he did.'

As Lisa listened to Nora's clear, unhesitating account of facts that had long been shrouded in mystery and speculation, her worst fears fell away. There was no joy in life, she thought, to compare with the bliss of relief from a long-haunting anxiety. Murray's account from this girl's lips rang true, and was absolutely convincing to Lisa. But when repeated and discussed there would be skeptics. It was Nora who first expressed recognition of this fact.

'There were no witnesses,' she said. 'Lots of people wouldn't understand why anybody would run away and hide, unless he had done something to run away and hide from.'

'That's true,' Lisa replied, brow knit and thoughtful. 'There are always doubting Thomases who demand proofs. Oh, how I *wish* we had something tangible to support Murray's word that he put up that fight for Briggs.'

'Do *you* doubt his word?'

'No. But that's because I know Murray. Others, like Jim Billings, for instance, haven't that insight. Jim insists that all the clues he found be kept so if Murray turns up he can account for them. He's even saving a piece of canvas with mysterious marks on it, which he salvaged when they patched the canoe.'

'Has this Jim Billings, with all his clues, got it in his mind that Joe knocked Briggs out?'

'It has occurred to him, but he believes the results were unintentional.'

'So Joe is up against *that*, is he? I suppose if this smart Jim Billings got a chance he'd accuse him of his horrid suspicions, wouldn't he?'

'No, Jim is our friend. He *wants* to believe Murray tried to save Briggs, but he's one of the doubting Thomases — a very important one, too. His conviction will carry great weight.'

'Oh, that type will never be convinced. When this darned war is over Joe and I will go and live in Australia, or New Zealand, or somewhere way off.'

'That won't be necessary. Let's just wait. Memories fade. People forget. *Time's* the great cure-all.'

'How many are there who are in the know about Joe?'
asked Nora.

'Jim Billings and his wife, Mr. Ben, my husband, myself,
Doctor Jaquith — six. And now you.'

'Who's Doctor Jaquith?'

'He is a psychiatrist and a very wise man. I often turn
to him for advice.'

'From what Joe said about you, I didn't suppose you ever
needed it. You're awfully different from what I thought.'

'How?'

'You're so — so un-dead-sure! Joe said he always used to do
what you thought best because he found it usually proved to
be best. I expected you'd be a terribly domineering mother.'

'Oh, dear!' Lisa exclaimed. 'What I want most in the
world is *not* to be a domineering mother.'

'Perhaps,' said Nora reflectively, 'a person can be dominated
by someone who is not domineering.'

'Just as one can be dominated by a false fear,' Lisa com-
mented.

'I don't think Windy is the domineering type either,' Nora
went on judicially, pursuing her own thought. 'He's just
sure of himself, yet Joe has always been dominated by
Windy, too. He was a sort of gilded image of perfection to
him, a model of what he'd like to be, and what everybody
was urging and trying to help him to be. I don't say it was
Windy's fault. It was just one of those things.'

'Why, Nora, how did you discover all these things about
Murray in so short a time?'

'It's mutual. We both have been discovering things.
We've been psychoanalyzing each other. We've swapped
even our kid nicknames. He knows now that one of my nicknames was "Tom Cat" (I scratched a boy's face in a fight
till it bled). And I know that one of his nicknames was
"Johnny-Jump-Up," and what it meant. If I were a real
psychoanalyst, one of the first things I'd do would be to dig

up a patient's nicknames and get them out into the open.
Nicknames are to blame for a lot of inhibitions and com-
plexes.'

'How did you ever know so much about psychoanalysis?'

'I don't, much. But one of the girls I live with in New York
was psychoed once, and everybody has seen *Lady in the
Dark*. I'd be pretty dumb not to know the rudiments. Look,'
she broke off, 'would you like to see my engagement ring?'
Her resistance to Lisa was fast disappearing.

'I'd love to see it.'

Nora pulled up the long sleeve of her flannel shirt and
stretched out her left wrist. Joe's watch was strapped on it.

'Joe said you gave it to him when he was eighteen.'

Lisa took Nora's wrist in her hand, gazing down silently
at the familiar watch. She couldn't trust herself to speak.

Nora misinterpreted her silence, 'Perhaps you don't like
my having it?'

'I love your having it!'

'It doesn't keep time. You can't even wind it. Joe never
had it repaired after grinding the stem against the canoe
for over an hour with Briggs' dead weight on top. He says
it's a wonder it didn't break the stem off.'

Lisa's heart seemed to skip a beat. 'Nora!' she exclaimed,
'You must give that watch to me!'

'What for?'

'It's our evidence!'

'Our evidence?'

'Yes. Listen, Nora. I told you about those marks on the
canoe. What made them is still a mystery to Jim. Perhaps
the stem of Murray's watch made them, Nora, when he was
holding Briggs' body onto the canoe. And it will prove he
put up a good fight for him.'

'Take it! Take it!' said Nora and began unbuckling the
strap, then stopped abruptly. 'But wait a minute! How are
you going to explain to Jim Billings where you got it?'

'I'm going to tell him exactly where I got it, and also the others who have known that Murray didn't die.'

'But you'll have to tell them that Joe's enlisted in the Navy! A private detective could track him down as easy as anything, if he wanted to. I don't think I want that done.'

'Nor I either, Nora. I don't want any circumstances to arise that will force Murray to acknowledge his name and family until the time is right for it. Even though it may be never.'

'Oh, do you feel that way, too?'

'What importance is a name and family as compared to a personality and its salvation? If Murray is a happier, freer and more useful human being as Eliot Jones, why resume a name and background that hampers and galls?'

'But,' queried Nora, brow puckered, 'isn't it sort of running away? Sort of — not facing the facts?' she groped.

'Perhaps. A little,' Lisa acknowledged. 'Of course I *hope* he'll come back!'

'So do I,' said Nora. There was a pause. Nora broke it. 'Well, here's the watch. Be careful of it. I want it back again.'

'You shall have it just as soon as Jim has compared it with the marks on the canoe. What is your address?'

'I'll write it here.' She reached for a sheet of paper. 'I won't be there long, but the girls I live with will know where to reach me.'

Lisa took both the watch and address, placed them carefully in a pocket of her sport shirt. There was a pause. Nora was gazing into the fire. Presently she looked up. 'Look here, Mrs. Firth, would you like to see your son? Because if you do, I can arrange it. He isn't far away.'

'That's dear of you, Nora. But I think not just now.'

'But you're his own mother!'

'Often an own mother must sit in the waiting-room and fold her hands while her child is wheeled off to the anesthetist and surgeon. I'm satisfied to leave him to you for the present.'

'You're right, I guess,' Nora agreed. 'It might upset the applecart. Have you any message for Joe? I'll be seeing him in a day or two.'

'Tell him I've fallen in love with you, too,' said Lisa lightly.

'I think you're a perfectly grand person, Mrs. Firth.'

'Will you wait here just a minute?' asked Lisa. 'I want to get something.'

She took the kerosene lamp, leaving Nora in semi-darkness, and went into the back room. From the corner of her suitcase she produced a small leather jewel-case, empty except for an extra pair of cuff-links and a diamond bracelet and brooch, which she had brought to wear evenings at the Laurentian camp. The brooch had belonged to Grandmother Vale, who almost invariably used to wear it at her throat at the bottom of her high stiff collars. It appeared in the Sargent portrait, life size, pinned at her bosom in the center of the wide off-the-shoulders rosepoint bertha. It consisted of a large diamond set low in gold surrounded by countless low-set satellites. Grandmother Vale had given it to Lisa in her will as an 'expression of approval,' she had stated. Lisa quickly wrapped it in paper and put it in an envelope, sticking the flap down tightly, then snapping an elastic band around it. Murray was familiar with the brooch. It would carry a message far more eloquent than anything she could say or write.

She returned to the front room and gave it to Nora. 'Don't open this until you see Murray, please. It is a little engagement present I'm giving you.'

31

CHAPTER

Lɪꜱᴀ sat in her upstairs sitting room writing letters. The fragrance of lilacs drifted into the open window. The white lilac bushes planted close to the house had grown so tall that she could see their white plumes waving just below the window sill and smell their fragrance. Occasionally she caught a breath from the pink hawthorn tree, and sometimes the heliotropelike scent from a bowl of viburnum which she had picked from the shrubs below. The combination was more delicious than any brand of 'Mille Fleur' that could be purchased in any shop, and was contributed gratis, not even as a reward for labor. None of the trees and shrubs, so generously pouring out their fragrance this morning, had received any labor or care worth mentioning since the beginning of the war.

Every Sunday for the last four years there were two letters which Lisa seldom failed to write at some time during the day. Both letters were mailed in envelopes with red, white, and blue borders; both bore airmail stamps, but they flew in opposite directions. One was addressed to Lieutenant Fabia Vale, and reached her somewhere in Italy at a hospital where she was a nurse. The other was addressed to Joseph Jones, C.Q.M., and reached him somewhere in the Pacific. His replies to Lisa were addressed to General Delivery, Boston, and she received them straight from the hands of a post office official.

The date Lisa placed at the top of her letters today was May 14, 1945. It was nearly six years now since Murray's disappearance, since his death, according to the public's assumption. Lisa wondered if suspicions hadn't occurred to certain members of the Vale family. Rosa and Justine had both expressed surprise that no stone had been erected as a record of Murray's death. Once, long ago, Lloyd and Hilary had suggested that the small pond where Murray's body was supposed to be imprisoned be drained so as to recover something in the way of identification or remains to bury in the family lot, and had thought her strong opposition strange. Charlotte had once gone so far as to say that she didn't feel at all sure that Murray's body was there! Charlotte had never repeated her skepticism. Perhaps, Lisa thought, because she had been aware it had struck some too-tender spot.

These few instances were the only indications Lisa had had that Murray's death had been doubted. The world-at-large had accepted it. It was just as she had predicted. Time had dulled the details of the tragedy. The war with all its suffering and outstanding acts of heroism had made the failure to rescue a drowning boy at a summer-camp fade into insignificance.

Murray's watch had accomplished its mission perfectly. Its ribbed stem had fitted the imprint in the paint like the glass slipper Cinderella's foot. Jim Billings had needed no other proof to be convinced that Lisa's account, as told her by Nora Brock, was true. Moreover, the knots in the handkerchief had been explained, and were added testimony that Murray had employed every means at his disposal to rescue Briggs.

Murray had departed for his first training-center in less than a week after Lisa decided not to see him. Lisa hadn't seen him yet. Nora had written Lisa from somewhere in the vicinity of Murray's first training-center, announcing that she had become Mrs. Eliot Jones, and was determined to follow Joe wherever he was sent, for as long as the powers-that-be allowed it. When he went overseas she had a plan up her sleeve to wangle her way to some port near his ship's activities. It was with this end in view that she had plunged into a six-weeks' indoctrination course in overseas club work in Washington, D.C. Joe sailed for the Pacific in March, 1942. A few weeks later Nora followed him with a Red Cross Canteen unit. She was one of the lucky ones to be sent to the area which she had stated as her preference.

The first Lisa knew of it was when she received a letter from Nora bearing a New Guinea stamp. She announced that she was now in uniform as well as Joe — a bona fide Red Cross club-worker.

'Most of the boys don't know I'm married and hanging around this port in case my sailor turns up.' Which actually happened finally! Joe's ship was tied up for a whole fort-night near Nora's canteen, and every time he had shore liberty Nora was on hand.

'With the result,' she wrote some months later, 'that I've lost my job, anyway temporarily. The Red Cross is packing me off to the U.S.A., because, believe it or not, I'm going to have a baby! I love to write it. I'd like to *shout* it! But I shan't be coming back East yet awhile. I'm going to wait for Joe on the coast nearest his ship. San Diego, I think. I have a hunch he'll be getting a furlough one of these days, and I don't want to waste any of the precious hours getting across the continent to him.'

Nora's baby was an eight-pound boy. On his birth certifi-cate he was Murray V. Jones. The V was for Victory, she told anyone who asked. In San Diego, Nora lived with a friend who also had a baby. As soon as Vee was old enough to leave with the friend for brief periods, Nora volunteered as a nurse's aid at the Red Cross chapter. She'd always longed to be a doctor. Nursing was the nearest thing to it.

Nora had remained in San Diego for three years, refusing

to leave for any long period for fear it might be just the time
when her presentiment that Joe would turn up again would
be realized. But she was not rewarded. He had never turned
up on these shores. A few months ago Nora had received
word that her father had had a serious operation and
couldn't live long. She had been granted a leave of absence
by the Red Cross and was now established in her father's
apartment in Detroit, nursing him herself, performing countless homely little tasks for him and rejoicing at Vee's devotion to his grandfather.

She had a nurse to spell her occasionally and had been
able to run down to New York for several short trips. Lisa
had met her there ten days ago, and they had arranged that
she should come to Boston over this weekend, stay at the
Ritz, and come out on Sunday for midday dinner — simply
as a casual acquaintance whom Lisa had met on one of her
vacation trips. Lisa was always extending hospitality to
casual acquaintances and Sunday noon was one of her favorite times for entertaining all sorts and varieties of people.

Lisa sealed the envelope addressed to Fabia, placed it on
the top of her desk, drew out another sheet of paper, dated
it, and began:

Dear Murray:
Sunday morning again, mid-May and the place is looking
just the same as when you last saw it, only everything is
weedier and shaggier, except the Sophora.

She paused and glanced out at the tree visible from her
window.

The Sophora is acting in its usual shy, backward manner
in the Spring. Not a leaf out yet. I've had your old tree-
house restored for Christopher and he adores it. So too will
Vee some day.
First a word about what is lying on my desk as I write.
Nora had an advance copy sent me. It's all her doings. All

I did was to suggest that she send the manuscript to Mr. Simms, a man I know connected with a New York publishing house. I wrote Mr. Simms that I'd run across the manuscript by mere chance one summer in Maine, and at that time the author's name was unknown to me. Each statement is literally a fact. An advanced copy has of course gone to you too, but books are so often delayed this letter may reach you first. The jacket on the book is pale yellow with several butterflies, some brown moths, a 'darning-needle,' and what looks to me like a wild honey bee flying across your title, 'Winged Animals I have Known,' and the author's name 'Eliot Jones.' There are several pages of colored reproductions of your specimens and many of your sketches. Mr. Simms had a Naturalist check up on your facts and references, and he told Mr. Simms that he thought your book was a real contribution to science. The other day Windy picked it up and remarked, 'Murray would have been interested in this,' then tossed it back on the table and nothing more was said. Nobody suspects you have the remotest connection with the book.

Also nobody suspects I have a son in the Pacific. A Grey Lady at the hospital where I work told me the other day that I was very lucky to have only a daughter in a base hospital in Italy to worry about. She said that I simply couldn't imagine the anxiety which *she* woke up to every morning of her life, thinking about her Teddy on a ship which might at any moment be attacked by one of those horrible Kamikazes. I wanted to tell her we couldn't all wear our hearts on our sleeves.

Lisa glanced up at the speaking likeness of Murray over the mantel. He was a petty officer now — a Chief Quartermaster, which Lisa had learned was one of the most responsible petty officers' positions on the ship. He was 'right-hand man' to the Captain, Navigator, or Officer of the Deck. His station when on duty was in the pilot house, chart house, or on the bridge. He must know the 'rules of the road,' and often stand quarter-deck watch. Still gazing at his portrait,

Lisa tried to visualize him on the bridge dressed in his Navy uniform. That soft, tender quality around his mouth must have disappeared now. There would be a stern look in his eyes instead of that expectant smile. He would be listening to the drone of an enemy aeroplane instead of to the song of a bird; peering through binoculars at mysterious specks on the horizon that might mean approaching death, instead of through his beloved microscope at scales on a butterfly's wings. Of how much greater value the service to his country if he had been in some laboratory searching for malaria germs. What a mistake to place a boy like Murray on the bridge of a ship. Yet it made her proud. His ship had been far behind the battle lines so far. Way back in '42 Murray had written Lisa that she need have no anxiety for his life. The Japs wouldn't waste any gunpowder on 'Old Whale.'

For four years 'Old Whale,' as Murray usually called his ship in his letters, had been a sort of concentration camp for its two hundred odd men, who were as crazy to see action as any bunch of good red-blooded American kids, who enlisted to serve their country and prove 'they'd got what it takes.' For four years the men and officers assigned to the *U.S.S. Cetus* had seen no action, unless they had managed to get transferred.

The *Cetus* wasn't a battleship, aircraft carrier, cruiser, destroyer, P.T., submarine, or minesweeper. On the Navy's list of ships and planes its type wasn't even mentioned as a rule. It was a Naval Auxiliary — a cargo ship — a big, bulky, slow-moving hulk, its hold filled with homely supplies to keep men's bodies covered, washed, and fed. It carried no troops, no planes, no weapons for the combat forces to kill the Japs with. It lacked all glamour. It tied up at ports which Murray's censored letters never called by their actual names, located far behind the active theater of the war. The crew was as completely cut off from its drama and excitement and applause as a crew of stage-hands, pulling ropes and turning cranks, offstage during a play, and not half as essential. His descriptions of the surrounding country were graphic. Reefs of coral, naked wastes of sand. For a man who loved the woods, Lisa wrote Murray, whose refuge when he was a boy was in the treetops, and whose chief interest was natural history — birds, butterflies, growing things — what a prison!

'Nothing of the sort,' Murray had replied in his next letter. 'There are plenty of growing things here. Every time I get shore liberty I bring back new specimens. Thank heaven I've brought my magnifying glass. I don't even have to go ashore for some of my specimens. At present I'm studying a fascinating species of animal life called *cimex lectularius,* commonly known as bedbug. I have a glorious supply of larvae and hundreds of perfect hatched specimens in a confined area allotted to me by our doc, who's got his microscope with him. He lends it to me occasionally. Our doc is a good man. He is "Nick" to me, when we're alone, and I'm "Bug" to him. We are great pals. Of course, officers aren't supposed to fraternize with enlisted men but many of the etiquette rules aren't enforced on "Old Hulk," by our Old Man.'

Even though Murray had no rank, his rating was as high as any man's on his ship. His estimate of his qualifications as a cook had not been shared by the Selection Department of the Navy. He had been assigned to quite a different type of Service School than that for cooks. His first billet on the *Cetus* was 'pharmacist's mate.' How he had found his way to a job on the bridge Lisa didn't know, especially in view of his eyesight. He explained that on the 'Old Whale' he guessed they were not so fussy about a man's qualifications. Besides, his eyes were better now.

Lisa reached for a fresh sheet of paper, then paused, looking off into space. She had come to the most important part of her letter and didn't know how to proceed. She wrote a line or two, reread it, then tore it up and took a fresh sheet. She repeated the false start and took a third sheet.

Last February the long delayed opportunity to prove his courage in a crisis had come to Murray at last. He had grasped it instantly. He made little of it to Lisa, referred to it briefly. 'All I did was to haul a man off a burning raft.' He had gone into only a few more details about the attack itself, which had at last broken the ship's virgin record of no action. 'There was plenty of action at last on board "Old Whale," from the first moment an enemy plane was sighted (just my luck not to have been on the bridge), till the Old Man's order "Prepare to abandon ship." Plenty of action afterwards too, though again it was my rotten luck to be out of a lot of it, stuck on a reef. "Old Whale" didn't sink after all. But it will be some time before she's in working order again and I hope my request for a transfer will be granted at last.'

In his letter to Nora he had been more specific about the man he had hauled off the raft. Nora had sent his letter to Lisa. 'I was in a life-boat when I first saw him,' Murray wrote, 'he was wounded and lying face down on the raft, inside a rectangle of flames. When I jumped overboard to get him it was my idea to bring him back to the life-boat, but it took quite a while, and I never saw the life-boat again, nor anything else to pick us up. After a while I decided to swim for a coral reef I saw in the distance. It was some undertaking. A squall blew up. The guy couldn't help any. He was absolutely out. For a long while I didn't know who it was. His face was smeared and his nose smashed in. I didn't think I was going to make it. I sort of lost consciousness at times. Funny, but I had the darndest feeling — almost conviction — that I'd found Briggs and was swimming for dear life back to that old dead tree with him. I was so mixed up that some of the old slogans came back, such as "You can do what you want to if you want to do it enough," and also that old Tamarack motto: "Protect the weak." I tell you it felt simply wonderful when I finally bumped head on into that old tree — or reef, whichever it was. This time I wasn't alone! This

time I had Briggs! And he was alive! I thanked God when
he began to gag and sputter!'

Lisa had hesitated in her previous letters to write freely
to Murray about the rescue, but now she decided to disregard restraint and give in to her impulse. This was her final
draft:

> Certainly now you can feel no more compunction for not
> having drowned with Briggs. If you hadn't been alive that
> young man on the raft would probably never have survived.
> Whatever debt you felt you owed to the human race, be-
> cause one man in your care died has been paid now by
> saving another, and whatever doubt you felt about your
> courage in a crisis has been removed. What reason is there
> now to conceal your identity? Isn't your object won? I am
> going to indulge in a quotation, just as if I were Mr. Ben.
> 'From fearful trip, the victor ship comes in with object won.'
> That's a line from 'O Captain, My Captain.' Forgive me for
> waxing poetical, and sentimental, too, all in one paragraph;
> but I very much want the family and the world to know
> about the book, and Nora and Vee, and that you're in the
> Navy with the combat forces in the Pacific. I long to tell
> that Gray Lady friend of mine that I've as much reason as
> she to wake up in the morning anxious.

She paused and gazed off into space. It had been nine
weeks now since either she or Nora had received any letter
from Murray. Murray had been transferred to another ship —
another cargo ship, much to his disappointment, but at least
the ship was being sent into a danger zone, proudly he had
informed Nora. Lisa had avoided asking Nora questions.
They each had refrained from expressing anxiety about the
long silence. Lisa bent over the letter on her desk and continued:

> I wrote you last week of our plan for today. Nora is
> already at the Ritz. I called her up bright and early. Os-
> tensibly my party is in honor of Nichols. He is here on leave,
> having just returned by plane from England. He looks very

handsome in his Major's uniform. He's still in the Ordnance
Department with headquarters in Washington. Several
weeks ago he was sent to London on some important errand.
Aunt Rosa has been beside herself with anxiety for fear a
bomb might fall on his hotel.

Now I must go and make my beds. Beds and tubs are now
my daily exercise. We're very lucky to have old Delia to
cook and old Nellie to put the food on the table. Christopher is proving an excellent bus boy. No more now. I'll
tell you all about Nora's first visit here next time I write.

Love,
Mother.

P.S. Quite a while now since either Nora or I have had a
letter from you. But we know outgoing mails are infrequent
from atolls, and 'no news is good news.'

How the trite phrases helped!

It wasn't until this letter was mailed that Lisa wished she
had omitted that line from Walt Whitman's 'O Captain! My
Captain!'

When she quoted it the poem had been but a dim
memory. She remembered it chiefly as a hymn of victory for
a ship's triumphant return, and a tribute to an idolized
leader. She hadn't realized to what extent it was also a
lament for the captain who had died just before his ship
reached its home port. Later Lisa reread the poem to refresh
her memory. Immediately the possible analogy loomed large
before her. Immediately she dismissed it, or tried to. The
dirgelike refrain repeated at the end of each verse, 'fallen
cold and dead,' kept recurring to her at unexpected times
and places, like a pain which one tries to discount but which
persists. What if Murray —— 'Stop it! Stop it!' she admon-
ished herself. She wasn't superstitious. She didn't believe
in omens. Her intelligence told her that whatever the source
of that line which she had quoted to Murray it could have
no effect on the sequence of events in store for him. True,
true, but there was the possibility of a tragic coincidence!

32

CHAPTER

Lɪsᴀ's luncheon guests were all arriving by automobile in spite of the gas shortage. Nichols's contribution of one of his 'leave' gas coupons was an immense boon to Windy who lived fifteen miles out. Windy was to pick up June and Tuck and Aunt Charlotte.

Windy was surprised to receive a telephone call from June about nine o'clock. 'Have you seen the last edition of *Leader*?'

'No. Why?'

'Never mind. Go and look an page 47,' she said and rang off.

Windy went in search of the periodical but Frietchie said it hadn't been delivered.

Half an hour after June rang off Aunt Charlotte was on the phone. 'Hello, Windy. This is Aunt Charlotte. Does your mother take *Leader*?'

'No, *Newsweek*. Why?'

'I'm afraid something in *Leader* will upset her.'

'What's in it?'

'Well, you know how she has been talking about that nature book that's just come out, by someone by the name of Eliot Jones?'

'Yes, I've seen the book.'

'Well, I was suspicious when I saw how she acted and looked, sort of starry-eyed — almost teary. I was there when the book came.'

'Well, what of it? What's this all about?'

'A picture of Eliot Jones is in *Leader*, not as the author of the book, but in that column *Leader* is running now called "Heroes." He's just been awarded a medal and there's a picture of him receiving it. It looks like Murray.'

'Oh, you mean this chap has a strong resemblance to Murray? I don't think that will upset mother.'

'I thought it was just a resemblance, at first. But there is a scar on his left eyebrow, Windy.' There was a pause, then in a lower tone, 'You know Murray's body was never found. I've always wondered about it. Haven't you?'

'At first — a little,' Windy acknowledged. 'Look here, Aunt Charlotte, Frietchie and I will be right in and see you at June's.'

'Guess there's no doubt about it,' said Windy, gazing at the picture. 'I watched the doctor when he sewed up that eyebrow. I remember even the angle. This will be a shock to Mother.'

The picture appeared half-way down a single column of print headed HEROES in black capitals. Murray was standing very straight, his shoulders squared, while an admiral was pinning a medal on his chest.

'Read what it says, Windy,' said June, 'it's sort of stirring. Read it.'

Silently Windy's eyes scanned the lines. Afterwards he took out his handkerchief and blew his nose hard.

Lisa had arranged that Nora should arrive after the other guests had assembled and cocktails were under way. This would give her time to pave the way for Nora, make casual mention that another guest was expected, and provide the family with a few informatory facts about her.

Nora and she had talked over the details. They agreed it was wiser not to refer to the fact that she was Mrs. Eliot

Jones — the wife of the author of the book which Lisa had
had lying about in conspicuous places of late. It would be
playing safer to arouse as little interest in Nora as possible.
Fortunately Jones was a common name. It was decided to
introduce her as Mrs. Joe Jones as she was known in San
Diego. She preferred it to Eliot. Of course it was possible
that Windy and Christopher might recognize her, and possibly Nichols ('though he saw me only that one night at
Fiddle Pond at supper,' said Nora, 'when he was so snooty
and I got mad'), but it seemed unlikely in a different setting,
in different clothes, and under a different name.

Nichols arrived first, bringing his mother and father —
Lloyd and Rosa, and his unmarried sister, Henrietta. Shortly
after, Hilary and Justine followed in their ancient seven-
passenger limousine crowded to its wide running-board with
their three daughters and respective spouses. Windy's car,
bearing June, Tuck, Frietchie, Aunt Charlotte, and Thirp,
was the last to arrive. It had been decided that no reference
would be made to the article in the periodical until after
dinner.

'I'm expecting another guest today,' Lisa remarked when
Barry was refilling the cocktail glasses. 'A young woman I
met at a Maine camp. She's at the Ritz, and was to be alone
for dinner today, so I asked her to join us. She has been a
Red Cross worker in the Pacific somewhere and I think
we'll find her interesting.'

'Married or single?' Nichols inquired.

'Married, Nichols. Her husband is in the Navy, also somewhere in the Pacific.'

'What is her name?' inquired Rosa, sipping her tomato
juice.

'Jones.'

'Jones? Jones? What Jones?' Lloyd inquired frowning,
sipping *his* tomato juice.

'She says she is known as Mrs. Joe Jones in San Diego

where she now lives,' Lisa replied, 'which sounds to me like
an abbreviation of Joseph Jones.'

'Joseph Jones? Joseph Jones?' Hilary repeated, also frowning, also sipping tomato juice.

'You may remember her, Windy,' said Lisa, deciding it
wiser to anticipate the possibility and avoid a surprise. 'Her
name was Brock — Nora Brock. We met her that fall at that
place up in Maine where Nichols had to make a forced
landing.'

'Of course I remember her!' exclaimed Windy. 'A good-
looker, with a marvelous old scout of a father. Both wonderful sportsmen. I never saw a girl cast a prettier fly.'

'Nor a prettier shadow, either!' Nichols remarked. 'Though
she was well covered with dungarees the one time I saw
her. You don't mean to say she's the lady expected? She's
got a look in her eyes as fierce as an eagle's, if she doesn't
approve of your style. And she certainly didn't approve of
mine! She is the independent goddess type. A perfect Diana.
Utterly fearless.' He turned to Lisa. 'Put her beside me at
the table, will you? I'd like nothing better than to eat
humble-pie and get a soft look out of that girl!'

A taxicab drove up the curved driveway at this point.
Everyone looked out of the long French windows as Nora,
dressed in her Red Cross uniform, stepped from the car and
paused to pay the driver. A moment later she stood on the
threshold of the room facing them all, erect, poised and
self-possessed. Lisa felt a wave of inordinate pride. This
was Murray's wife — Murray's wife, and she made every
woman in the room appear drab and unimportant in com-
parison! Of course it was partly due to her uniform. She
was encased in steel blue, smooth and sleek like a coat of
mail. Most women not in uniform are uncomfortably aware
of the frivolity of their own costumes when in the presence
of one of their own sex who has eschewed feminine attire
for military, or that of some form of rigorous service, and

they often feel a sense of inferiority. Lisa was aware of this
reaction to Nora as she stood in the doorway. She greeted
Nora with older-woman ease and familiarity, grasping her
hand warmly in both hers.

'Hello, Nora, my dear. I've already told them all about
you. Here she is — Mrs. Joe Jones. I won't bother to call
them all by name to you, Nora. Come in, my dear.'

'Hello, everybody!' Nora said simply, calmly gazing at the
eyes upon her from beneath her visored cap, which she wore
straight, not tilted. 'Am I late?'

'No. Exactly on time,' Lisa assured her. 'Pass her the
cocktail tray, Tuck.'

'Won't you have a cigarette?' inquired Nichols, extending
his cigarette case spread wide open.

'No, thank you, I don't smoke,' Nora replied without
apology.

'What'll you have to drink?' asked Tuck, standing before
her with the tray on which were half a dozen filled glasses.
'Martini? Manhattan?'

'Tomato juice for me, please,' she said and reached for the
one remaining glassful.

'Independent as they come,' thought June. 'Doesn't give
a darn for us.'

'It seems to me we've met before,' said Nichols in his most
ingratiating manner.

'Oh, have we?' she inquired coolly. 'Where, Major? She
emphasized the last word slightly, glancing flatteringly at
the leaf on his shoulder. 'Overseas, perhaps?'

'No. At Fiddle Pond four years ago when a plane de-
scended unexpectedly upon the waters.'

'Were you one of *that* party?' she exclaimed wide-eyed.

'The humble pilot.' He bowed low.

'And not-so-humble owner of the plane, too, I seem to
recollect,' she flashed back but her reference was without
bitterness. 'We didn't exchange half a dozen words.' She

went on, 'And you weren't in uniform then, so I've got a good excuse for not remembering you right off the bat.'

'You remember *me*, I hope,' Windy broke in. '*We* exchanged more than half a dozen words.'

'Of course I remember *you!* You're Windy! Even if you weren't so famous I'd remember *you*. Dad took a great shine to you.'

'And I took a great shine to *him*. Her father is a wonderful fisherman,' said Windy, addressing the group, 'and has the best line of stories!'

'Do you remember *me?*' piped up Christopher.

Nora regarded him closely, brows knit. 'Now let me think —'

'You gave me two flies.'

'Oh, I remember the flies all right! I was trying to get your name. Isn't it Christopher?'

He gave a sharp affirmative nod, eyes shining.

'Did you ever get anything on those flies, Christopher?'

'No, but it wasn't their fault. They were good flies.'

Nichols bent toward Nora and spoke confidentially. 'I've asked to be placed beside you at the table,' he said. 'I hope you are in a forgiving mood.'

She gave him a straight look and smiled, 'I'm willing to start at scratch, Major,' she said.

'Come out to dinner, everybody!' sang out Lisa joyously. Nora had passed her first test.

33

CHAPTER

IT was after dinner when everyone was sitting around in the big square entrance hall after the coffee tray had been removed that the article in *Leader* exploded. It was due to an accident. Windy had put the magazine in the pocket of his coat. When reaching for one of his canes the magazine had slipped out, and before he could get it Christopher had picked it up. It was open to page 47, folded into an oblong. Christopher started to unfold it. Windy snatched it away from him.

'Why can't I look at it?'

'Pipe down, Christopher. For gosh sakes, keep still.'

'What's this all about?' asked Lisa, who had seen Windy snatch the magazine from Christopher.

'There's something in this magazine,' said Windy, 'that we were going to show you later, but Christopher has gone and spilled the beans.' He stopped. 'But you've got to know sometime.'

'What is it I've got to know sometime?'

Windy didn't know how to go on. As Lisa waited she had that sensation of dropping in an elevator. But she dropped only a few stories. She had learned how to put on the emergency brakes. Whatever the catastrophe about to befall her she was ready to take it.

'Go on, Windy. Tell me,' she said quietly. Everybody in the room was listening.

'It's nothing bad, Mother,' June burst out. 'Don't look like that!'

'It's just something we happened to run across in *Leader*,' said Windy. 'It may come as a kind of a shock to you, but — '

'For goodness' sakes, Windy!' Frietchie exclaimed. 'Give her the magazine.'

'Perhaps that *is* the best way,' said Windy, and passed it to Lisa.

She stood perfectly still for a moment gazing down at the picture, then remarked quietly, 'It does look like Murray, doesn't it?' and passed the magazine to Barry. 'It's quite a striking resemblance, Barry.' Charlotte saw the look that passed between them, straight in the eyes and penetrating, like that of two conspirators.

Barry's reaction to the picture was similar to Lisa's — controlled interest and not the slightest betrayal of the secret knowledge they shared.

'It looks very much indeed like Murray,' he remarked. 'Quite a coincidence!'

Lisa took the magazine from Barry and walked over to Nora

'Perhaps *you'd* like to see what our son Murray looks like. This picture resembles him closely,' and she passed the magazine to Nora.

Nora looked at the picture a moment then said lightly, returning the magazine to Lisa, 'What a handsome son you have!'

Charlotte, still closely observing, thought she saw a conniving look pass between Lisa and this strange Mrs. Jones. Jones! The name of the author of the nature book was Jones. The plot thickened.

'Let *me* look at the picture,' said Christopher.

'Very well, dear.' And Lisa held the magazine down for him to see.

'Look! Look!' he exclaimed in his eager treble. 'He's even got a scar on his eyebrow like Murray's!' He glanced up at his mother with an expression of alarm. 'What does it mean?'

'There are often cases of mistaken identity, Christopher. I'll explain what it means later.'

'Lisa,' said Charlotte, 'this is less of a surprise to you than to *us*, isn't it?'

'What do you mean, Charlotte?'

'Listen to this, Mother,' Christopher interrupted, and blurted out Charlotte's discovery. 'His name is Jones! Eliot Jones! That's the name of the author of that book that was sent you by the publishers.'

'Lisa,' Charlotte went on, 'there's no use pretending with us any more. Several of us here have had doubts about what became of Murray, and have kept our doubts to ourselves. But we can't any longer. Barry, you've known, too, haven't you?'

Barry smiled, slipped his arm through Lisa's and said, 'I guess the cat's out of the bag, Lisa.'

Lisa said quietly, but accusingly too, 'And who let it out? *I* didn't! *You* did, Barry!'

'No, Lisa. Murray did. He should never have gotten himself awarded medals for heroism if he wanted to keep his cat in the bag. Let's hear what the article says.'

'We'd all like to hear it,' said Lloyd. 'Read it out loud, Lisa.'

'You read it, Barry,' said Lisa and passed him the magazine. Barry moved over nearer to a window so that the light fell on the page.

'Above is a picture of Eliot Jones, from Millinocket, Maine, formerly a guide in the Maine woods but now a Quartermaster in the United States Navy. He is known as "Joe Jones" on board his ship, the *Cetus* and is called "Joe" or "Bug" by his intimates. We are proud to publish Joe's

picture as our war hero of the week, along with the account
of his extraordinary heroism received only a few days ago
from our correspondent in the Pacific.

'Joe enlisted in the Navy before the attack on Pearl
Harbor. For four years he has been serving his country on
board a Navy Auxiliary — a cargo ship — plying between
ports located somewhere in the backwashes of the Pacific,
far removed from the battle-line.

'Joe is one of the hordes of young men who enlisted in
the Navy expecting to fight for their country, but who instead were assigned to monotonous jobs in outlying God-
forsaken, war-forsaken districts, and left there indefinitely
to grin and bear it, or else crack. Joe is one of those who
didn't crack.

'Joe, quiet, unpretentious, reserved, is liked and respected
by every man and officer on board his ship. But the U.S.
Government does not award medals for popularity, or yet
for the superior performance of normal duties. It was not
until the *U.S.S. Cetus* was in combat last February that Joe
had an opportunity to prove the stuff he was made of.

'Joe is extremely modest. He says the act for which he
was decorated was not due to heroism. Joe rescued a
wounded comrade from a burning raft. Joe was ignorant
of his comrade's identity. He protests that when swimming
to safety with his helpless burden he was impelled by an
inner compulsion which had nothing to do with the war, the
service he was rendering, or heroism. The Captain and
other officers of the ship, also the Government, were of a
different opinion.

'The text of the citation accompanying the Award for
Chief Quartermaster Jones is as follows:

' "For conspicuous gallantry and intrepidity at the risk of
his life above and beyond the call of duty while serving as
Chief Quartermaster in the United States Navy, when his
ship had been fiercely attacked by enemy Japanese aircraft.
After the order to abandon ship had been carried out and
Chief Quartermaster Jones was seated in a lifeboat surrounded by burning wreckage, undeterred by the over-

whelming odds against him, he left the lifeboat and went to
the rescue of a shipmate whom he saw lying unconscious
face down on a burning raft. After pulling him off the raft,
Quartermaster Jones, cut off from the lifeboat by exploding
ammunition, struck out for a distant reef, waging a lone,
long and successful battle with the waves of a furious squall.
Not until he had been swimming for some distance did he
discover that the man whom he had rescued was the Execu-
tive Officer of his ship. Quartermaster Jones's cool judgment, initiative and heroism in the face of almost certain
death was an inspiration to all the officers and men of the
U.S.S. Cetus. His valor and invincible fighting spirit were
in keeping with the highest tradition of the United States
Naval Service." '

Barry stopped. No one spoke. Christopher looked around
at the staring faces, perplexed. 'Who is Eliot Jones, father?'
he inquired.

'Eliot Jones is a name Murray has been using while doing
brave things, Christopher,' Barry replied.

'And while writing clever books,' said Charlotte.

Christopher turned to his mother, brow puckered. 'Is
Murray alive, Mother?'

'Yes, Christopher,' said Lisa. (Please, God, she added to
herself, as the black shadow of fear swooped low. Nine
weeks and no word!)

'Is he coming back again?'

'I hope so, some time,' Lisa replied, and after a pause, 'he
has already come back in one way.'

'In what way? He isn't here,' Christopher objected.

'The truth about him is here,' said Lisa. 'There's nothing
for him to hide from any more.'

'What was there once for him to hide from?' asked
Christopher.

'It's a long story. I'll tell you some time.'

Suddenly Nora spoke. 'There was nothing for him to hide
from, ever, Christopher. Nothing at all!'

'Do *you* know Murray?'

'Yes, better than anybody in the world knows him! And he was always heroic and brave and wonderful,' her voice quavered a little.

'Who are you?'

'I'm Murray's wife, Christopher.' She spoke with such simple straightforwardness that everyone was stirred.

Finally, however, tongues were unloosed, questions released. How long had Lisa known that Murray was alive? How had she found out? Who was Jim Billings? It was Barry who told them about Jim Billings, his private detective flair, and his final conclusions based on the clues he had found and the testimony of the watch stem. Nora stretched out her arm for them to see her 'engagement ring,' strapped to her wrist. The ribbed stem of the watch was far more precious to her, she said, than any solitaire.

They were all gathered around Nora when Lisa was called to the telephone.

'It was Doctor Jaquith calling from New York,' she announced. 'He wanted to know if we had seen the article in *Leader*. He said Mr. Ben had just called him up about it and what do you think Mr. Ben had to suggest, Windy?'

'What?'

'That the chapel which we planned to give in *memory* of Murray's heroism be given now, in *recognition* of it, and that it be dedicated as a war memorial to the Tamarack boys who will never come back.'

'That's a grand idea! I'm all for it!' Windy exclaimed.

'Lisa, I have something to say,' announced Lloyd, abruptly stepping forward. He paused and waited for everyone to be silent.

'Yes, Lloyd?' Lisa observed he was holding Murray's book in one hand.

'This has been a very impressive afternoon,' he continued ponderously in a deep sonorous voice, as if making a speech.

'Very impressive indeed. We are all proud of Murray. He has brought honor and distinction to the family, not only because of his war record, but because of this.' He tapped the book. 'I am told it is an extremely intelligent book.' He raised his eyes to the portrait of Grandmother Vale. 'Mother would be proud of Murray, too.'

Lisa hoped she wasn't going to cry. She started to speak. Any effort would help maintain her control. But Lloyd held up his hand.

'When you were at the telephone,' he went on, 'I spoke to Hilary and Charlotte. All three of Mother's children agree that Murray's portrait should now occupy the place of honor in this house.'

'Thank you, Lloyd,' Lisa managed to reply.

When Christopher came home from school late the next afternoon it was too early for the lights to be lit, but dusk always fell early in the entrance hall. Its corners and recesses were already wrapped in their familiar afternoon shadows when he entered by a side door. There was an unusual glow emanating from over the mantel, like the glow from beneath it when the logs were lit.

He walked over in front of the mantel. Murray's portrait was hanging there. Lisa had turned on the light at the base of the frame and the spotlight too. The combination made the portrait come alive as it never had in her room upstairs.

Christopher stood staring up at Murray for a long time. Lisa found him there when she came downstairs. She walked over to him, and in silence they both gazed up at the reinstalled portrait.

'I guess I see what you meant now, Mother,' finally Christopher remarked, 'Murray has come back.'

'Yes,' said Lisa, and after a pause, 'the ship is in its home port.'

THE END